"WILL YOU KISS ME?
I MEAN *REALLY* KISS ME,
UNTIL I'M WEAK?"

Taking her at her word, Nicholai kissed Lisette thoroughly, with an intimacy that stunned her until a sudden jolt of pleasure shook the center of her being.

His strong, sure embrace, the heady male scent of his bronzed skin, the thrill of his warm lips moving over her own, his tongue probing her mouth in a way that made her answer, needing more . . . all these sensations combined to ignite a fire of desire within Lisette.

She was twenty-one years old, yet lived the chaste life of a nun . . . the part of her that was meant to love had lain dormant. Now, as Nicholai kissed her, the fire spread, surging through Lisette's ripe body.

She had never been naked with a man before, but tonight she felt utterly mad and didn't care if sanity ever returned . . .

Spring Fires

Cynthia Challed Wright

BALLANTINE BOOKS • NEW YORK

For my extraordinary parents,
Gene and Priscilla Challed.
I love you!

Library of Congress Catalog Card Number 82-90862

ISBN 0-345-27514-4

Manufactured in the United States of America

First Edition: March 1983

CAST OF CHARACTERS

LISETTE HAHN—proprietor of Han's CoffeeHouse in 1793 Philadelphia

NICHOLAI BEAUVISAGE*—a man who has been driven back from France, after a decade, by the Revolution

ERNST HAHN—Lisette's ailing father

HYLA FLOWERS—Lisette's co-worker and friend

JAMES STRINGFELLOW—CoffeeHouse barman and friend

PLUS some familiar faces from past books—

From *CAROLINE:*

ALEXANDRE and CAROLINE BEAUVISAGE—Nicholai's brother and sister-in-law

ÉTIENNE, NATALYA, and KRISTIN—their children

JEAN-PHILIPPE and ANTONIA BEAUVISAGE—Alec's parents

NICHOLAI*—the younger Beauvisage brother

KATYA BEAUVISAGE—the youngest sister, now Lisette's best friend

RANDOLPH EDWARDS—Katya's fiancé

PIERRE DUBOIS—Alec's valet

From *TOUCH THE SUN:*

LION and MEAGAN HAMPSHIRE—a couple now married four years

MARCUS REEMS—Lion's half-brother

BRAMBLE—the Hampshires' cook

WONG—Lion's valet

ANNE BINGHAM—a wealthy Philadelphia socialite

GEORGE WASHINGTON—the President

From *SILVER STORM:*

ANDRÉ and DEVON RAVENEAU—a sea captain and his wife

MOUETTE and NATHAN—their children

HALSEY MINTER—André's first officer

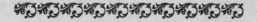

❦ Part One ❧

They meet but with unwholesome springs
    And summers which infectious are;
They hear but when the mermaid sings,
    And only see the falling star,
        Who ever dare
    Affirm no woman chaste and fair.

What madman, 'cause the glow-worm's flame
    Is cold, swears there's no warmth in fire?
Cause some make forfeit of their name,
    And slave themselves to man's desire,
        Shall the sex, free
    From guilt, damn'd to bondage be?

WILLIAM HABINGTON
(1605–1654)

❧ *Chapter 1* ❧

March 17, 1793

Smoky rose light filtered hazily through the dormer win-dows. Under a mound of colorful quilts, Lisette Hahn was curled in resistance to the wintry dawn. Long golden lashes brushed her cheeks, though behind them, she was awake and dreading the prospect of rising to face the chilly morning. Her pretty mouth curved down on one side, then parted to allow a groan to escape. The quilts were pushed aside, and Lisette swung long graceful legs to the icy floor while running a hand through her sunbeam-colored tousled hair.

Hurriedly, she built up the fire to a cheery blaze, lit a candle and went downstairs for fresh water. She washed herself with the aid of the exquisite pitcher and bowl that her mother had brought from Austria; they were made from the finest porcelain, patterned in red and silver on a white background. Lisette could still remember her mother chatting idly to her as she packed them for the crossing to America. She had daydreamed aloud about the new life that lay ahead for them in Philadelphia, and the lovely home that awaited the Hahn family.

Seventeen years had passed since that day, but Lisette's eyes still burned whenever she remembered her mother's sweet, hopeful expression. Their ship had been attacked by an overeager English brigantine and all the money and treasures belonging to the Hahns were confiscated. Lisette's distraught mother sickened with a strange fever and died before ever setting eyes on Philadelphia. Penniless and grief stricken, Ernst Hahn and his daughter had arrived alone in a foreign world. The long years since had been crammed with numbing work, but the fruits of their labor were visible in the CoffeeHouse they owned, which had become a tremendous success since Philadelphia had been designated America's capital in late 1790.

Bradford's London CoffeeHouse had long been the favorite, but Lisette's beauty had intensified apace with her skill as a cook, and the Hahns' establishment drew larger and larger crowds. There were no women allowed in the Coffee-Houses, which were cherished havens of male conversation and negotiation, so the fair and remote Lisette was a sweet diversion. Customers were fascinated by her ability to combine intelligent charm with an inaccessible aura that frustrated and yet tantalized her admirers. In an atmosphere where men bragged of their conquests, real or exaggerated, there was not one who dared claim to have sampled Mistress Hahn's tempting and succulent favors. The Austrian beauty became the ultimate challenge.

The fire was blunting the chill edge in the air now, and Lisette could see the sun rising over the Delaware River, dripping its hot crimson juice into the frosty water. Pulling a clean tan cotton frock over her head, she could feel the sore muscles in her arms and back. The past few weeks had been exhausting. There had been the birthnight balls for the president on February 22, and then the second inauguration on March 4 with all its accompanying festivities. Hahn's CoffeeHouse had been full to bursting with celebrating citizens since before Christmas and straight through the New Year of 1793 to this day in mid-March. There were signs that the pace in Philadelphia was slowing, if only because everyone was utterly exhausted.

Brushing up her saffron curls, Lisette wondered idly how many tortes she had labored over in the past dozen weeks. Hahn's CoffeeHouse owed a large portion of its success to the fact that it, unlike its competitors, served meals. Lisette did most of the cooking, with the help of two rather inept young girls, and her talents were becoming legendary.

After selecting a clean folded apron and kerchief from her drawer, Lisette closed the door of her bedchamber and started downstairs. Pausing at her father's door, she could hear his rumbling snore; she smiled indulgently before con-

tinuing on her way. A tiny part of her couldn't help thinking that the more work there was to do, the older her father
became and the less he was able to help. Still, she loved
Ernst Hahn fiercely, and was determined that even if he
was completely undone by the cruel ravages of time and
could help her only with his wisdom, she would go on with
the CoffeeHouse. Lisette smiled as she came into the huge
sun-dappled keeping room, thinking of the probable reaction of her friends if they knew of her intention to defy
convention. None of them could understand how hard she
had worked for this success. . . . Lisette swore that she
would never surrender any part of her life simply because
she was a female.

Early morning sunshine was splashing across another bedchamber in a dwelling just miles from Hahn's CoffeeHouse.
North of Philadelphia, off Germantown Road, sprawled the
grand estate known as Belle Maison. Its master and mistress
were as celebrated as the house itself, and the handsome
couple was just then waking up.

Alexandre Beauvisage blinked turquoise eyes against the
glare of morning light and rolled in the opposite direction,
enraptured by the sight of his enchanting wife. Caroline's
honey-colored curls were spread across the satin pillow,
haloing a face that was half-awake and irritable. She
wrinkled her nose and squeezed her eyes more tightly shut
just as Alec slid muscular walnut-brown arms around her
and pressed warm lips along the line of her soft throat.

"Mmm." Caro protested halfheartedly, and was answered
by a low chuckle from her husband. She shivered as his
fingers slid the straps of her bed gown from her shoulders
and caressed her full sleep-warm breasts. Alec kissed the
rosy nipples tantalizingly and they hardened beneath his
tongue, while Caro pressed nearer, her fingers twisted in his
raven hair, her breath warm on his brow. Easily, Alec removed the gown and when his hand crept up her thigh to
find the warmth between her legs, Caro did not protest, but
moaned sweetly instead. She could feel his rigid manhood
pressing against her soft flesh and reached toward it just as
Alec forced her back into the pillows, moving above her,

palms on her cheeks as he kissed her hungrily. As her silky thighs spread in welcome, and her arms rounded his wide, hard shoulders, a faint knock sounded at the door.

"Papa?"

"Argh!" said Alec to Caro, black brows knitting above flashing eyes. She repressed a giggle as he swiftly shifted back to his pillow only moments before the door swung open to reveal two of their three children. Eight-year-old Étienne held the hand of five-year-old Natalya, whose tiny chin quivered warningly.

"What the—" Alec began testily, cut off by Caro's hand over his mouth.

"What's wrong, you two?" she inquired softly.

As a fat tear escaped Natalya's aqua eye, Étienne explained, "It is my fault, Maman and Papa. I called Talya a name."

"P-p-potato face!" she supplied, then burst into tears and ran straight to her father, who cradled her close and glared at his stalwart son. The boy was his double, except for his eyes, which were a deeper blue. Natalya's were closer in their soft aqua, but otherwise she was her mother all over. In Caro's early days with Alec, she had also cried with alarming frequency.

"Étienne, why would you say such a thing?"

"I'm truly sorry, Papa. I told her so. It just slipped out. She drew on some of my papers and made a terrible mess, and it just slipped out!"

"Oh, Alec," Caro interceded softly, "he's awfully good to admit it. Talya shouldn't be encouraged in these tantrums."

"The entire episode sounds ridiculous to me!" Alec burst out, patting his daughter's honey curls all the same. "Henceforth, I expect you two to settle these petty matters between yourselves, and do not come bursting in on your mother and me at such an early hour!"

"Yes, sir," quavered Étienne.

"Don't call me sir!"

Talya giggled at this and slid off her father's lap. Her brother grinned in relief, caught her hand, and the two of them scampered out of the bedchamber, closing the door as they ran.

"Children!" Alec growled, emerging naked and magnificent from the testered bed.

Caro laughed. "Charming, aren't they? Shall we lock them up somewhere?"

Alec grinned wickedly from the washstand. "Now, there's a brilliant idea!"

Caro watched as he shaved, thinking how handsome and irresistible he was at forty, no less than he had been at thirty-one. She remembered clearly watching him shave from this bed during that first winter of their marriage, and if anything, he seemed even harder and leaner now, the new lines about his eyes and mouth lending him a new dimension of magnetism missing in his younger days. If anyone had told her then that he could improve, she would have thought it impossible, but it was true. And their love had also grown more vibrant, passionate, and mellow with each passing year.

"What are you dreaming of, *chérie*?" Alec inquired with amused affection, bending to rinse the last traces of his shaving lather. "A huge breakfast or perhaps an elegant new frock?"

Caro arched a toffee-hued brow. "Just for that, I should insult you, but truthful as ever, I must confess I was dreaming of my husband."

"The lucky rascal." Alec smiled. "What are your plans for today? Have you time to exercise the horses with me?"

"I would love to, but I fear I promised to appear on Meagan's doorstep by ten o'clock. We're going to plan and shop for the party."

"Party?" Alec threw himself back onto the bed, still naked, and let out a loud lazy groan. One long arm bent and dropped across his eyes.

"The party for Philadelphia's newest senator, Lion Hampshire!" Caro retorted with mock formality. "Honestly, your memory. I spoke to you about this several times last week and even checked with you about the dates!"

A dramatic snore rumbled beside her, causing her to break off with a grin. He was impossible. Caro lay back against the pillows and let her mind drift, thinking nostalgically of the past and the changes that a decade had wrought. They continued to live at Belle Maison and sleep in the same bed, but large pieces had shifted in the puzzle of their lives. Two of Alec's sisters, her good friends, had moved from Philadelphia. Danielle Engelman and her family now lived in New York, and Natalya had moved to Charleston with her new husband over seven years ago. Alec's dear *grandmère* had passed away the previous autumn of 1792 after a very long and exceptional life. Her death had left a gaping tear in the fabric of their lives. And, Nicholai Beauvisage had gone off to manage the family château and vineyards in France in late 1784 and had not been seen since. He and Alec had been close as brothers, in spite of Nicholai's ardent affection for Caro, and his absence was still sorely felt. Contributing to the pangs the couple felt for Nicholai was the French Revolution, which had lately reached a fever pitch. The rumors that crossed the Atlantic were frightening. The king had been imprisoned, France was at war with several of her neighbors, countless aristocrats were losing their heads to the wicked-sounding guillotine, and a republic had been declared. Nicholai's parents were openly worried, for the last male Beauvisage to live at the château—*Grandmère*'s husband, Étienne—had been a marquis. Caro pretended all was well, but in truth, she thought of her brother-in-law constantly. He had been so carefree and charming . . . it was impossible that any harm could befall him. Besides, he was a Beauvisage: strong, quick witted, and courageous.

A cool finger touched her cheek and Caro glanced over, catching a glimpse of Alec's raven hair before warm lips captured her own. A hand snaked out to whip back the quilts, then he was over her. Caro melted as crisp chest hair brushed her nipples; she grew warm and eager, pulling him close, fitting her legs to his.

"M'sieur?" a voice queried beyond the door. "I have your coffee."

"Oh, for Christ's sake!" shouted Alec. "Go away!"

When Pierre replied, his French-accented voice was choked with embarrassment. "I beg your pardon, m'sieur! The children—they told me you and Madame were astir." The valet coughed, stalling. "I *do* have news of some importance . . ."

Grumbling, Alec turned and shifted back to his pillow once again, then readjusted the covers. Caro sighed as her husband barked, "Come in, then!"

The impish, earnest little Frenchman did as he was bade, scurrying to the bed with a silver tray bearing a fragrant coffeepot, a plate stacked with cranberry muffins, and a dish of butter. Pierre's blush darkened when Caro did not scramble for the food, but remained under covers to her neck.

"Give us this earth-shattering news before the suspense does me in," Alec suggested sarcastically.

"They've killed the king," Pierre said. "Louis has been guillotined. The middle of January."

"Oh! Dear lord . . ." breathed Caro. "I pray that Nicholai is safe! Alec—?"

The scowl of irritation had vanished from her husband's face. His vivid turquoise eyes were focused at a point on the far wall, and they mirrored the shock and tide of worry that was growing inside of him.

"It's that bad in France, then . . ." he whispered. "The entire country must be a bit insane . . . and I fear matters will worsen before the people regain their sensitivity." Alec blinked, suddenly conscious of the pressure of Caro's hand on his taut forearm. "It won't do any good for you to carry on about Nicky, *chéri*. You can take comfort in the fact that he is neither a royalist or an aristo, in the strict sense of the word. If he keeps his wits about him, I've little doubt he'll emerge unscathed."

Caro nodded, but her expression remained pained and anxious. After all, Nicky had been such a sweet and trusting boy, rather like an eager puppy, and always more easygoing than Alec. All too human, she feared.

❧ Chapter 2 ❧

March 17, 1793

The keeping room for Hahn's CoffeeHouse was located in the rear of the large brick building. Lisette loved the long hours she spent cooking there, for the room was buttery gold with firelight and rich with heavenly aromas and caring conversations. It seemed that every inch of space was filled. There were rough-hewn shelves above the hearth crowded with stoneware, baskets, and assorted vessels of copper, iron, and tin. A medley of cooking tools was displayed on hooks, and fragrant bunches of herbs dangled from the beamed ceiling: savory, tansy, sage, sweet marjoram, and costmary. Beyond the double doors sprawled the public room with its patchwork of heavy scarred tables and bow-back chairs, banistered partitions, tin chandeliers, and two giant hearths. By mid-afternoon, the room would reverberate with animated masculine conversation.

Hyla Flowers, a woman of dissipation and raw charm, was in charge in that noisy "jungle," as Ernst Hahn affectionately called it. She had been a "lady of the evening" before and during the war, but after a bad experience with two Hessian mercenaries, who had beaten and robbed her, Hyla had turned to more honest work. After fifteen years at the CoffeeHouse, she clucked like a possessive mother hen around Lisette. The two serving girls, sisters named Purity and Chastity, helped Lisette cook in the morning and filled orders under Mrs. Flowers's direction for the rest of the day.

The cage-topped bar was the domain of James Stringfellow, an irrepressible and gregarious Englishman who had come to Philadelphia two years before with an acting company. One night he had stopped in the CoffeeHouse for a jug of ale and hadn't left since. His dark-haired, wiry good looks combined with an engaging smile and quick tongue to make him well loved and respected by all.

Lisette's father worked and mingled in the CoffeeHouse, but today he occupied his favorite comb-back chair near the kitchen hearth, pale hands clasped over the stomach that had once been generous and hearty.

A long sawbuck table, bleached, stained, and piled with vegetables, stood in the center of the room. Lisette labored over it, perched on a rush stool, her blond curls tied up in a kerchief and her lovely form concealed by a cotton apron.

"Papa?" she ventured softly, studying his sad profile. He had once been a fine-looking man, tall and erect, with sandy hair and sensitive, determined features. Now, all of him seemed to droop. "If you feel unwell, perhaps you should return to bed. A nap might—"

"Lisette. Please do not say those words." Ernst Hahn spoke perfect, if stilted, English, with an accent that enchanted Lisette. It reminded her of her mother. "Do you wish that I should pull up my blanket and wait for my death?"

Horrified, she could only stare. *Death!* His words and the expression on his dear face made her want to weep with anguish. "Oh, Papa, please—"

The rear door swept open, letting in a blast of cold, sunny air and a pretty dark-haired young lady.

Katya Beauvisage crossed the wide-planked floor, bending to kiss Mr. Hahn's cheek and whisper in his ear, then reaching Lisette, who rose to hug her friend. Katya was the baby of the Beauvisage clan at eighteen, and a charming blend of her petite Russian mother and dark French father. She was keenly intelligent, and Lisette's closest friend since their years together at school.

"Randolph is in the public room," she confided, peeling off her dark blue pelisse and kid gloves before taking a stool beside Lisette. "He is having coffee with Lion Hampshire."

"The new senator has been here more and more often since his election," Lisette observed, pushing a pile of carrots toward Katya, along with a knife.

"That's not surprising. More politics is discussed here than in government sessions!"

"Is Randolph thinking of a new career?" Lisette teased. Since Katya had abandoned her books for the full-time occupation of lovesick fiancée to Randolph Edwards, a young attorney, Lisette couldn't hold her tongue.

The two girls chatted on, but Katya was preoccupied, thinking of a conversation she and Randolph had shared while walking to the CoffeeHouse. He had commented with enthusiasm on the beauty of Lisette Hahn, and her mystical appeal for the men who frequented the CoffeeHouse. But *why* was she still unattached at the age of twenty-one? Was she peculiar?

Katya had denied and dodged, but the questions had stirred up the matter of Lisette's love life, reminding her anew of the heart-to-heart talk the two girls had shared a few months before. Katya had probed and Lisette eventually revealed the reason for her lack of interest in men: a broken heart.

At eighteen, she had been wooed by a dashing congressman from the South. Naive and eager for love, Lisette had tumbled headlong into romance. She had spent long hours talking of books, politics, and far-off places with her new love, confiding her dreams and becoming so lovesick that she frequently neglected the CoffeeHouse. Telling the story to Katya, she bitterly remarked that it had been fortunate her father was well enough then to manage without her; guilt over her thoughtlessness still ate at her. Lisette told of the nights she had lain awake, spinning fantasies of the future and wondering about the strange feelings she had when her sweetheart kissed her, or even touched her hand.

The dream had been shattered one spring evening when the congressman had taken her to his house on Vine Street. Supper had been prepared and Lisette drank a good deal of wine, recklessly ready for adventure. Tears came when she told Katya of the sudden terse confession that saved her from meaningless ruin. "He stopped when I was in my chemise, and told me he couldn't do it—that he cared too much for my future, that he had a wife and two babies back home . . . !" Angry, galling tears interrupted her tale, but control returned quickly. "I was so certain! I trusted him, thought I knew him, but the lesson was well taken. Listening to the men who come here, I've daily reaffirmed my conviction that men are self-important, vain, shallow creatures for the most part. They take our hearts and suck us into some mad physical spell that drains away all our spirit. I have work to do, and I'll not be bewitched or used by any man, ever again!"

The married congressman had been defeated in the recent election and had returned to his trusting family. Lisette's stubborn determination had not diminished, but was so effectively masked that she continued to captivate the Coffee-House patrons with her golden beauty. Her charm was genuine but she was as multifaceted as a diamond. The next room was crowded with men who dreamed of winning the mysterious Lisette, and thinking of this, Katya smiled ironically. Perhaps men were fools and Lisette was right, after all.

Yet . . . growing up in a family of Beauvisage men, she believed there were no easy generalities. And she trusted Randolph. He, at least, had lived here all his life, and *couldn't* have a hidden wife! He respected and encouraged her intelligence, too, which never ceased to surprise her.

Glancing up, Katya found Lisette's beautiful eyes watching her. It had taken a long time, but Katya had finally learned to read them. Generally, they were a rich cornflower blue, but when Lisette was sad they shaded toward gray, and when she was angry or excited, they sparkled like sapphires.

"Are you mooning over Randolph?" she asked playfully, her eyes twinkling with just a hint of teasing.

Katya flushed. "No. No! Really, Lisette, you say that as if you believe me rendered witless! Do not smile! I—I was thinking about Caroline, my sister-in-law. She stopped at our house today to leave her children with Maman for a few hours. She was with Meagan Hampshire and mentioned that they might stop here."

"Whatever for? Mrs. Hampshire cannot join her husband. Those men wouldn't allow even a senator's wife to intrude on their private refuge!"

"Caro said they wanted to speak with you. I know you are fatigued, so perhaps I should warn you . . . Caro is planning a party for Lion Hampshire and means to ask you to make several tortes for the occasion."

Lisette pushed aside the heap of sliced onions and started on the potatoes. "Not another party!"

"Well . . . Caro and Sacha are very close friends of the Hampshires. They know how long Lion has dreamt of this —Meagan, too. Caro feels they deserve a chance to shine."

"That is really very nice. I like Senator Hampshire—and I suppose a few more tortes won't kill me, though I *may* go insane!"

They laughed together at this, then Lisette continued, "I have heard that Mrs. Hampshire is expecting a child . . . she must be very happy."

"Yes! I understand it is due the end of August. Although, as delighted as Meagan must be, I'll wager she feels like a fish out of water. She is so full of energy, somehow I cannot see her as an expectant mother."

The back door swung open again as Chastity and Purity came in from the courtyard garden with a basket of fresh herbs. Lisette asked them to see to the tripe, veal knuckle, and marrow bones that had been simmering in a pot over the fire since dawn.

"Pepper pot?" Katya guessed, inhaling appreciatively.

The girls nodded vigorously. Ernst Hahn was dozing now before the hearth. Lisette turned the sliced and chopped vegetables over to the girls and went to fetch the necessary ingredients for several gallons of lemonade. Katya helped her bring the glass pitchers to the table, but stopped halfway back with her arms full.

"God's name! I almost·forgot! Did you hear about the king of France?"

"Why—no!" Anxiously, Lisette took some of the teetering pitchers from Katya and added a bit more calmly, "Do tell me!"

"Caro says he was guillotined! Of course, it happened more than two months ago, and Lord knows what has transpired since."

Lisette looked concerned. Setting the pitchers on the

table, she reached for her friend's hand. "Katya, isn't your brother living in France? Is he in danger?"

"Well . . . Caro and my parents are behaving with forced assurance about that. Nicky lives in our ancestral château and controls a huge expanse of vineyards, so I suppose he is suspect. No one there is behaving very rationally—I mean, killing the king! So . . ."

"How old is your brother now?"

"Oh, let's see . . . thirty-two or more, I suppose. Goodness, that is hard to imagine. I was a little girl when he left, not yet ten years old, but I remember him as a gay young bachelor—always ready for a laugh and plunging headlong into escapades. . . . It really is difficult to imagine him at this age, but I can't imagine he's changed very much. He must think they are simply *mad* over there."

"Well, aren't they?"

It was Caro, speaking from the doorway. She was clad in a beautiful pelisse of apricot wool, its hood haloed with red fox. At her side was Meagan Hampshire, who was already slipping out of her plum-colored pelisse, smiling to break the tension.

"I hope you don't mind this intrusion," she apologized, walking over to offer Lisette her hand. "I have heard such wonderful things about you from everyone, including my husband. I'm Meagan Hampshire."

It was Lisette's first close look at this legendary beauty who was barely older than she. Everyone knew the story of her aristocratic Virginia background and the masquerade she had practiced on Lion. Four years ago, they met when he, hoping to secure a Senate seat, became betrothed to a southern girl of respected lineage who was also Meagan's friend. Since Meagan's parents had just died and she was about to be shipped off to an old aunt, she decided to come to Philadelphia with her friend Priscilla, posing as her lady's maid. Meagan was an exquisite violet-eyed minx with long lustrous black curls and a winning personality. Lisette wasn't surprised that Lion had fallen in love with the "lady's maid," especially considering the fact that Priscilla Wade Reems, though stunning, was irritatingly shallow. After losing Lion, Priscilla had married his villainous rival, Marcus

Reems, but tragically died in childbirth at the age of nineteen.

Lion soon decided that he loved Meagan better than politics, and had retired to a quiet life for two years, but eventually, he was spurred on by his spirited wife, and his ambition had flared again. His new title of senator held great meaning for both Mr. and Mrs. Hampshire.

"It is a pleasure to meet you, Mrs. Hampshire." Lisette smiled. "I have heard a great deal about *you,* also! Senator Hampshire is a wonderful man."

Was it Lisette's imagination, or did Meagan's eyes cloud momentarily? The smile faltered for an instant before she replied, "You must call me Meagan! Lord, but that pepper pot smells heavenly! I thought that our cook was an expert with that dish, but I'm having second thoughts."

"Her tortes are even better," hinted Caro, launching into a carefully prepared speech that built slowly into an unrefusable plea for Lisette's help with the party. The beautiful Austrian girl smiled ingenuously, with secret enjoyment. Pausing to consider Caro and Meagan's request, she glanced at Katya and winked.

"Ladies . . ." She drew out the word and Caro cringed as if to ward off a negative answer. "I would love to help with the party. I'll make as many tortes as you need, whatever kind you like. I am honored to do this for the senator."

Caro gave a happy cry and turned to Meagan, who tried to match her smile but succeeded only in looking ill.

"Meagan, dear, are you all right?"

"Oh, certainly. I'm very thankful! I know Lion will be, too, and speaking of my husband—Lisette, I wonder if you might coax him away from the men? I would dearly love a moment of his time."

Lisette seemed surprised at this request, but nodded cheerfully, slipping off of her stool. She untied the kerchief with a slim hand and Meagan watched as a bright lemony waterfall of curls cascaded down her back. Off came the apron, revealing Lisette's lovely figure with its tiny waist and high ripe breasts. Meagan swallowed, feeling the swollen abdomen that made her stylish gowns fit tighter by the day.

While Lisette was in the CoffeeHouse, Caro and Meagan chatted politely with Mr. Hahn, while Katya started to work on the lemonade. It was nearly noon and the various beverages—wine, lemonade, chocolate, and coffee—had to be ready to serve in quantity to the crowds that would spill in for lunch.

After several minutes, the door to the public room opened to reveal Lion Hampshire, laughing down at the beautiful Lisette. Meagan paled visibly as she observed her dazzlingly handsome husband. At thirty-seven, he was in his prime: tall, hard, deeply tanned, with molten gold hair, ocean-blue eyes, and an easy star-white grin. His greatest appeal lay in an air of confidence, untarnished by foppish vanity or conceit. Meagan still loved Lion so intensely that it hurt when she observed many women openly pursue him as though he had no wife at all.

Lisette seemed at ease as she turned from the new senator to finish her lemonade, while Lion went to his wife with a roguish grin.

"What do you require of me, sweeting?" he asked lightly, bending to kiss her glossy black curls. Meagan blushed at what she interpreted to be an impersonal, fatherly gesture. Her own hands touched him possessively—his coat sleeves, shirtfront, waist.

"I thought you might be able to come out to an inn for luncheon with me," she whispered. "The sun is shining—and it seems so long since we just walked together. . . ."

Lion led her to a corner. "Meagan, you know that I would love to, but I have responsibilities now! When we discussed this again last night I thought you understood. I'm having lunch today with several important gentlemen—every conversation I have here teaches me something, and these lessons taken from others' experience are the most valuable of all. You *do* understand, don't you?"

He stared at her troubled face, but Meagan was looking past him at Lisette Hahn. "Will you be home for supper? *Please*, Lion!" Tears welled in her eyes, startling Lion.

"Yes, of course, fondling. And we will talk." This pregnant Meagan seemed like a stranger, full of contradictions, childish tears, and even depressions. The woman he had married was strong willed, feisty, and proud of her unique independence among the throngs of simpering females. Lion was totally confused and more than a little worried.

"Talk?" Her chin trembled. "Yes, of course . . . talk."
She wished he would whisper in her ear that they would
have supper in bed and stay there for twenty-four hours.
"Well, I don't want to keep you from your friends."

"I will see you in a few hours." He ran a dark finger
along her chin and smiled before turning toward the public
room. Meagan wanted to sob as she watched him pause to
taste the lemonade, laughing with Lisette the way he used
to laugh with *her*.

❦ *Chapter 3* ❧

March 25, 1793

The bedchamber hadn't been changed at all during the decade of Caro and Alec's marriage; it was still innocently lovely, a reminder of the sweet girl with no memory who had come to Belle Maison as Alec's ward. The furniture was upholstered in moss green velvet or silk, except for the splendid cherry field bed with its snowy net canopy and white counterpane. Many a night Caro had lain awake there, thinking and dreaming of Alec, but now the bed was slept in only by guests.

She sat on the counterpane now in her satin chemise, while Meagan occupied one of the Queen Anne chairs before the fire. Rose, the maid, was repairing a small tear in the hem of her mistress's gown, and Alec was drinking brandy with Lion in the library down the hall.

"It is so kind of you to give this party for Lion. He is very pleased and proud," Meagan was saying.

Caro stared at her friend. On the surface, she was as enchanting as ever, clad in a fashionable gown of dusky rose velvet and white silk. Milky pearls set off her ivory throat, while more were scattered among upswept raven curls. Yet, the sparkle was gone from her violet eyes, and there was a listless, sad quality about Meagan that was completely out of character.

Slowly, Caro rose and crossed to a nearby chair. She touched Meagan's cool hand and implored, "Do tell me what is troubling you! Are you ill? Is it the pregnancy? Is there a problem that I could try to help you solve?"

"Oh, Caro . . ." Her voice quavered miserably. "I *do*

need to talk, but I'm afraid you'll think I've gone mad!
Sometimes I'm convinced I've cause for worry, other times
I'm certain my imagination's to blame—"

"Meagan, start from the beginning."

She closed her eyes for a moment. "Part of the trouble
is the pregnancy. It came at the wrong time, even though
we'd hoped in the past. . . . When Lion won the election, I
wanted to be able to stand beside him, to share this new life
. . . and then *this!* I began to vomit every morning, I lost
my appetite and energy, I grew pale and weepy, and now
I'm getting so *fat!* I had to have this gown made for tonight
because nothing else fit!"

"But dear, you would have done that in any case, and
you've never been vain before—"

"That's not the point!" shrilled Meagan.

"But everyone grows fat when they are pregnant. You
can't put the baby in your pocket!"

"I know that! And, if it had happened earlier, when Lion
and I were together all the time, I'm certain I would be
having fun with all these symptoms. As it is, Lion is gone
every day, into a world that cannot accommodate me, like
this, and he barely has time to think of his baby . . . or me
either, I fear. He's always at that CoffeeHouse—with—"

"With?" Caro urged, baffled.

"Never mind. In addition to my other current faults, I've
developed a runaway tongue as well. You must not worry
about me, Caro. I've struggled with worse problems . . .
and as they say, the honeymoon can't last forever."

When Meagan stood up to study the field bed, Caro followed her tense figure with anxious eyes. Whoever had said
that about honeymoons was terribly wrong, and there was
no reason on earth for Meagan's marriage to add fuel to
that cruel myth.

Then the hall door opened and Katya's pretty head poked
inside. "Hello, lovely ladies! Caro, I've brought your frock.
You'd better hurry now; it's getting late and other guests
will begin to arrive soon."

Caro took the priceless gown of cream satin embroidered
with seed pearls and tiny diamonds and slipped it up her
legs. Meagan helped her fasten the back as Katya remarked,

"I saw Pierre arriving with Lisette when Randolph and I left our carriage."

"Oh, good. Pierre left to get her three hours ago and I'd begun to fear they had had an accident! Fortunately, we don't need the tortes until later, so the delay won't be felt."

"Caro, Lisette went on to the kitchen, but Pierre stopped to tell me that her father is worse and she was reluctant to leave him. I'm terribly concerned for her sake."

"I am surprised she would allow this party and a few silly tortes to interfere," Meagan said, her tone unusually harsh.

"Lisette gave her word," Katya replied coolly.

At that moment, there was a short knock at the door that connected the bedchamber to Alec's dressing room.

"Come in, Alec," Caro called. "Everyone is decent!"

He laughed, walking into the room. "Damn! We're too late!"

Lion was behind his host, and his appearance could leave no doubt that he was the most handsome senator in America. Ben Franklin had predicted years before that Lion's looks would be a drawback in politics, but he had overcome them, as well as the scandal of his broken engagement to Priscilla and his wedding to Meagan. He'd learned that no amount of scheming could secure the Senate seat; maturity and competence radiated a glow that could not be contrived.

"My goodness! Don't you two look wonderful!" Katya sang out. "Where is Randolph?"

"We left him reading something in the library," replied Alec, who was resplendent in a black velvet coat over pearl-gray breeches and waistcoat. He went straight to Caro, gazing at her appreciatively until she blushed when he bent to kiss her neck.

Meagan's eyes were fastened on her husband; his devastating looks still had the power to set her heart racing. Could he possibly feel the same? His eyes were warm and intimate, smiling into her own, but Meagan felt flustered. She fussed with a tiny crease in his caramel velvet coat until Lion caught her hand.

"Have I told you tonight that you are beautiful?"

"Yes."

"Then why do you act as though you believe I don't mean it?"

"I suppose because I don't feel very beautiful. I feel fat and ill tempered and unfit for civilized company."

"Really?" A smile tugged at one side of his mouth. "That doesn't say much for my powers of perception, does it? As I recall, I married the loveliest, wittiest girl at President Washington's first inauguration."

"That was a long time ago," Meagan muttered, wanting to cry.

"You two stop this whispering now!" Caro ordered cheerfully. "We must all start downstairs—our guests will be arriving soon. I am going to run back to the kitchen to look in on Lisette and ask if she won't join the festivities for a while. Will anyone come with me?"

Katya volunteered immediately, and for a terrible moment Meagan thought that Lion meant to accompany them, but when he spoke, it was only to say, "You may regret turning Lisette loose on your party, Caro, for she could easily steal the night from the society belles!"

The kitchen was large, occupying its own building behind the main house. Tonight, the wooden floor was tapped like a drum by the feet of dozens of servants, who carried the meticulously cooked dishes over to the house. A mammoth fieldstone hearth spanned one wall; its fire warmed the room with yellow light, and Lisette chose a table nearby to do her work.

What a terrible night! she thought, slipping out of her pelisse with a grimace. Seemingly endless layers of tortes, in all flavors, were piled on the table before her, with the corresponding bowls of fillings and icings to one side. Mixing and baking these had taken hours; she was exhausted and dreaded even having to put them together. Worry for her father coupled with physical exhaustion had left Lisette listless and drained. Pushing back her unbound golden hair, she dropped into a chair just as the door opened to reveal Caroline Beauvisage and Katya. Three young serving girls nodded to their mistress as they hurried past into the night.

"Lisette!" greeted Caro. "I cannot tell you how grateful we are that you made this effort for us and for Lion. Katya heard of your father's condition and I would have certainly understood—"

"No, Mrs. Beauvisage—"

"Please! Caro!"

"I promised you that I would do this. I wanted to. There was nothing I could do for Papa . . . he must rest, and it was best that I leave so as not to disturb him."

"Well, we are very grateful."

Katya went to put an affectionate arm around her friend's shoulders. "Lisette is the best person I know!" she declared.

Lisette laughed. "How many glasses of wine has Randolph given you?" she teased.

"Time is short," Caro broke in. "I must get back, but I wanted you to know of our feelings . . . and that we would be honored if you would join us in the house when you are able."

Lisette shook her head. "I am not pretending to be subservient, Mrs.—Caro—but I am tired, improperly dressed, and I could not dance while my father is so ill. I shall go back into town when I am finished here."

Katya gave her another hug before returning to stand beside her sister-in-law. Caro's expression mixed disappointment with understanding. "Of course. That was thoughtless of me, but I wanted you to know how much we care for you. I would never pretend to be better than you are, Lisette; I admire you tremendously and am most grateful for all you've done to help us today."

"You are welcome, and I appreciate your feelings," Lisette replied with a warm smile.

The two richly garbed females bade her good evening, but no sooner was Caro out the door than she turned eagerly to Katya.

"She is so lovely! Why ever isn't she married or in love, Katya? I cannot bear to think of her slaving in that Coffee-House; we must devise a match for your friend Lisette!"

Katya laughed as they walked through the moonlit garden. "First of all, Lisette is not a slave. She prizes her independence; working allows her to be self-sufficient. Secondly, she is not receptive to romance. She was badly hurt two years ago and has built up some formidable barriers. She is still warm and sweet, but there is a strength in her that declares: 'I can take care of myself without a man's help.' She believes men are shallow and arrogant for the most part, and finds their egocentricity highly amusing."

"My goodness!" Caro blurted. "A most unusual female! Are you suggesting that she doesn't *want* to fall in love?"

"That's right . . . and to hear Lisette explain her point of view, you'd believe she's the only sane one among us!"

❧ Chapter 4 ☙

March 25, 1793

Belle Maison's entryway and stair hall were laid with English brick running in a diagonal pattern, the walls richly paneled. A graceful arched pair of doors divided the two areas; servants were posted in the entryway to greet the Beauvisages' guests and take their wraps before they proceeded through the doors to greet the host, hostess, and the guests of honor.

Most of the smiling, opulently garbed arrivals were mere acquaintances, but there were those few who were dear friends or relatives. Caro especially relished the opportunity to bring those closest to her and Alec together all at once. It was a rare, delicious treat.

Among the first to arrive were Alec's parents. Jean-Philippe's hair was snow white now, his face more deeply creased, but he continued to exude a magnetic charm despite his nearly seventy years.

Antonia had aged more. She was past sixty now, still petite and lovely, but thinner. Strands of silvery white were scattered through her russet hair and tiny lines were etched around her mouth. The dashing Frenchman's Russian bride had come to him as pirate's plunder over forty years ago. Although they continued to love each other with a vibrance that inspired younger couples' envy, their life was quieter now. With the latest dark developments in France, both Jean-Philippe and Antonia seemed to move under a cloud of worry. Caro could see it now as she kissed them and asked, "Is there news?"

"Well." Antonia smiled slowly. "Natalya writes that she

is certain there is a baby on the way! But as for Nicholai
. . . I regret to say that we have heard nothing."

They went on into the brightly lit parlor just as Anne and
William Bingham appeared in the doorway. They were little changed since the days when Meagan had lived in the
servants' wing of their luxurious Mansion House as Priscilla Wade's lady maid. Since the government had come to
Philadelphia, Anne had been known as "Queen of the
Republican Court," and it gave Meagan a sweet satisfaction
to stand in the receiving line, greeting the beautiful, snob-
bish Mrs. Bingham as a guest. For a moment, she felt a
surge of her old mischievousness return.

"I hope you do not mind that I brought a guest along?"
Anne inquired a trifle haughtily, pulling forward a pale,
birdlike girl whose cheeks reddened with her nervous giggle.
"This is my cousin, Ophelia Corkstall, who is visiting us
from England. Ophelia, may I present Mr. and Mrs. Beauvisage and Senator and Mrs. Hampshire."

The girl tittered again before offering her hand. She
stared openly, first at the dark, rakish Alec, and then at the
golden, dazzling new senator.

Marcus Reems managed to distract Ophelia, coming up
from behind to wrap a familiar arm around her narrow
shoulders. His amber eyes met the clear blue ones of his
half brother, Lion Hampshire. Only Meagan was aware of
the real reason for the feud between the two men, and although Lion could not be accused of stirring up trouble,
the darker sibling was constantly looking for some new
point of conflict.

Lion was the bastard son, reunited with his father and
brother upon his mother's death when he was fourteen. He
should have been the outcast, but somehow the roles were
reversed, with Lion the brighter and more magnetic of the
two sons. The father had favored him, and though the old
man was long dead, Marcus had never stopped trying to put
Lion in the shade. Everyone else thought that the rivalry
was rooted in simple dislike, though Lion did nothing to
encourage it. Meagan knew that her husband continued to
hope for a softening in Marcus Reems's bitter heart.

Lion watched his half brother proceed into the parlor,
chatting animatedly with Anne Bingham and Ophelia.

Slanting a sardonic look at Meagan, he whispered, "Marcus is as dense as ever. He thinks to make me envious of his social connections, when in fact I pity him for having to endure the company of those two."

"You know that Anne's influence is considerable," Meagan reminded him with a teasing smile.

"I can do without it," he snorted before straightening to shake the hand of Philadelphia's mayor, Samuel Powel.

The Powels were followed by President and Mrs. Washington, a fact duly noted by Meagan and Caro. Gossip was thick concerning the close friendship between the coquettish Eliza Powel and the aging president, who had always appreciated a winsome lady. No one cared to suggest they were lovers, but they enjoyed each other's company to an unseemly degree.

Musicians were tuning up in the north parlor. It was a lovely room, decorated in varying shades of green, with a patterned English rug, priceless Chippendale furniture, and a spectacular glass and ormolu chandelier. People milled about, spilling into the south parlor and the huge dining room, where food was already being arranged. As the late arrivals tapered off, Alec and Caro decided it was time that they and the Hampshires joined the party. When they appeared in the parlor, the musicians began to play; the harmonious mixture of harpsichord, violins, flute, and harp set the tone for the lighthearted evening ahead.

Back in the kitchen building, Lisette was alone. The last of the servants had disappeared into the house and only she and the desserts were left, though Pierre had promised to return to carry the tortes.

Usually, Lisette had little time for melancholy, but tonight she could feel it steal through her body in uneasy waves and stinging pangs. The music drifted back from the house and she could see that each window was ablaze with candlelight; laughter seemed stirred into the night air. Looking down at her simple peach-colored frock and the full-length cream apron that covered it, Lisette wondered what Meagan Hampshire, Anne Bingham, and all the other elegant women were wearing tonight. Were their curls artfully upswept, and studded with jewels? Did they smell of jasmine or gardenias? Tiredly, Lisette pushed back her loose curls, set down the wooden frosting spoon, and closed her eyes. Images flickered through her mind of the richly garbed people dancing, laughing, and chatting with witty sophistication.

I don't envy them, she reminded herself, *but tonight . . . it would be nice to feel beautiful, to be free of worry and responsibility, to feel alive . . . even to be in love.*

The last thought was so out of character for the usually rational, realistic Lisette that she smiled at herself and what she decided must be utter fatigue of brain as well as body. She opened her eyes, blinked in disbelief, then closed them tight before taking a second look.

A strange man stood in the doorway. Actually, he leaned indolently against the frame, regarding her with emerald eyes that sparkled like real jewels.

Lisette's heart quickened. The man could not be a guest, for he wore a leather coat over a casual dirt-streaked shirt, fawn breeches, and knee boots that were unshined and mud spattered. His face and hands were deeply tanned, dark hair curled where his shirt was open at the neck, and his flashing smile was as rakish as a pirate's.

"*Bonsoir*, mademoiselle," he said in a husky voice that unaccountably sent a delicious shiver down Lisette's back.

"Are you employed here, sir?"

He seemed to find this question highly amusing. "No, I am not."

Lisette wondered with a start if he was a highwayman or a criminal of some sort. Perhaps he meant to rob the guests at Belle Maison of their valuables—he might even do her physical harm.

"I must insist that you tell me who you are," she commanded, "and why you are here!"

Slowly, with graceful strength, he crossed the kitchen's planked floor. In the firelight, Lisette could see that his hair was a rich chestnut color with bronze highlights apparently caused by long exposure to the sun. It was not queued, but cut into ruffled layers that grew away from his face and ended with gleaming curls that negligently bent over his collar. There was a long fresh gash across one dark cheek. In spite of the dusty condition of his clothing, Lisette realized that the man beneath was quite clean. Tall, lean, and muscular, he smelled pleasantly of salt water, horses, and night air, and his hair gleamed as though freshly washed. To her surprise, the stranger reached out to catch her frosting-smudged hand, lifting it to his lips for a kiss that startled her by its sensuousness.

"Nicholai Beauvisage, at your service, mademoiselle," he said with wry jauntiness.

Lisette was stunned as she tried to absorb this news. *"Nicholai Beauvisage?"* she echoed. "I—but—why, I don't believe you!"

"You don't?" Both eyebrows flew up over the wide emerald eyes. "I am devastated to hear you say so, mademoiselle. And, now that we have that matter settled, I believe it is *my* turn to insist that *you* identify yourself."

Seated, Lisette felt at a disadvantage. The man towered over her, seeming to mock her somehow, so she wiped her hands on her apron and stood up. It was disconcerting to find herself only even with his wide shoulders, for Lisette was taller than most of her female acquaintances.

"My name is Lisette Hahn."

"Hmmm . . . that seems to—" He broke off, snapping his fingers in amusement. "I have it! Hahn's CoffeeHouse. I was there tonight for a jug of ale and I was surprised to learn that I could get supper as well. The stew was like ambrosia after the food I ate at sea. Are you one of *those* Hahns?"

"As a matter of fact, I am. I am pleased that you enjoyed my stew, sir."

"Why the devil are you here?"

"As a favor to your alleged brother and sister-in-law. I made these tortes for this party tonight." When he moved to the window, gazing back toward the house, Lisette persisted, "I still don't believe you are Nicholai, but *if* I did, I would want to know how you came to be here tonight."

He looked down at the lovely girl who stood at his shoulder. Moonlight streamed in through the window, shooting her long pale curls with silver lights. Nicholai was unaccustomed to seeing a female in public with her hair loose and flowing this way, and there was a direct, intelligent glint in these blue eyes that he found intriguing. She smelled of vanilla and butter, yet was utterly appealing: slender and graceful, with an exquisite neck and soft rose-tinted lips. It had been a long time since he'd had a woman. . . .

"It is quite simple, Lisette. The situation in France has become rather uncomfortable, so I decided the time was ripe for a visit home. My ship, which was less than luxurious, docked tonight. Since my house in town is closed up, I went to my parents' to see them and fetch the key, only to learn they had come *here*. So, I procured a horse and rode out. As long as I must make such a public reappearance, I thought it might be better if I could look presentable. I saw the light on back here and decided to take a chance on finding a familiar face. Where are Mrs. Forbes and Pierre and all the rest?"

"They've all gone to the main house. Dinner will be served momentarily, so they are busy with that. As you can see, I'm left with the last course—and I had better finish up before Pierre returns to fetch these."

Nicholai's eyes lit up at this. "Pierre is coming? *Bon Dieu,* it will be wonderful to see that old elf. Do you know, I've been gone ten years . . . and it suddenly seems a lifetime."

Lisette regarded him from the corner of her eye as she arranged the third layer on the last torte. He certainly did sound authentic. "I don't think you will find your family much changed. Have you been in touch?"

"Letters, yes—until a few months ago, when I was forced to leave my château for Paris. I've been duly informed of all the births, weddings . . . and Grandmère's death." He perched on the edge of the table and stared into the fire. As she spread orange icing, Lisette's eyes wandered over Nicholai Beauvisage. His profile was perfectly chiseled, but there was a hard strength about his face that was very unlike the description Katya had given of her brother. Fun loving, easygoing, vulnerable—those were the adjectives people had used in reference to the younger Beauvisage brother. But if this was indeed Nicholai, it was obvious that the decade he had spent in France had carved out a very different man. The lines of his body were steely; muscles and tendons showed in his bronzed neck and were outlined beneath the clothes that concealed the rest of his body. All outward signs of a rock-hard inner man, Lisette thought.

"You are staring, mademoiselle," Nicholai told her sardonically. "Do you find me odd looking?"

The last torte was done; Lisette put the wooden spoon into an empty bowl and gave him a wry smile. "Not at all, Mr. Beauvisage. I was thinking that, although you may not see many changes in your family, I would wager that they will be astounded by the transformation *you* have undergone!"

❧ Chapter 5 ❧

March 25, 1793

While waiting for Pierre to arrive, Nicholai Beauvisage worked up a craving for Lisette. Six long weeks had passed since he had bedded a woman—whose face he had already forgotten. It was his experience that females of the serving class were eager to please men of breeding and grateful for the attention. Smoothly, Nicholai eased into a more charming attitude. He began to compliment Lisette and look for excuses to touch her.

She, however, did not respond in the expected manner. Instead of becoming a shy coquette, the chit turned wary and cool. After receiving the second barbed set-down, Nicholai traded charm for rudeness.

"Hasn't anyone troubled to teach you manners?" he demanded harshly.

Lisette was washing the bowls and looked altogether frosty. Not bothering to look up, she retorted, "My dear Mr. Beauvisage, I see no reason to be polite to a man who wants something from me that he could pay for on the docks."

"Your tongue is sharp, mademoiselle," Nicholai muttered in a menacing tone.

"What do you expect? You would like it if I batted my eyes at you and unfastened my gown, wouldn't you? You've a lot of nerve, questioning *my* manners! Would you be trying to charm me into your bed if I were one of those ladies dancing in the parlor?"

Her cheeks were flushed with anger and Nicholai's face

hardened at her insults, but before either of them could speak again, Pierre burst in.

"Mon Dieu!" he cried. "The tortes! I have been so busy!" The little white-haired valet scurried toward the confections that lined the table, but halted in mid-step and seemed to freeze. His mouth gaped for several seconds before he managed to croak, "M'sieur Nicky! Can this be? Are you a ghost?"

The younger, much larger man came forward with a grin to embrace Pierre. "Christ, but it's good to see a familiar face! You look just the same!"

As much as both men would have enjoyed a leisurely conversation, time did not allow it. Nicholai needed a bath and a suit of clothes before he would venture into the party and the reunion with his family. Lisette solved several problems by insisting that she would transfer the tortes to the house while Pierre prepared the bath and hunted down a suit for Nicholai's use.

A blanket was strung up across a back corner of the kitchen, a bathtub concealed behind it. Lisette hurried in and out with the tortes while Pierre heated water and filled the tub. She made a grand effort to ignore the proceedings and avoid Nicholai's mocking green eyes.

Finally, the last torte was handed over to a crisply dressed maid in the main house and Lisette started back to the kitchen. She almost collided with Pierre in the garden.

"I cannot take you back to Philadelphia, mademoiselle, until I see to M'sieur Nicholai as well as several other matters. I am sorry to make you wait—but—now I must find a suit!" He was hurrying on, but stopped to add, "This is such a wonderful night! Everyone will be so happy!"

"Pierre, does Mr. Beauvisage seem the same to you?"

The Frenchman's eyes were wide in the darkness. *"Mais, non!* Truly, he is a man now. Greatly changed. The family will be astounded."

Lisette nodded slowly as she watched Pierre disappear into the moonlit garden. For a moment, she wondered whether or not to return to the kitchen, even though Nicholai and his bath were concealed behind a curtain.

"Am I to stand out here in the cold?" she whispered,

deciding at once. A few more steps and the kitchen was at hand; Lisette opened the door purposefully, only to find the bathtub in full view. The blanket lay in a heap on the floor.

"It fell," Nicholai said with a mischievous smile.

Lisette was astonished to realize that she was blushing. She had believed herself beyond shock or embarrassment after her years at the CoffeeHouse; she met men each day who said and did things no other virtuous girl had to deal with. They make jokes about her aloof mien . . . how could her composure disintegrate *now*, when she needed it most?

Realizing that to look away would be the worst thing she could do, Lisette counted on the dusky firelight to hide the color of her cheeks. "I am certain that the position of that blanket could not matter less to me, Mr. Beauvisage," she said coolly, meeting his amused gaze.

Nicholai grinned. "You don't mind if I get out, then?"

"Please, do *not*." Lisette strove for a disgusted tone, but could not help noticing the strong neck and wide shoulders that glistened with soapy water. The man was more deeply tanned than even Lion and Alec, and his arms and auburn-haired chest were steely with muscles.

"You are an intriguing paradox," Nicholai decided, enjoying this light banter that chased his thoughts from France and the recent past.

"I haven't the faintest notion what you mean, sir."

"The infamous Mistress Hahn—a woman who has no interest in any man—nor *need* for one." The emerald eyes glinted with gentle perception. "Isn't that so? You would have me believe that, mademoiselle . . . believe that no man could send a chill down your spine or cause your heart to race with physical craving for his touch, kiss—"

"Mr. Beauvisage!" Lisette burst out, angry to feel her cheeks burn again. "You have been living in France too long—and I think that you would not dare to speak this way to a female of what you'd consider your own station. Not that *I* believe you are in any way above me—"

Nicholai laughed. "I have no interest in this class nonsense, mademoiselle. If I believed in it, I would doubtless have lost my head, literally, long ago. But back to my observations . . . the other side of your paradoxical nature is this: I see, opposing your coolness, that utterly beautiful face and body that seem to cry to be made love to. I see the fire in your eyes when you are angry, I feel the genuine passion of your character."

"You are inexpressibly insolent," Lisette told him in her iciest tone.

"Which side of you is real?" he continued, ignoring her insult. "You know you can confide in me; I won't tell a soul."

Lisette stared at him in fury, noting that his own gaze had hardened in challenge. "You are a rude, odious man and you have further spoiled an already disagreeable evening."

"Well, I would ordinarily beg for forgiveness on bended knee, but am prevented by my state of undress and the fact that my *own* day has been somewhat less than idyllic."

Lisette noted that the light tone was gone from Nicholai's voice. Eyes averted, he slowly soaped the strong expanse of his chest, and for a moment looked poignantly weary. Before Lisette could ponder the ordeal of his escape from France or speak in a gentler tone, Pierre burst in, brandishing a handsome suit of sage green, a fawn waistcoat, and a snowy starched shirt with pleated cuffs.

"Voilà!" he cried happily. "You will look magnificent, monsieur! The colors are much better for you than for your brother; he has only worn this suit two or three times."

As the little Frenchman bustled about, Lisette went out to the dark garden. Pacing the brick walkways that divided up the intricate boxwood-edged flower beds, she wished that Pierre would hurry with his duties so that she might return to the CoffeeHouse. Tense and bone-tired, Lisette felt that the irritating appearance of Nicholai Beauvisage had stretched her nerves to the snapping point.

Without even realizing her direction, Lisette had come within a few yards of the main house. Light and music and the movement of richly garbed guests assaulted her senses; she recognized Annie Bingham through the french doors, twirling coquettishly in the arms of President Washington.

"Lisette? Is that you?"

She whirled to find Lion and Meagan Hampshire coming out of the darkened garden from a different direction. "You startled me, Senator!" Lisette managed a smile. "Good evening, Mrs. Hampshire. You are looking very beautiful tonight."

Meagan's expression was doubtful. "Thank you."

"I strayed a bit too near the house, I'm afraid," Lisette went on. "I wouldn't want anyone to see me wandering about looking like this. I'm just waiting for Pierre to take me back to town."

Lion smiled. "Don't apologize, Lisette. Even with icing on your nose, you are lovelier than most of the women inside."

In the darkness, Meagan's haunted look went unnoticed, and the next moment all three were distracted by the sudden appearance of energetic Pierre and a tall, darkly handsome stranger whom neither Lion nor Meagan recognized.

As the little Frenchman made introductions and the Hampshires enthusiastically told Nicholai how many tales they had heard of him and how happy they were to see him safe at home, Lisette scrutinized the arrogant Mr. Beauvisage.

In the shadows, gilt edged with chandelier light, Nicholai was devastating—there was a raw, wild quality about him, despite the elegant clothing. He was a man who belonged outdoors: deeply bronzed skin, sun-streaked hair, and a tall, steely-lean body. Yet, his green eyes were brilliant with intellect and a sure wit, and his firm mouth quirked confidently as he kissed Meagan's hand with all the grace of a native Frenchman.

One auburn brow arched in a tiny insolent salute to Lisette before Nicholai allowed Pierre and the Hampshires to pull him into the house. Lisette shivered in the night air as she watched him disappear into the crowd. What a happy night this would be for all the Beauvisages and their friends . . . ten years was a long time.

Shivering again, Lisette wrapped slim hands about her arms and started back to the kitchen to wait for Pierre.

Nicholai accepted another snifter of brandy from Alec and smiled with weary pleasure. His face ached from smiling; it was not an expression he'd had much use for of late. It was a shame he was so damned tired tonight . . . the happy reunion with his family seemed like a dream; somewhat blurry. It was difficult to comprehend that his brother, now forty, had an arm around him, and Caro, his first fierce one-sided love, had been rushing over to hug him every five minutes. Little Katya was nearly a woman, engaged to be married . . . how could that be? Maman and Papa stood nearby . . . older, yet seeming to shed years each time they looked at their long-lost son.

"I suppose you're exhausted," Alec murmured.

"God, that is an understatement. This seems a fantasy, Sacha. Very . . . odd. It's as though I've been asleep for a decade. It sounds ridiculous, but I think I expected all of you to have remained frozen in your good-byes to me all these years. No changes . . ."

Alec chuckled at Nicky's self-deprecating tone and expression. "*You* are the one who has changed, little brother."

"You think so?"

"One hundred eighty degrees. It's eerie."

Nicholai dismissed this with a shrug and drained his glass. "I suppose I grew up. Boy turns man . . ."

Anne Bingham could be seen steering her cousin through the crowd. She had already found three separate excuses for Ophelia to speak to this dashing mysteriously returned Beauvisage, but obviously another tactic had occurred to her.

"I wish your hidden door was in this parlor rather than the other one," groaned Nicholai.

"It's impossible to talk here, but we do have years of conversation to catch up on. What do you say to a late breakfast or lunch tomorrow?"

"I say yes."

"I'll burst in and rouse you around eleven?"

Nicholai grinned. "I look forward to it. Old times, *mon frère*." As Anne's fingers closed over his arm, Nicholai glanced sideways to see Alec give him a smile of evil glee before leaving to dance with his wife.

"Nicholai," coaxed Anne, "as we have said, my cousin Ophelia is English. We have just found ourselves *filled* with questions about France. Isn't that so, Ophelia?"

The girl nodded with frantic brightness. Fascinated and amused, Nicholai watched her, thinking that she bore a striking resemblance to a wood thrush.

"Well, ladies, there is very little that I feel at liberty to discuss. I left the country immediately after the king was guillotined, and any number of events may have transpired during the intervening weeks."

"Now, Mr. Beauvisage, aren't you being the least bit evasive? We heard you promise to take tea with the president not ten minutes ago, assuring him that there was a great deal of information you could pass along about France. You mustn't tease us—Ophelia would adore a deep conversation with you, for she's very quick about politics and world events. Couldn't you possibly come to Mansion House for a quiet supper this week?"

"Mrs. Bingham, you are very kind to invite me, but I've just arrived in Philadelphia tonight and I feel it's too soon to set dates for social engagements." Nicholai mustered a polite smile, hoping it didn't reflect the extent of his distaste.

"Poor Ophelia is so disappointed, aren't you, dear?"

"Honestly, Mr. Beauvisage," Ophelia spoke up, "I would adore a long conversation about the inherited traits of the Bourbons—"

Mayor Powel elbowed in at this point. He lived next to the Beauvisage family home, and had known Nicholai since childhood. More evasive chatter about France. Young ladies with surnames such as Penn, Allen, Oswald, and Chew sidled up to receive introductions to the handsome mystery guest. Nicholai could scarcely snatch a moment alone with his parents, though he did manage to stop long enough to get his house key and promise his mother to come for dinner the next night.

Finally, with a strange girl trying to coax him into the crowd of dancers while another tugged at his other arm, Nicholai, on the verge of saying something either vulgar or rude, firmly excused himself. He paused only long enough to refill his brandy snifter, then headed out into the chilly, blissfully still garden. Occasional twin shadows occupied secluded stone benches, offering their whispers to the gentle night sounds.

With near-savage relief, Nicholai tore off his well-cut jacket and untied his cravat. When he reached the kitchen building, he opened the door without a knock, somehow relishing the prospect of Lisette, with her unembellished beauty and fresh honesty.

"Oh, my God!" she cried. "I'm so glad—I was about to look for Pierre—I must get home. You will take me. Hurry!"

She was wearing her pelisse and tossing one bowl into another, ignoring the enormous clatter they made.

"What the hell is going on?" Nicholai demanded.

"My father!" She was shrill now, her great blue eyes glittering. "The boy—he just rode in and brought me the message from the CoffeeHouse. Papa is worse—much— will you help me with these, please?"

He moved quickly then, taking her dishes and catching her elbow in his other hand. The horse he'd ridden to Belle Maison was in the stable, so all they needed was to borrow a chaise and leave word with the stable boy to explain to Alec. He'd help Lisette and save himself from that party all at once.

Minutes later, Lisette clutched Nicholai's hard arm as he tooled the chaise on a wild course over the moon-silvered Germantown Road, south to Philadelphia.

❦ Chapter 6 ❧

March 26, 1793

Lisette's fatigue was replaced by a strained energy, spiral-ing up from some inner reserve. Gone was the cool, self-assured girl Nicholai had bantered with; in her place was a tense daughter, wild eyed with worry.

Reaching the outskirts of Philadelphia, Nicholai tried to ask a few tentative questions, which Lisette answered tersely. By the time the chaise drew up behind the CoffeeHouse, he had a rude sketch of her past, her current life, and her father's deteriorating health.

His own life in France had hardened him to death and unspeakable tragedy. Nicholai had seen friends lose their ancestral homes and hide shamelessly like rabbits, not to mention those whose heads were dropped into baskets by Madame Guillotine. His own emotions—love, trust, and most of the others that had been so carefully nurtured by his family—were crushed like the grapes in his Touraine vineyards. He could empathize with Lisette, but his own thick shell was a great help now, for he could guide her along as a silent, strong stranger and that was precisely what she needed most.

Nicholai's emerald eyes were sharp with interest as Lisette led him through the back door, into the darkened keeping room where a low fire crackled in the stone hearth. Briefly, he wondered why he *was* intrigued with her life and not bored by its mundane flavor. Then, Lisette was pulling off her pelisse and yanking furiously at her apron strings, which Nicholai moved to untie. Touching her, even

the peach cotton dress that nipped her small waist, gave
him a start. As she pulled the apron forward, her butter-
hued curls tossed toward his face and he inhaled their
vanilla fragrance.

A tiny flight of steep wooden stairs led upward, and he
followed her silently. A blowsy, frizzy-haired woman ran to
meet Lisette on the landing, dry eyed but obviously stricken.
She ignored Nicholai, instead gripping Lisette in a crushing
embrace as the two of them went down the gray-shadowed
hallway.

Disconcerted, Nicholai went back down the stairs and
into the noisy, smoky CoffeeHouse proper. The man in the
caged bar, earlier a cheery sort, was now subdued, but
found a brandy for the stranger when Nicholai produced
an extra two shillings. Carrying his drink, he went back to
the stair landing and sat down to wait.

"Oh, my papa . . ." Lisette's voice was a tiny plaintive
wail. "Please, Papa. I love you so . . ."

His eyelids, like crinkled parchment, fluttered but remained closed. Lisette wet a cloth with water from the
pitcher and touched it to her father's dry, cracked lips, and
the gentleness of her touch bespoke her love. She held his
hand, concentrating on its feeble warmth rather than on
the more noticeable limpness. As long as he was breathing,
she could stave off the terror of being alone. Her father
meant so much to her; not only did she adore him because
of the unselfish love he had given to her all his life, but his
presence sheltered her from the world. Even if she did all
the work, he was there, supporting her, approving, and
serving as the symbol of the CoffeeHouse to the city of
Philadelphia. As long as she did her work, she was insulated
from the world by the name Ernst Hahn. If he died, Lisette
would be losing a great deal more than the precious love
and company of her kind, gentle father. As she listened to
the rattling echo of his breathing, cold panic swept Lisette,
and the independence she prized suddenly seemed to swell
to such huge proportions that she would never be able to
grasp hold of it again.

"Papa . . . you must try—try to get well. . . ." Tears dripped onto his blanket.

Pale blue eyes opened, mirroring her sorrow. "*Liebling*, forgive me. If I had been more courageous after we lost your mother, I might be strong today. I've been so weak—"

"*No*, Papa! Look at me." Now she was vibrant. "Have I turned out so badly? How can you talk that way? I hope that people will know what a fine person you are by knowing me, because I learned all about living from you. . . ."

"You learned all about living because you were forced to compensate for the things I didn't do—not because I set such a wonderful example. . . ."

"Papa, I love you! I will not let you berate yourself. You have done your best—this CoffeeHouse stands as proof of your hard work—and you are a wonderful, caring man. I wouldn't change one detail about you."

Smiling a tiny bit at her ferocity, Ernst Hahn turned his head toward the lovely hand that held his and brushed a kiss across it. "You are a beautiful girl . . . and you have developed a strength far more durable than my own." He stopped suddenly, wincing with pain, and had trouble getting his breath. "Lisette, I—you must promise me that you will not be so strong that no man can penetrate your armor. You have so much . . ."—he panted briefly, and tears prickled Lisette's eyes—". . . so much to give. I don't want you to be alone because you are afraid of pain—the way I was. I want—you—"

She watched his face contort with the effort to say these last words, but they were lost. His eyes spoke sharply, then froze, and Lisette felt one last squeeze of his dry fingers before they went slack.

After several long, stunned minutes, Hyla Flowers came up from behind to comfort the girl, but Lisette pulled away. "No! Please—I don't want to think about it yet—"

"Baby, come out into the hall. You can't stay in here. Stringfellow and I will see to your papa now; you needn't worry about a thing."

Lisette was on her feet. "I have to go out for a while. Thank you for taking care of Papa . . ."

"But—sweetheart." Hyla followed her down the hallway. "Where will you be?"

"Mr. Beauvisage?" Lisette was calling. "Could you come downstairs with me?"

Hyla watched as the tall bronze-shaded man stood up and took Lisette's arm. Was this one of *those* Beauvisages? "Lisette Hahn," she admonished sharply, "have a care!"

Lisette wasn't listening. Every muscle tensed, she gripped Nicholai's arm and murmured, "Please . . . take me away. I can't bear any more. . . ." As she stepped forward, her knees buckled without warning.

Effortlessly, he lifted her up and carried her out to the chaise, and Lisette loved the ensuing sense of unreality. This was a perfect escape: a stranger who would take her away from Papa, the CoffeeHouse, and everything that made her hurt inside.

Minutes later, she was being lifted into strong arms and carried again, through a dark walled garden. A key clattered in a lock, then Lisette found herself in a moonlit marble-floored hallway.

"*Chérie,*" Nicholai whispered absently in French, "sit in here. I must light the fire, some candles—" He looked around in wonder. "*Bon Dieu!* it has been so long . . ."

As he arranged and lit the fire, Lisette became aware that she was in a small, cozy study at the back of Nicholai's house. Obviously the house had been cared for in his absence; white dustcovers enveloped the sofa and chairs, but the desk, books, rug, and tables were virtually spotless. The room's colors were terra-cotta and molten gold, highlighted by the patchwork walls of books. Exquisite brown-and-cream delft tile faced the fireplace.

Nicholai reentered the room but paused in the doorway to look at his guest, wondering what to do with her. Glassy-eyed, Lisette faced the fireplace, arms folded and knuckles white as her hands gripped the sleeves of the peach dress.

"What can I do?" he asked simply, crossing to her side. "Lisette, you must give me a clue. Would you like a drink?"

She nodded suddenly and whispered, "Yes. Brandy."

Nicholai found his decanters full, clean glasses turned

upside down in a curve around them. He poured a small
portion of brandy for Lisette, but she drank it down, wincing, before he could sit. "More, please," she said, and he
complied, pouring a glass for himself as well, then settling
down beside her on the sofa.

"Lisette . . . I wish that I knew what to say," he ventured. "I've seen so much death myself these past months
that I've become reconciled to it as a natural part of life.
It's inevitable . . . and the way the world turns today, it
seems that we're all just lucky for what we can get."

Lisette turned to meet his gaze, her own eyes wide and
midnight blue with utter pain. "Papa had a hard life. After
my mother died, he never found the sort of job he should
have. He deserved happiness, but too much work—for my
sake—"

"Now, Lisette," commanded Nicholai, "you must not
blame yourself. When someone close to you dies, there is
enough to deal with . . . guilt just muddies the grieving
process."

Abruptly, she pressed her fingers to her eyes, hard.
Nicholai watched as her lovely face crumpled, quivering,
then slowly smoothed out again. When her hands went
down, Lisette looked at him evenly with splintered ice-blue
eyes.

"You are right, of course. I'd rather not discuss this anymore, but if it's not too much of an imposition, I would
like to stay here for a bit. You must be eager to look around
your home—and I would like to see the rest of it myself."

Nicholai stared at this gracious stranger for the briefest
instant before taking his cue and responding in kind. "I
insist that you keep me company for as long as you like,
Lisette, and it would please me enormously to show you my
home. Are you hungry? If I know Maman, she's kept the
kitchen stocked with a few staples. My sister, Danielle, and
her family use this house when they visit Philadelphia."

Lisette stood up straight and smoothed her wilted frock.
"Well, that accounts for the freshness of the air and everything else. I wondered—ten years of standing empty!" She
smiled like a china doll. "I don't believe I can eat right
now, but perhaps a bit more brandy . . ."

Taking her glass, Nicholai wondered if he were actually asleep and in the midst of some eccentric dream. "Lisette, are you so accustomed to drinking brandy?"

"As a matter of fact, I rarely even take a glass of wine, but I must say I feel fine. Don't worry, Mr.—"

"Nicholai. Please." He refilled both their glasses, and decided that she must be in such shock that the liquor served to cushion her from the stabbing pain. *He* damn well needed all the help he could get to survive the rest of this incredibly strange night.

Touring the house, Lisette commented on each room with all the polite grace of a society matron. The dwelling was narrow, three floors tall, and extraordinarily unique.

The other highlight of the ground floor was the large dining room, which boasted built-in corner cabinets with semicircular tops carved in a shell design. Nicholai then led Lisette toward the front door and the vestibule and waited for her reaction to the focal point of his home: an elliptical flying staircase that rose as if by magic to the third floor. She stared upward and let out one eloquent gasp. As they climbed the steps, Nicholai held a chamber stick aloft, and the single flame danced eerily over the curling carved balusters and railings.

"What an amazing house!" Lisette said, awed. "I confess I am more impressed by these special surprises than I am by potent grandeur. Once, I went with Katya to the Bingham's Mansion House, and I found all that gold and marble and the rest too overpowering."

As they entered the parlor, which was built across the entire rear of the house, Nicholai echoed, "Katya?"

"Why, yes, your sister. She's my dearest friend."

"She is?" He cocked an eyebrow at this news, while circling the room to light a few candles. "I barely had a chance to speak to her tonight, but I must admit I found the change something of a shock. She was a little girl with a long fat pigtail when I left for France."

"I know . . . she's mentioned you often, but none of it seems to apply anymore."

"Everyone keeps repeating the same observation,"

Nicholai remarked with sardonic amusement, then fell silent as he set and wound a beautiful walnut tall-clock.

Standing next to him, Lisette looked briefly around the elegant shadowy parlor, then allowed her eyes to rest on Nicholai. An odd current of warmth ran through her body; she felt as if she had been transported into a fairy tale, complete with flying stairways and a dashing prince who had swept her into his arms when she was unable to walk.

Nicholai studied Lisette in return, thinking how utterly delectable she looked, with her tousled moonlit mane and her great wide eyes the color of the night sky. Her body, even clothed, bespoke satiny, graceful length, and Nicholai wondered what her legs would look like if he could see them . . . or her derriere. . . .

"Mr. Beauvisage," Lisette whispered impulsively, "you are looking at me in a way that seems suggestive!"

He showed no sign of embarrassment, but laughed aloud, white teeth flashing in contrast to the shadowy bronze of his face. "If my gaze is 'suggestive' of my admiration for your beauty, then I must plead guilty, Lisette." One finger reached out to softly trace the long line of her neck, sending a deep and unexpected shiver through Lisette.

"I—thank you for the compliment, Nicholai." Blushing, she looked away and stepped toward the doorway. "Is there another room on this floor?"

"A bedchamber. A suite, really, for guests." He crossed the hallway and threw open the door to a huge room, where candles and a fire had already been lit. The bed hangings were fluffy white muslin, the counterpane quilted green silk, and the sofa and chairs that circled the marble fireplace were upholstered in single shades of green, pink, and white velvet, complementing the needlepoint carpets and brocade drapes. The furniture was priceless Queen Anne, clean and elegantly simple.

"I had the room done with my sisters and mother in mind in case they ever wanted to visit me, and on one occasion Maman actually did come for a night when she was angry with my father! Caro helped me choose the colors and fabric, after she came to Belle Maison as Sacha's ward . . . but God knows *that's* another story."

Nicholai's voice was low and ironic, as if he was surprised at himself for mentioning Caro. "I lit the fire earlier on the chance that you might want to rest here tonight."

Lisette stared at the lovely, inviting bed until Nicholai put a hand to her cheek so that each fingertip brushed her skin individually. His gesture had begun as one of sympathy and comfort, but when he felt her velvet-soft skin prickle under his touch, a searing wave of desire broke over him.

In a cloud, Lisette looked up into his emerald eyes and murmured with someone else's voice, "That is very kind of you, Nicholai, but I would really like to see *your* bed-chamber."

Before she reached the third floor, Lisette vaguely realized that the brandy was having a definite effect. It had helped to numb her aching heart, but it also colored her cheeks and infused her with a reckless dizzying warmth.

As he lit the fire in his spacious bedchamber, Nicholai glanced over at Lisette Hahn and shook his head again in disbelief. Her hair gleamed like spun gold in the soft light; she looked like a runaway princess from a fairy tale. Sighing, he reached for his brandy and sat back on his heels to make sure the fire took hold.

"I love this room," Lisette remarked with a smile. "It fits you. The house is really perfect; like a dream."

"Thank you—again."

Almost laughing, she trailed over to the massive Hepplewhite four-poster and perched atop the feather tick. The entire room was decorated in forest green and creamy tan, with brass and polished wood accessories, all underlaid by a rich Persian rug. Nicholai looked quite devastating in this picturesque setting. His shirt was partly open, and auburn chest hairs glinted in the firelight that played over the dark chiseled planes of his face.

"Lisette," he asked, gently ironic, "what do you mean to do tonight?"

She looked fragile and somewhat forlorn to him, sitting in the middle of his bed with her tumbled tawny curls and her wrinkled cotton frock. From the parlor below them came the echo of the tall-clock striking midnight.

"If I ask you a favor, will you say yes?" Her tone was bold.

"It's entirely possible," Nicholai replied dryly.

"Will you come over here and kiss me? I mean *really* kiss me, until I'm weak."

❦ Chapter 7 ❧

March 26, 1793

Nicholai blinked once; his left eyebrow arched, then slowly straightened again. *Curiouser by the moment!* he thought, but stood up anyway.

"If you are certain it will help, I'll do my best."

Lisette ignored the slight mocking note in his voice, feeling her heart begin to pound as he approached the bed. With deliberate, excruciating slowness, Nicholai lifted Lisette to her knees and softly stroked her face, smoothing back wayward curls and tracing her delicate cheekbones and the curve of her throat. As his fingers caressed her, Lisette began to tremble. Briefly, she caught a last glimpse of twin emeralds that flashed in the shadows before his hard arms encircled her back and Nicholai bent to capture her eager mouth.

He kissed her thoroughly, with an intimacy that stunned Lisette, until a sudden jolt of pleasure shook the center of her being. His strong, sure embrace, the heady male scent of his bronzed skin, the thrill of his warm lips moving over her own, his tongue probing her mouth in a way that made her answer, needing more . . . all these sensations combined to ignite a brush fire of desire within Lisette. She was twenty-one years old, yet had lived the chaste life of a nun . . . the part of her that was meant to love had been chilled by heartbreak. Now, as Nicholai kissed her, the fire spread, surging through Lisette's ripe body, obliterating her grief, guilt, and fears.

Nicholai turned one brief wondering thought to Lisette's sudden abandon. She seemed ravenous; he could scarcely believe it was the same girl who had coldly accused him of flirting with her and being "insolent." Was this the same woman who had appeared so frosty only a few short hours ago? Now, as Lisette pulled frantically at his shirt, he almost disengaged himself to speak, but her mouth was too luscious, her slim vanilla-scented neck too tempting; he could already feel her breasts swelling warmly through the stretched cotton of her frock.

After weeks of enforced celibacy, Lisette seemed an extravagant fantasy. She was artfully made, as delectable as rich caviar and the finest champagne, but she wouldn't let him savor her. Agressively, she nipped at his collarbone, nuzzled his furry chest, and stroked the muscled expanse of his back as she returned to search his mouth with her tongue. Nicholai paused for a split second, then reached around to deftly unfasten her gown. If she wanted to play tigress, he thought, then he intended to match her frenzy. Obviously, either the chit had two distinct personalities, or he had seriously underestimated his appeal.

Soon, Lisette's dress and muslin undergarments were removed, followed quickly by Nicholai's boots and breeches. When he pressed her against the taut length of his body, it seemed that her own flesh caught fire. She had never been naked with a man before, but tonight she felt utterly mad and didn't care if sanity ever returned. When his lips slid over her shoulder, brushed the full curve of one breast, then kissed the taut pink nipple, Lisette heard herself gasp. She shuddered and clung to him as his mouth worked a blissful torment over her breasts; there was a frightening tingly cluster of sensations blossoming in the hidden place between her thighs. Lisette gripped Nicholai's gleaming hair, wondering if she would die. She pressed her hips searchingly against his body, shaking, pulling him back for kiss after kiss, drowning in the magic.

Nicholai, too, felt somewhat dizzied by the sheer force of Lisette's passion, but he forced himself to resist her urgency. With deliberate, lingering sensuousness, he alternately kissed and brushed his lips and tongue over the ripe curves and hollows of her body. Lisette was never still or quiet; she flinched as if shocked, gasped, moaned, and reached for him, but could not stop his progress. She was certain that she would be a mass of tiny burn marks, for his mouth scorched her soft skin and intensified the strange fire in her loins.

"You are ravishing," he whispered hoarsely, tracing the line of her hip. "Do you know how beautiful you are?"

"No—please!" Lisette's voice broke on a sob and her fingers fluttered at his broad muscular shoulders. "Please! Love me. *Love me!*"

She began to weep when he shifted upward, kissing her slowly as his hand explored the sweet wet place that yearned so desperately for something she couldn't name. "Please!" she implored, trembling.

"Don't cry, *chérie.*" Nicholai, faintly alarmed despite his own fever pitch, paused to kiss away her tears. "Will you help me?" Gently he guided her apprehensively eager fingers to the hard length of his manhood. For a moment, Lisette was shocked by its size and pulsing warmth; then instinct took over. She pressed him between her legs, shifting her hips to receive him and crying out with painful ecstasy as he drove up seemingly to the core of her soul. Crazily, she welcomed the pain as a kind of purge, and as Nicholai's maleness filled her again and again, Lisette felt the grieving void grow warm. The fiery ache where their bodies joined intensified, and then finally seemed to explode. She quaked involuntarily with tingling contractions that caught and released Nicholai's hardness. Her blue eyes were wide with surprise; then he tensed and Lisette saw corded muscles tauten in his golden brown neck and shoulders. When he lowered his body to crush her tender breasts, she realized that they both were covered by sheens of perspiration that mingled now.

"Shh," soothed Nicholai. He put up a hand to smooth her silky blond hair, sensing somehow that she was teetering on the edge of some precipice. Still holding her, he slid to one side, cradling her face against his wide chest. Strangled small sobs rose from deep in Lisette's throat, and Nicholai assumed that she was thinking of her father. There was no doubt in his mind that Lisette was far from the ice maiden she had first seemed to be, but he couldn't believe her a common tavern wench, either. Obviously, her abandon tonight must have been precipitated by her father's sudden death . . . whatever the reason, this tumble they had taken together was one to remember. Lisette's passion had almost cleared his mind of painful memories of other nights with—

"I'm so cold," whispered Lisette, and indeed, Nicholai realized that she was shivering in his arms. Wordlessly, he disengaged himself to pull back the pine green velvet counterpane, then the quilts and linen sheet. The bed smelled fresh and cool, and the sight of the plush pillows reminded Nicholai of his own bone-deep fatigue. The two of them crawled between the covers and Lisette allowed him to hold her close against the crisp hair that covered his hard brown chest. Absently, the fingers that had touched her so intimately minutes before now caressed her brow as if she were a child. As soon as she was certain he had fallen asleep, Lisette moved away from Nicholai's masculine warmth to lie alone, staring into the coral gold fire.

A fine, dreary rain misted the windowpanes. It masked the sun, allowing Nicholai more sleep. When at last he did awake, his exposed torso was chilled and instinctively he burrowed back under the quilts.

Alec's borrowed clothes were scattered over the floor, but there was not a trace of Lisette. Had she left? It still seemed early. Nicholai was compelled to meet the chilly gray morning, rising to search for his waistcoat and the watch lodged in its pocket. Locating it, he stared in disbelief. Nearly eleven o'clock!

"Argh!" he groaned, and retreated to the warm bed. As he pulled back the covers, his eyes met an even more startling sight, for there were bloodstains on the side where Lisette had slept.

"Oh, Christ . . . it couldn't be!" Whipping up the velvet counterpane, he inspected the scene of their lovemaking, only to find two more definite reddish streaks. Nicholai got into bed, dazed. It simply was not possible . . . no virgin, especially one of twenty-one years, could be capable of such wanton passion. And when he had entered—she had displayed neither fear nor pain; in fact, she had seemed as sure of her movements as he was of his!

"What girl in her right mind would give her virginity to a virtual stranger?" he muttered aloud, continuing to puzzle over the matter until a distant knocking sound distracted him. Hastily, as the noise intensified, Nicholai pulled on breeches and hurried down the elliptical staircase. The black and white marble floor of the vestibule was cold beneath his bare feet, but he paid no mind to the discomfort, intent on ending the insistent knocking. Perhaps it was Lisette Hahn, back to explain herself. . . .

Nicholai threw open the door and found his brother standing on the stoop, his black hair damp with mist.

"I am so flattered to find that you have been anxiously awaiting my arrival!" barked Alec, yanking off his wet cape as he stepped inside.

"Now, dear brother, do strive to be more understanding . . . one would think you were not overjoyed to have me back in the bosom of my family!" Nicholai smothered a grin and recognized his own impulse to retreat into his one-time role of the cheerfully mischievous little brother.

"It would appear that someone from our parents' house tried to rouse you earlier," Alec went on sarcastically, gesturing back to the trunk that rested on the stoop. "I gather you left that thing at our parents' when you came on to Belle Maison in search of your key last night."

Nicholai smiled. "Well, I couldn't very well take it along on the horse!"

"And you were obviously far too occupied with Lisette Hahn to stop for it on the way back!"

"Now, Sacha—" Nicholai pulled the wet trunk inside and closed the door. "You've heard about her father, haven't you? I was only trying to help in Lisette's hour of need."

"Help her into bed, I'll wager . . . though I'm also certain you learned the unpleasant truth about the beautiful but cold Mistress Hahn." Taking hold of one end of the trunk, Alec helped Nicholai carry it up the curving stairway. "What about her father?"

"He died! Quite suddenly, I gathered . . . poor man. I never saw him, but my heart went out to Lisette; she was devastated."

Alec was stunned, but kept silent until they reached the

bedchamber, whereupon he settled into a tan-and-green-striped wing chair while Nicholai selected clean clothes from his trunk.

"Nicky, am I wrong, or did you just meet Lisette Hahn last night?"

"That's right." He peered in the mirror above his washstand. "I had a bath and shave last night at Belle Maison . . . do you think I can pass for now?"

"God, yes—no one will know who you are, anyway. Will you tell me how you two came to be so well acquainted?"

"Lisette and I?" Nicholai flashed a decidedly adult grin while buttoning a fine linen shirt. "She was building those tortes in the kitchen, which is where I went first last night so that I might get a bath and some decent clothing before presenting myself to that ball you were giving. We talked; the chit intrigued me. Later, when all those eager unmarried females began trying to pull me apart, I returned to the kitchen to catch my breath. Lisette had just gotten word that her father was on his deathbed, so I took her home. I've been wondering how she is . . . and what she'll do now about that CoffeeHouse."

"Mistress Hahn is very independent. The last few years, as her father's health has deteriorated, she's practically run the place herself."

Dressed, Nicholai brushed his burnished chestnut hair back in curly disarray. "By the way, Alec, what did you mean by the 'unpleasant truth' about Lisette?"

"I mean that it is common knowledge that, for all her succulent and tempting beauty, the lady has passed twenty-one summers without consenting to share any man's bed. And, believe me, nearly the entire male population of Philadelphia has tried to thaw the maiden's shield of ice."

Nicholai's eyes gleamed attentively. "Why, do you suppose? Doesn't she like men?"

"Not particularly, at least not on intimate terms. She's unfailingly friendly and witty with her CoffeeHouse customers, but it never goes beyond that. The challenge of Lisette is an important factor in the growing success of that CoffeeHouse!

"Are you ready?" Alec stood up. "I hope you won't mind the fact that I told Lion Hampshire he could join us for luncheon. It seems that he has something he's anxious to discuss with you."

"Ah, yes—the senator! Where are we bound for this mysterious meal?"

Alec grinned a trifle wickedly, watching for Nicholai's reaction. "Coincidentally, Lion asked us to meet him at noon . . . at Hahn's CoffeeHouse."

Nicholai's only response was an enigmatic smile and a fleeting sparkle of his emerald eyes.

Chapter 8

March 26, 1793

The two brothers, each uniquely and magnetically hand-some, walked side by side down the elegant stairway.

"The house looks splendid," Nicholai murmured. "I mustn't forget to give Maman a kiss for taking such care of the place. Now I suppose I must hunt for a few servants."

"Let Maman do that when she offers. She'll be delighted to help. As you might guess, she and father are dying for you to come to supper tonight and fill them in on your life this past decade."

"And Caro?"

Alec glanced sharply at his brother. "She's as anxious to hear all as the rest of us—insisted that we come into town for dinner as well, ostensibly so that you can meet your nephew and nieces."

"Nieces?" he echoed in the midst of locking the front door.

"The newest Beauvisage was born October twentieth. We named her Kristin, which you may recall was Caro's real name, and she looks *exactly* like me. Now, Talya, on the other hand, has beautiful honey hair like her mother, and I'm certain you'll take to Étienne immediately. He's *eight*! You know, Nicky . . . I wrote to you the instant Kristin was born, and sent it with a packet I knew was bound for Brest . . . it's odd that the letter missed you."

They strolled through the mist, east along Spruce Street toward the Delaware River. It was a quiet day, with few people or carriages venturing out into the damp gray cold, and Nicholai looked around at the familiar brick row houses while his brother talked.

"Philadelphia doesn't seem very different," he observed. "Now that it's the capital, I expected a tremendous transformation."

Alec made a derisive sound. "In many ways it *has* been transformed. The population has swelled far past fifty thousand, I'd wager, and the edge of town creeps nearer the Schuylkill by the day. Water Street is a deafening mess of carts, drays, and six-horse wagons from the country, though I would be a hypocrite to complain about the boom in sea trade, since it has quadrupled the Beauvisage fortune in the last few years. . . ."

"Sacha—" Nicholai interrupted suddenly, stopping on the brick footpath and gazing intently at his brother. "I'd better tell you—the reason why I never received your letter in France is because I left the château in August and wasn't able to return before I sailed from Le Havre in January. I couldn't even say with any degree of certainty whether the vineyards still belong to our family or not. . . ."

"Nicky, what the devil are you talking about?"

"I've been unsure how much to tell father and Maman . . . let me tell you all of it, and perhaps you can advise me whether to bare all tonight or wait out the Revolution and hope for the best."

"For God's sake, man, get on with it!"

"You know, Sacha, I got the impression last night— listening to everyone rave so cheerily about the situation in France—that you may all think it's like our own fight for independence."

"I suppose that's a fair generalization. There's been a good deal of cockade wearing, singing of French marching songs, and for a period it was in vogue to call one another 'citizen.' The news about the king is causing people to think twice, however."

Nicholai grimaced as he walked along slowly, searching for the right words. "I didn't want to write stories home of how horrendous it had actually been, but in truth it is a miracle that I'm alive! Before the Revolution began, nearly every nobleman I ever knew of left his château to be part of the court at Versailles . . . ultimately embittering the people of the provinces. I was disgusted by the whole place! The queen saw me as a challenge and invited me frequently, though I only made three short visits . . . thank God. I managed to elude her most of the time, but I did meet the sister of a prominent marquis during my first stay at Versailles in 1787, and she bewitched me instantly. Gabrielle came to my château several times the following year, even after her brother had forced her to marry a pompous, perfumed *comte*."

"What happened to those aristocrats?"

"I'll get to that . . . I know we haven't all day, so I'll try to condense my story. As you know, France has always been divided into three classes: the nobility, the clergy, and the third estate—everyone else from bankers to peasants—and it was that last group who paid the taxes to support the other two estates. I never considered myself a nobleman, which everyone in Touraine knew. I paid taxes and worked in the vineyards just as they did. They were aware that I could have easily played the aristocrat, yet I shunned Versailles and the soft life at Court.

"At any rate, there was always unrest and resentment simmering under the surface, but at court it was bad form to take things too seriously. Though the economy was a shambles, the king was spending nearly a thousand pounds a year just for his damned *lemonade*! It took the hellish, torturous winter of 1789 to bring the boil to a head. Louis finally focused his eyes for a moment in May and called an Estates General to solve the problems. I was elected as a delegate for the third estate, and though we all had high hopes, it turned out to be a *farce*!" Nicholai's entire body clenched at the memory, his green eyes turned jewel-hard. "With the clergy and nobility to back him up, Louis refused to accept most of our reforms . . . and it was the last straw. There was a terrible drought that summer, and the revolution began in earnest when the people took matters into their own hands and stormed the Bastille—"

"Nicky, you sound as if you were all for it!" interrupted Alec.

"At that time, I was—emotionally, at least. But it's all gone mad. The Girondists and the Jacobins are constantly jockeying for power; there is no order—the quest for change and freedom has become, in my opinion, a chaotic bloodbath. And it's getting worse. There is no respect for human life. A person can be sent to the guillotine for no reason at all! During the September Massacres, the 'trials' lasted one *minute* at most and the prisoners were hacked down en masse in the prison courtyards . . . I could tell you grisly stories that would keep you awake at night."

Alec gazed at Nicholai's haunted face. "How can you be so certain that you have not heard exaggerations?"

"Because I was there! Gabrielle came to me in July to tell me that her brother had been imprisoned and to beg me to come to Paris and arrange his escape. The September Massacres were methodically planned in advance for the simple purpose of convincing the troops that they should leave Paris for the front. It was a way to show them that the aristocrats were not relieved from fighting the war by being in prison—and also that they wouldn't break out and overturn the Revolution when the army left town. Over a thousand people were murdered—butchered!—and I was almost one of them. In August, they began rounding up people to fill the prisons, and on my first night in Paris Gabrielle and I became victims of the infamous house-to-house searches that were carried out all month. Supposedly, they were looking for her husband, who was hiding in the provinces, but they settled for *la comtesse* and her lover."

"You." whispered Alec.

"Yes. Instead of rescuing Gabrielle's brother, I watched her stuffed into a prison wagon . . . that was the last time I ever saw her. I've no doubt the marquis and she were both killed in the massacres. *I* was only saved by a freak encounter with Maximilien Robespierre on September second, the first day of the massacre. He appeared in my prison during the shamtrials and recognized me. We had talked at length during the Estates General, to which he was also a delegate. Fortunately for me, he remembered my stand on behalf of the third estate despite my opportunity to be part of the aristocracy . . . and he had me set free. I pleaded with him to spare Gabrielle as well, though I had no idea to which prison she'd been taken, but Robespierre has no heart."

"What have you been doing since then?"

"I lived those five months in Paris, spending as much time as I dared with the fanatics that steer the Revolution's course, hoping to subtly influence them with a sane idea or two. Robespierre liked me since I had studied Rousseau, though God knows I didn't absorb it in the warped fashion he did! I hoped to find Gabrielle alive and keep the king from being murdered, but I accomplished neither. I argued recklessly with Robespierre, Marat, and Danton the night before Louis was guillotined; I pushed too hard, they perceived me for what I am, and I knew that if I had stayed in Paris past that twenty-first day of January, I would have been disposed of. I was on my way to Le Havre less than an hour after Louis the Sixteenth went to the guillotine. . . ."

Although they had reached the CoffeeHouse, the brothers remained standing outside in the fine, cold rain. The noise of horses and wagons and boisterous shouts had nearly drowned out Nicholai's bitter voice, but Alec was mesmerized, staring at his younger brother in awe and fascination. "I can scarcely take it all in," he murmured. "Now I know . . . what has caused the change in you. I sensed that it was more than simple maturation. You've been hardened by these last years in France."

Nicholai shrugged, his expression poignant with weary pain. "When a man lives in a world of insanity and meaningless killing, he learns to use his wits—one either grows hard or is crushed."

Inside the CoffeeHouse, Lion Hampshire withdrew his pocket watch to note the time. At nearly half-past twelve, he began to wonder if Alec had forgotten their appointment.

Restlessly, the handsome senator surveyed the smoky, crowded room. At the center stood the coffee urn, where men borrowed money and traded goods. Behind the cage of his bar against the east wall, James Stringfellow watched the movements of each person, all the while keeping up a fast and frisky repartee with Hyla Flowers, Purity, Chastity, and the occasional customer who came over to say hello or to fetch his own wine, liquor, or lemonade. Cheerful orange fires blazed in the two mammoth hearths, and the sprawling room was made cozier by the voices of men who enjoyed gossip and the lively art of conversation. By the time several different and prominent citizens had waved at Lion, inviting him to move to their tables, he was beginning to feel foolish for turning them down.

Suddenly, Alec and his brother appeared, working their way between the tables and pausing to answer the greetings of old friends.

"At last!" Lion said, uncharacteristically annoyed.

Alec and Nicholai looked at each other and laughed, then slid into the booth opposite Lion. "That's exactly what Sacha yelled into my face when I opened my front door this morning," the younger Beauvisage explained. "I apologize for our delay, Senator. I was telling Sacha the tale of my years in France and I fear I grew rather long-winded."

The amazed expression returned to Alec's face. "You cannot imagine what he's been through, Lion—what has been going on over there—"

"Sacha, if you don't mind, I'm rather fed up with the entire subject, and I'm certain the senator has more pressing matters to discuss."

Lion studied Nicholai Beauvisage more closely. There was no doubt that his charismatic good looks equaled Alec's, but there was something else about him that Lion couldn't label. There was a natural confidence in his bearing and voice, and a cynical gleam in those brilliant green eyes that belied his polite charm . . . Lion sensed a steel edge beneath the pleasant smile.

"Nicholai, I insist that you call me Lion. I've been your brother's friend for years and I hope that you and I will come to know one another very well, too."

Nicholai appraised the young senator steadily and expertly concealed his own thoughts. Flashing his most friendly smile, he took in the details of Hampshire's striking physical appearance. He wondered what sort of man Lion really was, under the immaculate white shirt and cravat and the expensive blue gray coat. Was it possible that he could not be conceited and egotistical, considering his looks and his new position? Did Lion imagine he could manipulate Nicholai with the power of his office and the fire of his smile?

"I would be pleased to count you as a friend—Lion, but I know that you must be a very busy man. Why should I be singled out to 'get to know you very well'?" There was an unmistakable caustic undercurrent in Nicholai's pointedly polite voice.

Lion grinned, delighted. "You're wonderful, perfect! Marcus is much too poor a judge of people to see beyond your smile, charm, and family connections. Please, Nicholai, you must promise to be frank and open with me. You can trust me and I need to know what you're thinking and feeling."

First perplexed, then astonished, and finally outraged, Nicholai leaned forward and snarled, "Right now, I'm *thinking* you're a raving, arrogant lunatic and I'm *feeling* a great stab of regret for not staying home in bed!"

Alec looked at Lion, then gave a bemused smile and a sigh. Lion laughed in return, rubbing dark hands together with excitement.

"What the hell is wrong with you two?" Nicholai demanded. "Sacha, I'm beginning to think you're as demented as your *friend* here—"

He was interrupted by the voice of Hyla Flowers, asking what the gentlemen would like to drink. Instead of her usual gaily striped frock, she wore one of dismal gray, and her puffy face was unpainted and pinched.

"Hyla," Lion chided, "you look as if you've lost your best friend! Cheer up, woman! By the way, where is Lisette today? I haven't seen her once since I came in."

"Good God!" Nicholai broke in. "You're an even bigger dolt than I'd imagined! Don't you know that Lisette's father died last night? I'm amazed that the CoffeeHouse is open at all today, and I'm sure we'll not see Mistress Hahn in our midst for a long time."

"Nicky!" admonished Alec, fearing that his brother would carry his insults too far.

"This man—Mr. Beauvisage, ain't it?—speaks the truth about Master Hahn," Hyla said, her voice shaking, "but he's all wrong about our Lisette. She's a fighter, as you well know, Senator, and her work will be what sees her through her pain. Stronger than a dozen of you men, she is!" Hyla finished with a venomous glare at the stranger whom she imagined had taken advantage of Lisette's grief and shock. Hyla had been wide awake when her young mistress crept up the stairs before dawn, though she knew better than to mention those lost hours to Lisette, ever.

Lion Hampshire was too stunned by the news of Ernst Hahn's death to acknowledge either Nicholai's rudeness or Hyla's odd treatment of the younger Beauvisage. "I—I cannot believe it! So that's what became of Lisette last night. . . ." His handsome face tightened with genuine sorrow and pain. "She must be hurting terribly."

"You know Lisette, sir—she doesn't let on. There's even oxtail soup and warm gingerbread with raisins and hot lemon sauce. I told her she didn't need to fix nothin'. . . ."

Subdued, the men ordered food and hot coffee to fortify themselves against the wet, dark weather. Nicholai decided that Lion Hampshire might deserve a second chance; the sincere emotion he'd displayed had impressed Nicholai.

"Look," said Lion, "I don't feel much like discussing anything right now, but there may not be another opportunity. You're mistaken about me; your brother will tell you that I am neither arrogant nor demented. I'm a normal man, like you, who has developed certain strengths and learned to overcome some of my flaws. I'm honest and fair and I believe in this country, so becoming a senator has meant a great deal to me. I want to help."

"It's true, Nicky," Alec confirmed. "Lion's a fine man; he's my friend and I'm for him. You can trust him."

Nicholai sighed. "I may have been too hasty, but my own life has been so erratic of late . . . sometimes I tend to think the world has gone mad, and after my experiences in France, its easy for me to think the worst when I meet someone new. I used to be very trusting. . . ." His voice trailed off bitterly.

"I probably confused you when I mentioned Marcus earlier," Lion smoothed. "I got ahead of myself; I don't blame you for thinking me unhinged. After I met you last night, I began to wonder if you might not be able to help me with the one chronic problem in my life. Alec told me that you had returned to Philadelphia because of the situation in France and that he wasn't certain what course you would follow next. It occurred to me that what I have in mind might provide you with an interesting diversion while you make a decision about your future."

Chastity put heavy bowls of soup on the table, then added pewter spoons, a loaf of warm bread, and a crock of butter. After pausing to taste the soup, Nicholai met Lion's penetrating gaze.

"You've intrigued me! I gather this problem of yours concerns this Marcus character?"

Alec made a rude noise at the mention of Marcus Reems, but Lion ignored his friend. "Yes. It's an incredible story, but I'll try to explain as simply as I can. You see, I was born out of wedlock and didn't know my father until my mother died when I was fourteen. He came for me then and was thrilled to find that, unlike his legitimate son, I resembled *him*. Later, when he realized that school and life in general came easily for me, my father heaped even more attention on me—yet, no matter how he tried, he couldn't force me to love him. That other son, my half brother, is Marcus Reems, and he's gone through life trying to outdo me, especially since our father died a dozen years ago. No doubt, if he pursued his own abilities, he could excel also, but he invariably challenges me at my own game. Ridiculous situation, isn't it? Unfortunately, Marcus takes it all quite seriously and more than once his sport has taken a dangerous turn. He thought he'd won when he stole my fiancée away and married her—only to learn later that I'd been in love all along with someone else, who is now my wife . . . his bitterness subsided a bit until I won the election last fall. Since then, I can see him gnashing his teeth each time we meet! I am angry with myself for wasting so much time wondering what the hell he's plotting. Since his wife died, tragically, in childbirth two years ago, he's begun to act rather deranged, and I never know what to expect."

"How can I help you?"

Lion's smile warmed. "You are new on the scene; no one knows where you stand or who you call your friends. To be blunt, you would be the perfect person to keep an eye on Marcus—"

"*Spy* on him?" Nicholai pressed, grinning wickedly.

"That's a strong word—but apt, I suppose." Lion's voice grew serious. "I can just sense that he is up to something; if you could learn what it is, there's an excellent chance it

might save my life. I wouldn't put murder past him anymore, even though eliminating me would end his sport."

Nicholai saw the sad regret in Lion's eyes and nodded
slowly. "Certainly, I'll help if I can. As you said, it would
be an interesting diversion."

Alec had been munching on a chunk of buttered bread
and looking out the window, trying to seem inconspicuous
while the other two men talked. Now he suddenly straightened. "Lion—speak of the devil, he's on his way up the
street and appears to be headed this way. You certainly
don't want your '*spy*' to be seen with *you!*"

"Thank God you were looking in the right direction,"
moaned Lion with relief. Standing up, he reached over to
grasp Nicholai's hand. "Thank you. We'll have you to dinner soon and we can talk at length. I'm going to be a father
in a few months and I find I've become more protective of
myself. I want to see my child." He picked up his cape,
slung it over one arm, and exited through the door that led
to the kitchen.

"He seems to know his way around," Nicholai observed,
remembering the way Hyla Flowers had alluded to Lion's
familiarity with Lisette's nature.

Alec propped his booted feet on the opposite booth and
took a long drink of coffee. "I think he does. Lion was a
friend to both Ernst and Lisette Hahn." He inclined his
head toward the doorway. "There he is—Marcus Reems.
The tall one with the black hair. Can you see his eyes?"

Nicholai watched as Reems passed, in the company of
two other men. When he was seated, safely out of earshot,
Nicholai said, "His eyes looked *gold* to me. Strange!"

"Well, there's Lisette now," Alec said, staring past his
brother. "The classic tragic beauty."

Nicholai's head snapped around; when he spotted her his
breath caught for a moment, an occurrence so odd that he
paused to wonder what was amiss with his body. Lisette
was crossing the large, crowded room with a tray filled with
plates of gingerbread. She wore her hair in a high braided
crown that emphasized the graceful perfection of her face
and neck, and even the severe cut of her midnight blue
frock could not hide her lithe curves. As she set plates on

tables and smiled at the men who greeted her or offered expressions of sympathy, Nicholai was conscious of a sharp sensation in his chest. Unbidden, the memory of Lisette's hypnotic kiss invaded his mind and he saw her again, naked, clinging to him, begging him to . . . love her.

She was only a few feet away now and there were two plates left on the tray. Alec stood, extending his hand to Lisette, telling her how sorry he was to hear of her loss.

"Thank you, Mr. Beauvisage. I appreciate your kindness."

Nicholai stood next to his brother, expecting Lisette to look up into his eyes, to say some small thing that he would understand. She carefully set the gingerbread and two forks on the table, but when she glanced at Nicholai, her eyes were as remote as a stranger's.

"Good day to you, Mistress Hahn," Nicholai said, thinking to be kind and break the ice for her.

Lisette had already begun to turn away when she answered, with cool finality, "Good day, sir."

Chapter 9

March 26, 1793

Nicholai wouldn't have allowed Lisette to get in the last word if Marcus Reems hadn't intervened.

"Mistress Hahn, may I have a word with you?" The tall man with the gold tiger eyes rose partway, smiling warmly at Lisette as he gestured for her to come toward his table.

After reseating himself in the booth, Nicholai watched as Alec attacked the fragrant dessert. Lisette was only inches from Marcus Reems's face, bending closer to listen to whatever it was he was saying; Nicholai could almost smell the vanilla and butter that scented her skin, clothing, hair. . . .

"Sacha, what the devil is the wench up to, now? First she pretends not to know *me,* and then she cozies up to the man I've just been told is the blackest of villains!"

Alec put another bite of gingerbread in his mouth and chewed thoughtfully. "I was going to ask *you* what happened to the flourishing friendship between you two . . ."

Watching Lisette return to the keeping room, slim shoulders straight, the golden crown of hair gleaming in the candlelight shed by tin chandeliers, Nicholai pondered his brother's gentle gibe. Though he was puzzled and vaguely annoyed, a spasm of fury twisted in his gut when he saw Marcus Reems get to his feet, glancing furtively around to see if he was observed, and follow Lisette's course toward the back of the building.

Not wanting to explain to Alec the major reason for his interest, he muttered, "For our friend Lion's sake, I believe I'll look into this a bit more carefully."

"But, Nicky," came the mock-plaintive protest, "don't you want your dessert?"

Nicholai pushed the plate over to Alec as he stood up. "Oh, I insist!" He grinned, then added, "Don't wait for me. I will see you and Caro and your entourage of children tonight at our parents'."

With that, he set off, toward the front door.

Leaning against the brick wall, Nicholai rubbed five knuckles over his stubbly jaw. He wished now that he had shaved again. Only a quarter hour had passed, but a clear veil of mist covered his auburn gold hair and the cold seemed to seep closer to his bones by the minute.

I must be getting old, he thought with a little groan. *What the hell is he doing in there?*

As if in answer, Marcus Reems appeared from the CoffeeHouse's back door. The fact that he hadn't chosen to return into the public room merely confirmed Nicholai's suspicions. However, as he started toward the rear door himself, after Reems was safely out of sight, Nicholai had more than one matter to discuss with Lisette Hahn.

He entered without knocking, thinking to put her on the defensive, but as it turned out Lisette did not see him at all. She was feverishly pouring hot lemon sauce over two large rectangular gingerbreads while Purity lined the worktable with small plates. Hyla Flowers was dishing up oxtail soup from the pot over the fire, handing the full bowls to Chastity.

Nicholai paused for a moment. He was beginning to wish he'd never seen this enigmatic, beautiful girl . . . had it been less than a day since they met? Not once in the intervening hours had she behaved as he anticipated; all of his considerable experience with women was going to waste in his dealings with the contrary Lisette Hahn.

"Do you mind, sir?" Her voice, cool and clear, broke into his thoughts. "I have a business to tend."

Nicholai met the challenge in her blue eyes and felt his self-assurance return. Who, for God's sake, did the wench think she was?

"I shall wait, mademoiselle, until you have a moment to spare me—as you had for Marcus Reems." Negligently, he took a rough-hewn chair far across the keeping room and leaned back, emerald eyes piercingly warm as they contemplated Lisette's face and form.

She forced herself to ignore him, keeping her head bent over the gingerbread so that no one would see the blush that suddenly heated her cheeks. It was as much a mystery to Lisette as the tidal wave of events last night, but she had reached one hard conclusion while walking home before dawn—there was no room in her life for this uncontrollable side of her personality, this physical being who would not listen to the shouted orders of her mind. Lisette had resolved to steer clear of Nicholai Beauvisage, or any other man who tempted her to forget her work and the necessary discipline of her life. It was going to be difficult enough to continue with the CoffeeHouse, simply because she was female.

When the dessert was cut and transferred to the plates, Lisette watched Purity crowd them onto a huge tray, which she then lifted with shaky triumph. Hyla held the door, then followed the two girls as the last servings of food were carried into the CoffeeHouse. Suddenly alone with Nicholai, Lisette hurried over to remove the empty kettle from the fire. She grasped the handle with two thick towels and had begun to turn when a pair of dark, well-made male hands took it from her and set it on the hearth with ease.

Something snapped inside Lisette. Her blue eyes blazed as she confronted Nicholai, determined to settle the matter between them. "Sir, I have made it plain that I do not want you here. I would hope that you could show me the courtesy of taking the hint without forcing me to call for assistance."

He returned her stare, his own eyes penetrating and slightly amused by her effrontery. "Lisette, how can you say such a thing? I thought I took your hint rather well last night."

She drew her hand back as if to slap him, but stopped in midair. "You are a rude, inconsiderate cad! I do not wish to discuss last night or any other subject with you." The firelight haloed the plaited crown atop her head, suffusing her beauty with golden light. "Please leave my Coffee-House."

Nicholai caught her wrist when she began to turn away.

"Lisette, what is it? Are you going to pretend that we didn't make love last night? I don't want you to hate me and you mustn't worry that I think you common or that I would tell anyone what transpired between us. If you are angry because you feel I used you—"

"*You* used *me*?" One delicate brow arched derisively as she pulled her wrist free. "You men are really incredible! Did it ever occur to you, Mr. Beauvisage, that I used *you* last night? Women have physical needs, too, and you were conveniently available to ease mine. I am not a simpering coquette, like those you must have grown used to in France —I am an independent, hardworking woman, and though it may be a difficult concept for you to grasp, I neither need nor *want* to be swept off my feet and taken care of by you or any other self-important man!"

Though momentarily stunned, Nicholai felt a bubble of delight rise in his throat. "Do you mean to say that I was just one of many? Another dispassionate conquest for you?" His dramatic tone was heavy with amusement.

"Boor!" Lisette hissed disgustedly. She averted her face and took two steps toward the worktable before Nicholai caught her in his arms. For a moment, he held her fast, laughing softly as she struggled and cursed, then he murmured, "You are remarkably hard-bitten after only a few hours' practice at being a woman of the world! Tell me— how did you satisfy your 'woman's needs' *before* last night, when you were still a virgin?"

The sudden widening of her eyes was answer enough for Nicholai. Smiling, he cut off her denial with a warm, leisurely kiss, and Lisette gasped at her body's reaction. Reason was swept away, her slender arms encircled broad shoulders, graceful fingers touched thick, damp hair that smelled of fresh rain and the maleness of Nicholai. Over and over, they kissed, animosity replaced by hungry passion. Lisette let herself drown in the intoxicating pleasure of his hard embrace, the deft magic of his touch, and her tired body drew strength from his.

"Sweetheart, have you lost all reason?" Hyla Flowers demanded in a hoarse voice from the doorway.

Lisette broke away, flushed and glowing, and stared at Nicholai in disbelief. "I don't know, Hyla . . . since

Papa . . ." She turned wide cornflower blue eyes on the older woman. "I'll be all right—I just need some time to adjust. . . ."

Hyla came over and patted her cheek, glaring at Nicholai. "That's right, baby. You keep yourself away from people who'd take advantage of your grief!"

"I'll try, Hyla." Lisette smiled weakly. "Mr. Beauvisage, what I said still stands. I would like you to leave."

He raked a hand through bronze-streaked hair, one side of his mouth quirking ironically. "As you wish, mademoiselle. But first, there is another matter I would like to discuss with you—for Senator Hampshire's sake. Could you spare me a few minutes in private if I give you my word to behave . . . as a gentleman?"

Lisette ignored the sudden grin that flashed in his deeply tanned face. "Hyla," she sighed, "I'll speak to Mr. Beauvisage in the study if you will take over for a few minutes. Perhaps this will put a permanent end to his business here."

Nicholai waited as she removed her snowy apron, then he followed her across the keeping room to a door opposite the stairway. Lisette opened it to reveal a charming room, more of a retreat than a study, with cream-colored walls and a fine worn oriental rug of ocher, blue, and gold. An old cherry secretary stood tall against one wall, its front lowered to reveal pigeonholes neatly filled with various papers, and an open ledger with a silver inkwell and quill beside it. There were two windsor armchairs, a handsome corner chair, miniatures on the walls, a bookcase with overstuffed shelves, and finally, under a window, a faded red chaise upon which were two pillows, a sewing basket, a man's shirt, and an open book.

Lisette closed the door and the two of them sat down.

"I apologize for kissing you just now, Lisette. I took unfair advantage of my physical strength."

"I don't want to discuss that kiss or any other. Can't you hear what I've been saying to you? Tell me whatever it is that concerns Senator Hampshire, then go home to your flying staircase and let me return to my work!"

"This looks like your room," he commented, stretching out and crossing long booted legs. "Something of a haven?"

"Papa was sick for a long time. After I began taking care

of the accounts, the study took on more of my personality."
Suddenly, she stood and retrieved the shirt from the chaise.
"This was his. I started to mend it two days ago, but I
didn't finish because of the party at Belle Maison—all those
tortes. I can't believe . . . tomorrow Papa will be buried,
under the cold ground." Slowly, she raised it to one cheek
and Nicholai saw the tears, like moonlight in her eyes.

"Lisette . . . you have to be able to cry. It won't go away
if you keep it inside, it will only fester—" When he reached
for her hands, she pulled away violently, as if from a fire.

"Don't touch me!" Angrily, she wiped her eyes, then
looked at him, sitting tensely with the shirt clutched in her
hands.

Nicholai shrugged fleetingly and his eyes seemed to
change, becoming cool and unreadable. "Have it your way,
chérie. If you are so closed off that you cannot accept a
hand in friendship, your problem is worse than I imagined.
I will make this brief so that you won't have to suffer my
company much longer."

She had paled visibly, but managed to reply, "Thank
you."

The smile he gave her was openly cynical. "I want you
to tell me what you and Marcus Reems were discussing so
cozily. Is it personal, or related to business?"

"What concern is it of yours?"

"It is not my concern, I assure you! Lion Hampshire has
cause to mistrust M'sieur Reems and he asked me to learn
what I could. I shouldn't even tell you, but for some reason
I cannot make myself believe you desire any association
with Reems."

"That's your male vanity," Lisette retorted, and then
smiled a little. "I am too tired to argue with you, and since
I abhor Marcus Reems, I'll tell you what he wants from me.

"As you may know, he is a banker, and seemingly well
aware of the large loan my father drew several years ago,
most of which we still owe. Mr. Reems believes that the
bank will not accept me alone as their client, and in any
event, he also believes that the CoffeeHouse is doomed if I
intend to be sole proprietor." Her eyes flashed in recollection. "The toad! Ever so silkily, he offered to buy the

CoffeeHouse for an incredibly high amount—to relieve me of this 'tremendous burden.' "

"I gather that you refused?"

"Of course! I'm perfectly capable of solving my own problems, and I certainly don't care to be rescued by Marcus Reems!"

Nicholai lifted an eyebrow. "Somehow, I knew you would say that. I might try to discuss the reality of your position here, with the CoffeeHouse, but I know you would summarily reject any advice I might offer, so I'll leave it to someone for whom you have a higher regard."

He stood, but waved her down when she moved to join him. "No, no, I can find my way out." Casually, Nicholai leaned over, took Lisette's slim hand, and pressed his mouth to her palm. With satisfaction, he saw the tiny blond hairs on her forearm rise up. "Don't worry, I won't attack you. It has been . . . interesting knowing you, Lisette, and I do hope that if, in the future, you are overcome by 'womanly needs,' you won't hesitate to *use* me again. I've decided it would be worth the shame."

Lisette, for once, was speechless. She stared as Nicholai straightened the sleeves of his leather coat and paused in the doorway to add an irrepressible emerald wink. Then he was gone.

❧ *Chapter 10* ❧

March 26, 1793

The fashionable gown of sky blue velvet sailed through the air, landing in a heap at the foot of the testered bed.

"Damn!" swore Meagan Hampshire, standing in the dressing room in her satin chemise. Still frustrated, she pressed her lips together and stamped a bare foot as hard as she was able.

At that moment, the door to the bedchamber opened and Lion came in, eyes alight with mock fear. "Dare I enter?" he called, peeking into the dressing room. "Are you having a tantrum, fair wife?"

"Oh, hush!" Meagan reached for another gown from the long line adorning her side of the narrow chamber. After their marriage, Lion had moved his off-season clothes into a separate closet and Meagan had done the same. They enjoyed bumping into each other, nearly naked, each morning in that dressing room. Usually, Lion substituted a return to bed with Meagan for his second cup of coffee.

"You know, fondling, I believe you are losing your sense of humor," he commented now, an edge of irritation sharpening his own voice. "That might be serious . . . perhaps I should call Dr. Rush."

"Oh, Lion." Slowly, Meagan turned to face her husband. Her violet eyes glistened as Lion's fingers slipped into her shiny curls; a wave of relief swept her when her cheek found the clean frill of his shirtfront and she felt his other arm encircle her back. "I know I've been a shrew; I get so mad sometimes when I realize how sorry I've been feeling for myself. People tell me it's part of pregnancy—and if that's true, I wonder if the whole idea wasn't a mistake. I can't wear a single one of my gowns—all the beautiful new ones you had made for my Christmas present after the election. I was so *happy* then—"

Lion felt Meagan's tiny back shake as she began to sob. "Sweetheart, this is madness. . . ."

"Oh, that's easy for you to say," she gulped through her sea of tears. "You're having a fine time, strutting like a peacock because your sweet little obedient wife is pregnant. But *I'm* the one getting fat, trapped in this house—" She almost added "losing you!" but stopped herself in time.

"Meagan! That's a devil of a thing to say to me! Do you honestly believe that I'm behaving like a *peacock*, for God's sake?"

She gazed up at him, searching his face, seeing the familiar expression of the man she loved. "No, no, of course not. It's not your fault—it just seems that our life has changed so much."

Lion blotted her tears with his handkerchief before tightening his embrace and covering Meagan's salty lips with his own. Startled by the eagerness of her response, her arms tight around his neck, he let the kiss deepen recklessly and slid his hand around to her side, then higher to caress the ripe swell of one satin-covered breast.

Meagan groaned softly, but Lion lifted his head as a distant knocking grew more insistent. "What? Who is it?"

"Missa Lion," cried Wong, the Chinese butler, from the hallway, "you allight? Supper leady—getting cold! You and Missy come now or Blamble be fulious!"

Meagan clung to his arms. "No!" she pleaded. "Ignore them—"

"Sweeting, you know I'd prefer to stay here and make love, but we do have all evening! I'm ravenous; I only had half my lunch this noon, so please indulge me this once and let me go downstairs and stuff myself. Besides, you know how Bramble is about her food; if we ignore supper now, she's liable to lock the kitchen!"

Meagan tried to return his smile, but turned away instead to search out a loose robelike gown that would accommodate her swollen waistline. Frantically, she pulled it on and suffered the touch of Lion's fingers as they fastened the back. He hung up his coat and loosened his cravat, then put a brotherly arm around her shoulders as they went down to eat.

As always, the table was set with the finest china, silver, and linen—Bramble's indirect salute to Lion's new office. The sour-faced, loyal cook now made certain that Wong wore his best formal suit and striped waistcoat when he served the courses. Watching him stiffly place bowls of celery soup in front of them, Meagan resolved again to tell Bramble firmly that such starchy displays must cease unless she personally requested a formal meal. Longingly, she remembered the casual suppers they used to eat before the fire, in the garden, or on trays in bed. Sometimes, they had gone to their country home, Markwood Villa, for a week at a time alone, leaving the servants here in the city. The first two years of their marriage she and Lion had spent almost exclusively in the country, either in Virginia on her ancestral plantation or at the villa. Now, Meagan could not coax her husband away from Philadelphia for even a day.

When Wong returned for their soup bowls, he cast a doubtful eye on Meagan's nearly untouched portion, but bit his tongue when she turned a challenging glare his way.

For the main course, there was pheasant stuffed with wild rice, mushrooms, and almonds, as well as buttered acorn squash. Meagan pushed her food around and sipped her wine.

"How was your day?" she asked hesitantly.

Briefly, Lion spoke of the news in the Senate, then looked up in sudden sober recollection. "Meagan, have you heard? Ernst Hahn, who owned the CoffeeHouse, died last night."

Her heart twisted as she listened to his sensitive expression of sympathy for Lisette, and the wine emboldened her to ask: "Have you seen her today?"

"Yes, I spoke to her after I heard the news. Lisette's a brave girl—independent, much the way you were when we met—but I worry about her all the same. One can see that she hides her emotions, and I am afraid that she may force herself to work harder than she should."

Meagan nodded mechanically, still hearing that phrase, "independent—the way you *were*." Tears burned her heart, but she refused to cry anymore. Lion ate wholeheartedly, and went on to mention his encounter with Nicholai Beauvisage, offering a few observations, without divulging any of their conversation.

There were baked apples for dessert, with a sweet mixture of nuts, butter, and cinnamon melted over them and down the tunnels where the cores had been. It was a favorite dessert of Lion's and its warmth, topped with rich cream, was soothing to Meagan.

"Lion, couldn't we go to the villa this Friday? I miss it so. . . ."

"I don't know, fondling. It will depend."

To herself, Meagan decided that was the same as a refusal. Any number of things could arise—each apparently more important than Lion's relationship with his wife.

It was then, at the worst possible moment, that Wong answered a knock at the front door and returned to the dining room with an envelope for Lion. Quickly, his keen blue eyes scanned the note before looking up at Meagan.

"I'm sorry—I have to go out for a short while." Already he was folding his napkin.

"Oh, *really*?" Meagan heard the shrill note in her voice, but couldn't make herself relax.

"I shouldn't be away long, two hours at the most."

She stood when he did, following him when he started toward the door. Wong, ever the model servant, waited with a fresh coat, hat, and cape. When Lion turned back to embrace his wife, she held him at arm's length and asked, "Won't you tell me where you are going?"

"I would rather not, sweetheart."

"What kind of appointment it is that you cannot tell me about it? Is it at the CoffeeHouse?"

"Meagan, I don't know what the devil's gotten into you, but whatever it is, I'm fed up with it." His hands fell away from her arms. "I don't even know you lately."

"Oh!" Meagan's violet eyes sparkled as she let out a laugh that stung his ears. "That's odd, because I feel exactly the same way about you!"

Lion started to answer, but bit back the harsher words. Instead, he went into the entryway, ripped the garments out of Wong's hands, and strode out into the cold, misty night.

When the wind reached Meagan, she began to tremble. Still shaking, she went upstairs to their room, found her washbasin, and wept as she vomited into it.

Two hours later, Lion and Nicholai emerged from the latter's house on Spruce Street and paused under a flickering street lamp.

"I'm sorry if I interrupted your supper," Nicholai said. "It looks as though I'll be late to my parents' as it is, but I couldn't think of another time for us to talk."

"That's fine, Nicholai—in fact, I'm grateful to you for contacting me so quickly. As I've told you, this action of Marcus's can be best interpreted by me; after nearly two dozen years, I'm beginning to make a perverse sort of sense out of his approach to life."

"I'm glad to be of any help."

"It would seem that the logical course for you to take would be to keep the lines of communication open between you and Lisette. If she will confide in you—"

Nicholai gave a snort of laughter. "At this point, that's doubtful! She isn't particularly fond of me; in fact, I believe she meant her good-bye to me today to be permanent."

"Lisette is very wary about trusting people—especially men." Lion smiled.

"I've noticed that!" He laughed again, dryly. "Ordinarily, I wouldn't let myself in for more abuse from such a female, but in this case, I'll make an exception. Lisette Hahn will require subtle, skillful handling, so you must not expect immediate results."

"Any results at all will be better than none," Lion assured him. The two men shook hands, then parted in the darkness. Nicholai turned north, and Lion south, back to his home on Pine Street and his thorny, perplexing wife.

* * *

Antonia Beauvisage waited and watched for her younger son to arrive, illogically anxious that he might disappear again.

From the mist-shrouded footpath, Nicholai saw his lovely petite mother framed by light from his childhood home. Feeling strangely bittersweet, he realized that until he had gone to France at the age of twenty-three, he had lived his entire life in or near this house. Now it seemed as if he had been catapulted back ten years and tonight was just one more meal with his family. Nicholai smiled slightly, recalling that even after he had moved into his own house, he'd taken shameless advantage of Mrs. Reeves, the cook his parents employed, stopping to eat with them almost daily.

"My dear!" Antonia stood on tiptoe to hug and kiss her son, then looked up, her emerald eyes mirroring his. "You will never know how we've missed you—and *worried,* since the trouble began in France. I still feel I'm dreaming, it's so difficult to believe you are really *home*—"

Nicholai held her close, caressing his mother's silver-veined chestnut curls. "Maman, it is *your* home, but I am happy to visit." The smile he gave her was a man's and it startled her. "I'm not the Nicky you knew a decade ago . . . and you must not expect me to be. So, where is Father?"

Katya appeared first, pulling Randolph after her, and Nicholai laughed to think that his intellectual sister had truly been bowled over by love. Jean-Philippe came into the stair hall next, greeting his son with the sort of hug he'd been unable to give last night at the crowded party. After a long minute, Nicholai drew away just enough to meet his father's gaze.

"I must be looking quite ancient to you, *mon fils,*" Jean-Philippe murmured with a wry smile.

"Father, you look exactly as I hope I shall after seventy happy years of life." It was true. The tanned face was generously lined and his silver hair gone white, but the senior Beauvisage stood straight and lithe, flat bellied and blessed with his own strong teeth and humorous blue eyes that seemed to hold the answers to all of life's questions.

"You seem to be growing more tactful as you age— except that I am only sixty-nine!" Jean-Philippe laughed.

"And *you* have changed considerably. There are a few obvious physical alterations—you have definitely lost all the remnants of youth. But now that I have an opportunity to study your face, voice, manner . . . I can see that your character has ripened as well."

Nicholai smiled, warmed by his father's approval. "We have a great deal to discuss. When you hear more of my life in France, you'll understand the influences that forged the change in me."

"Papa!" scolded Katya. "Are you going to monopolize Nicky here in the stair hall all evening long?"

"You sound and look like Natalya did the last time I was here," Nicholai told her. "It may be difficult for me to adjust to her absence—and the incredible transformation *you* have undergone!"

Katya took his arm and smiled coquettishly. Clad in a new gown of lilac watered silk, her black curls bound by an ivory silk bandeau, she was well aware of her kittenish appeal. "It is no miracle, dear brother—ten years have passed and I've made a perfectly normal progression from child to woman."

"I can see that!" Nicholai laughed.

Caro sat on the green and ivory brocade settee, watching the affectionate exchange between Katya and her long-lost brother. The had reached the parlor threshold, but Nicholai was looking down at her teasingly, and Caro took the opportunity to study him.

Clad in his own expertly tailored clothes, Nicholai looked even more devastating than he had last night at Belle Maison. He wore toasty brown leather knee boots, fawn breeches and waistcoat, and a coffee-colored coat. Caro took in the sharp contrast between Nicholai's snowy pleated shirt and cravat and the deep tan of his chiseled face. He seemed so much older . . . there were tiny lines around his mouth. . . .

"Caro!" He greeted her with a smile, but she could see the glint of irony in his eyes as he came forward to hug her. He smelled as deliciously masculine as Alec.

"Hello, Nicholai." She kissed his cheek, then sat down, hoping to distract him from her blush.

"You're looking very beautiful." He touched the pale yellow velvet of her skirt and the creamy lace that spilled from her sleeve. Caro's hair was a riot of loose honey-hued curls, set off by a bandeau of leaf green silk. "The years have improved on perfection."

She smiled warmly, realizing that the compliment was sincere and to the point. "I'm pleased that you think so, Nicholai. To be honest, I was just thinking the same thing about you!"

He cringed with amusement and sat down beside her on the settee. "I know, I know—I've *changed*! That is all I've heard these past twenty-four hours. Everyone is so astounded to find me an adult that I have been trying to remember if I was in short pants and riding a hobbyhorse before I left for France!"

"No, that was definitely not the case. You were quite grown up . . . I should know." Caro put a hand out to touch the lean line of his jaw, remembering the night Nicholai had started to declare his love for her. If Alec hadn't come into the garden, he probably would have kissed her. She could still see a shadow of that handsome, fun-loving young rogue in Nicholai's face; a decade ago Caro had felt an aching remorse, knowing she had been the first person to hurt him and wake him up to the fact that life could be cruel, hard, and confusing. Now it was evident that Nicholai had survived many, much worse tests. . . . Alec had told her a bit of the horror he'd endured in France, but only now could she grasp the extent of his ordeal and its effects.

Nicholai held Caro's small fingers against his cheek, then shifted, pressing warm hard lips to her palm. "You look thoughtful." He smiled. "I suppose you're regretting choosing Sacha rather than me!"

Standing a few feet away, in conversation with her husband, Katya, and Randolph, Antonia glanced up, momentarily alarmed when she heard her son's teasing observation.

Caro laughed and pulled her hand from his grasp. "Nicholai, you are as outrageous as ever! And you know, even though I must say in honesty that I think you are indecently handsome, I was born to love Alec."

"That is aptly put, Caro, and I would be the first to challenge any man or woman who tried to damage your marriage in any way." He paused to accept a brandy from his hovering mother. "Speaking of Sacha—I think your presence has made me forget him! Where is he—and this trio of offspring I've been hearing about?"

"They went out to the kitchen just before you arrived." Caro smiled. "Mrs. Reeves was anxious to see how Kristin has grown, and I think Étienne and Talya were planning to help her cook."

Nicholai laughed. "Typical Beauvisage strategy!"

Caro watched him, wondering about the women in his life and whether he had known love and contentment with any of them. Alec had been a heartless rake until he fell in love with her, but by the time he was Nicholai's age he was married and Étienne was born.

Voices—Alec's and the children's—came to her from down the hallway, shaking her out of her contemplation. Caro started to speak, but no words came out when she met Nicholai's eyes and found them both penetrating and interested.

"That is the second time you have done that, Caro, and now I truly wonder what you can be thinking about. Will you tell me?"

She heard her children giggling as they neared the parlor, but didn't take her eyes from Nicholai's. "I was thinking about the past and how I broke your heart. You were so surprised by the pain . . . remember how long it took you to recover your balance and begin to enjoy life again? Then, I see you today and realize how much you've changed. You are a survivor now, Nicholai. . . ."

"And?" He watched Caro closely, scrutinizing her expressions and memorizing each word.

She sensed Alec's presence, watching them from the doorway, but felt compelled to finish this dialogue with her brother-in-law. "You mustn't think I disapprove . . . and I can see that, although you've hardened, you have the sort of perceptivity to people's thoughts and actions which a true survivor needs."

"Caro, if I hadn't cultivated a new set of instincts, I could not have stayed alive in France," he reminded her.

"I know." Unexpectedly, her eyes stung with sentimental tears. "But . . . Nicholai, I worry that your openness has been crushed; I keep wondering whether any person on earth could ever hurt you again."

❧ *Chapter 11* ❧

March 26, 1793

Nicholai enjoyed the evening with his family immensely.
He began to see the connection between Caro's poignant
words and the love and trust he felt for the few people in
this house. Perhaps she was right . . . it seemed that only
with his family could he lower his guard and open his heart.

The hours passed quickly. Before supper, the children
had become acquainted with their uncle. Talya sat on his
lap, staring up at Nicholai adoringly, while Étienne unreeled
endless facts about his school, horse, friends, and his father's
ships. Finally, after relating a story about going to tea at
the president's house with his parents, Étienne allowed
Antonia to interrupt with the news that supper was ready.
Kristin, now five months old, sat at the table in an oak high
chair, between Nicholai and her doting grandmother. Alec
had told the truth: the baby was blessed with raven hair
and black-lashed turquoise eyes exactly like his.

While they ate a meal that could have been a Christmas
feast, Antonia and the others gave Nicholai detailed news
regarding his sisters, Danielle and Natalya. It was almost
as difficult for him to imagine Natalya a wife and mother
as it was to realize that Katya was now a young woman.
Learning that his younger sister was happy and that her
husband lived up to the fantasies of her youth pleased
Nicholai.

"It would seem that I am the only one of your children
who isn't safely embraced by true love, Maman."

His mouth curved with casual amusement, but Antonia

did not see the humor. "That does seem to be the case," she replied, eyeing him speculatively.

"Oh, no—don't you start drawing up a master plan to marry me off, Maman! I can already see into your mind; you are perusing your list of available maidens in search of the first one to invite to supper on an evening when I will be attending." He scolded her affectionately and the rest of the family laughed at this accurate prediction of Antonia's behavior. She played meddling matchmaker only in extreme cases, when her children went for long periods of time without romantic progress of their own. Her methods were so subtle that frequently the victim wasn't even aware of any manipulation.

"Speaking of maidens," Nicholai continued lightly, "how is Mary Armstrong?"

Caro watched him, trying to decide if his tone masked a deeper feeling. Mary had been his sweetheart for several months, mending the tear Caro had made in his heart. Until the day Nicholai announced he wanted to begin a new life in France, they had all hoped he would make Mary his wife.

"She's no longer a maiden, I fear," Jean-Philippe was saying. "She married Timothy Barcroft at least two years ago. He is a professor at the Philadelphia Academy."

Nicholai smiled, apparently genuinely pleased. "Good. I hope that life is treating her well; she deserves happiness."

Antonia and Caro exchanged perplexed glances, remembering how Mary had waited nearly eight years for Nicholai to return from France, until she was twenty-five. Although she did seem content with life, they both were convinced that she had only accepted Timothy's offer out of desperation when she realized she was slipping into spinsterhood.

Dessert was being served and there were exclamations of delight from the children when they saw that Mrs. Reeves had made ice cream. The cook smiled broadly at Nicholai as she placed the largest portion in front of him.

"I remembered 'twas always your favorite, Master Nicky," she said. " 'Tis my welcome-home gift to you."

Nicholai stood partway, leaning over the high chair, and gave Mrs. Reeves a hug. Something was whispered in her ear that made her turn pink and give him a playful swat; then she hurried back to the kitchen.

Nicholai sat down just as Kristin put five plump fingers into his ice cream, gave a gurgling laugh, and patted her uncle's sleeve. Ignoring the sticky mess on his expensive coat, he took her little hand and kissed it.

"Kristin, my sweet, I am truly glad to be here tonight with you—and all my family." The grin that flashed in contrast to Nicholai's bronzed face held no trace of mockery.

Alec poured brandy into two snifters and joined his brother in the other crewel wing chair that faced the library fireplace. For a slow minute, they sipped the warming liquor and regarded the leaping yellow flames.

"I know Father is anxious to join us," Nicholai said at last, "so I had better tell you what has happened. Lion feels that you should be kept abreast of this situation with Marcus Reems."

"Nicky, don't say that you already have news!" exclaimed Alec. "You just saw the man for the first time a few hours ago!"

Nicholai loosened his cravat with two dark fingers and sighed dramatically. "It *has* been a full day. . . ."

"I understand," Alec replied sarcastically. "Do you think you can manage to tell me about it before you expire?"

Laughing, Nicholai nodded acceptance to his brother's offer of a cheroot and watched as he lit two of them on a candle. "Actually, I stumbled onto Marcus's trail. You recall my early departure from the CoffeeHouse—and your gluttonous dispatch of my gingerbread? Well, I waited outside until I saw Reems exit—from the back door—then I had a little chat with Lisette Hahn."

"Really? Did she remember you this time?"

Nicholai repressed a smile, and drew on the thin dark cheroot instead. "As a matter of fact, she did. I have a theory that Mademoiselle Hahn is pretending indifference in an effort to conceal a shameless passion for me."

"I would say she ought to go on the stage. Her performance at lunch certainly convinced me!"

"Please!" Nicholai protested with a laugh. "My confidence is melting away as you speak!"

Alec's only answer to this was a doubtful snort.

"At any rate, Lisette was eventually persuaded to confide in me—"

"Her tongue was doubtless loosened by her famous desire for your body," Alec rejoined agreeably.

"Doubtless!" He narrowed his green eyes. "Lisette told me that her father owed a large sum of money to the bank where Reems is employed. He tried to frighten her by saying the CoffeeHouse could never survive with a female in charge and offered to buy it from her for a very generous sum."

"Lisette refused?"

"Oh, yes. She's a headstrong, independent woman, as she reminded me today in no uncertain terms. Her favorite phrase is, 'I do not need one of you self-important, pompous, vain *men* to take care of me!'"

Alec smiled at Nicholai's falsetto imitation of Lisette. "Are you certain we are talking about the same girl? I always thought she had a soft, sensuous voice. . . ."

"You haven't heard her when she gets angry."

"If she sounds like *that*, she won't have to worry about any man trying to take care of her." On the word *that*, Alec's voice mimicked Nicholai's imitation of Lisette.

"Sacha . . . haven't you learned yet that there is a time and place for unending tasteless jokes?"

"My apologies. I will try to restrain myself. Did you discuss Marcus's scheme with Lion?"

"Yes—that's why I was late tonight. He came over to my house and we talked at length. I like him immensely, Sacha, and admire his honesty and insight. He seems to know exactly what Reems is up to."

"I would trust his instincts."

"I do. Lion thinks that Reems feels he lost the prestige of his wife's fine old family when she died—which he, in his own view, would need to overtake Lion now that he is a senator. Don't ask me how he plans to beat *that;* perhaps he intends to become president! At any rate, since the CoffeeHouse is the gathering place for political figures to hold informal discussions, as well as all other local negotiations and gossip, Lion is certain that Reems wants to own it so that he can orchestrate all these power conversations. Does that make sense?"

"It sounds as if Marcus wants to trade family prestige for local power. Friendships with the men who count, hmm?"

"Exactly. And Lion is convinced he has a darker goal in mind . . . ownership of the forum where he could subtly spread rumors about Senator Hampshire."

"With an eye toward taking that Senate seat himself, I'll wager—after he's created a cloud of scandal over Lion's name."

"It would seem so."

The door opened then and Jean-Philippe's white hair appeared. "Am I still banished?" Antonia's petite form crowded in beside her husband. "I won't be left out either, you scoundrels. I want to hear everything!"

Their sons laughed, calling to them to enter, and the quartet sat for over an hour around the fire, drinking brandy and discussing the progress of the Beauvisage ships, especially since the China trade had opened. Nicholai was telling his parents about France, beginning with the family château and vineyards, when Caro suddenly appeared.

"I'm sorry—I didn't mean to interrupt—it's just that Étienne and Talya will not go to sleep without a kiss from their uncle."

Alec began to rise automatically, then Caro's words sank in. Dropping back into his chair, while Nicholai crossed the room, he experienced the same unsettling twinge that he had felt earlier. He had stood in the parlor for minutes before Caro and Nicholai had been able to stop talking and gazing at each other long enough to acknowledge his presence. Now Alec's children wanted their *uncle*. His mind trusted Caro implicitly and told him to relax . . . but there was a nagging ache in his chest.

Little Natalya and Étienne were exhausted, and after a last hug from their uncle, they snuggled together in the canopy bed and closed their eyes. A cradle swayed nearby, where Kristin lay on her tummy, rosy cheeked and dreaming.

Nicholai continued to whisper to Caro in the hallway. "Where is Katya?"

"Nicholai, the door is closed. You needn't whisper! And Katya and Randolph went out to the theater a half-hour ago. She told me to give you a kiss for her, but I think I will leave that to Antonia."

"Damn! I wanted to talk to her."

"Can I help?"

Nicholai shrugged with studied nonchalance. "Well, it's not a matter of any real importance. I merely wanted to talk to Katya about Lisette Hahn, since I understand they are good friends."

"Oh! Well, perhaps I can substitute. I'm quite well acquainted with Lisette myself, and Katya and I had a good long talk about her just last night."

When Nicholai felt Caro's watchful brown eyes on him, he wished he'd never mentioned Lisette Hahn to her. When it came to male-female attractions, his sister-in-law had the instincts of a bloodhound.

"Oh, Caro, you needn't bother yourself," he said indifferently. "I just felt a momentary twinge of curiosity and hoped Katya could satisfy it."

"Come on, Nicky." She took his arm. "Let's go into Antonia's sitting room and have a nice chat. To tell you the truth, I find Lisette Hahn an intriguing enigma and shall be interested to hear *your* opinions."

The room was decorated in muted shades of green, gold, and cobalt blue, blending tastefully with the cozy collection of Queen Anne furniture, various ornaments, books, and needlework projects. Caro sat down on the green-striped settee and pulled Nicholai down beside her.

"Do you find it odd," she began, as though the conversation were her own idea, "that Lisette is so aloof with men? She is beautiful and intelligent enough to attract any bachelor in Philadelphia, yet she is twenty-one years old and rebuffs every man who approaches her."

"Yes. I *do* find it odd," Nicholai echoed sardonically.

"Alec said that you took her home last night after word reached Belle Maison that Ernst Hahn had been stricken. I suppose you got to know her quite well."

Nicholai studied a pleated shirt cuff and casually lifted his russet brows. "As you have said, she is an enigma. A raving contradiction, to be exact."

Struggling to squelch a smile, Caro answered, "Katya told me a few things last night that might help you to understand Lisette—in case you should have cause to deal with her in the future. Your sister maintains that Lisette wants to be self-reliant . . . and I gather that her opinion of men in general is not terribly good."

"I know all that!" Hearing his voice rise, Nicholai paused to take a breath and continued evenly, *"What I want to know is why!"*

Caro noted the way Nicholai's profile had frozen to hard-molded bronze. She couldn't guess what had transpired between him and Lisette Hahn, but whatever it was, it had left him anything but indifferent.

"I shouldn't tell you, but I know Katya will if I don't. She said that the reason Lisette is unreceptive to romance is because she was *badly* hurt two years ago. Whoever it was must have destroyed her trust in men."

Nicholai regarded Caro for a long minute, then his mouth drew up in a suggestion of a smile. "So, Caro, it would seem that Lisette Hahn is of a breed I should understand."

"What do you mean?"

"Correct me if I am wrong, but I would swear that you think Lisette is as true and as bitter a survivor as I am!"

"Oh, Nicky." Stung by his tone, Caro put out a hand and touched one dark tense cheek. "Please, you must—"

"I do hope I'm not intruding—again," a voice interrupted from the doorway. It was Alec, and his expression and tone belied the smooth apology.

Caro came forward to greet her husband, but could see the jealous anger in his eyes, even from a distance. Inwardly, she groaned, knowing that it would take more than a logical explanation to quell Alec's suspicions.

"Sacha," Nicholai was saying, "I've appropriated your wife far too often this evening, and do you know, I've suddenly realized how exhausted I am. Before I fall unconscious on the rug, I think it would be wise to bid you all good night and be off to my own home and bed." He was careful to give his sister-in-law a chaste kiss on the cheek, then patted Alec's shoulder and disappeared into the hall-way.

Caramel-warm eyes locked with splintered turquoise.

"You are being very foolish," Caro told her husband in a soft, even voice.

"I hope so." Each word was weighted with meaning. Then Alec pulled Caro roughly into his arms and kissed her with all the angry heat his love could generate. Feeling Caro's response, the way she molded her body to his, tightened her arms around his neck to keep their lips joined, and moaned almost inaudibly, Alec shed his doubts. They drifted away and disintegrated in the fire of passion, and he raised his head enough to murmur, "Madame, I think we should repair to Belle Maison and our bedchamber with all possible speed. In addition, I am convinced that our children are overdue for a few days' visit with their grand-parents."

Caro stood on tiptoe, nuzzling the line of his brown neck that showed above a snowy stock. "I concur wholeheartedly, sir, on both counts."

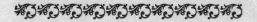

Part Two

Oh, how hard it is to find
The one just suited to our mind;
    And if that one should be
False, unkind, or found too late,
What can we do but sigh at fate,
    And sing 'Woe's me—Woe's me?'

Love's a boundless burning waste,
Where bliss's stream we seldom taste,
    And still more seldom flee
Suspense's thorns, suspicion's stings;
Yet somehow love a something brings
    That's sweet—ev'n when we sigh
        'Woe's me!'

THOMAS CAMPBELL
(1777–1844)

❦❧ Chapter 12 ❧❦

April 9, 1793

Nicholai was naked beneath the covers, and his lean, mus-
cled torso was exposed as he reclined against three plush
pillows. The current *National Gazette* was spread open
over his lap, and sweet early sunlight splashed across the
empty teacup on the lowboy and Nicholai's golden brown
shoulders.

He could smell the boxwood, hyacinths, and strawberry
bushes that scented the morning breeze. Sighing, he folded
the *Gazette,* set it aside, and closed his eyes.

The days since his return had slipped away in a blur of
gradual routine. There were servants now, hired by his
mother, who greatly simplified Nicholai's life in the house
on Spruce Street. There was Oliver, the butler-valet, a tall,
dignified Negro, and the easygoing, rotund cook, Welcome,
whose daughter, Felicity, did the housecleaning. For several
days after their arrival, Antonia seemed a fixture in
Nicholai's home as she made lists of her son's habits and
tastes and taught the new servants their duties.

Leisurely, Nicholai grew accustomed to life in Philadelphia. He talked to shopkeepers, old friends, and the men at
the CoffeeHouse, learning the changes in America's texture.
Amelia Purdy, the restless wife of a wealthy merchant, provided uncomplicated sexual diversion, and Nicholai also
spent frequent evenings with different family members. Last
week, Katya and Randolph had been his first dinner guests.
Old relationships were restored and new acquaintances
made, including those of President Washington, Secretary

of State Thomas Jefferson, and the secretary of the treasury, Alexander Hamilton.

Nicholai was intrigued by the resentment and conflict that existed between Hamilton and Jefferson, each of whom wielded power exceeded only by the president's. Jefferson detested Hamilton, believing him to be corrupt and a monarchist at heart, and he further opposed the genteel, class-oriented Federalists. It seemed that Hamilton's influence pulled Washington in one direction, while Jefferson, whose Republican party stood for unqualified democracy, pulled the president the opposite way.

Perhaps, thought Nicholai wryly, they cancel each other out. There were constant rumors that either Jefferson or Hamilton would resign, but it was doubtful that one could countenance leaving the other with the president's undivided attention.

The Congress had adjourned in March for the summer and, just a few days ago, Washington had traveled south to Mount Vernon. Nicholai had met the president the night before his departure and felt that the careworn man's cheerful mood had been born of his eagerness to be home again. Washington carried the unsought burden of the presidency with stoic dignity; Nicholai sincerely hoped that he would find true peace and pleasure during his respite at Mount Vernon.

With this generous thought, he stretched and threw off the warm quilts. The new staff was well trained. Each morning at eight o'clock, Oliver woke Nicholai and prepared a scalding bath that would take one-half hour to become bearable. Welcome bustled in next, delivering a cup of tea with lemon and the day's newspaper. If Nicholai had not stirred from under his covers yet, she would cheerfully make a great show of rolling up the paper to apply to his "backside," but as yet she hadn't dealt one swat, for Nicholai always managed to moan and growl his way to daylight.

Now, he padded naked across the elegantly colored Persian rug. Diffused sunlight played over his strong bronzed body. The shaving stand was ready for his use and he attacked his face and neck, barely glancing at the mirror. Before the fireplace the bathtub steamed invitingly, and in minutes, Nicholai was easing himself into it with a sigh of pleasure.

He took his time and soaked unhurriedly in the soothing warmth. These lazy mornings were a luxurious contrast to those he'd spent at the château. For ten years he had risen with the dawn in order to make use of each daylight hour outdoors. From the planting of new vines to the latest superb vintage, Nicholai had contributed direct supervision and his own strong back to make certain that each bottle of wine was as close to perfection as he could make it.

But this current easier life gave him no pangs of guilt. After the pressures of the Revolution in France and the squalid voyage across the Atlantic, Nicholai saw these weeks as his respite . . . and felt he deserved one as much as President Washington. He would let his life right itself, trusting it to show him a direction for the future, and in the meantime, he fully intended to enjoy slow mornings, active days, and evenings filled with friends, good food, and wine.

Voices in the hallway attracted Nicholai's attention. His hair was just rinsed and a few quick squeezes of the sponge dispersed the last bits of soap from his shoulders and chest.

"I'm sorry, sir, but I cannot allow you to enter the master's bedchamber," Oliver was saying.

"Look here, dear chap, you needn't concern yourself! I'll take the blame—I haven't time to spare, waiting for your *master* to powder and perfume himself!"

As Nicholai recognized the British accent, his mouth quirked in amusement; then, he wondered what on earth James Stringfellow could want. Could this urgent mission be connected in any way with the mysterious Lisette Hahn?

Stringfellow was knocking agitatedly on the door, while Oliver made sterner protests. Nicholai stepped onto a blotter of linen towels and found two more draped over a chair back.

"Mr. Stringfellow," he called, drying off, "I beg a moment's indulgence."

The wiry Englishman launched into an anxious exhortation, but before he could finish, the door opened and Nicholai waved him into the bedchamber. Stringfellow blinked; his host wore only a large white towel, which was knotted snugly against his tanned, flat belly. In his hands was a second towel, which was being applied with vigor to wet chestnut hair.

"Good morning," said Nicholai, giving him a brief smile before resuming the hair massage. "Have I forgotten our breakfast engagement?"

"Mr. Beauvisage, you know bloody well that I have no reason whatever to be here—that *you* are aware of." He watched Nicholai cross the room and look at the clothing assembled along the far side of the bed.. "Hyla would have my head on a platter if she knew I was confiding in you, but this is one time when I think my instincts as a man are superior to hers."

Nicholai dressed slowly in buff breeches, brown boots, a cream linen shirt and cravat, and a well-cut frock coat of wheat-colored broadcloth. As he drew on his clothing, he listened attentively to James Stringfellow's account of the most recent events at the CoffeeHouse. In a nutshell, it seemed that Marcus Reems had been barging into the keeping room, unannounced and uninvited, with increasing frequency. Stringfellow declared that Reems was an overbearing sort whose manner rubbed Lisette the wrong way. Although she had refused his offer to buy the CoffeeHouse, he continued to badger her. Last night, he had arrived with Ernst Hahn's loan record, which he waved ominously under Lisette's nose.

"Hyla is especially agitated because she fears that Lisette is beginning to sway. I never thought I would be saying this, but her self-confidence is eroding."

Nicholai brushed back his thick, gleaming hair so that it looked appealingly ruffled. "Perhaps she's simply in need of some rest. Everyone has an emotional limit—grief, overwork, and financial pressure may have brought your mistress to hers."

"That may be true, Mr. Beauvisage, but I never saw her waver before, so this is a devil of a sign. Lisette has always had a mind of her own and has never allowed anyone to bully her—"

"Stringfellow, what is it you want from me? Since that night Ernst Hahn died, you and Hyla Flowers have been glaring at me suspiciously—and I would think you'd both be overjoyed by my recent indifference toward your mistress."

The Englishman colored awkwardly. "We only want what's best for Lisette. Hyla doesn't trust you, but I've some ruddy intuition that tells me that you're a decent man. I thought that, if you had wronged Lisette in any way—as Hyla suspects—then you might want to make up for it."

"What sort of help do you mean? Emotional or financial?"

"That's for you and your conscience to decide, sir. Lisette is far and away too proud to ask for assistance from anyone, so I'm asking for her."

"I doubt that she'll appreciate your gesture of loyalty," Nicholai muttered sardonically. "All right, Stringfellow, I will pay another visit to Mistress Hahn—and if she does me physical harm with one of those evil kitchen tools, *you* shall suffer the consequences!"

Tendrils of golden hair curled softly around the oval of Lisette's face, framing her luminous blue eyes, flushed cheeks, and rose petal mouth. For over an hour, she had worked with Chastity, Purity, and Hyla in the public room. Now that the floor, the hearths, and the tables were clean, she paused to lean against a banistered partition. The fatigue was there, hovering nearby, but she could not allow herself to relax—too many things required her attention.

"Well," she said, "now that the end is in sight here, I believe I'll see to the food."

"That's right, baby." Hyla nodded vigorously. "You sit yourself down and rest. There's lots of time yet."

Knowing that rest was impossible, Lisette only offered a crooked smile in reply. She went through the door to the keeping room, absently brushing the worst dust from her beige-and-gold-striped muslin gown, and was only a few steps from the worktable when her tired eyes focused on Nicholai Beauvisage.

"Good morning, Mistress Hahn," he greeted her with a slightly insolent smile. Since arriving in Philadelphia, he had worked to break the habit of using French terms of address; to his own ears they sounded pretentious.

Lisette stared in surprise. Nicholai was perched on one

of the high stools in front of the worktable. He was coatless, and the sleeves of his cream-colored shirt turned up to reveal strong sun-darkened forearms. After his initial greeting, he returned to the array of turnips and potatoes he was slicing.

Recovering, Lisette demanded, "What do you think you are doing?"

"Oh, I was just passing by and thought I would visit you. Not wanting to make a nuisance of myself, I decided to help you with your chores while I waited for you to appear."

She regarded him with frank suspicion, remembering the lame excuse Stringfellow had offered when he left the CoffeeHouse that morning. Lisette knew that he and Hyla had been worried about her, especially since her latest confrontation with Marcus Reems.

Besides, Nicholai had made a point of his detachment from her each time she encountered him in the public room these past two weeks. Why would he turn up here so suddenly, all easy good humor and affectionate audacity, unless there was a tangible reason?

She fetched her apron from its hook and slipped it slowly over her gown. "Why so thoughtful and solicitous *today*, Mr. Beauvisage? I've heard no more than a casual word of greeting from your lips in the space of a fortnight."

Nicholai set down the knife and a turnip and swiveled to meet Lisette's sly gaze. Without a word, he pulled her between his knees, facing away from him, and tied the apron strings into a bow. Caught off guard, Lisette didn't try to break away. Nicholai's position on the stool put his head only a fraction above hers, and now he slid his hands all the way around her slim waist, easing her tense body back into his.

"So, you've been missing me, eh?" he murmured, gently teasing.

Lisette felt the steel of his chest and his muscular buff-covered thighs that held her prisoner. When his mouth touched her ear, she flinched and gasped. His warm lips grazed traitorous places along her nape, sending long hot shivers down Lisette's spine. Her head dropped back as Nicholai's mouth moved to burn a tantalizing trail over her throat, and when he turned her into the curve of his embrace, she eagerly received his kiss. Dizzy with passion, Lisette felt the fiery throb swell within her body. The rigid evidence of Nicholai's desire pressed against her, unmistakable even through her gown and petticoats, and her hips moved involuntarily.

Nicholai's mouth left Lisette's reluctantly, as he whispered hoarsely, "I am nearing the point of no return, my dear . . . but since, unfortunately, we are not in my bed with the door locked, I am forced to put this matter into your hands."

Icy reality jolted Lisette. Her eyes were like saucers as she pushed free of him, astonished and confused by her own behavior.

"What is *wrong* with me?"

Nicholai sighed. "I gather that means our interlude is at an end." With mock despair, he glanced down at his lap, then turned back to the vegetables. "You know, Lisette, at the risk of being turned into stew along with these turnips, I would have to say that there's nothing at all wrong with you. Frankly, I find these bursts of *response* much more normal than your usual pose as the indestructible, self-sufficient woman."

She wasn't sure how to take this opinion; whether to believe that Nicholai truly felt this way, or to distrust him and believe that he was interested only in whatever physical entertainment she was foolish enough to provide.

"It's kind—I suppose—of you to say so, but honestly, I cannot fathom what sort of demon must possess me—"

"It's the same demon that saw to it that you and I were created, Lisette."

"That is *not* the same thing at all! I am not married to you, and furthermore, I frequently find your very presence quite unnerving."

"Really?" He finished the vegetables and transferred them to a plate, which he took to the kettle.

"No, no!" Lisette interrupted. "Don't put those in! I have to separate the meat from the stock first." After fetching a huge bowl and a long sharp fork, she joined him and allowed him to spear the meat while she held the bowl.

First came a large chicken, followed by a piece of boiled beef, and finally another type that looked rather like beef, yet . . .

"*What* is this?" demanded Nicholai.

"Bear." Lisette smiled.

"*Bear!* What the devil are we making?"

Deciding to ignore the "we," she replied, "It's succotash. I've yet to add the pea beans and corn. One of the Coffee-House patrons brings me the bear meat when he visits Philadelphia, and since succotash is his favorite food, I make a kettleful to say thank you."

Nicholai eyed the inert meat doubtfully. "I wonder how grateful your other patrons would be if they knew what they were consuming?"

"You'll change your tune when you taste it. It's delicious." Her delicate nose went up a bit, proudly. "I am an excellent cook and have yet to hear the feeblest complaint."

"I beg your pardon, Mistress Hahn." Nicholai's voice was solemn, but mischief danced in his eyes. "And it would be a privilege to sample this latest masterpiece, but to do so I would have to remain here until the noon hour. . . ."

"Your subtlety amazes me," Lisette retorted, looking up at him with soft eyes. Bathed in fire glow, he was like a magnificent statue brought to life, cast in varying shades of warm bronze.

Lisette swallowed hard. "You may remain here and share a plate of succotash with me, Mr. Beauvisage—on one condition."

"Name it!"

"You must not take me lightly; I am quite serious about this. What madness possesses me when you—well—I mean that I do not have the time to ponder it, nor do I want it to happen again."

"*It?*" Nicholai echoed in innocent confusion.

"You know very well what I am trying to say, so please do me the kindness of not forcing me to use more explicit language." Frustrated, Lisette bit her lower lip and averted her eyes from his. "You may stay and chat with me until the succotash is ready, but you must give me your word that you won't touch me again or taunt me about my idiotic behavior."

"Oh, Lisette . . ." His jaw tensed in annoyance. "Look at me! What is wrong with you? Why should a beautiful, strong-minded girl like you be so blind about the natural pleasure your body can *give* and *take*? Those are *needs* you feel, fighting to be satisfied, just like your appetite for food, or sleep—"

"Stop! What you say is fine, but unfortunately, there are other circumstances involved. Emotions, pride, reputation, dignity . . . I will not be used, my body and heart wrung dry, and then left behind to be the subject of gossip. As I told you before, I satisfied my *needs* that night at your house, but I cannot allow an encore. If *your* appetite is making demands, I suggest that you seek out some equally ravenous female who has already forfeited her self-respect."

A muscle moved near Nicholai's mouth and his narrowed eyes bespoke his vexation, but he bit back a fresh argument. "Fine. I can see that it is hopeless to try to reason with you. Your head is as hard as that kettle." When she moved to walk away, he gripped her slim forearm and went on evenly, "I believe, my dear, that you've repressed more appetites than one. Don't you ever get hungry for affection or laughter?"

"I cannot spare the time, Mr. Beauvisage," Lisette shot back. "Unlike you, I have more pressing worries than the gratification of every emotional craving."

"It's a pity you must neglect them completely, because that won't make them disappear. All those needs are inside of you, growing by the day, and the time will come when you won't be able to ignore them any longer—they won't let you."

Chapter 13

April 9, 1793

By two o'clock, Lisette's face was flour smudged, but the keeping room was suffused with the sweet aroma of apple pie. Nicholai smelled of apples himself, for he had done all the slicing. Hours ago, he'd removed his stock in defense against the heat. Now Hyla and Chastity were busily spooning the last of the succotash onto plates—vegetables and meat on separate halves, with the rich stock over all—while Lisette and Nicholai sat in comb-back chairs before the fire.

"Uhhoh . . ." she groaned, stretching white-stockinged feet. When her gown caught, displaying her right calf, she readjusted it with a rosy blush.

Nicholai lit a cheroot, regarding her with his mouth quirked on one side. Lisette remembered then how *much* he had already seen and touched of her now-clothed body. Her blush grew hotter.

He smoked silently and wondered if she was actually softening. Was it his imagination? The last time they had conversed in this keeping room, he wouldn't have believed Lisette susceptible to embarrassment. Earlier, when he'd kissed her and she'd succumbed to passion, he had been less defensive during the aftermath than in the past. All-out verbal or physical attacks were Lisette's previous style— total denial of her own response. She was still resisting their chemistry, but it seemed that her inner struggle was less frenzied.

Then, Nicholai remembered what Stringfellow had said about Lisette's resolve weakening where Marcus Reems was concerned. He'd put it down to simple exhaustion . . . what conceit made him believe this wasn't also the cause of her softening toward *him*?

"That's a rather acid smile on your face, Mr. Beau-visage," Lisette remarked. "Are you plotting the downfall of another maiden?"

One chestnut brow arched high above the glint of his wide offended eyes. "Mistress Hahn, you *wound* me!"

Lisette's lips twitched in response to his mock-innocent pose. A deep dimple appeared in her left cheek; then she gave in to genuine delighted laughter.

Staring in disbelief, Nicholai leaned toward her. "I am in shock. That is the first time I've ever seen you *smile*, let alone laugh. Look at this!" He touched the dimple with a dark finger, then shook his head again. "It may take me days to recover! Whatever it was I said, you must tell me so I can write it down to refer to in the future."

"Please," Lisette muttered, allowing him his point with a wry smile. "You needn't make a speech; I *am* perceptive, in spite of my antagonistic disposition."

Nicholai leaned back again and slowly drew on the cheroot. "Well," he replied, exhaling the fragrant smoke, "it is simply a huge relief to discover you *can* laugh. I was beginning to worry that you were afflicted somehow—perhaps an exotic disease had destroyed your sense of humor or disabled your mouth so that it was unable to curve upward—"

"I'm so glad you are enjoying this. Your state of high amusement should improve the taste of this bear meat."

He saw the wicked sidelong glance Lisette slanted at him as she stood to fill a pewter plate with succotash. The fact that she was still playing, her irritation infused with mischief, astonished and pleased him.

"You are bent on retaliation, I see," Nicholai accused when she presented him with a large helping of bear meat. "Childish tactics on your part, Mistress Hahn."

Lisette's beautiful face lit up with another impish smile, blue eyes sparkling in the firelight. "How true, Mr. Beau-visage. Now, eat! You must know that I have only tolerated your company these long hours so that I could watch you savor your first bite of bear meat."

Cheerfully, she dropped into her seat and propped an

elbow on the chair arm. Chin on palm, she gazed back at him. Nicholai's brow was furrowed as he looked from Lisette to the bear meat, then put out his cheroot with a sigh.

"Your pleading little-boy expression won't help you," she grinned. "I know you too well. Eat."

So he did, with great reluctance. The taste of bear was not the best meal in his life thus far, but it was far better than he had expected. The vegetables, pea beans, and stock were memorably flavorful, and the meat was tender. The cook could not be faulted.

"Shockingly adequate," he told Lisette after several slow bites. Dancing emerald eyes relayed the bulk of the compliment.

While he ate, Lisette moved around the keeping room in her stockinged feet, arranging soiled dishes, cutlery, and empty pie tins. All would be washed before she began to cook again for the evening crush.

"What do you think about the war news?" she asked, bringing Nicholai a cold mug of ale.

"*War* news?" he echoed.

"Why, yes! Didn't you hear? Mr. Jefferson stopped here for some coffee about eight o'clock and he told me that it is definite. France has declared war on England, Russia, Spain, and the Netherlands."

"How would I have heard?" he demanded. "I came from my own bed directly here—and I've been chopping apples and eating bear rather than being in *there*"—he gestured toward the public room door—"where I could learn the news of France!"

"Well, for heaven's sake!" Lisette cried, hands on hips, "I certainly didn't invite you to spend the day with me! You needn't behave as if I'm to blame!"

This silenced Nicholai as he remembered that she believed his visit one of pure chance or his own choice.

"I beg your pardon, Lisette. I spoke without thinking."

She shrugged and returned to the clutter of the worktable. "I suppose you must feel strongly about France," she allowed.

"Yes." Nicholai's eyes were on the orange embers in the hearth.

Pausing for a long minute, Lisette regarded his stern profile. What was he thinking? "No doubt this will stir things up here in America as well."

He nodded slightly.

"You know, the Federalists and Republicans are already constantly at odds. Mr. Hamilton's party distrusts the Revolution; they are so shocked by the terrible violence in France that it seems that they're for England."

"No doubt," was Nicholai's distant reply. Lisette clattered a few plates together, to no avail.

"Mr. Jefferson," she went on blithely, "feels that in spite of the horrors occurring, liberty everywhere is caught up in France's fate. I argued a bit, but he insisted that he would rather have one-half the world destroyed than to see liberty fail. Don't you find that a rather chilling sentiment?"

"It's no different than the one Americans fought and died for. Have you forgotten Patrick Henry's battle cry: 'Give me liberty, or give me death'? You are only shocked by what Jefferson says because there has been such cold-blooded slaughter in France in the name of liberty. Liberty is what he has based his life on—and if he feels freedom is worth *any* price, he is entitled to his opinion."

Lisette drifted back to the hearth. She had perched on a footstool, eye level with Nicholai's booted legs, before she realized that she still held a pie tin.

"What do *you* think?" she queried, her expression suddenly intense. "You have lived in France for a decade, and though I don't know what you've experienced during these past years of the Revolution, I'm certain it was enough to shape an opinion. Who is right—Hamilton or Jefferson?"

Nicholai's eyes were hooded, masking his emotions. Most of the succotash was gone, so he leaned over to set the plate on the floor, then reclined with his ale mug. "Neither of them is right, naturally. And in France, no one at *all* is right! Christ, the situation there is too insane to be borne—but that's an entirely different topic of conversation."

Lisette interrupted. "*Neither* is right? If that is so, then what shall we do? What will happen in America?"

"Well, obviously, the first thing the president must consider is the effect this war will have on sea trade. Certainly, England will rush to blockade France, and if we attempt to run the blockade, our ships and their crews will risk destruction or capture."

"Won't the president be forced to choose Hamilton's or Jefferson's position then?"

Nicholai shrugged. "Not necessarily. There is always neutrality, my dear. In a case like this, colored with so many shades of gray, that may be the only course. The question is, how to approach it in view of our best interests."

"Poor President Washington," Lisette sighed. "It seems that the Federalists are on one side of the fence, the Republicans on the other, and that he's teetering on the fence itself. How can he choose?"

"If he is as fair and thoughtful as he seems, he will form an opinion based on his own judgment."

They were silent for a few minutes; then the muffled rumble of voices and hammering footsteps began seeping through the public room's wall. Lisette considered Nicholai's succinct presentation of the problems facing the president and compared them to the convoluted discussions that filled the smoky air of the public room all day. When she glanced up, she found Nicholai's penetrating eyes pinning her to the stool. Finally, he stood to light another cheroot and remarked, "I pity the president. I saw him before he left for Mount Vernon and he seemed as delighted as a boy to escape this town. Doubtless this latest crisis will force him to return before he's barely pulled off his boots."

"You're right! Mr. Jefferson mentioned that he posted a letter to the president yesterday and broke the bad news. Isn't it a shame—"

Lisette was interrupted by a sudden flurry of cool wind and a burst of sunlight as the door to the rear court swung open. They both turned their heads to meet the sinister gaze of Marcus Reems.

"A thousand pardons," he said smoothly as he entered. "Ah, Mr. Beauvisage, this is certainly a surprise." He swept off his top hat and made a short bow.

Nicholai's face was indifferently courteous and altogether unreadable as he stood to offer his hand. "I agree, Mr. Reems."

"Look here, Beauvisage, I enjoy a bit of witty conversation as much as the next man, but the fact is, I can't spare

the time. If you'll excuse us, there is a business matter I
should like to discuss with Mistress Hahn."

Momentarily at a loss for words, Lisette looked from
Nicholai to the black-haired intruder. "I—"

"That's very strange," Nicholai was saying, "since I made
an appointment with Mistress Hahn myself for this very
afternoon." He bent a look of dismay at Lisette. "Mademoiselle, could you have been so remiss as to arrange conflicting engagements?"

Recovered by now, she replied, "As a matter of fact, Mr.
Beauvisage, I did not invite Mr. Reems, nor did he inform
me of his intention to visit in advance. So, in view of the
fact that my time is limited, I suggest we repair to the
study, where we can finish our discussion without further
interruption."

With that cool snub, she dismissed Marcus Reems and
made an elegant exit. Nicholai followed Lisette in silence,
sensing Reems's impotent rage, thick as wood smoke in the
atmosphere.

When the study door was closed, they sank down on the
plush chaise and shared a conspiratorial smile. Lisette's
dimple winked at Nicholai, and sent a rush of warmth
through his chest.

"Please—don't look at me that way," she begged, all too
aware of the beginning magnetic pull.

"I don't mean to seem a lecher, Mistress Hahn. I thought
you were beautiful and desirable from the moment we met
at Belle Maison, but since you've begun favoring me with
these enchanting smiles, I'm hard pressed to contain my—
er—admiration."

Lisette assumed a prim expression. "If that's the case,
then I must remember to be ill tempered at all times when
you are present."

"A cruel threat."

"Besides, I don't believe your professions of uncontrol-
able longing. Look at me! My hair is coming down, a lock a
minute, I'm covered with spices and flour from head to toe,
my face is bare, and my gown"—she swallowed, disconcerted by his sensual gaze—"my gown is pathetic—worn,
homemade. . . ."

"Your unembellished beauty is the core of your appeal—

and your mystique," he countered, smiling at this uncharacteristically feminine play for flattery. "The fact that you are confident and aloof enough not to paint your face and dress fashionably makes you much more fascinating. Men are constantly besieged by predatory females who use their good looks and fashion as sly weapons. You, Lisette, are a lovely, refreshing enigma . . . you know perfectly well how much desire you generate each time you appear in that public room."

"There are always ill-bred men who think they must conquer every moving skirt . . . and it just happens that I am the only possible victim, save Hyla and the two girls. Don't imagine that those obnoxious attentions make me purr to myself! And that's beside the point, for I was speaking of *you*. No doubt you've women fawning over you constantly—"

"Flocks of them," he confirmed. *"Herds."*

"So why do you persist in bothering me—you've already proven that you could seduce me!"

"Is your opinion of men so low that you cannot see us as individuals? I find it is very insulting that you should toss me into your pot of men who view females only as bed partners. Do you imagine that when I hold you in my arms I do so only to gratify my ego?"

Uneasily, Lisette stood and paced across the study. "No —well, I don't know." How had he put her so far on the defensive? She took a deep breath. "What are you implying? Be plain, Mr. Beauvisage, and tell me what I *should* imagine!"

"For God's sake, call me Nicholai!" He ground out his cheroot in a candy dish, leaned forward, and rested his forearms on his knees. "For such a bright girl, you are appallingly ignorant concerning human relationships. Must I feel only lust or love? Can a man not feel a mixture of emotions of varying strengths? There are many qualities that I like in you and feel an urge to explore. You are complicated and I enjoy puzzles. Yes, there's the physical tug . . . and I have known enough women to be aware of the rare intensity of the current running from your resisting body to my own. You can feel it now, can't you, Lisette?

Even with the entire room separating us." He saw her tense against a blush, but ignored it. "I also have found myself wondering how you are coping here at the CoffeeHouse— and what your financial situation has become. I would like to help . . . perhaps I could lend you the money to pay off the loan to Marcus Reems's bank."

Lisette felt an alarming weakness steal over her as she listened to Nicholai and let herself believe him. However, his last words triggered an automatic response in her mind, which also alerted her to the erosion of her strength. This was dangerous. Not since her involvement with the congressman had she felt quite so light-headed—as though there were no world outside this room. She'd nearly forgotten the CoffeeHouse and her responsibility that other time—and had her heart broken in the end. She forced herself to heed the painful memory.

"You can't conceive of the possibility that I, a mere woman, could manage here alone, can you? So the big brilliant man comes to rescue me from my blundering predicament." Gathering steam, she crossed the rug until she was standing over him. "You would love to hear me admit defeat and then sigh adoringly while you skillfully unravel the snarls I've made in my dim-witted femininity!"

Nicholai had stared in surprise when she began her tirade, but now he was coldly furious. Roughly, he reached up to grasp her waist and yanked her over onto the chaise, pinning down her shoulders. Lisette struggled wildly and spat out threats and insults, but Nicholai merely hooked a leg over her own to hold her still.

"Be quiet!" he ground out. A muscle twitched above his tense jaw and tendons stood out in his neck. "You perverse, hardheaded bitch! What does it take to dent that armor of yours? Are you totally impervious to reason!"

"Are you planning to beat some sense into me?" Lisette shot back, blue eyes blazing. Tangled gold curls poured across the chaise, emphasizing her angry beauty.

"No."

Lisette paused to catch her breath and was jarred by a sudden awareness of Nicholai looming above her. His cold rage was reflected in his icy green eyes and the tense

112 ──────────────────────────── SPRING FIRES

chiseled strength of his dark face. There was something
about the virile expanse of his chest, exposed by his open
shirt, that made her heart pound.

Nicholai's hands slid over Lisette's arms until his steely
fingers encircled her delicate wrists. She was mustering a
fresh burst of outrage when suddenly it was too late; a hard
mouth crushed her own with scorching intensity. There was
no trace of the familiar leisureliness of past kisses, no deft
coaxing of her response. When his tongue abruptly invaded
her mouth, Lisette trembled. She tried to refuse the kiss, to
remain stiff under his assault, and to remember how bar-
barically arrogant he was. . . .

Nicholai continued to kiss her with savage intimacy until
her mouth answered hungrily. He surveyed her flushed
cheeks, sparkling eyes, and the pulse at the base of her
throat before shifting her wrists above her head, where he
held them with one hand. His other hand roughly moved to
unfasten Lisette's bodice; he could feel the drumming of her
heart against his fingertips. Nicholai thought how predict-
able she was in this one way . . . someday she would get
the point, more likely from this argument than from any
words he could use.

Unsympathetically, he tore the front of her chemise to
reveal full firm breasts, their nipples taut with arousal. In
the daylight, Nicholai blinked at such creamy beauty, almost allowing his heart to soften. He ran his tongue around
the puckered edge of one nipple slowly, feeling it tense.
Finally, he covered it with his lips, kissing and tugging
gently until Lisette moaned and fought to free her arms.
Nicholai's mouth seared a trail to her other breast, and
then he released his hold on her wrists. Aching to touch
him, Lisette buried her fingers in his gleaming hair and
endured the sweet agony that transmitted itself between her
tingling breasts and the throbbing place beneath her skirts.

At length, craving another potent kiss, she urged him
upward with her hands. Nicholai did shift so that his forbidding face was above hers, but there were no kisses.
Deliberately, he moved the rest of his body so that he lay
between her legs; then he pressed his hips to hers. Through

her gown, Lisette felt Nicholai's tantalizing rigid maleness against the core of her own hot ache. Swallowing a tiny whimper, she moved her hips hesitantly, and prayed he would lift her skirts and end this torture.

"You want it, don't you?" he asked harshly.

She saw the ruthless glint in his eyes, but couldn't help nodding. After all, he knew it was true. "Yes," she whispered.

Nicholai swung his legs free and stood up. "Dear Lisette, you must make a record of this, for it is certainly a milestone—not only have we discovered an undertaking that you were not *quite* self-sufficient enough to complete alone, but I've also witnessed your first request for *assistance*." Rolling down his cuffs, he never looked at her, but continued caustically, "However, knowing how adamantly you reject all forms of rescue from *men,* my conscience will not allow me to interfere. You may have weakened momentarily, but later you'll certainly be pleased to be standing alone."

Seething with angry humiliation, Lisette stood to face Nicholai, and promptly slapped him across the face as hard as she could. "You arrogant, odious beast!"

Instantly, his hands gripped her sore wrists with crushing strength. "Knowing your views on equal treatment for women, I ought to return that slap. Strike me again and you will be repaid."

"Let go, before I call for Stringfellow. I must fasten my gown and return to work." When the task was done, she stared murderously up at Nicholai. "I'd have been better off with that villain Marcus Reems!"

"Mistress Hahn, may I remind you that *you* wanted to continue this little—interlude, and it was *I* who called halt. Your pose as victim will not alter the facts."

Lisette opened her mouth to reply, but was cut off by a quiet knock at the study door. She glared at Nicholai and went to answer it.

"Hello, Lisette."

It was Lion Hampshire. His eyes quickly took in her state of dishabille, then fell on Nicholai.

"Well! Hello, Mr. Beauvisage. I'm sorry if I interrupted your conversation—" He searched Nicholai's face for a hint of the situation.

"No!" countered Lisette. "He was just leaving."

"Please—stay a moment," Lion said to Nicholai, raising blond brows meaningfully. "I'll be brief."

"As you wish," Nicholai said tonelessly.

"The fact is, Lisette, that Hyla spoke to me today and told me that Marcus Reems has been harassing you about a loan, and pressuring you to sell the CoffeeHouse to him."

"That is correct, Senator—but I think Hyla should tend to her own affairs."

"She is concerned, Lisette—and so am I. For an hour, I've sat alone in a corner of the public room, considering this matter. I know that you want to keep the CoffeeHouse in business on your own, but after all, it was your father who took the loan. Shouldn't you be able to begin with a clean slate?"

"Please sit down, Senator." Lisette offered him the corner chair, then seated herself opposite. In the background, Nicholai lounged against the far wall and listened.

"My offer is simple. I would like to loan to you the amount due on Ernst's note, so that you will be able to free yourself from Marcus Reems. I attach no conditions except repayment as you are able. You will be able to tell Marcus Reems that you stand alone and will not need his contribution."

To Nicholai's incredulous amazement, he heard Lisette reply, "Senator, I wish I were in a position to say no, but I am not. I am honored to accept your kind offer—and I shall repay you with all possible speed."

Nicholai's reaction was immediate and brusque. "I must leave. Good day." Passing them, he nodded once at Lion, but ignored Lisette completely.

Back in the keeping room, he was oblivious to Hyla Flowers's curious stare as he retrieved his cravat and jacket. Pulling them on while he walked, Nicholai went through to the public room. Stringfellow was winding his way between the tables when he felt an iron band grip his arm. The tray almost slipped and he looked around crossly.

A dangerous-looking Nicholai Beauvisage narrowed jewel-hard eyes at him and growled, "Stringfellow, don't you *ever* again consider me as a possible savior for your Lisette-in-distress. If she makes a mess of her life, it won't be more than she's striven for and deserves!"

. . Stringfellow was still rooted to the spot, staring and clutching his tray, a full minute after Nicholai's broad shoulders had disappeared through the CoffeeHouse door.

Chapter 14

April 18, 1793

The baskets of crimson strawberries were a pretty sight in the twilit keeping room. Lisette sat on her stool, rinsing and cleaning them with uncharacteristic languor, pausing at intervals to sample a particularly plump berry.

Across from her, Hyla Flowers was polishing silver. *Thank God for Sundays,* she thought. *Without a day to catch our breath, we'd never survive.* She pushed back a lock of frizzy coral-tinted hair and regarded Lisette. How listless she seemed! Her thick-lashed blue eyes were dreamy and sad, and each breath she took was nearly a sigh.

"What's wrong, honey?"

"Hmm?"

"I said, what ails you? Are you sick?"

"Oh—no, no, Hyla." She managed a weak smile. "Perhaps it's spring fever."

"I know what you need," Hyla decided. "You spend every waking moment cooped up in this CoffeeHouse. The only fresh air you ever get is when you go out to the market. I think the best thing you could do would be to treat yourself to a nice long walk. It's a rare evening and you'd have a chance to just relax and clear your mind."

Lisette started to decline, then paused. "Do you know, Hyla, I believe you are right. It isn't healthy for me to stay in here all the time; I *will* go out for a stroll."

Grinning with pleasure, the older woman sent her upstairs to wash and put on a fresh gown. A quarter hour later, Lisette was waving good-bye, clad in a soft butter-yellow frock with a fichu of white gauze, her tousled blond curls intertwined with a yellow muslin fillet; against these sunny colors, her eyes sparkled like sapphires.

It did feel wonderful to be outdoors. The smells of the waterfront were a welcome change, and it was fun to pass people on the footpaths and exchange smiles and greetings. As the flaming sky shaded toward violet blue and lamps were lit, Lisette meandered up Front Street to Walnut, then strolled south along the bends of Dock Street. She watched the handsome three-story brick row houses turn inward for the night, curtained windows burnished gold, and wondered where Nicholai was—with whom was he talking . . . laughing?

A woman?

She wondered, leaning against a dogwood tree, what sort of life he led. Since the day in the study, when she accepted Lion Hampshire's loan, Nicholai had not set foot in the CoffeeHouse. Lisette knew, because not an hour passed that she did not find an excuse to tour the public room. Her mind insisted that she was well rid of his disruptive influence, but her heart and body found him difficult to forget. At night, when she lay in bed, blurry eyed with fatigue, she remembered what he had said to her about "needs," the expression on his face when he'd said that she possessed qualities he wanted to explore, and the offhand tone with which he'd offered to lend her the money to pay off Marcus Reems. Alone in the darkness, Lisette tried to ignore the nagging inner voice that insisted that she had erred in the way she'd handled *that* situation. In fact, it seemed that she hadn't ever said or done the right thing in Nicholai's presence . . . she'd been shrewish, moody, stubborn, childish— and shamelessly lacking in willpower.

With a bitter sigh, Lisette continued to walk alone through the night, south toward Spruce Street. She blinked back the tears that stung her eyes and tried to convince herself that she was better off without emotional involvements . . . especially with a man like Nicholai Beauvisage.

At that moment, Nicholai was seated in a wing chair in his study, smoking a cheroot and staring at a message just arrived from Lion Hampshire.

It is important that I speak with you tonight. May
I come to your house at eight o'clock?

L.H.

Nicholai scowled at the words. He could guess what was
on Lion's mind, for he hadn't gone near the CoffeeHouse
or Lisette Hahn in more than a week. There was simply no
possible way for him to continue this charade of keeping
track of Marcus Reems, for he refused to endure another
meeting with the maddening Mistress Hahn. Lisette had
believed his visits to be products of his entrancement with
her, and after her cutting acceptance of Lion's loan, Nicholai refused to flatter her any further.

But how to explain to Lion? Why couldn't Marcus
Reems's scheme have involved some other female? Nicholai
truly wished he could help Hampshire—but not at a sacrifice to his own self-respect. And he couldn't explain to Lion
what existed between himself and Lisette Hahn.

"Damn it!" he swore. The note from Lion was crushed
in his fist and he tossed it into the fire. After shifting the
chair around to the handsome fall-front desk, Nicholai took
quill in hand and wrote:

Sorry, NO.

N.P.B.

It seemed that the only solution was for him to be so
rude to Lion that there would be no questions. It was simpler to be thought callous and irresponsible than to expose
his chaotic relationship with Lisette.

Oliver was summoned to deliver the message, and when
he was gone, Nicholai relaxed with a brandy and the remainder of his cheroot. A strange night indeed. He had
wriggled out of an invitation from Anne and William Bingham to share supper with them and the unlovely Ophelia
after Caro begged him to join them at Belle Maison. However, it had been nearly a week since he'd been with his
lady friend, the restlessly married Amelia Purdy, and when
her message arrived yesterday informing him that her hus-

band would be away for tonight, Nicholai canceled his plans at Belle Maison. He was more in the mood for unemotional sex than for another performance of Caro and Sacha as the consummate married couple. If there was any justice in the world, he'd be at Amelia's now and be spared the problem of Lion's request, but it seemed, as of an hour ago, that Mr. Purdy had a last-minute change of plans.

Nicholai ground out his cheroot and drained the brandy. He should have found another woman or two by now; this business with Amelia was ridiculously unpredictable, and besides, she wasn't his match under the sheets. That would have to be his spring project now that he'd rid himself of the Reems-Hahn enterprise. It was cheering to look forward to lovely, uncomplicated coquettes who would gaze at him adoringly and melt in his embrace. Just the thing. Much more enjoyable and relaxing than trying to get close to the prickly, fitful Mistress Hahn. Let her eat bear meat until kingdom come—*he* certainly didn't care.

There was a knock at the front door. Welcome and Felicity had already retired to their quarters attached to the kitchen building behind the garden. Oliver usually slept in a chamber located in front of the study, but tonight he had asked if he might pay a visit to his sweetheart after delivering the message to Lion Hampshire.

Sighing, Nicholai rose and glanced in the mirror. His cravat was loosened casually, his hair ruffled even more negligently than usual, and he wore no jacket, only a waistlength, unbuttoned fawn waistcoat. Deciding that, as master in his own home, he had a right to be as disheveled as he pleased, Nicholai went down the marble hallway.

When he pulled open the door, he found Lisette Hahn standing there, looking humble and utterly lovely in her yellow gown.

"Lisette?"

"Had you forgotten me?" She gave him a hopeful smile.

"Of course not! But what is it? Is something wrong?"

Still on the doorstep, Lisette noted the appearance of his clothing. "No, nothing is wrong. Is there a woman here? If you were busy, I will go . . . it was foolish of me to knock at all—"

"Of course there isn't a woman here!" Nicholai chided

in mock dismay. "Come in. I am breathless with curiosity to learn why you are here."

He took her back to the study and Lisette looked around the narrow, cozy room while Nicholai poured some wine.

"I like your furniture much better without the dust covers." She smiled. The camelback sofa was upholstered in a Chinese pattern of terra-cotta, gold, and dark green, while the chairs were velvet covered in matching solid colors.

"Thank you." Nicholai's entire approach was wary, from the humor in his voice to the amount of wine he poured. *What the devil is the vixen up to now?* seemed his one coherent thought. "Let's sit here before the fire while you tell me what has prompted this *most* unexpected visit. I wasn't aware you ever wandered more than a few feet from the CoffeeHouse."

"You have endowed me with several peculiar traits, Mr. Beauvisage. First you believed me unable to laugh—"

"Nicholai. For the hundredth time, call me Nicholai." Somehow, he felt that she used this formality to keep him at arm's length, to prove her indifference, rather than as a sign of polite respect. "And, since we are in my house, before *my* fire, I must take a turn at naming the conditions to be met if you remain."

Lisette strove to show no reaction. Was he going to try to trick her into another night in his bed? The mere thought of this threw her senses into conflict. A part of her was shocked and outraged, but another part—the one born the night Nicholai taught her the splendor of lovemaking—was frankly excited by the prospect.

"All right, I accept."

"Fine." Nicholai's brow was arched slightly, as if he could read her mind. "I want you to tell me, *honestly*, why you came here tonight. That is all I ask."

A little crease formed down the bridge of her nose.

"The truth," Nicholai pressed.

"I heard you!" She glared at him. "All right. I came here because I had been thinking about you. I regretted the unfortunate way our last encounter ended—" Her voice broke off as she swallowed the more humbling reasons.

"Not half the truth, Lisette, *all* of it."

"You are a vile man! I will say the rest, but I've changed my mind since I felt this way!" She took a deep breath. "I had considered some of the things you said to me—about the appetites I'd neglected, and about your friendly feeling towards me. It seemed that you put out your hand to me more than once, offering me your friendship and help, and it was mean spirited of me to strike it away. I think, now, that it was a reflex—to protect myself from hurt and rejection." Lisette no longer looked vexed. She met his gaze and felt a spreading current of relief now that the words were being spoken. "I've realized that I have been a coward, which is not to say I accept all the blame, for you have behaved badly as well. And, I don't plan to leap into your bed now or weep a confession of love. I just wanted you to know I've been working to fix my 'hard head' . . . I apologize for my childish scenes, and . . ."

"And you have been lonely? It's not much fun to exist in a world where there is no special intimacy with another person, is it?"

"No." Her chin quivered.

Nicholai put his hand against one side of her face and queried gently, "Did you miss my aggravating visits just a bit?"

After a moment, Lisette nodded, and tears glittered in her thick lashes. "I—I kept remembering the succotash . . . how you made me laugh in a way I hadn't known for so long. It wasn't just a reflex—it felt *good,* because the laughter bubbled out when I tried to keep it inside. Just talking, about politics and the other everyday things was a treat for me. I used to chat by the hour with Katya, but she's always with Randolph now, or planning her wedding and that's as it should be. I suppose"—her voice quavered as a few of the tears flicked free—"I had forgotten the pleasure of stimulating conversation, instead of just going through the motions with Hyla or the customers . . . even Papa. But there, I did try; he was so withdrawn toward the end."

Nicholai carefully gathered her into his arms, cradling her close as she wept. He sensed that she'd broken down a few of the barriers, but not all—when that happened, there would be a flood of tears rather than this trickle.

"It's hard to admit, to you," Lisette whispered brokenly, "but I think the only times I have felt really alive lately have been in your presence. I couldn't put a name to it, but there's no doubt that you stir me up somehow . . . Nicholai."

He smiled against her soft vanilla-scented hair. Tonight there was a hint of strawberries in it. "That is good, Lisette. We all need a bit of stirring up from time to time."

"Promise me—promise that you won't use my confessions to embarrass me. I couldn't bear it if you were constantly laughing at me with your eyes, reminding me that I've told you of my secret feelings. I—"

"Lisette, will you never learn? If you mean to embark on a—friendship with me, you mustn't continue to harbor these suspicions, particularly aloud—to my face! It's *very* insulting and makes it difficult for me to remain patient with you."

Lisette drew back to look at him, relieved to find the sardonically amused undercurrent in his voice reinforced by a quirk on one side of his mouth. "I am sorry." She grinned.

"Please, no more apologies! Just one, coming from you, will take me all evening to digest."

Suddenly, she moved up, wrapping her arms around his wide shoulders. Their eyes met, inches apart, for an instant, before Lisette kissed Nicholai's mouth. It was a tender, lingering kiss, and their tongues played in a nonverbal truce. The gentleness of Lisette's kiss merely heightened the sensitivity of Nicholai's body . . . he burned and ached, but somehow managed to control the urge to take charge. When she drew back at last, Nicholai groaned, "*What* were you doing?"

Lisette disengaged herself from his arms, smudges of color across her cheekbones. "I had a sudden urge to find out if I would be affected differently now that we are no longer antagonists."

"I see. And what have you deduced? Has the fire been quenched?"

Lisette put up her hands as if to ward off an attack and murmured, "No. It's the same."

"*Bambine,*" he accused in French. "There will be no

more cruel experiments conducted on *me*. That is like
dangling a leg of lamb before a starving man to see if he
salivates, then snatching it away!"

"What does *bambine* mean?" Lisette demanded.

"Brat!" He drained his wineglass to hide a smile just as
another knock came at the front door; Nicholai's mood
switched to one of annoyance.

"Oliver, my butler, is out, so I must see who it is. Excuse
me."

Lisette gave him a feline smile, and curled up with her
wine. "You are excused."

Shaking his head, he went back down the hall to answer
the door. This time, standing on the step and cloaked in
darkness, was Lion Hampshire.

"Beauvisage, what sort of rudeness is this?" He held up
the blunt note Oliver had delivered.

"I'd hoped it would speak for itself."

"Very amusing. May I come in?" He did so, and the two
men faced each other in the lamp-lit vestibule. "I see you
are home! I might be more understanding if you had been
called away—"

"Senator, is my time not my own? Am I at the beck and
call of you and every other self-important citizen of
Philadelphia?"

"Damn it, this is important!"

"If it's about Marcus Reems, I have nothing to say. I
should think you would know better than I what is afoot,
since you leaped to the fore with your generous loan to
Lisette Hahn. You ought to be better able than I, at this
point, to learn what Reems intends to do."

"Will you allow me to explain?" cried Lion. "It's not
about Marcus. President Washington arrived back from
Mount Vernon tonight and there is a cabinet meeting tomorrow to decide what we should do about France."

"Cozy. Hamilton and Jefferson, with Washington in the
middle. Interesting."

"That is why I am here. It would seem that you made a
definite impression on the president. He has asked that you
visit him tonight—*now*—so that he can discuss the situation
in France with you."

"I don't have any easy answers," Nicholai warned.

"None are required. He only wishes to *talk*."

Sighing, Nicholai capitulated. One could not deny the request of President Washington.

"I will fetch my coat." To dissuade Lion from following along, he added, "Please, have a chair. I'll be just a moment."

Back in the study, Nicholai drank in the lemon and cream vision of Lisette and muttered a particularly vulgar French epithet.

"What is it?"

"Shh . . . I assume you don't want to be discovered by Senator Hampshire—the circumstances *are* suspicious. And, it's damned bad luck that I'm forced to go out for a while. Someone wants to hear my firsthand account of life in France; according to Hampshire, it can't wait."

Lisette watched as he swiftly retied his muslin cravat, buttoned his waistcoat, and pulled on a forest green coat. When Nicholai turned from the mirror to find her looking so disappointed, his heart lurched just a bit.

"Oh, Lisette, you mustn't pout. I'm not going to send you back to the CoffeeHouse! Why don't you take a nap while I am gone—I can see that you are exhausted. Curl up, close your eyes, and when you wake up I will be here. This shouldn't take more than an hour, two at the most, and the evening is young."

She looked doubtful. "If I stay, that doesn't mean I intend to share your bed again."

"Have I been less than a gentleman tonight?"

"Well, no . . . but how long can you go on?" Lisette smiled playfully.

"Gad, what conceit!" He chuckled. "We will talk. That's all. And, if you should be seized by an attack of physical craving—"

"You will do your best to oblige."

They laughed together softly. "I must go now, before Lion begins to search me out. I hope you will stay, Lisette."

"Perhaps. Thank you for your wine—and sympathetic ear."

"And lips." He bent to press a chaste kiss to her brow before exiting to join Lion Hampshire. Minutes later they were on horseback, riding north up Third Street. They were so preoccupied that neither glanced to the left while passing the Binghams' Mansion House, lit up behind its ornate gates and the curtain of trees that lined its circular drive.

However, wrapped in darkness on the other side of the gates, a figure on horseback watched Lion and Nicholai ride by. He had left the Binghams' gathering to escape the cloying attentions of Ophelia, but now his mood lightened. No one could have been more intrigued by the sight of Hampshire and Beauvisage, deep in conversation, than Marcus Reems.

❧ Chapter 15 ❧

April 18, 1793

Lisette couldn't decide whether to behave rationally and return to the CoffeeHouse or to be frivolous and wait for Nicholai. When several minutes of internal debate failed to provide an answer, she decided to give her weary mind a few minutes' rest. After all, there was no rush. . . .

The sound of a voice caused her to open her eyes, focusing first on the fire. It had been burning with antic cheer the last time she had looked . . . but now there were only orange embers against the blackness. Nearby oil lamps provided flickering light—just enough to illuminate Lisette's golden drowsy beauty.

"I *said*, where is Nicholai? Wake up, wench!"

Lisette blinked. A few feet away, shrouded in shadow, stood a tall, slender woman with black hair and ivory skin.

"Who—who are you?" Lisette struggled to sit up.

"My name is Amelia Purdy. You needn't bother to introduce yourself; I have no time to socialize with kitchen wenches. I was looking for Mr. Beauvisage and saw the light from this room. Do you not agree that your master would prefer you to be awake to open the door for visitors, rather than slumbering in his study as if you own the place?"

During this speech, Lisette became fully alert. Indignantly, she stood to face Amelia Purdy and glared at her with eyes of sharp blue ice. "I shall introduce myself all the same, *Mrs.* Purdy. My name is Lisette Hahn; I do not labor in Mr. Beauvisage's kitchen—I spend more than enough time in the keeping room of Hahn's CoffeeHouse." Seeing the angry confusion in the other woman's face, she explained, "*I* am the proprietress." A wickedly sweet smile came next, then, "And what do *you* do, Mrs. Purdy?"

The Washingtons' home in Philadelphia belonged to Robert Morris, who was said to be America's richest man. Located on High Street, west of Society Hill, the three-story mansion was tastefully elegant. Both tables and doors were made of polished mahogany, the brass locks and hinges were startlingly bright, and the beautifully decorated rooms were artfully and neatly arranged. Nicholai recognized various paintings and *objets,* as well as the superb pieces of furniture, many of which were embellished with silver or inlaid with sandalwood.

Also prominently displayed, in the main parlor, were two gifts Washington had received from his dear friend the Marquis de Lafayette: the key to the Bastille and a drawing of the fortress's destruction. During his first visit, Nicholai learned that the president had also hung an engraving of Louis XVI so that he would not appear prejudiced, but it was removed when word came of Louis's encounter with the guillotine.

Tonight, Tobias Lear, Washington's secretary, led the two men up to a private study on the second floor. The sixty-year-old president was seated in a plush velvet easy chair, clad in a long burgundy dressing gown. His pale hands were clasped over his belly, the thinning-gray-haired head tilted to one side to allow an occasional snore or moan to escape. Nicholai could see ashy smudges under the sleeping eyes.

"We can return tomorrow," he whispered to Hampshire.

"No!" came the hissed reply. "Tomorrow is the cabinet meeting. The president has just returned from Mount Vernon this evening to deal with the war situation in France. Since nearly all of the Congress is away during this recess, I have been involved in the discussions held by the cabinet these past ten days. I mentioned you several times and it seems that either Jefferson or Hamilton must have

passed my comments on to the president. Nicholai, he *needs*
to hear every intelligent opinion available if he is to make
the right decision."

"Absolutely!" President Washington agreed. Wearily, he
hoisted his tall body into a sitting position and smiled.
Though his false teeth, fashioned of hippopotamus ivory,
were wine- and tea-stained, Nicholai felt the full impact of
the president's goodness.

"We weren't aware you had awakened, Mr. President,"
Lion apologized, bowing in an informal manner. "I regret
this disturbance, but I understood you were anxious to speak
to Mr. Beauvisage."

"Indeed I am!" Washington gripped Nicholai's hand. "I
trust you are well, sir, and enjoying the high life of Philadelphia? Has Mrs. Bingham yet maneuvered you into pro-
posing marriage to her English cousin? Before I left town,
my good friend Eliza Powel assured me that that was
Anne's intent!"

Nicholai chuckled, acknowledging the twinkle in the
president's eyes. "No, but that's not for lack of effort on
Mrs. Bingham's part, Mr. President."

After a few more minutes of pleasantries and the pouring
of Madeira, Washington settled down to discuss the current
dilemma involving France and her neighbors. First, he
asked Nicholai for a detailed account of his own experiences connected with the Revolution. All was revealed save
the true situation involving Gabrielle and their romance; he
merely said that someone close to him had not shared his
luck in surviving the September Massacres. The president
listened closely, then spoke of his own pain. Lafayette,
whom he loved as a son, had been forced to flee to Austria,
where he had been imprisoned by aristocrats.

"I know the marquis," Nicholai replied. "I admire him
greatly, and his efforts to bring about beneficial change
through moderate means. This growing extremism, which
embraces farcical trials and executions, eats like a cancer
at all the noble core of the Revolution. The mad injustice
of it makes my blood boil! Sir, you have never known such
a twisted group of men as those who struggle for control in
France—both Jacobins and Girondists. Each man is slightly
insane in his own fashion, and because of this, scores of

people who committed no crime save that of gentle birth are spilling their blood in the place de la Révolution."

"I have heard that cattle refuse to walk there because of the blood," whispered the president.

"I assure you, sir, that no words can convey even a fraction of the revulsion and horror one experiences if he lives through a block of time in France."

"Are you against the Revolution, then?" queried Washington, his eyes sharp. "Would you favor England's side?"

"Hell, no! I *believe* in the original concept of revolution in France. The system was horrendously off balance—the poor lived in squalor while the king spent thousands of pounds on shallow pursuits and luxuries. Revolt was inevitable, as you well know, though I am proud to say that I managed my own estate in a democratic manner. I would even suggest that I am alive today because of the loyalty and affection of those who labored in my vineyards. They were never bitten by the rabid discontent which is cured only by the murder of the resident aristo."

"In your opinion, Mr. Bêauvisage, how do you expect it will end?"

"I hope that eventually sanity will rear its head and the snarl of madness will untangle itself. *But*," Nicholai added in a steely, bitter voice, "I fear that more blood has been shed than can ever be bleached or covered over. The stench and stain will cling to democracy in France forever . . . I for one hope that is the case. If, in centuries to come, people can learn from the stories and dark blot of the Revolution, I might be able to believe it wasn't all meaningless."

"Mr. Beauvisage, if you were in my place, what would you do?"

"I would keep America's meddling fingers out of that mess in Europe. There is no right side. We must continue to hope that democracy and liberty will emerge triumphant in France, but we cannot condone the slaughter going on now. At this point, I pray that the Revolution succeeds— for if it were to collapse under the pressures of war, all the death and despair would be completely without meaning. However, the chaos was created without aid from America and I am convinced that France must see her own way clear."

"Are you aware that we have signed certain treaties which obligate us to provide forms of assistance to France should she become involved in war?"

Nicholai made a derisive sound. "Mr. President, you know as well as I that, since the king's execution removed all traces of the old government, men currently in power could never hold you to those treaties."

Splaying his fingers, Washington let the tips of right and left hands bounce against one another. "Have you heard that the new French minister, Genêt, is on his way to our shores? What do you propose I should do? Some people urge me to ignore him, since receiving him could be construed as an acknowledgment that those treaties we made with Louis are still binding."

Nicholai made a face and whistled softly. "I am acquainted with Citizen Genêt, and I believe you will find him difficult to ignore. He is very—ah—*visible,* a man of oft-voiced opinions that are usually quite unorthodox. He has been connected with the royal family for years, but I know it was his troublemaking past that allowed him to find a place with the new government. Mr. President, if you refuse to receive Genêt, he will make an ungodly fuss here in America . . . and you know how much pro-France sentiment exists."

"The situation calls for careful handling," Washington said, smiling.

"No more than your usual tact, Mr. President," Nicholai replied, white teeth flashing against his dark face.

"I fear I shall need an extra supply tomorrow when the cabinet convenes. If I cannot convince those men, with their monumental differences of opinion, to unite and support my decisions . . . I shudder to think of the various disastrous possibilities."

"It is unfortunate that the weight of this must fall on you, Mr. President, rather than on Congress."

"I wish there were *time* to reconvene the Congress, Mr. Beauvisage . . . this sort of crisis deserves their attention. However, it *is* a crisis, and requires immediate action. In less than a week, there would be so many Americans outfitting privateers to help the French that any declaration of neutrality from me would come too late."

They chatted on for another hour. In spite of his tired appearance, Washington was involved deeply in this conversation; he apparently deemed it more important than a solid night's sleep. Finally, when Tobias Lear peeked in to mention that it was eleven o'clock, the president bade Nicholai and Lion a reluctant good night. He stood and walked down the hall with them, telling Lion that he wished him to attend the cabinet meeting the following morning. Then, he paused at the stairway and grasped Nicholai's hand. His deep-set eyes studied the younger man's face for a full minute before he spoke.

"Will you return to France, Mr. Beauvisage, or remain here with us in America?"

"I cannot say, sir. My heart is torn, and my feelings for France are mixed. She is like a woman whom one loves blindly and believes to be good and true—then one day she betrays you, and your disillusion seems to sour all the beautiful emotions that went before. Yet, one cannot forget. There is a mystical bond that connects me to France, to my land and my home which I love as you love Mount Vernon. The day may come when I will be drawn back whether I want to be or not."

Washington had planned to urge Nicholai to stay in Philadelphia, thinking that he had the kind of intelligence and insight needed in their government, but instead he only nodded. "I understand, Mr. Beauvisage. I wish you peace, whatever choice you make."

Nicholai and Lion rode slowly down High Street. The heart of town was quiet and they passed few people except for the watchmen who stood on the well-lit footpaths.

"How is your lovely wife?" inquired Nicholai after a long silence. "I understand she is expecting a baby."

"Yes." Lion's smile was thoughtful. "Meagan isn't quite herself these days, I'm afraid. The baby had forced her to curb her activities—a difficult order for a high-spirited girl who is used to being my full, visible, and vocal partner."

"Has she suffered any of the maladies common to women in her condition? I remember that when my mother was expecting Katya, we were never able to predict what she would say or do."

"You cannot imagine . . ." Lion sighed loudly. "She cries, she pouts, she is alternately restless and lethargic. I feel as though I am living with a stranger."

"Well, I understand those symptoms fade away after the first few months, so take heart, my friend."

"I must confess, I haven't helped the situation much. Meagan begged me to take her to our country house, south of town, and after the president left for Mount Vernon, I resolved to leave the preoccupations of government behind and spend a few weeks alone with my wife."

"I can guess how that has turned out—since this business about the war in France has come up."

"With the Congress in recess, I could not avoid being drawn in. The hell of it is, I cannot confide in Meagan beyond the sketchiest explanations of what keeps me in Philadelphia. Thank God our relationship has such a solid base of trust."

They drew up before Nicholai's house and reined in the horses. Dismounting, Nicholai handed his borrowed horse over to Lion so that he might return it to his Pine Street stable.

"Cheer up, Lion! Tomorrow the cabinet will meet, and with luck, all will go well and you'll be free to smooth your wife's ruffled feathers."

"Meagan is not so easily placated, I fear, but I shall hope for the best. For now, I must return this horse and ride for my villa. It's nearly midnight, which means I am seven hours past the time I told Meagan I would be home."

Nicholai laughed sympathetically. "I will not keep you then, Senator. *Bonsoir*."

"Again, my thanks for meeting with President Washington."

With that, Lion nudged his red roan with his knee and they started off toward Pine Street, leading the other horse. Nicholai went into the house with a sleepy yawn. Shrugging out of his coat and loosening his cravat, he walked first to the study. Of course, Lisette was gone; it *was* half-past eleven, after all, but what surprised Nicholai was the prickle of disappointment he felt. The fire had gone out; only a few reddish embers remained to cast their glow on the half-empty wineglass Lisette had left behind.

Upstairs, his bedchamber was dark. When Oliver was at home, he lit a candle or two, turned back the counterpane, and placed a brass bed warmer beneath the quilts. The queer pang in Nicholai's chest intensified as he closed the door and undressed in darkness. For a moment, padding naked across to his bed, he wondered if loneliness caused his bleak mood. The thought was dismissed quickly . . . how could he be lonely when in truth he could scarcely snatch a moment of solitude? If he did feel let down, obviously bone-deep fatigue was the culprit.

After drawing the drapes to shut out the stray moonbeams, Nicholai groped for the bed and slid beneath the cool silky sheets. He groaned, stretched, and burrowed into the down-filled pillow. It felt as though fingertips were on his back, skimming from lean-muscled buttocks to the hair that curled over his nape. A chill rushed up, then back down his spine.

There was another hand now, turning his face from the pillow. Nicholai's eyes refused to open—though the darkness would have kept him blind. Full hard-tipped breasts touched his chest; a tongue flickered at his mouth; the fingers slid down, sending a shock through Nicholai when they brushed over his erect manhood.

"Good God, Lisette! What's come over you?" His eyes flew open. "I cannot *believe*—"

"Believe what, Nicky darling? Don't you want to finish your thought?"

He had broken off at the sight of the shadow-blurred face next to his. Pale skin, the smudge of lashes, indistinct mouth —and hair much blacker than the night that served as its backdrop. Of course, the moment she spoke, his confusion was dispelled.

"Christ, Amelia, it's *you*." He sounded as though he'd been hit in the chest.

"I apologize, darling, for giving you such a fright. Silly of me not to realize there are any number of doxies who might be waiting in your bed this way! I'm such a vain creature."

"Amelia—"

"Oh, my, don't apologize! No doubt an occasional bruise is good for my ego."

Nicholai let out a harsh sigh and fell back on the pillow. Briefly, he'd been caught in a web of exquisite, torturous desire—but the instant he realized the true identity of his seductress, the sad emptiness swelled up again in his heart. This bitch was an expert at saying just the right thing to paint herself the victim and make him feel like the most coldhearted of beasts. Perhaps Amelia's dim-witted husband took the bait, but Nicholai was intuitive enough to recognize the venomous undercurrent in her voice.

"What the devil are you up to, Amelia? I thought you weren't going to be able to escape Clarence tonight."

"Well, I did!" She turned openly petulant. "I came over to surprise you—"

"Amelia!" Nicholai's head jerked up; he tried to discern her expression. "Was there someone here when you arrived?"

"Why, *no*—in fact, I had to let myself in! You are so lax with those servants of yours, darling—they will lose all respect for you." The words came out in a flurry. "I would think you'd be so pleased I waited here all this time for you to come home. I had a long heavenly bath before supper . . ." She rubbed against him like a cat. "Do you smell the bergamot, darling? I've been begging for a vial of scent to surprise you. Does it make you warm? Here—just inhale—"

Nicholai's nerves were strung tight with frustration and a dozen other conflicting emotions. He was annoyed with Amelia, and angry with himself for being so galvanized by his yearning for Lisette . . . now, as Amelia nuzzled his neck, then flicked her pointed tongue against his mouth, he wanted to shove her away. Yet a voiceless instinct suggested that, once she was ejected from his bed, his house, he would be left alone with no outlet for his aggravation.

Amelia moved so that her breast brushed Nicholai's lips, furious that he had not groaned in surrender. Suddenly, white teeth caught the rosy point, nibbling at first and then almost biting it as strong hands gripped Amelia's hips. When his mouth relaxed, he pulled her down and proceeded to kiss and caress her bruisingly. Amelia was shocked; Nicholai had always been so skillful and civilized in bed. As much as she adored and burned under this rough treatment, a tiny part of her was detached enough to realize that this was not love play. Nicholai was angry. It might as well be a weapon that he drove up into her with such force. Amelia cried out with mingled passion and alarm . . . she tried not to wonder how that proud yellow-haired chit figured into Nicholai's violent mood.

Nearly a half mile northeast of Nicholai's house on Spruce Street, someone else was holding angry frustration in check. Lisette Hahn, veiled by wavering candlelight, sat alone in her tiny bedchamber above the CoffeeHouse. She pulled her brush through her tumbled golden curls with a vengeance.

Damn Nicholai Beauvisage! That conceited rutting defiler of maidens! She would gladly carve out his lying tongue and serve it in tomorrow's stew! Amelia Purdy could go in as well—whole and dressed, for all she cared. That high-flown adulterous slut! How Lisette had longed to claw out those arrogant eyes tonight in Nicholai's study. . . . She seethed at the memory of Mrs. Purdy's brazen admission that *she* was Nicholai's mistress.

"He makes love to me until I think I shall die of rapture," Amelia had purred. "We have waited for tonight with such anticipation . . . I'm certain, dear girl, that you wouldn't care to watch us try to contain our passion while making silly chitchat with *you*. Hadn't you better run on back to that CoffeeHouse? There must be *one* man out of all those dozens that frequent that *place* who would do whatever it was you needed Nicky for."

Now, in her fury, Lisette could take a moment's satisfaction in the memory of her own flawless performance. She was certain her expression had betrayed no hint of the humiliation and outrage that made her ache inside. The epitome of frosty contempt, she had fixed her most intimidating stare on Amelia Purdy before replying.

"Don't imagine that you have frightened me away, madame . . . I've simply a low threshold for tasteless people and petty conversation." Aware of the elegant line of her slim neck, Lisette had held her head high as she swept past Nicholai's mistress. "Good evening."

As the memory crumbled, she stopped brushing her hair

and restlessly crossed to the narrow window. A street lamp flickered over the cobbles of Front Street. Lisette pushed the casement open, arching her throat to accept the night breeze's caress. *Well,* she mused, *I've got my pride . . . so what?* Her mind pulled her unwillingly through the memories of the conversation she and Nicholai had shared a few short hours ago. How recklessly candid she had been—and he had reacted with a gentle encouragement that melted her defenses. It was as close as she had come in years to vulnerability . . . why was disillusionment the inevitable consequence?

Lisette's eyes, luminous in their sadness, gazed over the dark rooftops toward Spruce and Second streets. Was Nicholai making love to that sharp-tongued harlot? Kissing Amelia in the same scorching way he kissed her? Why he had begged her to wait for him if he had made an appointment with another? . . . Was that his cowardly male way of communicating his preference for casual attachments?

❦ *Chapter 16* ❦

April 19, 1793

"You are looking absolutely radiant!" Caro proclaimed for the second time. "Oh, Meagan, I'm so relieved to see that you are yourself again!"

Meagan lifted her cup for a sip of tea so that Caro would not notice her faltering smile. As her fifth month of her pregnancy drew to a close, she was undoubtedly the picture of rosy-cheeked good health, but unfortunately the glow was only skin-deep.

"I am grateful to you for coming all this way on such short notice, Caro. It seems like three months, rather than three weeks, since we came out here to the villa . . . and I've missed your unselfish and sympathetic ear."

"I have missed *you* as well, silly goose! Besides, a ride into the country and a visit here make a wonderful spring outing." Her eyes swept the sunny parlor, which was decorated in rich shades of dove gray and cranberry and accented by ornaments of polished brass. Barely four years ago, Markwood Villa had been a deserted and musty shell of its prerevolutionary grandeur. Mr. Markwood, killed in a duel, was rumored to haunt the place, so until Lion bought and restored it, no one would come near.

The two women were seated in wing chairs that flanked a sun-drenched Palladian window. As Caro sipped her tea and surveyed the garden, Meagan found herself staring at the blood red moreen of her chair, remembering the day, four springs past, when she had chosen the fabric. Lion had been engaged to Priscilla then, and he still believed Meagan to be a common serving girl. They were in love, but to avoid scandal as they planned and shopped for Markwood Villa, she had masqueraded as a boy. The risk and adventure brought them closer together than ever, and she had been Lion's partner in transforming the villa.

"You are certainly looking pensive!" Caro said.

Meagan's smile was sad as she smoothed out a wrinkle in her lavender silk gown. It was part of a newly completed wardrobe that flattered her blossoming waistline. She couldn't blame her dejection on ill-fitting gowns any longer.

"I was thinking about the first spring Lion and I had together, when we worked out the new interior for this house. Life is so perverse . . . then, I believed that to marry Lion would mean eternal bliss. It seemed that, if we could ever untangle the problems and obstacles that complicated our lives then—"

"Well, you *did*," Caro broke in, wondering what Meagan meant. There was an odd faraway look in her violet eyes. "Lion chose you over Priscilla—even before he knew your true identity. Not only were you married, but Lion has become a senator despite the scandal, and now . . . there will be a child born of your love."

"I am very fortunate."

"Meagan! You look like you have lost your best friend! What is it? Now that the Congress is in recess and Lion has brought you out into the country for the time alone you craved, I thought you would be ecstatic!"

"But I wanted time alone with him!"

Caro blinked and set her teacup on the pembroke side table. "I don't understand—"

"Lion is scarcely here at all!" Tears welled in her eyes as the swollen dam that held in her misery finally gave way. "When we came down here, to be together and enjoy the spring, I was so h-happy! But, after a few days, Lion began to make trips into Philadelphia that he wouldn't explain. They have become more frequent and longer. . . ." She accepted the gauzy handkerchief an anxious Caro held out and pressed it to her eyes. "Last night, he didn't come home until m-midnight! I was so miserable, I pretended to be asleep, but then, when I woke today and found he'd left again—there was just a vague note on my dressing table—that's when I knew I had to t-talk to someone. . . ."

Caro watched helplessly as her friend soaked the lawn handkerchief. "Meagan, sweetheart, I cannot believe—" She knelt beside the other wing chair and embraced Meagan, patting the ebony curls that fell down her back the way she would with one of her own children. "Please, you are going to make yourself sick! Try to calm down a bit, and then we can sort out this madness. You have not told me what it is about Lion's absences that devastates you so. I feel certain that whatever takes him into Philadelphia must be related to the Senate—"

"The Senate is in *recess*," Meagan reminded her flatly. She sat back, dry eyed, and Caro retreated to her own chair. "And even in March there were mysterious absences at night. If he were going to meet with Mr. Jefferson, for instance, why could he not say so?"

"Where do *you* think he goes?"

"Lion is—" She swallowed. Her head throbbed, her eyes stung, and her face was hot from weeping. "Lion is involved with another woman."

Caro gaped. "What! Oh, no, I cannot—"

"It's true. I haven't wanted to believe it myself, though I've suspected for weeks. . . ." Two fat tears slid down her cheeks. "I have proof now . . . and after last night and today . . . !"

"Oh, Meagan, no wonder you are so distraught. But, unless you have seen him in bed with this other woman, you cannot be certain. I know how easy it is for the female imagination to run wild—please, tell me about your proof."

"I—I've wondered for weeks, pushing it back in my mind, hoping one day I would awake and find Lion his normal self again . . . until today, I haven't been able to say the words."

"I'm glad you are finally talking about it, sweetheart."

"I told myself it was the pregnancy, the Senate, my imagination—but after we came down here and he made the first trip into town and wouldn't tell me why, my heart just sank. Last night, trying to distract myself, I thought I would clean the drawers in our bedchamber and put in fresh sachets. And I found it."

Caro held her breath.

"A note. It was a note recording a huge amount of money he had given Lisette Hahn . . . on that first day he went back into Philadelphia."

"I don't—understand! You aren't suggesting that Lion is having a love affair with *Lisette*?"

"Oh, yes, I am! You needn't look so stunned—she hasn't two heads, after all. She is gorgeous! I'm not too proud to admit that she is more beautiful and elegant than I—especially now that my waist grows thicker by the day."

"Meagan, this sounds quite mad to me! I fear that your suspicions are rooted more in your own pregnancy than in reality. Don't you think that there must be another explanation? Perhaps you are just unaccustomed to his new routine; it is difficult for you to share him with the Senate—"

"This is much more than a normal working day. What about these nighttime absences and the time he has spent in Philadelphia during the Senate's *recess*? His colleagues are far away, tucked in at home with their families—why, even the president has fled this city. Before we married, although Lion was promised to Priscilla, I knew that he was ruled by his love for me. Now . . . I couldn't say if he cares for me at all."

Caro looked pained. "Sweetheart, it's a rare marriage that doesn't experience an occasional drought! But—how did you ever concoct this notion about Lion and Lisette?"

"I knew who she was before Lion became a senator. I can even remember *him* talking about her—the mysterious, unapproachable Mistress Hahn. Then . . . after the election, he began to spend more and more time at the CoffeeHouse. When a wife feels the distance growing between herself and her husband, it doesn't take long for her to wonder if another woman has captured his eye. Especially in my case." Meagan slanted a miserable look at her middle. "The first time I saw him with her, last month when you and I went to the CoffeeHouse, I felt ill. They laughed together —and she was so lovely and graceful. Afterwards, Lion began to go out at night—and of course, now there is the note for all that money. It would seem that her elusive favors are not bestowed unconditionally."

"Meagan, it seems to me that your evidence is very circumstantial! You have let your imagination run wild . . .

and besides, I happen to know that my brother-in-law, Nicholai, has a serious interest in Lisette himself. What do you say to that?"

Her eyes were frosty amethysts. "I would say that Mistress Hahn is a busy young woman . . . and most undeserving of her reputation for aloof purity."

"You do not even sound like yourself, Meagan Hampshire! I am going home now, because I want you to think this over very carefully. Try to remember that your only competition for Lion's time may be the United States Senate—and also that the trust between a husband and wife should not be so quickly discarded. You may regret your hasty doubts later on."

Caro kissed her friend and urged her to remain in her chair, to rest and consider all they had discussed. She herself was so preoccupied as she passed through the entryway and opened the front door that she failed to notice the tall man with the gold hair and stormy face who stood back in the shadowed hallway.

Meagan, aching with fatigue after the tearful ordeal with Caro, sat back in the wing chair and stared at the willow-canopied garden until she fell asleep.

Dusk was enveloping the villa when Bramble shook her mistress's arm in an effort to revive her.

"Ye cannot wish to remain in this chair all night!" exclaimed the dour cook. Though Meagan was now her mistress, Bramble never quite forgot the days when the girl had masqueraded as a lady's maid and taken orders from *her*.

"Oh—no—" Meagan blinked sparkly eyes and rubbed her neck. "Goodness, I am so stiff!"

"Supper is nearly done," Bramble warned.

Standing up, Meagan stretched and sighed. The cool twilight and lingering sleepiness did nothing to lighten her mood. "I shall go upstairs and freshen up, Bramble."

"Good." Bramble kept her voice sharp as she watched her mistress leave the parlor, but she did allow herself a tight satisfied smile.

Ascending the stairs, Meagan tried to repress the tide of sadness that washed over her. Lion had been gone nearly twelve hours . . . didn't he even care enough to come home and play the dutiful husband? Did he want her to suspect his infidelity?

When she opened the door to their bedchamber, she found that the plum-tinted dusk was warmed by a bright fire and the golden light of several candles.

"Good evening, fondling."

Meagan gasped in surprise. "Lion!" He was sitting on the huge four-poster, leaning back into a pillow propped against the headboard. He wore only a dressing gown of tawny velvet that accentuated the bronzed warmth of his skin and shining gold of his hair. As Meagan gaped, Lion gave her a caustic smile and drank from a goblet of white wine.

"You seem surprised to see me! Is there somewhere else I should be?"

Meagan arched her eyebrow. "What a question! It seems to me that you have been *here* very little!"

"Through no choice of my own."

She made a derisive noise, but managed to refrain from putting her feelings into words.

"Dearest wife," he implored, sweetly sarcastic, "do sit beside me so that we can look into one another's eyes as we talk." Lion patted the plush ivory satin comforter.

Meagan saw the dangerous gleam in his eyes and wondered at it, but reminded herself that he was the sinner and she the victim. Gingerly, she perched near him, beside the other pillow.

"Ah, sweeting, I have missed you so today," Lion declared. He hooked an arm around her and pulled her against him, tipping her chin up with his other hand. His mouth closed over Meagan's, kissing her with scorching intensity. She gave a little sob and pushed him away.

"Stop it! Somehow you are ridiculing me, and I won't allow it!"

"You think that I would play you false, dear wife? Are you certain you can read a lie in my eyes?" Roughly, he turned her face back. "Let us put your intuition to the test. I shall tell you two things—one lie and one piece of pure truth. Concentrate and then tell me which is which."

Meagan's expression was wary, but she met the challenge and felt her own anger and resentment bubble to the surface. Whatever game he was playing now, she knew that this would be the night they would have it out. No more silent brooding.

"All right, Lion. I will take your test."

"Excellent." There was a trace of venom in his flashing white grin. "Here is the first statement." He stared into Meagan's amethyst eyes with an intensity that unnerved her. "You are my wife, my friend and my passion; the warm glow that propels me through life. I love you far too much to ever betray you in *any* way."

Lion's expression flickered from intense to cynical. He lifted blond eyebrows and inquired, "How do you like the test so far? I suppose it is ridiculously easy for someone as intuitive as you are, but let us continue with part two anyway. Ready?"

Vaguely alarmed, Meagan nodded.

"Fine. I just wanted to tell you that I place no value at all on our vows now that you are pregnant with my child. I find your body disgusting! Now, Lisette Hahn is another matter altogether . . . you know how we men love a mysterious challenge! I could scarcely tear myself out of her bed to come home last night, and of course, I spent all day today right back under her sheets. It is wonderful to make love again to a woman with a flat belly—it really doesn't matter *who* it is."

Meagan wondered if her mind had been cauterized by Lion's fiery blue eyes. She was numb with confusion and a hundred questions crowded her mind.

"What is it, dear wife? Can't you decide which statement reflects the real me? Perhaps you merely refuse to believe that I could be repulsed by your new body. Let me show you how difficult it is for me to touch you."

When he gathered her into his hard embrace and kissed her with leisurely finesse, Meagan felt her nerves begin to tingle, and her bones seemed to melt. She could feel the hammering of her heart as Lion pressed a searing kiss to her throat. As he unfastened her lavender silk gown, Meagan closed her eyes rather than meet the piercing question in his gaze. His fingers, touching the batiste and lace of her chemise, were deft and gentle, and Meagan remained utterly still as her breasts were uncovered.

"Meagan," Lion whispered sternly, "look at yourself. Open your eyes and look!"

Swallowing a whimper, she looked down at her creamy rose-tipped breasts, swollen and proud as they marked the progress of a growing baby. Lion put out a dark finger, caressing the curving outline of each breast. The nipples peaked in response to his touch; he kissed each one lingeringly in turn and Meagan heard herself sob.

"Repulsive, aren't you?" Lion asked. There was no doubt about the iciness of his voice any longer. "Really, I think I deserve some sort of medal for this!" He eased Meagan into a more relaxed position against the pillows, then proceeded to remove her clothing until she was completely naked. "We will keep the candles lit, just so there is no mistake about the extent of my revulsion."

Meagan turned her face into the pillow. "Lion, please— *why* are you doing this? I don't enjoy being the object of a joke—"

"Believe me, sweeting, this is not a joke! In fact, I have never been more serious."

He made love to her then, with excruciating slowness, and Meagan was too entangled in the web of her own yearning to protest. His fingers worked a magic spell on her soft bare skin; they traced the line of her belly as lovingly as a sculptor with a fine piece of clay. When the baby answered with a fluttering kick, Lion put his cheek to the spot and listened to the restless movements of his child.

Eventually, after bringing Meagan to a feverish plane of readiness, he joined his hard body to her own and she responded with eager passion. At last, drifting downward together from the peak, they were wrapped in a warm embrace of love.

"Meagan," Lion breathed against her tiny ear. "I love you. Never allow yourself to doubt that, or my fidelity to you, ever again."

Weeping, she tightened her arms around his neck with such fervor that Lion laughed softly. "I'm sorry—and confused," she said, between sobs.

They remained close and silent for a few minutes; then he drew back the comforter and sheets. Before rejoining his wife, Lion lit a cheroot and closed the gray and ivory bed curtains so that they were totally isolated. He settled back and pulled the covers over his naked torso, then turned to find Meagan staring at him.

"You are ravishing," he said, smiling. And she was. After love, she always had a dusky, contented glow, but now it was more alluring than ever. Glossy black curls framed her fragile face; luminous thick-lashed eyes of violet regarded him with wonderment. "You are curious to learn what lies behind my words and actions, aren't you?"

Meagan nodded. She fitted her neck into the bend of his arm, but kept enough distance to watch Lion's face. "Explain to me . . . how you knew, how you feel . . ."

"I came home, through the back of the house, hours ago while you were talking to Caro. I heard it all—your misery and worry over my absences and your angry suspicions about Lisette Hahn." Momentarily, he averted his eyes and drew on the cheroot. "I cannot describe how I felt, hearing you say those things . . . it was as if you were talking about a stranger. I thought, she can't mean *me*! I found it so incredible that you should suspect such things . . . let alone be convinced of their truth! But what shocked me most was your own opinion of *yourself*. I knew that you had felt blue about the changes in your body, but I thought it was all an emotional reaction. Today, I heard the voice of a Meagan I didn't even know. . . ."

"You took the old reliable me for granted," she whispered.

"You were always the voice of reason . . . the antithesis of someone like Priscilla, who acted solely on female impulse. She rode her emotions like a child on a hobbyhorse, with no regard for logic or another person's viewpoint. I never expected *you* to believe anything but the truth . . . I thought you were so wise and reasonable."

"Lion, we all have times when life catches us off guard. I was completely unprepared for the changes of these past months—the Senate, the pregnancy, our altered lives. Everyone tells me that all women are subject to emotional upheavals during pregnancy—"

"Sweetheart," Lion interrupted warmly, "the point is that I had no right to count on unwavering maturity from you. You have as much right to cry or abandon reason as anyone . . . my expectations were quite selfish."

"But it was unfair for *me* to think that your election to the Senate wouldn't change our life. My mind knew that you had to be away during the day, but my heart resented you for it."

"I've been terribly insensitive to your needs, sweeting. I can see that now. Today, hearing you proclaim that I had abandoned you for Lisette, my first reaction was total rage. I was furious with you! Fortunately, you fell asleep; that gave me time to reassess the situation. I realized then that I was as much to blame . . . I was so wrapped up in my new life as senator that I *did* put you on the shelf. I think I expected you to stay in limbo until I got over my initial fascination with my novel occupation."

"I know you well enough . . . I shouldn't have been so resentful!"

Lion laughed softly. "We are each certainly anxious to take all the blame! The fact is that, though I am angry and hurt that you could believe I would turn to another woman, I do see that I helped push you toward that belief."

"I suppose that the truth is—we both have made mistakes. Mistakes that fed upon themselves. I think that suspicion has made me a little irrational. . . ."

He was holding her now, close against the wide warmth of his chest. "Oh, Meagan, how could you think I would cast you aside—"

"In some ways, even though you didn't turn to another woman, you *did* cast me aside!" Tears spilled onto the mat of golden hair covering Lion's chest. "I needed you so much—more than I ever needed you before—and you weren't there!"

"Meagan, I am so sorry. Never, never again . . . you are my life—nothing matters without you, you know that—"

When they kissed, her tears mingled with his.

Later, according to Lion's earlier instructions, Bramble brought a dinner up of turkey stuffed with oysters, squash, hot cornbread, and green beans mixed with bacon. To drink, there was a lot of cold champagne, and Lion and Meagan toasted their cook, their love, their house, their bed, and, several times, their child.

It was past midnight when Meagan shook her husband awake. "Lion! You forgot to explain! Why *have* you made all those trips to Philadelphia . . . and why did you give so much money to Lisette Hahn?"

Lion made a sound that combined laughter with a deep, sleepy groan. "Can't this wait until morning?" His hair shone in the moonlight as he burrowed back into the pillows.

"I don't like secrets."

He growled and pulled her into his arms. "All right! Tomorrow it will all be out in the open. Since France declared war on half of Europe, there has been a great deal of controversy about our country's role. There were questions about the effect blockades will have on our ability to trade, and the dilemma of how to treat the new government in view of our past loyalty to France—the issues are endless. Before privateers are manned and sent to help France, the president had to take a stand. He returned from Mount Vernon yesterday and met with the cabinet this afternoon. That's where I have been lately—and before Washington's return, I was meeting with Jefferson and the others. There wasn't time to call back the Congress, so every available voice counted. The neutrality proclamation is being drawn up right now."

"I'm sorry . . . no wonder you've been preoccupied."

"No excuse." He yawned. "I wish I could have shared it with you—but, in any event, I should have worked harder to reassure you."

"And Lisette?"

"A long story. Essentially, I tried to save her from Marcus. He has been threatening her with a debt of her father's . . . wants to own the CoffeeHouse himself." He drowsily kissed Meagan's warm, pliant mouth. "Lisette is beautiful and enigmatic, but I love you far too much to become attracted to any other female. *You* are a full time occupation! Besides which, you hold my heart, fondling, and I cannot break it into pieces and expect it to thrive."

"I believe you."

"Of course." Lion smiled and closed his eyes again.

He had just drifted off to sleep when Meagan whispered, "Are you asleep?" No response. "Lion?"

"Yes, I'm asleep!" His eyes were open, like blue stars in the darkness.

"I have been thinking . . . about the way the past few months have affected me."

"And your conclusion?" he prodded sleepily.

"I've decided that I became so upset because of the way society is structured. There is no room for a woman in the world in which you work all day. I was like a candle suddenly deprived of air, sent home to make a baby and do needlework."

Lion was awake now, staring as Meagan's voice rose and sparks began to fly from her eyes. "It isn't fair. The day you became a senator, society managed to shut me out completely. No wonder we lost touch with one another!"

"Meagan—it's you! You're back!"

She saw the flash of his grin in the dark. "I am going to *do* something about this, Lion. *I mean it!* . . ."

"I can see you are ready to rush into the night and take action, but please don't be in too much of a hurry. I'm selfish; I have plans for you." Lion kissed her tenderly. "Tomorrow, and the next day, and the next. . . ."

Chapter 17

April 25, 1793

*It was not a ball or even a party. Antonia Beauvisage pre-*ferred the word *gathering* to describe the impromptu assembly of interesting, diverse people. There was a sumptuous array of food: soups and meats, pastries, candied nuts, and floating island, among numerous other colorful dishes. Now, as the evening advanced, more and more guests were mingling around the table, plates in hand.

Antonia, gowned in burgundy velvet with lace trim and a sash of ivory satin, stood near the doorway of the chandelier-lit second-floor ballroom and surveyed her guests. Jean-Philippe was deep in conversation with William Bingham and Samuel Powel, who was not only Philadelphia's mayor, but also their next-door neighbor. Meanwhile, Eliza Powel was seated on a love seat against the far wall with a revived-looking George Washington. The president's fascination with the bright and coquettish Eliza was long-standing; she brought out the charmer in him and made him forget the burdens of his office.

Anne Bingham was standing with Alec and Caro as all three sampled the floating island, and poor Nicholai was trapped in a corner with Ophelia.

"Mr. Beauvisage, what are your views on the House of Bourbon?" Ophelia was asking, her eyes bird-bright. "What I mean to say is, what personality traits do you feel are inherent in the line and consequently led to the downfall of the royal family?"

Nicholai stared at her, so thin and intense in her ill-fitting pink gown, and took a large swallow of wine. "Well, Mistress Corkstall, that is a solemn and important question which deserves a thoughtful answer." He glanced around, casually searching for an excuse to escape. When Mary Armstrong appeared in the doorway, his excuse was valid, but the sight of her caused him to forget Ophelia anyway.

"Mary!" As Nicholai crossed the ballroom, he marveled at how her beauty had intensified in ten years. She had been pretty in their youth—dimpled, blond, and petite—but now she had the glow of a ripe peach. She was a woman. When her china blue eyes rested on him, Mary gasped and made a sound of delight.

"Oh, Nicky, how wonderful to see you!"

They embraced, and as he was feeling tempted to forget the rest of the world and kiss her, Mary broke free and gestured to a strange man. "Timothy, do come and meet Nicky, the prodigal Beauvisage son! He has been in France these past ten years, and—well, you have heard me speak of him before. Nicky, this is Timothy, my husband."

Extending his hand to greet Timothy Barcroft, Nicholai expected at least a twinge of jealousy or regret, but felt neither. Mary's husband was tall and sandy haired, with an easy smile—a hard man to resent—and when Nicholai saw them together, he was glad to realize someone dear to him had found happiness. So, the three of them chatted, telling tales of their different and separate lives, while Nicholai remembered the long-ago days when Mary had been exuberant and naive and he had been recklessly fun loving. So many kisses . . . he had *tried* to love her. All the ingredients were there; he had lined them up a dozen times, but the recipe never turned out.

Antonia appeared, begging Mary and Timothy to play a duet for the other guests. This seemed a usual occurrence and Nicholai soon learned the reason. Timothy was an expert at the harpsichord; Mary's talent with the violin had improved with age, and the two of them obviously played together a great deal. Soon, the guests began to dance. When Ophelia caught his eye and made an attempt at smiling flirtatiously, Nicholai reached for Katya's arm as she and Randolph passed by.

"Darling sister, I beg for
moment alone in days!"

Katya laughed at her broth
dear, I was breathless with fear
ask me, sir!"

When they were alone together,
Street window, Katya asked softly, "
seeing Mary? Are you sad?"

Nicholai shrugged in the midst of his
forward to touch Katya's hand. His perfor
chanical, his mind on other matters. "No—n
I was startled by her good looks and shaken
rushed back, but it was never real love for
could I begrudge her a full life with Mr. Barcroft?
it was I who left for France alone. My ego is
swollen, I hope, that I expect every woman who has
for me to go to her grave pining."

Katya's laughter was gentle. "Let us sit down—here
the corner."

He was grateful to obey. "If Ophelia Corkstall comes
over here, you must pretend to be confiding a serious and
private secret."

"Yes, Nicky!" Smiling, she settled down on the love seat
and appraised her brother's appearance. How handsome he
looked; his clothes were expertly cut—pale yellow breeches
with black knee boots, a short double-breasted waistcoat of
smoky quilted silk, and a frock coat of dove gray over a
snowy white shirt and a high cravat. In contrast, Nicholai's
face was masculine and cynically expressive. He was the
only man in the room whose hair was not queued.
Nicholai's auburn gold hair was cut and combed away
from his face in appealing rakish disarray.

"You must have every female in Philadelphia pursuing
you," Katya said bluntly.

He laughed. "At least! I believe there are a few from
New York and Baltimore as well."

"To be honest, I am glad to see you don't take it too
seriously. I couldn't bear for you to become a conceited
bore!"

He pretended to be hurt. "I appreciate your opinion!"

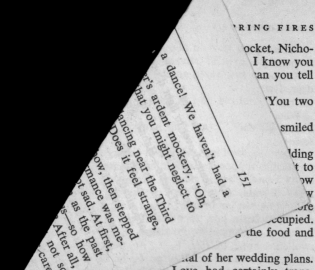

ocket, Nicho-
I know you
an you tell

You two

smiled

lding
t to
ow
w
re
ccupied.
the food and

151

...al of her wedding plans. Love had certainly trans-, her only passion had been books. ... she was devouring Shakespeare and ...ussian and French, but now he doubted that ...d concentrate long enough to read one page. Yet, ...e was happy . . . for the present, at least.

As Katya started her description of the house she and Randolph would live in after their marriage, Nicholai stiffened at the sight of Clarence and Amelia Purdy entering the ballroom.

"Katya! What the devil are the Purdys doing here?"

Startled by his interruption, she broke off. "Why, I'm not sure. I believe Mrs. Purdy has been rather overfriendly to Maman lately. I think she even had them for dinner, so perhaps this is Maman's reciprocation." Appraising Amelia's appearance, she added, "That woman is certainly glamorous! Her black hair and white skin are dramatic enough . . . but I think she is trying too hard to compete with Anne Bingham."

Nicholai's smile was sickly. Seeing the way Amelia's carnivorous eyes scanned the room, he bent over and pretended to look for something on the floor.

"Oh—oh, Nicky, I think I see Anne herself coming this

way, with that horrid English cousin in tow. Am I wrong, or are you their target?"

He sat up abruptly. Katya was correct; they were threading their way between the dancers, while, at the other side of the room, Mrs. Purdy was scrutinizing the crowd with growing agitation. "Beautiful sister, I believe you are right, and rude as it sounds, I'm not up to another discussion of the genetic flaws in the House of Bourbon." He stood up and kissed her hand. "I believe I shall escape into the garden for some fresh air. Why don't you tell Anne and her cousin, and anyone else who might ask, that I left because I felt another attack coming on."

"Attack!" Katya's eyes widened. "What sort of attacks do you have?"

Nicholai spluttered with laughter. "I don't have *any* sort, dear sibling! But, if you say that I do, looking serious and quite worried, it might scare them off!"

Katya laughed as he exited, quite inconspicuously for such a tall, broad-shouldered man, then murmured ruefully to herself, "I wouldn't depend on it. . . ."

Walking down the stairway in the home where he had grown up, Nicholai felt strangely empty. Yet, even in the ballroom, surrounded by smiling people and sweet music, he had felt alone. The surfeit of romance rubbed him the wrong way. Everyone was so much in love, or at least enamored or in search of romance, that he felt out of place. Mary and Timothy, Katya and Randolph, Caro and Alec, and even his own parents. He couldn't question the validity of Antonia and Jean-Philippe's love, but as for the others, he wondered how long it would be before a few of the stars in their eyes began to dim. Lisette probably had the right idea . . . love was a troublesome affliction that only served to confuse the real struggle of life.

Pausing to refill his glass from a decanter on the table, Nicholai heard a soft giggle. Through a crack in the double parlor doors, he glimpsed Alec and Caro standing in that firelit room, bathed in coral shadows. Alec was passionately kissing his wife, all the while unfastening the back of her peach and beige muslin gown. When he shifted to bury his face in her neck. Caro laughed again and whispered a half-hearted protest. The sudden sight of one full gorgeous breast shocked Nicholai into turning his head, but before he continued out to the garden, he silently eased the parlor door closed.

Outside, he gulped first night air and then brandy, conscious of his own heartbeat. Why were his thoughts full of Lisette? Nicholai knew that he felt more than a yearning to make love to her; the image of her evoked feelings of anger, curiosity . . . even a strange sort of fear. Lisette was a mystery fraught with risks, not the least of which was rejection.

Comparing her with lovely, contented Mary, Nicholai realized why his former sweetheart held no stronger allure for him. In his mind, he could see and hear Lisette, eyes flashing with determination—standing before him to declare that *she could do anything!* The searing heat of her sudden passion had branded him, and he remembered the soft, emotional confession she had made in his study as if it had happened only moments ago.

With a sigh, Nicholai sat down on a bench and gazed around at the starlit flowers. It seemed that Lisette was more exotic than any of these blooms, opening unexpectedly to dazzle him with a beauty much deeper and more complex than her outward perfection indicated—then, closing abruptly, just as he moved toward her for a closer look, a touch. . . .

Plucking a blossom from a white moonvine, Nicholai inhaled the lemony fragrance and muttered with dismay, "Women!"

Stars glittered high above the CoffeeHouse as Lisette made her keeping-room rounds. Though the public room would remain open for two more hours, her work was done. Stringfellow had an ample supply of beverages, the last meal had long since been served, the dishes were washed, and the keeping room was clean. Bone-tired, she longed to bid this kitchen good-bye for a few hours. There were pigeon and chicken pies to make at dawn, but for now, her bed beckoned.

Still, after banking the fire for the night, Lisette lowered herself into the comb-back chair to watch the flames dwindle. Her thoughts drifted to her father. In his last months, Ernst Hahn had been a virtual fixture in this chair . . . she'd felt his absence much less than she'd expected. It seemed strange that he had seldom entered her mind more than fleetingly. Obviously, the incessant routine of hard work had helped lessen the pain of her grief, yet—it wasn't right for her to push him out of her thoughts completely. Did her insatiable appetite for work leave no room for *feelings?*

Lisette pushed off her shoes and stretched delicate ankles and feet toward the fire. It didn't seem so long ago that her mama had been alive and all three of them were living in Austria. She had been less than five years old, but she could remember her parents laughing, her father embracing her mother, the times when they whispered their adult conversations rather than allow her to understand. Her mother had made room for a high-blooming love and hard work at the same time, but then, she and Ernst had worked together; they had shared the same goals.

My situation is different, Lisette reminded herself stubbornly.

What was more easily recalled was the respect for work her parents had instilled in her. Her mother had been in constant motion, from dawn until long after dusk, and as a child Lisette learned the meanings of words like *constructive, discipline, satisfaction,* and *achievement.* Everything, it seemed, had been a result of her mother or father's labors—the bread she ate, the clothes she wore, the soap she washed with . . . in Austria, her father had even built their furniture. The love was ever present, but precious minutes were seldom wasted on frivolity.

Ambitious dreams had propelled the Hahns toward America. Lisette wondered now if her parents had tried for too much, and overstepped some invisible boundary. Her mama's death was marked by the snuffing out of a vital and warmth-giving light in the family. Ever after, the Hahn family was crippled and cast in shadow. In America, Lisette grew to exquisite and charming womanhood, watching her father build the CoffeeHouse out of nothing but his own heartbreak. Work had kept him going. . . .

Lisette opened her eyes. The fire sent flickering shadows up to the beamed ceiling, where they danced as if cruelly amused.

"What did Papa get from his work, besides this place?" she whispered. "Papa . . . you never gave your heart another chance! If you had learned to love again—you might have found a share of contentment, a new warmth. . . ." Tears trickled down her cheeks. Instinctively, Lisette wished she could retrace the last few minutes, back to a point before she'd begun to examine her feelings. She knew all too well what had made her father keep life at arm's length: the uncertainty of what released emotion might bring. The risk of pain. She had learned all she knew about that from Ernst Hahn.

Remembering the still-tender wound left by her married congressman, Lisette could comfort herself with the reminder that she *had* tried once. Yet, something gnawed inside of her. Expelling a ragged sigh, she drew up her legs, wiped her tears with her apron, and closed her eyes. Images of Nicholai seemed to taunt her . . . it had been a week since she had sat beside him in his study, but it seemed months. How could a man seem so tender and caring, then let an entire week elapse as if she didn't exist?

Part of her wanted to jump incautiously into an adventure with Nicholai Beauvisage, but another, more familiar side of her shouted logical-sounding warnings. The general message was, *He's a magnificent man—witty, handsome, intelligent, and, yes,* magical, *but those are the most dangerous kind. No future, only pain. Pain.*

Those last words echoed in her head night and day. She pondered them again, and escaped a decision by drifting into sleep. Later, Lisette would wonder what had awakened her. Whether she had an accidental noise or her own internal alarm system to thank, she never knew. Only one thing was certain. When her azure eyes flew open, Marcus Reems was there, looming above Lisette and poised like a powerful snake about to strike.

Chapter 18

April 25, 1793

"Mistress Hahn! I was just about to wake you!"

Tensed and alert, Lisette appraised Marcus Reems. In spite of the smile that curved his mouth, she felt threatened. The room was nearly dark except for an orange glow from the hearth that heightened Reems's eerie menace, and, conscious of his piercing gaze and formidable strength, Lisette could not decide how to react.

"I don't recall inviting you to come in, Mr. Reems." Her voice was cool, effectively masking the panic that made her heart thump against her breastbone.

"My dear Mistress Hahn, I confess that, when my knock went unanswered, I could not contain my impatience. You see, I would like to discuss a matter that is of grave importance to us both."

Lisette wondered if she should simply call out for Stringfellow. This game of intimidation Reems played was not at all to her liking. A fortnight had passed since Lion Hampshire had lent her the money to pay off this cad, during which Lisette had waited smugly for Reems to return and renew his offer. What had kept him away—and why was he here now, at this hour, smirking as if the CoffeeHouse had already been sold to him?

"Mr. Reems, before we have your 'grave discussion,' there is a matter I would like to settle first." Marshaling her poise and courage, Lisette stood up. Her gold braids were pinned up in a crown and she wore a frock of blue-sprigged muslin that flattered her lissome grace. Following her back to the study, Marcus could think only that the jewelry would be too much temptation for such a splendorous creature. It did not occur to him that Lisette's beauty needed no embellishment.

There was one candle that continued to sputter in the study. Lisette lost no time in using it to light the remaining tapers around the room, then stirred up the fire and added a log. When she finished, she turned to find Marcus sitting in the corner and leering at her with undisguised lust.

"Mr. Reems, I do not appreciate your attitude. You seem to think that I am some mush-brained maiden who is made starry eyed by your forcefulness and rude ogling."

Marcus removed his cloak and flung it onto the chaise, then grinned at Lisette in a way that made her shiver. "Your manner is quite entertaining, Mistress Hahn! We will pursue that topic in greater depth after we conclude the business at hand."

"I have only one thing to say to you, Mr. Reems." Lisette opened the secretary and took out an envelope that bore Lion's seal. "Here is the money my father owed your bank. As far as I am concerned, that concludes our business. Can you find your way out?"

Marcus went pale and snatched the envelope from her hand. His eyes seemed to burn into the familiar seal stamped on the back, and a long moment passed before he broke it and withdrew a sheaf of hundred-pound notes. Furiously, they were counted, then recounted. Lisette waited, still feeling indignant and proud to have played her winning card so effectively. However, when Marcus Reems looked up and their eyes met, a wave of alarm broke over her.

"Do you think that you can pay me off so easily—with *his* money?" He was on his feet, his tiger eyes glowing with rage. "What did you do for *him*? What did you give *him*, virtuous lady? You pretend that you are too pure for me to look at; my presence offends you!" He caught her forearms in a punishing grip. "You should see your face now, Mistress Hahn! You don't look quite so superior anymore."

When she saw the way his lip curled in triumph, Lisette forced back the tide of her panic. "What do you want from me?" she asked evenly. "I have paid you the money. Why can't you leave me alone?"

"Because, as you must realize, it is not the money I want. I want this CoffeeHouse, influence over the leaders who come here to share secrets, and I want you, my yellow rose." To Lisette's horror, he suddenly pressed his wide, sensuous mouth against her throat. Nuzzling downward to the hollow at the base of her neck, Marcus could feel the drumming of Lisette's heart and took that as encouragement. "You are flesh and blood after all!" He chuckled. "Damn, how you arouse me. Even I am amazed! Tell me, Mistress Hahn . . . are you a witch?"

Though clenched teeth, she answered, "I certainly am *not*! Whatever fascination I hold for men is real only in their imaginations, can't you see? You are intrigued because I'm the only eligible female in the CoffeeHouse and I don't bed my customers. If I were playing the doxy while I served ale and stew, giggling and leaning over so that every man could view my bosom, I would be no more desirable to you and the rest of the customers than any tavern wench in Philadelphia."

Marcus was pressing hot kisses onto each delicately tapered finger, and paused now to give Lisette his best roguish smile. "You are quite right. I don't claim to be in love with you, Mistress Hahn. It is a physical infatuation, and no doubt it caught fire for the simple reason you just mentioned—that you are the antithesis of that common, ever-available tavern wench. With your crown of braids, you seem as pure and inaccessible as a virgin princess."

"I must ask you to release me, Mr. Reems." Lisette kept her voice low, for there was an element in this man's personality that sent an icy chill down her back.

"What intrigues me the most," Marcus elaborated, ignoring Lisette's request, "is the possibility that you might not be as perfect as you appear. After all, no one is *perfect*, isn't that so?"

"Of course! Mr. Reems, if you don't mind, I would like to say good night now and—"

"I am certain that you are a fine person, Mistress Hahn, but not stupid, I hope. I would like to offer you a better life, and I hope you will listen to reason."

Lisette wished she were a tall, muscle-bound man, so that she could hit Reems in the mouth and render him senseless.

"Mr. Reems, what you do not appear able to comprehend is the fact that the only better life I aspire to is one that I work toward and am entitled to."

He wasn't listening. "Look what I have here. I brought these tonight with the idea of giving them to you in addition to that generous sum I offered for the CoffeeHouse itself." From the pocket of his deep purple velvet coat, he withdrew a silken bundle, which he set on a nearby tea table and untied. Inside was a profusion of priceless jewelry. There were emeralds, diamonds, sapphires, and rubies of every size, mounted in settings of gold and silver; necklaces, bracelets, rings, brooches, winking and glittering in the candlelight. Still gripping Lisette's slim arm, Reems urged her closer. "Look at them. If you will sell me the CoffeeHouse, all of these pieces are yours. Have you ever seen a larger emerald?"

Lisette ignored the necklace he was holding to the light. "I suppose these belonged to your wife!"

"No, as a matter of fact, they did not. The person who owned them died and the collection came into my possession. For four years, I have kept all of these jewels locked in their case . . . and to allay my fear that they might be stolen, I had the case stored out of sight at my mother's home in New York State."

"Is that where you have been—?"

"Of course! I realized that money alone was not sufficient to convince you to sell the CoffeeHouse. Then I remembered the jewels. Their previous owner resembled you in many ways, although she was not nearly the woman you are. Still"—Marcus paused to leer knowingly—"I knew how ravishing you would look wearing these rare gems— around your exquisite neck, your fragile wrists, and graceful fingers. How stunning your beautiful face would become, set off by sapphires or emeralds in your ears or tucked among your golden curls."

Lisette could bear no more of this sly simpering. "I beg you, Mr. Reems, to cease." She tried once more to wriggle free of the hands that had caressed her arms during his speech. "I am sorry to disappoint you, but I am not as blinded by these jewels as you hoped. If, as you insist, my face and form are attractively made, then I shall be thankful for my good fortune and leave these decorations for a plainer maid who could make better use of them." Noticing that Marcus's swarthy face was growing pale and his grip tightening on her upper arms, she strove for a more conciliatory note. "I agree, fully, that these gems are magnificent, and it is quite probable that most women would be thrilled to own such a collection. But, Mr. Reems"—Lisette attempted to smile sincerely—"you can see that extravagant gowns and jewels have never held much allure for me. I realize that I am quite strange, but my tastes *are* different from the average woman's and I have accepted that." She hoped *he* would accept it. It was almost impossible for Lisette to disguise her contempt for Marcus Reems, but the queer look on his face warned her that he was capable of very irrational behavior. Once again, she wished that she were as tall and strong as a man, so that she could speak the truth and tell him to leave without worrying that he would take offense and snap the bones in her arms.

"You accepted money from Lion Hampshire," argued Marcus, "and you would probably take this jewelry if it were he who offered it! Why? What makes his money better than mine?"

"Please! You are hurting me! And, I would not take a gift like this from Senator Hampshire! He is happily married and asks nothing of me beyond friendship. He did not want to buy the CoffeeHouse from me, Mr. Reems; he loaned me money so that *I could keep it,* with no conditions attached. The senator is a fine, honest man and I resent your suggestion that either he or I would exchange help to a friend for sexual favors!"

"Christ, how ravishing you are!" Almost angrily, Marcus shifted his arms so that Lisette was caught against satin breeches. He kissed her with hot, cruel lips until she choked for breath. "All right!" he gasped, lifting his head enough so that she could swallow air. "So you believe that Lion Hampshire is a saint among men! I think, Mistress Hahn, that you play with me, goading me until I elevate my offer. Is it marriage that you are angling for?"

Still stunned by his sudden brutal kiss, Lisette could only gasp when she heard Reems's question.

"You needn't be surprised," he smirked. "I've known scores of women and am well versed with the sly ways they manipulate men. I'll admit that you are uniquely subtle. . . ." Once more, he kissed her, probing her mouth with his sharp tongue. "For the moment, I do not intend to remarry, but my appetite for you is voracious. I see no reason why we could not work out an arrangement whereby you would become my mistress after I take possession of the Coffee-House. Not only will I pay you and give you the jewelry, but I will then support you so that you needn't spend the money from the sale." He nibbled at her ear and mistook her shudder for trembling excitement. "In fact, you may live at Wadelands, the summer estate I own a few miles to the north. My wife was the last woman to sleep there. . . ."

His voice trailed off suggestively and Lisette reacted on impulse when she realized that he was going to kiss her again.

"No!" Her hands flew up and pushed violently at his chest. For an instant, Marcus's hold on her waist was broken and Lisette stumbled backward. "Leave me alone!"

She was only halfway to the closed door when Reems grasped her elbow so tightly that she cried out as he spun her around. Fury suffused his face, but Lisette was past caution.

"You are insane!" she spat. "Is it so impossible for you to realize that my only feelings toward you are contempt and revulsion? I do not play games with words—and if I suggested that Lion Hampshire is a 'saint among men,' then compared to *you*, he certainly is!" Aside from curling his lip and increasing the pressure on her arms, Marcus had not moved, so Lisette continued to vent her frustrated rage. "Allow me to clarify my position! I do *not* want to be your wife or mistress and I do not want you to touch me again. I do *not* want your money, your jewelry, or your summer estate. I will *not* sell the CoffeeHouse to you or anyone else, and I consider the subject closed. I dislike being bullied, and kissed against my will. I find your tactics extremely insulting." To emphasize her point, Lisette attempted once more to pull her arms free. "Mr. Reems, I demand that you release me and leave my CoffeeHouse."

"Are you quite finished, Mistress Hahn? Most entertaining!" Reems's face was twisted, his voice sneering and sarcastic. "Enjoy your brief taste of triumph because I do not intend to crawl out of here, hiding my head in shame. You are an exceptional woman, Mistress Hahn, but I am a *man*, and it will take more than words to rout me. Perhaps you will now face reality . . ."

"Which is?" Lisette interrupted icily.

"That you *are* a woman, and no matter how loudly you declare what you want and what you will allow, you can never control a situation the way a man can. You are so helpless right now, it is laughable! I'll wager you will wish you hadn't been so stiff necked with me—and friendly with Lion—because neither your cold insults or his money can help you now!"

His arms held her like suffocating bands of steel and the kiss he forced into her mouth went beyond mere revulsion to the frightening edge of violent assault. Initially, as she choked on the battering of his tongue in her mouth, Lisette was boiling with rage. Her efforts to push him away were fruitless and the pummeling of her small fists at his chest seemed only to incite and gratify him further.

How dare he! her mind screamed. *This is not fair! What can I do? There must be something!*

Then, Lisette's anger was burned away by a blaze of terror as Marcus Reems stopped kissing her long enough to reach around with one large hand and rip the bodice of her muslin gown.

"Don't scream," he warned in a frigid voice, "or I will choke you to death."

When he had torn her chemise so that her creamy breasts were exposed, Reems made a sound of gross appreciation. "Go over to the chaise and lay down."

For a moment, fear almost won, but Lisette could not allow herself to be beaten by this odious creature. Her head, with its braided gold crown, remained high and she did not move.

A strong dark hand came up, then struck her face with savage force. Lisette felt her neck snap back, but she remained upright and met Marcus Reems's cruel stare.

"Are you challenging me to break your will?" he demanded.

"I am challenging you to see me as a woman that you are attempting to violate. Have you no conscience, Mr. Reems?"

"I used to, but I conveniently mislaid it nearly two dozen years ago." As if to wipe the reminder of all decency from his mind, he yanked Lisette closer and kissed her again. In spite of the contempt that she radiated for him, her mouth was as sweet as wild-flower honey. The rest of the world receded as he kissed her repeatedly and became conscious of the firm naked breasts pressing against him as she struggled, branding his chest through the waistcoat and shirt. Keeping one arm securely around Lisette's slim back, he sought the pale curved globes with his other hand. He could hear his own rasping breath as he nuzzled her neck and squeezed one breast with cruel force.

Lisette swallowed a shriek of pain and felt her eyes pool with tears. Just as she was ready to sob aloud, something happened. Abruptly, Marcus Reems released her and Lisette stumbled back against the corner chair. The sound of her own frenzied weeping filled her head and eyes and it seemed that an eternity passed before she managed to discern Marcus Reems, lying on the floor. Through the blur of her tears, Lisette recognized the blood red trickle that ran down his chin, and then she focused on Nicholai Beaüvisage.

To Nicholai's dismay, her first question was punctuated by a convulsive sob. *"What are you doing here?"* she demanded.

Chapter 19

Midnight to Dawn, April 26, 1793

"For God's sake, Lisette, cover yourself!" Stepping over the dazed form of Marcus Reems, Nicholai pulled off his dove gray coat and put it on Lisette. The handsome garment hung loosely, its sleeves trailing past her fingertips, but it served its purpose by hiding her torn bodice and bare breasts.

"You needn't behave as if I undressed myself!" Lisette protested, as she stood, conscious of her knee-buckling weakness. Nicholai was conveniently close by and she let herself lean into his chest. "W-why?" she whispered.

"That doesn't matter now . . . just be glad I am here! It would seem that Mr. Reems is not a man who takes no for an answer," Nicholai observed. "You needn't be afraid to hold on to me—I promise not to tell anyone that the stalwart Mistress Hahn showed signs of feminine frailty."

Without replying, Lisette did press her face to his snowy shirtfront, holding fast to the fabric of his waistcoat as if to replenish her strength.

Several feet away, Marcus Reems stirred and tried to sit up. Nicholai stared at him over Lisette's crown of braids, watching as he shook his raven head dazedly and blinked several times. Finally, Marcus focused his eyes and met the icy stare of Nicholai Beauvisage.

"That was quite a blow you dealt me, Mr. Beauvisage."

"You deserved it."

His self-possession rapidly returning, Marcus got to his feet and pressed a lawn handkerchief to his bloody chin. "I resent your tone of voice almost as much as I resent your attack on my person, Mr. Beauvisage. What is your interest in this matter?"

"I am a friend of Mistress Hahn's."

"I see." Reems's tone was acid. Ever since the night he had watched Nicholai ride up Third Street with Lion, his vague dislike for the new Beauvisage brother had deepened into bitter animosity. "Are you in the habit of interfering in her affairs?"

Lisette broke in to reply, "No more than *you*, Mr. Reems. I wish that all of you meddling men would attend to your own business and let me attend to mine."

"Right now, Mistress Hahn, my business is with Mr. Beauvisage," Marcus replied coldly. "If he will apologize for his violence toward me, I will say good night."

Nicholai made a rude noise. "Apologize! I would sooner apologize to a rat in the alleyway! Considering your uncivilized, lecherous attack on Mistress Hahn, you are fortunate that I was able to restrain myself after one blow!"

Listening to Nicholai's contemptuous tone, Marcus Reems's face darkened. Purposefully, he stepped forward and struck Nicholai across the cheek with the back of his hand. "Such crude insults leave me no choice, Mr. Beauvisage. The preservation of my honor demands that I challenge you."

Lisette looked from one man to the other, noting the way their eyes blazed in a way that left no room for reason or logic. "This is silly! You two cannot be considering a *duel*?"

Neither looked her way. "I accept your challenge, Mr. Reems, only because, as far as I can tell, you bring nothing but trouble to those people whose lives you touch."

"I do hope you count yourself among that elite group," Marcus parried smoothly, "because I plan to bring the worst sort of trouble to your life, Mr. Beauvisage. Could we agree on weapons and location without the assistance of seconds? What is your choice?"

"You may save your threats. I would prefer rapiers, but in America I know that pistols are the rule."

"Excellent. There is a fine open meadow north of my summer estate, Wadelands. Tomorrow, at dawn?"

"I will be there with my second. Good night, Mr. Reems."

Marcus made a low mocking bow, his eyes on Lisette, then left the study. The instant the door closed, she burst out, "Have you taken leave of your senses? A *duel*?"

"What did you expect me to do? Decline? If I didn't believe that the world will be well rid of that slime—"

"What if you lose?"

"I assure you, I shall not." He said this in a way that left no room for argument. "For God's sake, Lisette, how do you think it made me feel, walking in to find him kissing you, touching you—your clothes half off? If I were less civilized, I would have killed him right here, at that moment!"

"How do you think *I* felt? That is the second gown in one month that has been torn past repair by a man!" Her eyes pierced him accusingly. "Do you imagine that I enjoyed being mauled, forced to endure his repulsive—"

"Don't you compare me to him!" Nicholai retorted. "And besides, if you feel that way, why are you against a duel?"

She sat down on the chaise, suddenly tired. "It doesn't seem right. It's like sinking down to meet him on his own horrid level."

"Sometimes that is what it takes when one is dealing with truly corrupt evil."

As he sat down beside her, Lisette saw the faraway look in his emerald eyes. "I am sorry . . . I'd forgotten about France. I suppose you learned a different attitude there. . . ."

"It was forced on me—a colder view of reality, a technique for survival. I stopped expecting bad people to see the light and become good; I am used to uncivilized types."

She sighed. How handsome and appealing Nicholai was . . . and his honesty was unquestionable. She trusted him. The impulse to allow him to take care of her was powerful . . . how lovely it would be to be free of the responsibility of decision making and position taking. Lisette felt weary, into her bones. . . .

"I care about you," Nicholai was saying in a husky voice

that made her tingle. "I think of you all the time . . . even when I'm trying not to."

She was pulled into his wry, wondering smile and felt herself smile in response. "I know. I feel—the same."

Nicholai's head bent; his mouth covered Lisette's with a gentle, lingering kiss that kindled a bright spark of desire within her. All the tense, traumatic agitation was washed away as if by magic, to be replaced by sweet, aching bliss. She answered his kiss as it deepened and felt her skin prickle when he slid a warm strong hand around the curve of her neck.

"Oh, God, Lisette, you are perfection."

Lisette wanted to ask how Nicholai would describe Amelia Purdy, but couldn't bear to stir up new trouble. "Nicholai, why *did* you come here tonight? You look as though you're dressed for a party."

Between kisses down her neck, he replied, "I *was* at a party, but I made the mistake of comparing the other women to you."

"But surely, with their beautiful gowns and jewels and dressed hair—"

"There was no contest. You are incredible."

This time, his arms went around her and he kissed her more insistently. Lisette wondered if a spell had been cast on her to cause such a keen response throughout her body. Everything about him aroused her: his scent, the texture of his skin, the cut of his clothes, the tone of his voice, the sparkle in his eyes, the cynical flash of his smile and wit, the magical way he kissed her and touched her with those wonderful deft fingers. . . .

Gently, Nicholai eased Lisette back to lie across the chaise. The hard length of his body was pressed along her left side; as he kissed her again, he was opening the frock coat she wore, pushing aside the torn remnants of her gown to find her soft breasts.

Suddenly, Lisette went rigid. Her hands left Nicholai's shoulders and flew down to push desperately against his chest. "Stop. Stop it!" she cried.

"What the hell—?" He was irritated, confused. To deflect

Lisette's attack, he sat up, but stared as if he believed her unbalanced.

"I am sorry—I just saw *him* when you touched me—I felt as if—"

"For God's sake, Lisette, you couldn't say anything that would insult me more!" Nicholai stood and angrily raked both hands through his auburn gold hair. "To equate me with that disgusting excuse for a man, after it was I who saved you from—"

"I said I was sorry! I can't help it if I do not care to be pawed twice in one hour! Or must I surrender my body to you out of gratitude for your 'rescue'?"

For a moment, it seemed that he might strike her, but instead he reached over, gripped her elbows, and lifted her roughly to her feet.

"It seems that we are once again unable to agree, Mistress Hahn. I only hope that, in spite of your aversion to my touch, you can muster a tiny kiss to send me into battle."

Stunned, Lisette opened her mouth to protest and explain, but Nicholai took that opportunity to deliver a bruising kiss that she would never forget. When Nicholai raised his head, she had time only to note the hard set of his jaw before he said, "Knowing you has been a charming experience, Mistress Hahn . . . and since this may be good-bye, I know you won't begrudge me my coat."

All Lisette could see was his eyes, flashing cynically as he watched her remove the frock coat. Then he was on his way toward the door, shrugging into the jacket as he made his exit, and still Lisette could find no words that would make either of them understand.

In the darkness before dawn, Meagan and Lion Hampshire lay snuggled together in their bed at the villa. Meagan was dreaming of Pecan Grove, her family plantation in Virginia. Tomorrow they were leaving to travel there for several months of companionable solitude; the plan was that they would remain at Pecan Grove until their child was two months old. Even Lion was looking forward to the dogwood and cherry blossoms, and he knew he could satisfy his craving for politics by exchanging visits with any of the collection of wise Virginia statesmen. Already, Lion was relaxed and feeling like his usual self; after a week of complete isolation, Meagan and he were closer than ever, and neither could bear to break the spell by venturing into Philadelphia.

Something was pulling Meagan's dream away—a noise—but she resisted, burrowing deeper into the quilts and closer to Lion's chest.

"Someone is pounding on the front door," he muttered.

"Shh. It is still night. Wong will answer."

A long minute passed; the knocking went on. A voice joined in, crying out their names.

"Wong is at the Pine Street house, fondling. *You* sent all the servants back there to pack our trunks."

Feeling him roll away as he summoned the necessary energy to face the cold darkness, Meagan made a petulant sound.

"Who could be so rude and thoughtless?" she demanded crossly.

Lion chuckled as he climbed out of bed and searched for his dressing gown. "You are as spoiled as a child, my love. Can you not bear a few minutes out of my arms?"

She laughed at this, watching as he lit a taper in the embers of the fireplace. A candle was then lit beside the bed, and Lion took his chamber stick out into the hallway.

The pounding was more frantic than loud; he guessed it must be a woman. Could something be wrong? Was someone ill or hurt? One of their servants? President Washington?

The patterned brick entryway was cold under his bare feet and the tawny velvet dressing gown scarcely reached his knees, but Lion was too preoccupied to feel the chill wind as he threw open the front door.

"Oh, Senator Hampshire, I was so frightened that you might not be here!"

He blinked in surprise at the sight of Lisette Hahn, haloed by candlelight. Her mane of primrose curls was wind tossed, and the cold air had colored her cheeks and lips a dark rose. Anyone but Lion might have been startled by her costume of snug breeches, riding boots, and a rough, heavy woolen shirt, but he was well used to seeing his irrepressible wife in such attire.

"Lisette! What on earth—"

Impulsively, she leaned against his chest and drew strength from Lion's warmth and steady heartbeat.

"I had to come. You are the only person who can help me!"

At the top of the stairs, the shadows were prickled by a wavering flame, followed by Meagan's clear voice. "Pray explain, Mistress Hahn!"

Chapter 20

April 26, 1793

Lisette, unaware of Meagan's once-thriving suspicions about her and the senator, broke away from Lion's arms without a trace of discomfiture and peered at the indistinct figure above.

"Mrs. Hampshire? I am so sorry to disturb you—both of you!—at this hour. I wouldn't blame you at all for being furious with me, but I hope you will allow me to explain."

Candlestick in hand, Meagan descended, looking enchanting in a robe of plum silk. Her ebony curls were caught up in an ivory bandeau, and, to Lion's surprise, she was smiling warmly. "I didn't mean to sound cross, Mistress Hahn. Seeing you in breeches, I have a feeling we were meant to be friends! Why don't we all go into the kitchen while I fix a pot of tea?"

"There may not be much time," Lisette murmured doubtfully, accompanying the Hampshires into the kitchen and taking a chair at the hearth. After lighting the fire, Lion put the iron kettle in place.

"Now, tell us what the trouble is."

"How soon will it be dawn?" Lisette asked anxiously.

"I glanced at the clock just before I left our bedchamber," Meagan said. "It was a few minutes after five o'clock." She stood up and brought over the teapot as Lion removed the kettle from the fire.

"Good. There is more time than I thought. I couldn't sleep at all last night, trying to decide what to do. Then, I remembered that Senator Hampshire seemed to have some knowledge of Marcus Reems. He seemed so bitter last night when he learned you had lent me the money to repay the loan. It seemed to involve—forgive my presumptuousness —a personal grudge. Somehow, I thought you might be able to intercede. I didn't want to go to Nicholai's family—"

"Lisette, slow down!" demanded Lion. "You are making no sense whatsoever."

She closed her eyes for a moment and took a deep breath before relating the events of the previous night. She told them about the jewels, Marcus Reems's apparent resentment of Lion, and finally, the way he had attempted to force himself on her. At this point, Meagan poured the steaming tea and Lisette squeezed in lemon juice. Between sips, she revealed the story of Nicholai's appearance, his angry quarrel with Reems, and their agreement to duel. Her story ended with the explanation of how she and Nicholai had parted on a harsh note.

Lion asked if she could remember any of the pieces of jewelry, and after hearing two descriptions, he pressed for more details of what Marcus had said about them.

Finally, Meagan spoke what was in her husband's mind. "Clarissa. All these years, Lion."

"Who is Clarissa?" asked Lisette.

"Ah—a young lady we knew before our marriage," Lion told her absently. His mind was elsewhere.

Meagan interceded. "I think you should know, Lisette, that Marcus Reems is Lion's half brother. They did not meet until they were almost grown, at which point Marcus developed an irrational jealousy concerning Lion—and it has only grown worse over the years. Marcus has never been able to best Lion, and as time has passed, he has eased his need for superiority by trying to tyrannize others."

"I should have never let it go after Clarissa," Lion declared. "How could I have been so foolish, believing that he might appreciate a second chance? If only he had not gotten Priscilla involved!"

"I don't understand!" exclaimed Lisette.

"It is a long, complicated story," Meagan said slowly, "but . . . Lion had been casually involved with Clarissa, before his engagement to Priscilla Wade. After Priscilla and I came to Philadelphia, Marcus joined forces with the vengeful Clarissa to make trouble for us all. Marcus thought he was very sly, breaking up Lion's engagement and marrying Priscilla himself—but in truth it allowed Lion to escape the situation and marry me."

Lion broke in. "Meanwhile, I discovered Clarissa's involvement in the calamities which had been befalling us. After we had it out, she disappeared with her jewelry case, which contained a ring that implicated her in all that had happened. It's too complicated to explain . . . at any rate, she was killed in a coach accident—the wheel very suspiciously fell off—and the jewelry case was gone."

"You suspect Marcus?"

"I had proof that he possessed the rubies from that ring, but I decided not to pursue it because by then he was married to Priscilla, and Meagan and I wanted her to have a chance for happiness." He sighed harshly. "I hoped for her sake Marcus would turn over a new leaf, but after she died, he redoubled his efforts to damage me in some way. Since the election . . . well, I can't go back and change the past, but I can do something today. In spite of everything, I cannot help feeling a bit responsible. If I had never been thrust into his life—"

"Oh, please, Lion, no excuses!" Meagan exclaimed. "Marcus forfeited any right to your understanding years ago."

He drained his teacup. "I cannot argue with that . . . Nicholai knows all about Marcus and me, Lisette. That's why he has been making such a pest of himself at the CoffeeHouse; I asked him to do a bit of spying for me, to learn what Marcus was up to."

She tried to absorb this. What did it mean? "Oh . . ." Had Nicholai been acting to win her confidence?

"Well . . ." Lion was saying, "one thing is certain—I can't allow Nicholai to risk his life after I instigated his involvement. He would never have been at the CoffeeHouse at all last night were it not for me!"

"Marcus just transfers his resentment for you to everyone else he comes in contact with," said Meagan. "Since he hasn't been able to best you so far, he has to build up his stature by bullying people like Lisette and Nicholai." She gave her husband a tiny ironic smile and reached over to thread her fingers through his. "This time I wonder, though, if Marcus hasn't bitten off more than he can chew."

"I'm certain that Nicholai thinks so," Lisette agreed. "Although he was angry, I doubt that he would have agreed to a duel unless the challenger was so thoroughly odious. I *know* that 'honor' is not his motive."

Lion rose abruptly to his feet. "I'll get dressed, then Lisette and I will ride up to Wadelands." When Meagan opened her mouth, he firmly laid his hand over it. "*No!* You are pregnant and I will not allow you to get involved." Then, more gently, "You know that you could come, if not for the baby."

Lisette walked to the back window and surveyed the graying sky. It's growing lighter," she hinted urgently.

Lion nodded in reply and left the kitchen.

"Would you like more tea?" asked Meagan.

"Yes. Please." Lisette returned to her chair. "I feel terrible, disturbing you this way."

"I truly don't mind. I admire the way you have acted, rather than weeping in your bed; I understand that. And, as for Marcus, we do feel a certain responsibility for him."

"You have never shied from challenges yourself, if the stories I hear are true."

"Thank you for not putting me on the shelf. I'm only a few months older than you, but of late I have felt quite matronly."

"You look *beautiful!*" Lisette protested. "A baby . . . I think it is wonderful. As for me, I shall probably be a spinster. Adventure is not routine for me, I assure you. I spend most—all!—of my time working in the CoffeeHouse."

"But you are very proud of your CoffeeHouse, aren't you? You are the undeniable equal of the men who are your customers."

Suddenly, Lion's shout came from the entryway. "Lisette! Let's go!"

Meagan hurried after the taller girl. In the doorway, she grasped her husband's hand. "Lion, promise me that you will not do anything dangerous."

"I shall try to think of a painless way to stop the duel. Perhaps I could remove Nicholai—claim that one of his parents is very ill." He kissed her quickly. *"Don't worry,* fondling. And stay here!"

Lion had brought a yellow post chariot around to the front door; he explained that it was merely a precaution in the event that anyone was injured. Before allowing him to help her in, Lisette went over to her horse and took something out of her saddlebag.

"The jewels. Marcus forgot them last night in his rage. I don't like having them around, especially after hearing your story. You must decide what to do with them . . ."

Lion lifted a blond eyebrow, but said nothing. Instead, he took the bulging pouch back to his wife, spoke to her softly, then hastened back to the post chariot.

Moments later, Meagan watched the graceful yellow vehicle roll swiftly down the drive. Dawn was rushing in from the east, and as she felt the weight of the jewels in her hands, a foreboding chill prickled the back of her neck.

The Schuylkill River had turned violet by the time Lisette and Lion sighted the Wadelands. The handsome country house had been purchased by Marcus Reems as an inducement to Priscilla Wade to marry him instead of Lion. Now empty most of the year, it looked rather unkempt, its lawn ragged and garden overgrown.

Lion stopped the post chariot well away from the grounds and tied the horses to a tree overlooking the river. An anxious-looking Lisette joined him.

"I can see the sun coming up—there." She gestured to the east. "Do you know where the meadow is that Marcus spoke of?"

"Yes. Just beyond that long hedge that borders Wadelands. Look, you can see the fresh path beaten down across the grass to that space between the bushes. Someone is already here."

Lisette matched Lion's quiet sprint as they crossed the lawn. Never had she known such terrible panic. What if Nicholai was dead? That agonizing thought even blotted out Lion's revelation about the true reason for Nicholai's visits to the CoffeeHouse.

A few feet from the hedge, Lion stopped and withdrew

a well-made pistol with engraved brass trim. "Shh," he cautioned. "I hear them talking."

Lisette gaped, horrified, at his weapon. "You aren't planning to use that? You told Meagan—"

"Quiet!" Lion hissed. "Fair play is not a philosophy to which Marcus subscribes!"

With that, he took Lisette's clammy hand and led her along the high bushes to the opening. Both of them peered around the branches just in time to watch Nicholai and Marcus handing their coats to their seconds, Randolph Edwards and William Bingham. In return, each was presented with a dueling pistol. Lisette could guess why Nicholai had chosen Randolph as his second; a more intimate friend or relative would never stand for this foolishness.

A long area had been cleared of brush; the center and each man's twenty paces were marked. Now, the two duelists stood back to back against the fire-streaked sky, linen shirts fluttering in the breeze. Randolph and Bingham retreated to a safe distance just a few feet in front of the sleepy-looking Dr. Wistar and his medical valise.

"Your diversion!" Lisette whispered to Lion.

"It's too late for any more diversions," he replied softly. "It was too late four years ago, but I was too blind to see." Someone was counting, slowly, and the two men began to walk in opposite directions while Lion checked his pistol. "Don't worry about Beauvisage—Marcus was never very good at this . . . or anything else."

As the distance widened between the men, they fell silent. Lisette's heart was hammering so hard that she felt she might suffocate; her palms were wet and icy.

"Seventeen . . ." Randolph intoned, "eighteen, nineteen . . . *twen*—"

Lisette gasped in horror when Marcus Reems wheeled around and took aim a split second before the command to fire was given. Nicholai had just begun to turn when there were two staccato cracks, two puffs of smoke in the pink sunrise—one from Marcus's gun, one from Lion's—and two men crumpled to the ground.

Chapter 21

April 26, 1793

Meagan was upstairs, freshly garbed and brushing her hair, when she heard the clattering wheels of the post chariot in the drive. It took all her willpower not to race madly down the stairs; she took the rail and descended as quickly as she dared.

Throwing open the front door, her eyes fell on the yellow carriage and the vivid drops of blood spattered across its side. There was movement inside—heads shifting in the muted dawn light; it seemed that whoever had driven was now leaning in the far door.

"Lion?" Meagan whispered the name, afraid to hear the worst.

Instantly, his head appeared inside the coach. "I am fine, sweeting." Sweat and dust streaked his dark face. "It is Nicholai. Will you run up and turn back the covers on our bed?"

A lump of relief swelled in Meagan's throat as she hurried to do his bidding. She was arranging the pillows when Lion and Dr. Wistar appeared, arms around Nicholai's back. A crimson stain blossomed over the left shoulder of his linen shirt and his skin was bleached under its tan. Carefully, they eased him onto the bed. Nicholai's eyes were closed, his handsome face clenched with pain. He made no sound as Lion began to cut away his clothing and the doctor prepared to remove the lead ball embedded in his shoulder.

Meagan stepped out into the hall. To her surprise, she found Lisette at the top of the stairs, leaning against the baluster and sobbing wretchedly.

"Oh, Lisette . . ." Meagan went to her and embraced her. Something that Caro had said came back to her . . . *"I happen to know that Nicholai has a serious interest in Mistress Hahn himself."* It occurred to Meagan that Mr. Beauvisage may have had another motive for visiting Lisette aside from spying on Marcus. "You mustn't cry for too long—you will make yourself sick. Here, sit down."

They sat together on the stairs and Lisette rubbed her eyes with the sleeve of her man's shirt. "Oh, that felt good. I have been in agony, but I couldn't let Nicholai know."

"Tears are hard to keep inside," Meagan agreed. "Can you tell me what happened?"

"Marcus Reems is dead," answered Lisette tonelessly. She pressed slim fingers to her hot eyelids and cheeks.

"B-but—dear lord! I—how? Usually those pistols are so inaccurate that neither man is hit—"

"Nicholai didn't shoot Marcus—Lion did. Marcus fired before the signal was given; we were behind some bushes, and when Lion saw what was happening, he raised his pistol and shot."

Meagan paled in horror. "Oh, my God . . . how terrible. Did Marcus know?"

"Yes. The strange thing was—he didn't seem surprised. When Lion and I came forward, I saw the look in Marcus's eyes. Calm. I went to Nicholai, but I saw Lion kneel and lift Marcus's head . . . he only said one thing before he died. So odd. It was 'Thank you.' "

Meagan shivered visibly. "I suppose we underestimated Marcus; perhaps he had no more control over his actions than Lion did . . . and was waiting to be stopped." Her violet eyes pooled with tears.

"The doctor says Nicholai will be all right," Lisette was saying. "I pray that he's correct. All that blood . . . the pain in his eyes . . ."

"I am certain that Dr. Wistar is right. A shoulder wound should heal easily enough with the proper care. If everything is kept clean, the dressings changed, and Nicholai rests and stays quiet, there shouldn't be any problem at all."

"If anything happens to him . . ." Lisette whispered to herself.

"I—didn't realize you two were so involved. . . ." Meagan

hated herself for prying, but she couldn't instigate her plan unless she was certain.

"Oh—well—" Suddenly, Lisette was flustered; blood rushed to her face. "Involved is not the right word. I just feel that—that the duel was partly my fault, since I was the cause of their argument."

"Mmm. Yes." She struggled not to smile. "You mustn't think that way, Lisette. If the blame were to be divided, all of us would receive a portion."

As she nodded, another tear trickled down her cheek. "It is so hard to realize that that silly quarrel last night could have ended this way. That a life can be lost so quickly . . . and Nicholai—it's impossible to believe that someone so strong could be disabled so easily."

Meagan put her arm around Lisette again. "You are exhausted. When Dr. Wistar is ready to leave, I think that you should go back to Philadelphia with him. Perhaps he can give you something that will help you sleep; I'll wager that a few hours in a soft bed will do you a world of good—"

"No! Oh, please, I can't leave Nicholai. Please, let me stay!"

Their eyes met and Meagan knew the truth. "Of course you may stay. Absolutely."

At that moment, a door closed down the hall. Lion and Dr. Wistar paused there, talking, then started toward the stairway. Without a word, Meagan rose and went to her husband. She was well aware of the turmoil that brewed under his calm exterior; the hand that took her own was cold and tense.

"Well, ladies," Dr. Wistar was saying, "I have done all I can. He's a magnificently strong man and I have every hope that he will come out of this without lasting damage. I will write down a list of instructions: how often to change and clean his dressing, how often he may be given medication for the pain. I have a few things from my bag that I will leave—salves and such. Don't expect him to be alert for two or three days. Before that time, he will need the laudanum to keep the pain at bay; sleep will be a kindness for him." The doctor fixed accusing eyes on Lisette. "If you

want to see Mr. Beauvisage just to reassure yourself, I have
no objection. He was looking for you."

"He was?" She seemed on the verge of tears again. "I
will go to him, then. Excuse me."

As Lisette hurried down the hallway, Dr. Wistar went to
the parlor to prepare his instructions, and the Hampshires
slipped into a sitting room to steal a few minutes alone.

Opening the door to the room Nicholai occupied, Lisette
thought that she scarcely knew herself. All her carefully
structured defenses had come apart, and the result was total
chaos. She wanted to weep with abandon, as if to share
some of Nicholai's pain, and then cry even more just for
the fact that she cared so acutely.

Sunlight streamed into the chamber; morning was just
beginning. Lion and Meagan's bed was enormous and beautiful, with embroidered bed hangings of ivory and dove gray
and a plush comforter of cream satin. Almost in the middle, his gold-washed chestnut hair gleaming against a satin
pillow, lay Nicholai. Lisette made her way around the bed
slowly. Impatient . . . yet afraid to discover the truth. The
top third of Nicholai's body was uncovered. Although his
dark skin contrasted with the snowy linen, there was no
doubt that he was pale. Clean bandages hid his left shoulder, as well as a portion of his arm and chest, from view.
Lisette was shocked to see how large an area had been
affected, but she took comfort from the rest of him—lean
muscled, warm blooded, and unmistakably alive.

"Nicholai?" she whispered, starved for the sight of his
bright emerald eyes and the appealing sound of his voice.
"Nicholai, I am here. It's Lisette."

Finally, she realized that he was not resting or lightly
drowsing, but asleep, and her heart throbbed with anguished
disappointment. Lisette stared at the splendid face, which,
even in repose, had an undeniable strength. There was a
vulnerability, too, that was new to her. Nicholai's firm lips,
parted to allow the passage of warm breath, offset the lean
square line of his jaw, while his cynically drawn russet
brows and arrogantly chiseled nose seemed less harsh in
view of the thick eyelashes Lisette had never noticed before.

"I am not going to worry about that one," a voice announced from the foot of the bed. Lisette drew a surprised breath and turned to find Antonia Beauvisage. Nicholai's mother wore a mask of stoic composure that couldn't disguise the anxiety in her eyes. "Nicky is strong."

Jean-Philippe was there, putting an arm around his petite wife. "That is so true. This will be like a scratch for Nicky."

Lisette edged away from the bed, but relaxed when she saw Katya and Caro coming toward her from the doorway. Alec and Randolph brought up the rear.

"Mrs. Beauvisage . . ." Lisette met the older woman's eyes. "I am so sorry. Has someone explained—"

"Randolph rode out to tell us," Jean-Philippe said. "We understand the circumstances, Mistress Hahn, so you must know that it is perfectly clear that you are in no way to blame." He guided his wife around the side of the bed and the two of them studied Nicholai as he slept.

Katya hugged Lisette tightly. "How terrible for you! Randolph says you were standing right beside Senator Hampshire when he fired at Marcus Reems!"

"He tried—he was going to try to stop—the duel." Lisette gulped back a fresh wave of tears. "I took the senator to Wadelands because I couldn't think what else to do!"

"You mustn't feel responsible in the least," admonished Antonia, turning to seek out Lisette's anguished eyes. "In a few days, he will be as good as new."

Lisette nodded bravely, then let Katya hug her one more time. She barely saw the men, or the keen speculation in Caro's watchful eyes, but she was suddenly conscious of the fact that everyone in the room belonged to the Beauvisage family but her.

"I—I am terribly thirsty." She looked around. "If you'll excuse me . . ."

After Lisette had left the room, Caro went over to stand beside her mother-in-law. She gazed at Nicholai and touched his brow; then, satisfied that he would recover, she lifted delicate brows in Antonia's direction.

"Well?" Caro whispered. "I hope that you have decided to follow Meagan's advice regarding Lisette Hahn!"

*   *   *

Lisette found the kitchen on her own; there was no sign of either the Hampshires or any servants, which seemed quite odd for a house so large. Her hands shook as she poured water into a cup and drank, then poured and drank again. Finally, she drifted restlessly out the back door and discovered a sprawling, gaudy garden laced with paths of brick and punctuated by weeping willow and honey locust trees. The morning air was perfumed with boxwood, wisteria, hyacinths, and dozens of subtler flowers. Unable to stay still or examine the emotions that churned within herself, Lisette prowled the garden, pausing from time to time to look up at the window of Nicholai's chamber. Inexplicably, she felt acutely involved in his situation. She could almost feel his pulse in her own heart, almost sense the degree of his pain, his frustration, the confusion twisting about behind those closed eyes and deceptively peaceful body.

As the distant window curtains fluttered in the spring breeze, Lisette wondered, *Why do I feel I should be with him instead of his family? What madness possesses me now? I must leave him to his mother's care and return to my CoffeeHouse . . . I cannot doubt that it depends on me for survival.*

But Lisette was still in the garden when Meagan appeared, carrying shears and a large straw basket.

"I thought I would cut enough flowers to make an enormous bouquet for Nicholai's bedside," she announced. "I'm afraid that it will have to substitute for Lion and me when Nicholai awakens and needs cheering." Carefully nonchalant, Meagan clipped several daffodils and dropped them into the basket.

Lisette followed her. "I don't understand—"

"I'm afraid that we are going into Philadelphia this afternoon, and tomorrow we depart for several months' stay at Pecan Grove, the plantation in Virginia where I was raised. Our baby will be born there."

Watching as Meagan cut spicy moss-pink roses from a sloping terrace, Lisette attempted to mentally assemble this new puzzle. "Do you mean to have Nicholai remain here during his recovery—?"

"Well, naturally we wouldn't think of moving him; after all, we won't be using the villa ourselves."

"Will his mother stay to care for him?" Lisette tried to keep her tone conversational.

"Well, that's the problem." Meagan stopped and turned toward Lisette; she strove to sound casual. "It seems that Antonia and Caro both are so tied up in preparations for Katya's wedding next month that it is impossible for either one to move down here for the length of time it will take Nicholai to recuperate. And, of course, Caro can't just flit away and leave her children for days and days. . . ."

She paused. "Unfortunately, it looks as though one or two servants will have to look after Nicholai. A shame, isn't it?"

"It certainly is!" exclaimed Lisette in frustration. "If only I did not have so many responsibilities at the CoffeeHouse, I would be more than happy to look after Nicholai. You must know, Meagan, that he will be terribly restless! He could do something reckless if he has no one to make the monotonous hours pass a bit more easily—"

"That is exactly what has us, and his family, so worried!" Meagan bent to cut a crowded patch of yellow and violet pansies. "Nicholai really does need someone by his side who understands his moods and can help to stave off boredom. . . ." On cue, she straightened with an expression of sudden inspiration. "Do you know, I have just thought of two different solutions that I prefer vastly to the idea of servants tending Nicholai."

Lisette wished she could read Meagan's eyes to discover the direction of this conversation. "Really? I am terribly curious—"

"It suddenly occurred to me that there are several young ladies in Philadelphia who would be overjoyed to nurse Nicholai back to health. We could make inquiries and perhaps the volunteers could take turns spending the day here and trying to amuse Nicholai. I'd wager we could get the Misses Allen, Chew, Oswald, Penn—and, certainly, Anne Bingham's cousin from England. She is quite taken with Nicholai." Meagan bit her lip to keep from laughing.

Unfamiliar with Ophelia Corkstall, Lisette felt herself bristle. The idea of Nicholai being ministered to by a parade of simpering husband-hunting females was more than she could stand. "Have you considered the possibility that he might not care to be left at the mercy of some of those girls for hours and hours?"

Meagan could scarcely contain her glee. Turning to the flower bed on her left, she attacked some innocent lilies of the valley with her shears. "Well," she answered loudly, "I admit there are flaws, but at least it seems a feasible plan. My other idea is so farfetched—"

"What? What is it?" Lisette moved as close as possible, thinking that she would approve of savage Indians from the wilderness over the Misses Chew, Oswald, Penn, and Allen.

"You are bound to say no," Meagan insisted, "but it occurred to me that if the Beauvisages and I were to send a few servants over to the CoffeeHouse, that they could attempt to fill your many roles while you remain here at the villa and assume a new role—nurse and companion to Nicholai."

"Yes." Lisette's voice was emphatic with relief and what sounded to Meagan like elation. "I believe that is the best solution." She took another breath, intending to invent a logical-sounding reason for her willingness to stay with Nicholai, but Meagan lifted her eyes from the flower-filled basket to hold Lisette's with a clean violet gaze that destroyed all pretense.

"You don't have to pretend, Lisette," she said gently. "Though you and I are quite different—strangely enough, it seems that love strikes us both the same way. I know how you feel, even though you may not understand it yet, because I have struggled against the same forces." Meagan's dimples showed as she smiled. "If it is love, the current always pulls you under . . . you try to get a breath of reason, but it's hopeless. I can see that you don't want to be in love—I didn't either. My problems and obstacles were different from yours, but I can tell you one thing . . . love, that incredible magic, is more than worth the trouble . . . and once you've tasted it, the real world seems stale."

Lisette glanced up at the second-floor window with its fluttering curtains, and prepared to protest what Meagan had said. Meagan was wrong; she definitely did not love Nicholai Beauvisage. She had no intention of becoming ensnarled in the sort of predicament Meagan had just described. However, when she looked away from the window and opened her mouth to speak, Lisette found herself without an audience. She spied Lion, across the garden near the house; he was laughing softly as he met his diminutive raven-haired wife. They spoke and embraced while the basket slipped from Meagan's fingers, sending a bright shower of cut flowers over the lawn.

Nicholai felt as if he were trying to swim in a sea of mist . . . so strange, as though his limbs were free-floating, beyond his control. He tried to open his eyes, but they were too heavy. There seemed to be a layer of fleecy cotton covering his eyes, tongue, and the inside of his head, but he didn't care. It was protection, padding his brain against the wicked needles of pain that tried to invade and disrupt his dreams. So, he relaxed in the mist and let himself float, back to Paris. . . .

He was lying in Gabrielle's bed, with her cheek resting on his chest; he had studied the incredible plaster-ornamented ceiling with its circular painting of fat naked nymphs at the center. The ribbons and festoons of flowers carved above were as incongruous in this Paris of blood and sansculottes as Gabrielle herself. She belonged in a different world, insulated from reality and trouble. How he wished he could convince her to stop worrying about her brother and let him take her away from Paris, from France, to some place where she would be safe, swathed in satin and Alençon lace, until the Revolution ended. Her stubbornness was deaf to reason . . . the only time she could make Nicholai lose his temper was when she pouted, but he was unable to stay mad under her coaxing lips and skillful fingers. Gabrielle had skin like velvet, heady with the scent of gardenias she always wore, and when they made love Nicholai forgot all the gaps in his understanding of her, all the questions she laughingly deflected. For once, he held a beautiful woman who wasn't so eager she dampened his desire, or so obviously angling to trap him in marriage that he wanted only to get away. Gabrielle was a sensuous, luxurious mystery.

"Gabrielle . . ." Nicholai wondered if he had spoken. The layers of cotton wore away; the mist cleared. Pain—his shoulder burned and throbbed, sending knife-sharp currents down his arm, through his neck, and into his head. His chest was so hot; he couldn't move. Was Gabrielle here? Was this a dream? "Gabrielle."

Cool slim fingers touched his brow and cheek, smoothing back his hair with exquisite gentleness. It was a blissful sensation. Somehow he managed to open his eyes, only to find darkness. After a few moments, he discerned a window, framed by fluttering curtains and luminous with moonlight. A silhouette was etched against that silvery background . . . a female, slender and elegant, with a delicately drawn profile that was familiar to him.

She bent closer, tracing the chiseled strength of Nicholai's face with soft fingertips, and searched his emerald eyes. "It is Lisette, Nicholai," she whispered. "Do you remember?"

She smelled, not of gardenias, but of sweet meadow grass and—vanilla? He attempted a crooked smile. "Of course . . . I remember."

Lisette reached for a cup of wine from the side table and helped him to lift his head for a few welcome sips. "Better?"

"Much. Thank you." As his eyes grew accustomed to the dark, he stared at her as the pain receded. "The duel. I remember . . . my shoulder was hit."

"Yes, but the doctor says you'll mend without problem." Briefly, she reminded him about Marcus Reems's death and his current whereabouts, all the while continuing to smooth the crisp curls from his forehead.

"Your fingers are like feathers," he sighed. "I almost hate to ask, but why are you here instead of at the Coffee-House? It feels late—"

"Past midnight," she confirmed, smiling. "The Hampshires had to leave for Virginia, but they, and your family, have sent a few servants to the CoffeeHouse to substitute for me while I take care of you."

"Either I am dreaming, or this is a cruel joke," Nicholai groaned. "Do you expect me to believe that all those people have conspired to leave us alone here for an extended period of time? My *mother*? She barely knows you! Even more incredible is the possibility that you would elect to shut yourself up playing nursemaid to a temperamental character like me when you could be managing your Coffee-House. Why, you grow feverish when you're away from the place for one hour!" Nicholai was conscious of the intensifying pain in his shoulder, but somehow he felt removed from it. All that mattered was the sparks that crackled in the air between his body and Lisette's.

"I agree. Your mother and I have both behaved inexplicably today." Her voice was teasing, but her eyes were on the dot of blood that appeared on his white-wrapped shoulder. "Actually, I believe your mother was persuaded she could not take care of you because of the preparations for Katya's wedding."

"Are you making this sacrifice out of friendship for my sister?"

"No. And it's not a sacrifice. I chose to stay with you."

Their features were muted by the darkness, but Nicholai's eyes held her own until she shivered. "You must be in a great deal of pain. Let me get the bottle of laudanum."

His right hand snaked out and caught her fragile wrist. "I don't want the laudanum, Lisette. You can give me something that will kill the pain without numbing the rest of me."

"You mustn't make sudden movements like this, Nicholai. Dr. Wistar says—"

"Dr. Wistar has never been alone with you in a moonlit bed." His hand moved to her elbow, easing her forward.

"You are insane—and *we* are not in bed! Nicholai, you have been seriously injured—" She had to put her other hand on the bed above his shoulder to keep from losing her balance and falling on his wound, but this was just the move Nicholai had hoped she would make. Now her head was close enough for him to reach up easily and slide a hand around her neck. Lisette could not believe what was happening. She saw his eyes, two sparkling emeralds, as he pulled her down slowly until her lips were pressed to his warm mouth. The sensation sent a shock of pleasure through her body. She could feel Nicholai smiling as he kissed her, taking his time, caressing her throat, temples, and unbound curls with his free hand.

"I should have gotten shot long ago," he murmured at last, in a voice heavy with ironic amusement.

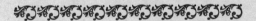

❧ Part Three ❧

Now the pleasant spring allureth,
    And both place and time invites;
Out, alas! What heart endureth
    To disclaim his sweet delights?
        After death, when we are gone,
        Joy and pleasure is there none.

THOMAS LODGE

(1556?–1625)

Chapter 22

April 27, 1793

Meagan leaned forward to look out the window of the post chariot as it turned into the drive leading to the villa. Her smile was more than a little mischievous.

"I wonder how Lisette is faring, now that she no longer has her work to hide behind. Nicholai Beauvisage may be injured, but I'll wager that she's acutely aware of him as a man."

Lion laughed softly and shook his head. "You're a sly minx, my love. Are you sure that you aren't going to all this bother so that Lisette will no longer be susceptible to *my* considerable good looks and charm?"

Turning on him, Meagan made a face and cuffed his arm. "I thought we agreed to forget my momentary derangement! Besides, I happen to like Lisette and I admire her . . ."

"But?"

"Well, she seems to have a tiny blind spot when it comes to men."

"And you are administering a cure?"

"In an indirect and subtle way," Meagan admitted frankly. "Love is difficult enough to discover and then keep . . . I can't see anything wrong with giving Lisette a tiny nudge in the right direction."

As the post chariot drew to a halt, Lion put a hand under his wife's delicate chin and leaned over to kiss her. "You are enchanting," he said sincerely. Meagan's gown of gray satin was set off by a cherry red sash around its raised waistline. Over it, she wore a pelisse of gray uncut velvet with a silken stripe, lined with cherry red satin. The ribbon encircling her neck and the fillet that wound through Meagan's glossy upswept curls were also of cherry red silk. She made a captivating picture as she stepped out of the carriage into the morning sunlight, while Lion went around to fetch a portable deer-hide trunk from the driver.

At that moment, the front door opened and Lisette came out to greet them. Since she had no other clothes, she continued to wear the breeches and shirt, but her hair and skin glowed from recent scrubbing.

"Good morning! So, you are off to Virginia!" Color crept into her cheeks. "I feel a bit strange, welcoming you in your own house. As a matter of fact, I feel a bit strange about a great many things!"

Meagan laughed as though it were all an amusing adventure. "You will adjust, and I'll wager that the change will do you good. Here you can sleep late and read and generally pursue some enjoyable diversions rather than working from dawn until midnight." She looked at Lion.

"Meagan is absolutely right, Lisette," he added hastily, stifling an urge to laugh at his wife's performance. "Think of it as a holiday."

Lisette raised an eyebrow, considering this, and Meagan asked, "But tell us—how is Nicholai? Are you managing all right? Has he been awake at all? Lucid?"

As they went into the entryway, Lisette replied, "He has made amazing progress. He has *definitely* been awake, and never more lucid." Her wry tone suggested that she was leaving much unsaid, but her further explanations divulged only that she had changed Nicholai's dressing, found the wound looking clean, and was able to persude him to take more laudanum only after he was unable to sleep because of the pain. The medicine induced a deeper sleep than Nicholai liked, but Lisette said that at least he seemed peaceful, his color improved.

"I hope you didn't deprive yourself of sleep because of us," scolded Meagan. "We could have tiptoed in and left your trunk, so quietly you would have never known!"

"Frankly, I *was* up most of the night," Lisette admitted. "It must have been three o'clock when Nicholai finally drifted off and I was able to retreat to my own bedchamber. However, my body didn't understand that it was on holiday, because I woke up at exactly the moment I always do, just before dawn." She laughed. "All morning, I felt odd . . . as if I'd forgotten something important. I'm learning that old routines are not easily abandoned!"

"Well, you needn't be concerned for the CoffeeHouse. Last evening, Lion and Alec rounded up three of our best servants to take over your duties. Bramble, our prize cook, is the most disciplined worker I know, so she will manage the kitchen in your place. Pierre, Alec's valet, will join your barman—"

"Stringfellow," Lisette supplied.

"A singular name! So, he and Pierre will take care of the liquor, repairs, and maintenance, all that sort of thing. Nicholai's mother has donated one of her prettiest serving girls to the cause—so you see, with the people you already had, this makes a fine staff!"

Lisette's smile was rather bleak. "I certainly appreciate the trouble you have taken. It's a relief to know that the CoffeeHouse will run smoothly in my absence."

"Mrs. Flowers packed your trunk," Lion told her. "I think she half-suspects that I have spirited you away into a den of lusting men. She asked questions the entire time I was there; her mouth never closed—she even followed me into the street when I left!"

Lisette laughed and felt herself relax as she watched Lion start up the stairs with the trunk.

"It is awfully generous of you to allow us to remain here in your absence," she said to Meagan, who was drifting across the parlor.

"On the contrary! We will be glad to think of the villa with friends inside, keeping the rooms warm and busy. For years, no one lived here; I'll never forget the cobwebs and must, that sad emptiness that hung over this place the first time I saw it. I feel less guilty about leaving since I know you and Nicholai will be here."

"Well, yes, but it will be only for a short while. Nicholai is strong and I'll wager he will be anxious to go home before a fortnight is out." She joined Meagan at the long window overlooking the garden. "By then, I am certain I will be impatient to resume my normal life. . . ."

Meagan saw that Lisette's blue eyes were fastened on the

tangle of spring flowers, so she made a face to vent her exasperation. "You never know . . . you might become spoiled and never want to go back!"

Sensing a tense undercurrent in Meagan's gay voice, Lisette looked over at her for a moment, puzzled. "Spoiled or not, I would have to return anyway—true? My time here is just an interlude . . . like Cinderella at the ball." She smiled. "Nicholai will get well and I will return to work if I want to go on eating, sleeping in a warm bed, and respecting myself."

Meagan literally bit her tongue. Unsolicited advice would only intensify Lisette's stubborn pride. Now that she had brought this reluctant couple together, alone, under one roof, it was up to them to find their own way.

Lisette took a breath as they heard Lion's footsteps on the stairs. "Meagan—I just wanted to ask you . . . do you know someone by the name of Gabrielle?"

Her brow puckered uncertainly. "Pardon?"

"Gabrielle. Does that name mean anything to you? Could it be someone in the Beauvisage family?"

"Why—not that I know of." Her husband came into the parlor and she greeted him with, "Do you know anyone named Gabrielle?"

"Hmmm . . ." He raked a hand through his gold hair, considering the name. "No, I'm afraid not."

"Is it important, Lisette?"

"Oh, no." She felt her cheeks grow warm as they crossed the room to join Lion. "In fact, it probably doesn't mean a thing."

"Well, if there's nothing else, I suppose we should be on our way—" Meagan's voice trailed off. "Mr. Stringfellow assured Lion that he would bring a supply of food out to you, and between the doctor and Nicholai's relatives, I should think you will have no shortage of contacts with the outside world if there is anything you need."

Lion opened the front door and followed the women back into the sunlight. "We insist that you treat the villa as your home, Lisette. There is a well-stocked library for you to enjoy, and you and Nicholai are welcome to the wine and liquor you'll find in the cellarette."

Meagan chimed in to enumerate solutions to any problems that might arise at the villa and locations of various items Lisette and Nicholai might make use of.

"Please, you mustn't worry. We will be fine, and the only thing on your minds should be the wonderful time you will have in Virginia. You certainly deserve a rest from Philadelphia, Senator."

Lion slanted an ironic look at Meagan. "My wife would be the first to agree with you on that point, Lisette! However, I fear that once we arrive at Pecan Grove, *she* will be the one behaving improperly! I have visions of myself spending the next five months trying to keep her off of her equally incorrigible horse!" Although he sighed loudly and gazed heavenward, his ocean blue eyes sparkled.

Joshua, their coachman, leaned down with a question then, and as Lion went up to confer with him, Lisette breathed, "I have never seen such love in a man's eyes! Not just love, but pure enjoyment. How rare! I hope you appreciate how fortunate you are."

Meagan's face burned as she listened to Lisette's awestruck, guileless words. "I can assure you that I shall never allow myself to forget again." She looked at Lion's splendid profile as he listened intently to Joshua's question. "It is good that we are going to Virginia now. Lion needs to put some distance between himself and Marcus. It will take him a long time to sort out his emotions . . . there is more guilt and grief inside of him than even he realizes. But he will resolve his feelings—and I'll do my best to help him."

"Soon he will have the baby to think about," Lisette said encouragingly.

Meagan nodded and absently rested a hand on the curve of her abdomen. "Yes . . . no one ever said that love was easy, but it certainly has its rewards."

"The road is beckoning, my lusty vixen, and we must be off," called Lion. "Say your good-byes."

Lisette and Meagan hugged and promised each other to take care and write a letter when there was news. "The next time I see the Hampshires, there will be three of you!" Lisette said, laughing.

After handing his wife into the carriage, Lion turned back and hooked an arm around Lisette's waist. "I shall miss you and your CoffeeHouse, dear Mistress Hahn." He smiled, then looked her over and shook his head in mock despair. "You must stop being so selfish—hoarding all this beauty! I will see you in autumn . . . and in the meantime, I hope you'll allow yourself to have a bit of fun and . . . dare I say it?" Lion arched a wicked eyebrow and stage-whispered, "Love!"

Lisette laughed as he gave her a last, fond wink and climbed in beside Meagan. After the door was secured and one more round of farewells was exchanged, the yellow post chariot rolled off toward the road to Gray's Ferry.

"Your eyes are full of devils," Lion said to his wife. He stretched out handsome booted legs and loosensed his cravat.

She bit her lip. "Poor Lisette. She doesn't know what she is in for! When I last spoke to Caro and Katya, they were having a wonderful time plotting ways to awaken Lisette's hidden feminine instincts."

He winced. "Please. I don't want to know. By the time Lisette receives the anonymous letter from my banker, she'll be the recipient of so much well-meaning meddling. . . ."

"Lion, what you have done is not meddling!" Meagan struggled out of her pelisse with his help, then lingered in his arms. "That letter from your banker will simply give Lisette a *choice* in the direction she takes in her life. You were right—if Clarissa were here, older and wiser, she would be pleased to see her jewelry used for such a worthy purpose. It can't undo the trouble Marcus caused in Lisette's life, but it can give her something in return."

"Well, it seems perilously close to tampering with fate, but on the other hand, I couldn't have those jewels around . . . and it did seem a proper solution. Rather like Marcus being brought to justice from the grave." Lion rested his tanned cheek on Meagan's lilac-scented ebony curls. "And now, if you don't mind, I would like to leave Lisette and Nicholai and Marcus and Clarissa and the Senate in Philadelphia. Let's spend this journey talking, playing, dreaming about our baby, and—"

"Yes." She turned to lie back in her husband's arms, violet eyes sparkling with mischief. "The 'and,' especially."

Lion bent his head to cover Meagan's sweet lips with his own. Their heated response grew with potent languor, sending currents between their bodies that made Lion think these kisses, forged out of years of struggling love, surpassed those they had shared in the first burst of their passion.

"Oh, Lion . . ." Meagan moaned, "you are cruel to do this when we are only minutes from the ferry." For a moment, as his mouth scorched her throat and the curve of one shoulder, she couldn't breathe.

"Certainly no woman could claim a crueler husband," he agreed in a tone husky with amusement.

"Do you think—oh, don't!—that, since we have conquered the first real crisis of our marriage, now we shall live happily ever after?"

Lion's head rose and one blond eyebrow curved high in his dark forehead. "God, I hope not. What a boring prospect!" His mouth quirked ironically as he regarded Meagan's winsome countenance, and he refrained from kissing her only long enough to add, "I offer Will Shakespeare's opinion as my last word: 'Ay me! For aught that I could ever read, Could ever hear by tale or history, The course of true love never did run smooth. . . .'"

❧ Chapter 23 ❧

April 27, 1793

The aroma of succulent chicken, simmering in a pot over the fire with a crowd of vegetables and herbs, made Lisette's mouth water. She hummed no particular tune as she finished cleaning the sawbuck table. Everything seemed perfect; Nicholai would soon be waking up, the soup smelled wonderful, and she was excessively pleased with her own appearance. Lisette had been a bit surprised to discover that Hyla Flowers had packed the lovely yellow frock for the Hampshires to bring, particularly in light of Hyla's opposition to any romance between Lisette and Nicholai. It would have made more sense if the deer-hide trunk had contained shapeless, raggedy dresses set off by patches.

Standing back to survey the now-immaculate kitchen, Lisette untied her apron and returned it to its hook. Still humming, she went into the hallway, where a beautiful oriental mirror graced one wall. It was difficult for her to acknowledge her own beauty, so instead she looked for needed repairs. Her shiny golden curls were being held up by hidden pins and a white muslin fillet; Lisette was pleased to see that the sprigs of lily of the valley she had inserted were still in place and not dangling precariously. She blushed at herself and returned to the kitchen.

Upstairs, Nicholai was tangled in the sheets, still asleep but slowly finding his way out of the laudanum-induced dreams. Hazy sunbeams filtered into the room to warm his face; eventually the light and heat combined to open one foggy green eye.

"Urrhhh," Nicholai groaned. His shoulder throbbed. He saw the dried blood on the bandages and felt the unpleasant heat that radiated from his wound. "Ahhrr." It seemed that he had been asleep for days. Stiff, damp with sweat, and plagued by burning eyes and a wretched taste in his mouth, Nicholai turned his head away from the bothersome sunlight and tried to go back to sleep.

The door creaked a bit as it opened. The faint, lovely essense of lily of the valley teased Nicholai's nose, then he smelled a heavenly chicken-vegetable-and-spice combination. Curiosity won out over lethargy.

There was Lisette, a tentative expression on her beautiful face, standing a few feet away from the bed. To his sleepy eyes, she was a vision, clad in buttery yellow, tiny white blossoms peeking from an upswept mane of blond curls. The crowning touch to all this aesthetically pleasing loveliness was the tray she held, which contained a china bowl of steaming chicken soup.

"I hope I didn't wake you. . . ." Lisette whispered. "I thought that by this time—"

"I was awake. Not particularly enthusiastic about it, but awake." Nicholai lay back on the pillow and emitted another ill-tempered groan. "My mouth tastes like hell. I'm hot, sweaty, and my muscles ache. All aside from *this*—" He spared a sideways glare for the bandaged shoulder. "You mustn't give me any more laudanum, Lisette. I would rather suffer insomnia than feel so cursed abominable upon waking; and I have my doubts that so much sleep is good for a person."

Placing the tray upon the side table, she perched on the edge of the bed. "I am truly sorry that you feel so wretched. Don't you think this soup should help?"

"I never thought I would see the day when Lisette Hahn would treat me with such solicitous deference. You have missed your calling! You should have been a nurse." Momentarily, a spark flickered in Nicholai's emerald eyes. "To tell you the truth, what I would like best of all is a long, scalding bath. Ahhh . . . I can feel it now. A slave to shave me as I recline, soaking, with my eyes closed—"

"It had better be a slave you can trust—else you might

find the blade slipping accidentally." Lisette stifled mischievous laughter. "Seriously, though, I am certain a bath is out of the question. It has only been a day since you were shot!"

"So it's soup instead, *n'est-ce pas?*"

Lisette felt sorry for Nicholai, but it was difficult to face just how deeply this and other emotions ran. She put a hand on his cheek, softly. "After you have some, I know you will feel much better, and then I will fill the basin with fresh water so that you can wash your face and hands."

"Will you help me with some of the other places I cannot reach?"

Lisette was distinctly relieved by the wicked white flash of his grin. "Incredible nerve. Absolutely not!"

Nicholai rejected her offer to feed him the soup, declaring that they would have it all over the covers and that would finish off his temper. By moving sideways to the far edge of the bed, he was able to spoon up the soup from the bowl on the side table, using his uninjured right arm. While he worked at this, Lisette dashed back to the kitchen to heat water for the basin. Soon she was back in the bedchamber with everything he would need, including a large white linen towel and a bar of sandalwood soap. Nicholai managed to wash and rinse his upper body quite deftly, and after a few moments' consideration, decided to let his beard grow during his convalescence. Lisette had just seated herself on the bed and begun to remove the bandages from his shoulder when a knocking began at the door.

"Who on earth could that be?" she wondered.

"I can think of a dozen answers to that, Mistress Hahn. More, in fact, if one takes into account your devoted clientele from the CoffeeHouse. They have probably arrived in force to take you back where you belong."

Lisette wanted to say, "This is where I belong," but smiled weakly instead and went downstairs. When she opened the front door, she found James Stringfellow and Dr. Wistar standing side by side. Stringfellow cheerfully explained that their paths had crossed for the very first time on the road to Markwood Villa.

"I was just beginning to change Mr. Beauvisage's dressing," Lisette told the doctor, who immediately stated that he would see to the injury and proceeded up the stairs to do just that.

"Now, then!" exclaimed Stringfellow, when he and Lisette were left alone in the entry hall. "You'll be telling me what you are up to, young lady! And I want the truth. If Hyla discovers a false note in the explanation I pass along to her, she'll be out here herself, in two shakes of a lamb's tail, and I cannot believe you relish that prospect!"

"Honestly, Stringfellow, you'd think you and Hyla were responsible for me! It is *I* who pays *your* salaries!"

"That is neither here nor there, as well you know, Lisette. The issue is our honest love for you and concern for your welfare." His eyes darkened with sharp emotion.

"All right, then! You needn't shout at me! It is very simple, really. I felt partially responsible for Mr. Beauvisage's injury. He needed someone to care for him during his recovery and it seemed that I was the only capable person available."

"If you, with a CoffeeHouse to manage, were 'available,' I would love to hear what the others are doing that qualifies them as 'unavailable'!"

"I chose to do this." Lisette's voice was low, final.

"A sense of obligation, eh?"

She examined a tiny chip in her fingernail. "That is correct."

"Blister it!" Stringfellow ejaculated, not altogether angrily. "You are here because you want to be as close to Beauvisage as possible. You're in love with the man, Lisette."

"That is just not true at all!" Her cheeks were flaming. How could he say that to her . . . right to her face?

"If you say so. Just—watch out for yourself, all right? The man is pretty harmless now, but as he begins to regain his strength—"

"I don't appreciate being treated like a child, Stringfellow."

"But, when it comes to love, that's what you are. Try to remember that when the air begins to heat up around here."

"Are you finished?"

"With the advice, yes." He smiled engagingly. "I brought

a wagon full of edible treasures. I'll bring it around to your kitchen door in back and unload." In the doorway, he gave her a chuckle and another smile. "Hyla's behind this. She worries that you will try to subsist on wild berries and infatuation."

Before Lisette could scold him again, Stringfellow darted off to the drive. A few minutes later, they met in the kitchen, and Lisette supervised as the Englishman marched in and out with the armfuls of "supplies." Hyla had even sent out pots that contained stew and applesauce and yams from the day before. All the while, Stringfellow dispensed news of the goings-on at the CoffeeHouse, particularly his opinions of Bramble, Pierre, and Nancy. He claimed to be reserving final judgment on the first two, but had nothing but fond words for Nancy, the little maid contributed by Antonia Beauvisage. Lisette listened with amused surprise as he described her beauty, charm, and pure spirit with fervent admiration.

"It sounds as if life won't be boring at the CoffeeHouse," she commented at last. "Between Hyla and Bramble locking horns and new romances in the air, I doubt that any of you will even have time to miss me!"

"Nonsense!" Stringfellow exploded. "It's you who bloody well won't miss us!"

"How can you say that? If you think I am out here mooning over Mr. Beauvisage—that I have abandoned common sense just because he happens to be a bit handsome and slightly intelligent . . . and moderately quick humored . . . well, you certainly underestimate me, James Stringfellow! Have you ever known me to lose my wits over a man before?"

"That is what worries me, m'dear," Stringfellow said gruffly. "I fear you're long overdue for a gigantic tumble."

Lisette glared. "Are you going to leave the rest of the things outside to spoil?"

He shrugged good-naturedly and exited, only to appear moments later with a large ham. "Do you know, I've a bit of other romantic news for you . . . to take your mind off the self-righteous anger you're building up for me. I may be a bit premature on this . . . but that Pierre fellow—"

"The valet from Belle Maison?"

"The same. I could swear that our own hard-boiled Hyla Flowers has been disposed to blushing overmuch in that Frenchman's company . . . and that he's ruddy well encouraging her!" Seeing Lisette's mouth drop open, he continued, "That's not all! The Hampshires' cook, Bramble, who is as withered and mean as any woman I've known, has been showing signs of irritation at these goings-on between Hyla and Pierre that *could* be interpreted, by a practiced eye, as jealousy!"

Lisette laughed in delight. "All of this sounds very amusing, but I hope that you won't all become so entangled in love affairs that the business of the CoffeeHouse is forgotten! I shudder to think what Bramble could do with a pot of dinner in the midst of an attack of jealousy! Or the sorts of mistakes you could make behind your bar if one wicked eye is following—"

"Nancy," Stringfellow sighed, grinning.

"Hmm. Yes. And Hyla—if she is blushing whenever Pierre glances her way, she will be dropping trays on the most important heads in Philadelphia!"

"If you are so worried, you might be wise to come back to supervise your incompetent staff. . . ."

Lisette's smile faded. "Please, make it easy for me to stay here right now—this is where I am needed most."

Stringfellow came around from behind the table and gave her a kiss. "You know that Hyla and I would give you the moon if we could, Lisette, and we'll bloody well make certain that the others work their hearts out as well."

"I knew that I could depend on you, *Mr.* Stringfellow." She returned his kiss, touching her lips lightly to his, and smiled when he flushed.

"Ahhh-*hem!*" Dr. Wistar cleared his throat so loudly that it sounded like a small explosion.

Startled, Lisette looked up and almost laughed when she realized that he must imagine that she and Stringfellow were engaged in a romantic tête-à-tête.

"Doctor!" She crossed the room to meet him. "Please, tell me, how is our patient?"

Oblivious to the mischievous twinkle in Lisette's eyes,

Wistar frowned. "I have spent several minutes searching for you, Mistress Hahn."

"Why, Doctor, you ought to know that the kitchen is the first place one should search for a woman!" She let an edge of sarcasm sharpen her voice. "Let me pour a glass of claret for you while you bring me up to date on Mr. Beauvisage's condition."

This gesture of hospitality caught Wistar off guard, and he softened somewhat as Lisette held out a goblet of crimson wine. "Well, Mistress Hahn, his physical condition is good enough. I am pleased to see that he has not developed a fever, especially, and to learn that he has been sleeping so long. However, his attitude is not the best. We must work to curb these restless, rebellious tendencies."

Lisette blinked, fighting an urge to smile. "How do you suggest we do that, Doctor?"

"First of all, you must make certain that he takes his dose of laudanum at the proper time. It will help him to get the rest he needs and will keep him quiet and peaceful when he is awake. Honestly, he became so agitated while speaking to me a few minutes ago that the veins in his arms and neck stood out, and that is just what that wound does not need if it is going to heal properly."

"But, Doctor, Mr. Beauvisage doesn't like the effects of the laudanum. He asked me not an hour ago to refrain from giving him any at all, even if he is unable to sleep."

"Is Mr. Beauvisage a physician?"

"Well, obviously not, but—"

"I do not have time to argue this point with you, Mistress Hahn. If you are going to attend Mr. Beauvisage's convalescence, I must insist that you follow my instructions."

Lisette clenched her teeth and tried to look as if she was yielding to his wisdom. "I shall certainly do whatever is best for Mr. Beauvisage, sir."

"Good." He drained the claret, picked up his medical valise, and started toward the door, explaining en route the procedure for changing Nicholai's dressing for the next few days. At the door, they exchanged farewells, and Wistar was halfway along the path to his phaeton when he stopped suddenly.

"Mistress Hahn!" Turning, he shaded his eyes and barked, "Under no circumstances is Mr. Beauvisage to move around the room, and especially not for the purpose of having a *bath*! That stubborn determination of his to do what I will not allow is the very reason why you must make certain that he has his laudanum—even if you have to put it in his tea to get it in his belly!"

Stringfellow came up behind Lisette as the doctor climbed up into his phaeton and started down the drive. He felt a twinge of undefined emotion when he saw the passionate light in her beautiful blue eyes.

"That man!" she cried. "I would feel like a criminal putting laudanum in Nicholai's tea and then watching him sink into that unnatural opium sleep!"

"Well, I don't doubt that the two of you will work out an alternate solution," he said weakly, knowing that Dr. Wistar had wasted his breath. "I should start now if I'm to reach the CoffeeHouse before supper."

"Yes, of course. I can't thank you—and Hyla—enough for bringing all that food . . . and yourself. It was wonderful to see you, Stringfellow. I shall be missing you . . . and everyone else at the CoffeeHouse."

"No more than we are missing you. It's just not the same, Lisette . . . but don't worry. When you come home, you'll be proud of us. You know that Hyla and I would do anything for you, just as we would have for your father. Blister it, you are our family!" He looked down at his buckled shoes, then averted threatening tears by exclaiming, "I'd quite forgotten one of the central reasons for my journey here—" Reaching into his waistcoat, Stringfellow produced a long cream-colored envelope. "This letter came for you this morning. Special messenger from one of the banks; he insisted I deliver it to you without delay."

Lisette was feeling too emotional to pay much attention to the mysterious envelope, and after Stringfellow's departure she absentmindedly carried it along upstairs and deposited it on the table next to Nicholai's bed. She was in the mood for a lively discussion with her patient; ready to repeat Dr. Wistar's impossible instructions, listen to Nicholai's cynical protestations, and finally to work out the "alternate solution" Stringfellow had spoken of.

However, one glance at the bed reminded Lisette that Nicholai was not feeling as well as usual; far from it. It had been only a few minutes since his argument with the doctor, but already his anger had dissipated enough to allow him to fall asleep. He was probably exhausted.

Lisette came around the far side of the four-poster and looked between the parted bed hangings. The window was open slightly to allow the perfumed breeze from the garden to caress the room, and warm gentle sunlight seemed to heighten the spell of spring. Nicholai had pushed away the sheet almost completely. One rumpled corner trailed over his muscular left thigh, across the bulge at the apex of his legs, and stopped an inch from the bone of his right hip. The spareness of the concealment was all the more noticeable because of the contrast between the snowy sheet and the bronzed darkness of Nicholai's body. Burnished by the late-afternoon sun, he looked like one of the Greek gods Lisette had read about in books.

An unnerving current of liquid fire coursed through Lisette's veins, leaving a tingling, hot chill on the skin above as it passed. Wary, yet helpless, she sat on the edge of the bed, afraid to touch him, yet unable to stop herself. First, she brushed her fingertips over the strong back of his hand —so softly that she barely made contact, yet she shivered as if she'd been kissed. Her eyes traveled over every inch of his nearly naked body, remembering the night it had been pressed against her own, steely and tender, magically evoking sensations that Lisette hadn't known herself capable of feeling. Before today, she hadn't allowed herself to think about those hours when she had lost control and begged Nicholai Beauvisage to make love to her . . . until now, the memories had been too painful. Yet, at this moment, she was hungry to recall every scorching kiss, every touch of his fingers, the way her skin had prickled when brushed by the soft hair that covered his chest and legs. Would he ever want to hold her again? She clearly remembered the words that had passed between them just two nights ago . . . she had shouted that she didn't care to be pawed twice in one night . . . and Nicholai's voice rang hauntingly in her mind, its bitter sarcasm intact—"*. . . your aversion to my touch . . .*"

and *"Knowing you has been a charming experience, Mistress Hahn . . . and since this may be good-bye—"*

The last time he had kissed her, his lips had been harsh, and the last time he had looked at her that night, she could have sworn there was hatred in his eyes. It suddenly seemed quite dangerous, this arrangement she had sought. Alone with Nicholai, miles from Philadelphia, she was losing all her defenses. After spending long years building and fortifying them, she was allowing them to crumble away in hours. Nicholai would probably be highly amused if he knew how she melted at the sight of him, how she craved the warmth of his skin and the familiar sardonic gleam in his eye. Staring at his face, Lisette had all she could do to stop herself from tracing the chiseled line of his jaw with kisses and sinking her fingers into his rich chestnut hair.

One eye opened tentatively, then closed. Lisette's cheeks flamed as Nicholai inquired huskily, "Were you staring at me, Mistress Hahn?"

"That's what I like best about you. You are so direct."

One side of his mouth quirked and he opened his eyes again. They were warm with amusement. "Don't tell me. Let me guess. You were struggling to suppress an attack of desire."

Wishing she could crawl under the bed, Lisette managed to retort, "Your conceit is undimmed even by this injury, I see. As a matter of fact, Mr. Beauvisage, I was just about to cover you up so that your mother or sister won't faint with shock if they should happen to pay a surprise visit."

"My mother and sister know what I look like without my clothes." He laughed, but pulled the sheet up to his waist. "At least, they did two dozen years ago."

"No doubt you spent your childhood running about naked!" Lisette said, nodding. Her heart was pounding.

"It certainly took a long time for you to decide how to cover me. Are you certain you weren't having a look yourself?"

"You are revoltingly insolent!" she cried. When he caught her forearm and pulled her over his face, she tried to put up a fight.

"Why don't we be insolent together?"

Their mouths were inches apart when a distant clatter came up from the floor below and a voice called, "Yoo-hoo! Lisette, it's Katya! I have brought two very eager young ladies all the way from Philadelphia to cheer up my brother."

Nicholai released her arm, his eyes sparkling devilishly. "What are you waiting for?" he asked the disconcerted Lisette. "Show in my guests! I am anxious to be cheered up."

❧ *Chapter 24* ❧

May 1, 1793

The candle's tiny flame cast a long, flickering shadow up the parlor wall. Lisette was huddled in one of the red moreen wing chairs, feeling chilly in spite of the quilt that covered her body and the hot tea that warmed her throat. When she paused to think, she knew that the cold came from her heart, yet she felt powerless to remedy it.

A slim volume of Shakespeare lay open in Lisette's lap. Since coming to stay at the villa, she had begun to read and had gradually worked up to the point where she now devoured books from the Hampshire library with ravenous speed. It had been years since she had read so much; there simply wasn't time at the CoffeeHouse for such frivolous pleasures. Now, she compensated for the long drought, and found that other people's stories kept her from constantly thinking about her own tangled life . . . and the enigmatic man who lay in the four-poster bed upstairs.

Evenings were hardest. After supper, Nicholai slept—without laudanum—for at least three hours, then revived for perhaps two before surrendering for the night. He had asked for a book of his own while awake tonight—something by Molière—and Lisette had left him. It wasn't often that he withdrew; usually he was glad to chat or play cards with her. He still teased her in a physical way, but had stopped any serious attempts to kiss her. This made Lisette more melancholy than ever.

The worst part was the parade of female visitors who traveled to the villa to cheer Nicholai up. Lisette seethed whenever she thought of them, simpering and flirting and casting venomous glances in her direction. Heiresses by the handful, from Philadelphia's finest families . . . each one clearly plotting to ensnare the dashing and mysterious Beauvisage. However, they did not irritate her half so much as Nicholai's response to their fawning attentions. He loved their visits! Lisette fumed when she thought of the way he played up to the conniving females . . . kissing their hands, laughing his most irresistible laugh, and apparently oblivious to the nauseating pretense of their personalities. Sometimes, Lisette wondered if it was possible that he behaved this way to nettle her—but considering the undeniable assets of the girls, her basic humility won out and she grew more despondent. The Lisette Hahn who had exuded confidence and easily put Nicholai Beauvisage in his place seemed a stranger lately. Was the sharp, intermittent pleasure of his company worth the pain and confusion she felt when she was alone—or watched him smiling into the excited eyes of Miss Oswald, Miss Chew, or Miss Penn? The thought that she might be one more in a long line of diverting flirtations was almost more than Lisette could bear. What was the truth? Was there anything in her world of which she could be certain?

The tall clock in the hall struck eleven, providing the needed impetus to send Lisette on her way to bed. As she prepared to close the book, her eyes fell on a sonnet that began with a familiar word:

> Love comforteth like sunshine after rain,
> But Lust's effect is tempest after sun;
> Love's gentle spring doth always fresh remain,
> Lust's winter comes ere summer half be done;
>> Love surfeits not. Lust like a glutton dies;
>> Love is all truth, Lust full of forged lies.

An invisible little knife twisted inside Lisette as she wondered which word described her relationship with Nicholai . . . and his feelings for her. Was it possible that this spring would never end for the two of them?

* * *

Clad in a soft, billowy, lawn bed gown, Lisette had just blown out her candle and was crawling between her quilts when she heard a strange sound from Nicholai's room. When she paused, listening, it came again, and she realized that it was Nicholai's voice. Frightened to think that he might be in so much pain that he would cry out, she scrambled off the bed and hurried through the dressing room that connected their bedchambers. Moonlight streamed across the bed, silvering Nicholai's sculpted face and body. Lisette could see that there was fresh blood on the dressings—and her patient was sound asleep. Then, he grimaced, eyes still closed, and whispered something. Was it "Gabrielle"? It alarmed her, the idea that another woman could mean so much to Nicholai that he would be unable to sleep because of her presence in his dreams.

There was real pain in his expression. Convulsively, he turned to the left and nearly rolled over on his wounded shoulder.

"Nicholai!" Lisette whispered loudly, crouching beside him on the bed, gripping his arms in an effort to keep him from complicating his injury. "Wake up! You are having a nightmare."

Gradually, he awoke. Lisette saw the volume of Molière caught in the sheet and pushed it aside; the obvious intensity of Nicholai's emotions swept away her own inhibitions. She held him fast, carefully avoiding the bandaged shoulder, and soothed him back to reality with the soft words her mother had spoken when Lisette had been plagued with bad dreams during the long-ago voyage to America.

After a few minutes, she knew he was awake and free of the nightmare. Lisette was embarrassed to find herself molded to the side of his hard body, his good arm around her back, her face against his hair.

"Are you all right? You frightened me, dreaming that way."

"Thank you for waking me," he replied in a low hoarse voice. "It was the Molière. I shouldn't have read it."

"Won't you tell me what you were dreaming that could upset you so?"

His face turned, nose and mouth pressing into the bottom

of her cheek and the side of her jaw. She could feel his heart beating against her breasts, the pulse of his blood flowing in the arm that circled her back, the gradual uncoiling of tense muscles in his legs. It almost seemed that their bodies were joined, and that sensation flooded Lisette with pleasure.

"It . . . isn't relevant to my life anymore. I don't think it would do any good to discuss it further."

"What a cowardly attitude!" Lisette whispered the words affectionately. "I think whatever it is must be very relevant if it is keeping you awake—or trying to—and if you reopen that shoulder wound, we won't be able to lightly dismiss your nightmare, will we?"

"I don't know if I should talk to you about this . . ." His voice held a weary note, as if he wished to avoid the conflict he felt Gabrielle might bring into his relationship with Lisette. It was already impossibly snarled. . . .

"Because of the woman? Gabrielle?" She spoke these few words as triumphantly as a cardplayer who suddenly lays down four aces. "You should know that I am bright enough to realize that you did not live in a monastery during your years in France, Nicholai."

A few minutes passed before Nicholai replied. The silence was thick, yet pleasurable somehow because they were embracing and seemingly caring for each other. "All right," he said at last, "I would like to tell you about Gabrielle and the things that happened to me in France. I suppose it is foolish and unrealistic for me to believe that I can shut the door on the past. Ghosts have a way of slipping through, don't they?"

"Yes," Lisette whispered sadly. "Inevitably."

Word by word, Nicholai revealed the events that connected to form his dozen years in France, inserting the characters who had affected his life. "It began so beautifully. The Loire Valley is like paradise . . . I'll never forget my first spring at the château. I felt, from the first moment, that I had found my true home. I slipped into the French language and culture as easily as a suit of clothes tailored just for me. I loved it, and I loved the vineyards . . . learning, growing, creating better and better wines."

Lisette's heart ached as she thought of him: young, filled with enthusiasm and energy for his new life, finding his niche . . . and then losing it all to the insanity of the Revolution. "I'm surprised you didn't marry."

He was silent for a minute, his eyes fixed on the flat ivory canopy. "For a long time, I was too busy and too far from Paris to meet very many eligible women. Not that there weren't some very diverting females close to the château— but they were either married to aged noblemen or were milkmaids; neither type was the sort of girl I wanted for a lifelong companion. Also, I wasn't really mature enough to be married myself until a few years ago, and by then I had become involved with Gabrielle."

"But you didn't marry her?" Lisette queried, and watched Nicholai's face as he smiled grimly in the darkness. "Please," she pressed. "I cannot bear the suspense."

Nicholai was sensitive to her tone, and it surprised him. "No, we didn't marry because her brother, a destitute marquis, arranged for her to wed a well-to-do *comte*. Gabrielle acquiesced, although by then we were in love, because she felt responsibility to her family. Unfortunately, it turned out to be a bad time to be an aristocrat, especially when doubled by marriage." He went on to sketch his first meeting with Gabrielle, five years before at Versailles, and though he tried to describe her looks and personality, he was kind enough to spare Lisette the details of Gabrielle's bewitching beauty.

"Well, I can't imagine being in love with one man and allowing myself to be forced to marry someone else. It sounds like a nightmare." Lisette's tone was disapproving.

"You have made a number of sacrifices in your own life, my sweet—for that CoffeeHouse, which isn't even alive."

"To me, it is," she argued. "Anyway, how could *she* give you up so easily if she loved you?" Lisette was incredulous at the thought of sacrificing Nicholai's love for any reason.

"Well, she didn't give me up. In France, such matters are more easily arranged and accepted. Gabrielle made frequent trips to my château, and we met elsewhere when her husband was occupied in Paris."

Lisette stiffened, noiselessly fighting for breath. Pictures of Nicholai engaging in a torrid, daring affair with *la belle comtesse* seared her brain. "She must have truly loved you, then, to have taken such risks."

"I . . . don't know about that. Part of the fascination Gabrielle held for me was her inscrutable personality. I never could be sure what she was thinking or feeling; somehow, even when she was in my arms, she seemed to be just out of reach."

Considering the way most women buzzed around Nicholai like anxious bees, Lisette found it easy to understand his fascination. Finally, she asked him about the Revolution and Gabrielle's fate, and painstakingly he revealed what those years had held for him . . . and for his exquisite lover. Lisette heard his voice grow choked with pain as he described the September Massacres, and the last time he had seen Gabrielle—the hot August night when they had been forced into separate prison wagons.

"Then she might still be alive!" she cried, softly reassuring.

"Lisette, I spent almost five months searching for some sign of her survival—even though I knew the odds were one million to one against it. If not for my freak accidental meeting with Robespierre and his recollection of me from the Estates General, I would have been a victim of the September Massacres myself—just like every other person who shared my prison wagon. What chance for escape did Gabrielle have? The sister of a marquis and the wife of a *comte*?" Nicholai's voice was bitterly ragged.

"I see now why she haunts your dreams," Lisette whispered.

"Sometimes I dream that she is being tortured—" His voice broke off. "But it doesn't help anyone for me to brood about it. I cannot undo the brutal bloodshed of the Revolution . . . the insanity of it. I will always be a victim of what I saw, heard, felt . . . but at least I am alive, and I don't intend to spend the rest of my days with tears in my eyes."

In the silvery shadows, Lisette saw Nicholai draw a bare forearm roughly across his face. The thought of him actually crying devastated her; worse, there was nothing she could do to lessen his pain. Jealousy was forgotten as Lisette gently kissed Nicholai's lips and cradled his strong dark head against her own cheek and throat. She caressed his temples, slowly and soothingly, until he slept again.

Chapter 25

May 5, 1793

It was a glorious day. Lisette wanted to sing along with the birds as she inhaled the fragrant sunny air and regarded the brilliant mosaic of flower beds. Following the maze of brick footpaths deeper into the garden, she paused under a giant weeping willow and set up her easel. It almost made her laugh when she thought of the difference between the way she had spent these recent May afternoons and those of other years. Spring seemed a new phenomenon to her . . . even the sunlight and the blue sky were more vivid than she had ever imagined during her long hours at work in the CoffeeHouse.

Carefully, she unwrapped a clean canvas and propped it on the easel. Next, she unlatched a wooden box filled with oil paints of every color imaginable. Katya had brought the painting supplies, remembering an idle wish Lisette had expressed the year before that she might one day have time to pursue such an avocation. Yesterday, she and Nicholai had discussed a related subject at length: Lisette's hidden talents. He suggested that she might find satisfaction in other ways besides working night and day. She was a woman of many talents, which were only now being tapped. Nicholai pointed out the insatiable enthusiasm with which she attacked literature and now art. Wasn't it a shame to extinguish these lights for the sole purpose of financial independence? Of course, he hadn't offered her any other solution.

The serenity and happiness of her life at the villa made Lisette feel that she was existing outside of the real world.

She would crash back down to earth only when some unwelcome visitor arrived to cheer up Nicholai. Even he seemed surprised by the quantity of women who were in competition for his attention, yet he played along gamely and Lisette grew increasingly frustrated. As if sensing her situation, Antonia had arrived a day ago with an entire trunk full of beautiful gauzy muslin gowns, which, she explained, belonged to her daughter Danielle. Rather than pack whenever she traveled to Philadelphia for a visit, the wealthy Mrs. Engelman kept an entire wardrobe at her mother's house. The oldest Beauvisage child was tall and slender like Lisette and the gowns fit as if they had been made just for her. The one she wore today blended perfectly with the willow tree and the two long rows of huge white lilies that swayed in the breeze behind her. Fashioned of white muslin, the frock was cut deeply at the neckline to display Lisette's seldom-seen and lushly curved breasts. Under the bodice ran a sash of cool green satin; the ends of the long slim sleeves were also edged in green. In her hair, Lisette wore a fillet of emerald-and-white-striped silk that contrasted beautifully with her loose randomly arranged curls, upswept to accentuate her elegant neck. It too was trimmed by a thin choker of green satin.

Just as she finished setting up her paints and allowed herself a glance toward the upstairs window, where curtains fluttered reassuringly, a voice broke the stillness of the garden and sent Lisette's heart drumming with startled shock.

"You are looking extraordinarily beautiful today, Mistress Hahn."

She stood, frozen, thinking that it simply could not be Nicholai; that was impossible—so who was this strange man who spoke from somewhere behind her?

"I had expected a warmer greeting . . . at least a few memorable words if you cannot manage anything physical."

It was Nicholai! Afraid to look, she turned slowly and found him leaning against a nearby honey locust tree with all the nonchalance of someone who spent every afternoon chatting with her in the garden. Lisette gasped. He wore snug buckskin breeches, the knee boots she had set in the kitchen to wait for their owner, and the white linen shirt she had soaked for two days to remove the bloodstains.

Nicholai's smile was wry, and his auburn gold hair, casually combed, gleamed in the sunlight.

"I would say that I am seeing a ghost . . . except, in your case, anything is possible," Lisette said hollowly. "I suppose I must assume that you have lost your senses."

He chuckled. "Oh. I see."

Her tenuous control slipped. "Are you mad, Nicholai? Do you want to kill yourself? After all the hours I have spent changing your dressings, watching you like a little child to make certain that you don't move too vigorously— and I even took the responsibility on myself to disregard Dr. Wistar's orders about the laudanum because I believed that, between the two of us, we might muster the necessary maturity to keep you quiet until that wound had healed sufficiently—"

"My ears hurt more than my shoulder!" Nicholai laughed. "Did it ever occur to you that I might have the good doctor's permission to come outside?"

"What do you mean?"

"Only that Dr. Wistar arrived while you were downstairs assembling your paints and he gave me the authorization to make the daring journey out the back door into the wilds of the garden."

"How do I know you are telling the truth?" Lisette asked warily.

"Come over here." Nicholai watched with less amusement as she approached, skirting the honey-locust tree uncertainly. "Here! I want you to look me in the eye."

"You aren't going to challenge me to a duel, I hope?"

He caught her slim arm so that their bodies touched, her muslin bodice brushing his linen shirt. "I ought to, wench! Look at me, Lisette, and see that, although I am not angry with you, I find no humor in being treated like a dishonest little boy. You aren't my mother . . . and if I choose to come into the garden—even *without* Dr. Wistar's approval —I shall damn well do so and there isn't a thing you could do about it! It is my body, not yours or the good doctor's, and I shall abuse it however the hell I please!"

"Well, then, why have I wasted my valuable time taking care of you? I should have let you jump out the window that first night, or leap out of bed and run back to Philadelphia into the waiting arms of all your sophisticated strumpets—"

Nicholai's lips twitched with delight; his emerald eyes sparkled. "Why didn't you, then?"

Lisette looked away, displaying her delicately etched profile, complete with long soft eyelashes that glistened with gold dust in the sun. "I don't know." Her voice was not quite cold enough to fool Nicholai.

"I do." His arm, curving slowly around her waist, burned through the thin white fabric of her gown. "You stayed because you love being here. You have had an excuse to play and be a woman without having to apologize for it . . . and you enjoy spending your time with a man, even one who is incapacitated—or perhaps *especially* one who is incapacitated." Nicholai's warm breath touched Lisette's brow tantalizingly. She was unnerved by the sensation of her nipples hardening visibly against her bodice, while her heart thumped so loudly she was certain Nicholai must hear it. "No angry retort?" he mocked. "No slap across my insolent mouth?"

"I am paralyzed with shock," murmured Lisette at length. "Honestly, your nerve . . ."

"Thrilling, eh? Let me give you fair warning, my beautiful, independent Mistress Hahn: *my* days of incapacitation are at an end. No longer will I be at your mercy, having to take an extra spoonful of soup when you hold it up to my mouth. As a matter of fact, there is something else entirely that I have been working up a powerful appetite for these past days. Weeks, actually." One chestnut brow arched satanically. "I realize that you think you are as strong as any man, but if you stay around here to test that theory, the results may surprise you."

"Is that a hint? Would you like me to leave so that you can import a more willing victim?"

He laughed softly and tightened his embrace. "On the contrary, my dear. I may play the gentleman and give you fair warning, but I certainly don't expect you to pay any attention to it! If you did"—his voice dropped to a dramatic bass for the next three words—"my *manly ego* would never recover."

Nicholai was so impudent that Lisette found it difficult to

feign outrage. Laughter and desire rose in her breasts; she opened her mouth to scold him, and warm hard lips came down to silence her. Lisette melted, then simmered helplessly in his arms. Boldly, Nicholai's tongue explored the softness of her mouth, sending little explosions to the parts of her body that had lain dormant since the last time they had kissed.

"Ahh-*hem!* Mistress Hahn! Is it possible that you are trying to reopen Mister Beauvisage's wound?"

Lisette's arms fell away from Nicholai's shoulders; she stepped backward, stumbled, and felt him reach out to catch her forearm. Dr. Wistar, his chin sternly lowered, was advancing toward them on the brick footpath.

"I only came back because I thought it might be prudent to confer with you regarding my decision to allow Mr. Beauvisage to leave his bed, just so there was no danger of my instructions being embellished." He cast a disapproving eye toward Nicholai, then returned his attention to the pale Lisette. "I can see, however, that *you* do not know the meaning of the word prudence! Furthermore, I strongly suspect that you ignored my instructions regarding Mr. Beauvisage's dose of laudanum! If you had administered it as I specified, it is highly doubtful that he would be so frisky this soon after his injury. I had hoped for at least another week of bed rest, but it is impossible to reason with him or to modify his energy. So, Mistress Hahn, I will leave you two to your—activities. I must warn you, however, that if Mr. Beauvisage should suffer a relapse, *you* will bear the responsibility!"

Nicholai released Lisette's arm and took a few steps toward Dr. Wistar. "I am not interested in wasting my time arguing with you, Doctor, but I do feel compelled to ask you never to speak to Mistress Hahn that way again. You have been unpardonably rude to a young lady who has sacrificed a great deal to care for me night and day at a time when my life depended on it."

"Hmm!" Dr. Wistar pursed his lips.

"Please don't hurry off before you've apologized," Nicholai murmured, smiling coldly.

The doctor blinked. "Well. I may have been a bit hasty."

He wet his lips. "I am sorry if I judged you too harshly, Mistress Hahn."

"You are forgiven, Doctor." Lisette repressed an urge to giggle. "Please, allow me to accompany you to your phaeton so that we may discuss Mr. Beauvisage's progress." She looked at Nicholai. "*You* go and sit down and behave yourself until I return."

He gave her a short amused bow. "As always, I obey, my lady."

Lisette pretended not to hear the high voice calling from the front of the villa. She resented any interruption of the serene enjoyment she and Nicholai had found in each other's company this afternoon. *Content* would have described her mood if not for the undercurrents of yearning that ran between them.

Two trays crowded with empty dishes occupied the stone bench at the end of the garden; between them reposed a long green bottle that had been filled with Burgundy wine just an hour earlier. Now Lisette and Nicholai were under the drooping willow. He was reclined against the trunk, his booted legs stretched out gracefully on the grass, tousled head tipped back. She, intent on capturing the line of his shoulder with her paintbrush, wondered if he was asleep. If he was, she could risk ignoring the female voice that persisted in calling from the drive.

"Lisette," mumbled Nicholai, "for God's sake, go and see who is out there." His eyes remained closed.

Lisette wanted to tell him to do his own investigating, and when she went through the house and discovered Anne Bingham and a girl who looked like a wren standing outside the front door, she wished she had.

"How do you do?" Mrs. Bingham began, putting up her lovely nose. "You must be Mistress Hahn . . . ? I have heard such admirable reports about your attempt to continue with the CoffeeHouse after your father's unfortunate death."

"I wouldn't use the word 'attempt,' Mrs. Bingham. I have been completely successful."

"Of course you have, my dear." Her smile was wooden.

"I would like you to meet my cousin, Ophelia Corkstall. She is visiting us from Britain, and has become exceedingly well acquainted with Mr. Beauvisage. We were out for a drive and just decided—very impulsively!—to pay a visit and let Mr. Beauvisage know how much Ophelia has missed him in Philadelphia of late."

Lisette exchanged strained pleasantries with Ophelia, who blushed and tittered at the mention of Nicholai's name. Feeling certain that her patient would not welcome this particular female guest, Lisette took wicked pleasure in showing Mrs. Bingham and her cousin back to the garden.

They found Nicholai pretending to touch up Lisette's painting; his eyes were full of mischief as he held the paint-brush in the air and tossed a nonchalant glance over his shoulder at them.

"Why, Nicholai Beauvisage, I didn't know you were a painter!" exclaimed Anne Bingham.

He shrugged modestly, put down the brush, and turned to kiss her slim, pale hand. "There are many things you don't know about me, Mrs. Bingham." He turned his attention to Ophelia, who was looking especially like a wood thrush in her taupe gown and concealing fichu. "Ah, Mistress Corkstall, how are you? I have sorely missed our discussions about the House of Bourbon!"

Lisette gaped as she watched Nicholai press his lips to the girl's hand for an indecent length of time. She could have sworn he was watching her from the corner of one twinkling eye, but this seemed to be conceit on her part. It was more likely that the rogue went through life gazing at each woman he met as if she were the most ravishing and fascinating female in the world. After a few eternally long minutes, Lisette fabricated an excuse and took their luncheon trays back to the kitchen. By the time she heard the carriage, which was pulled by four perfectly matched grays, roll down the drive, she was in her own bedchamber behind closed doors, furiously mending a torn chemise.

After a few more minutes, Lisette heard Nicholai slowly ascend the stairway and come down the hall. Moments later, there was a knock on the connecting door between their rooms.

"Lisette—is there something wrong?"

"How could you possibly imagine that anything could be wrong?" She aimed for indifference, but heard the sarcasm that dripped from each word.

"Please, open the door."

She prayed for the strength to resist his eyes, the expression on his face, the powerful physical tug of his body, and opened the door . . . just a tiny bit. "What do you want?"

"I didn't expect you to react this way, Lisette. I was just having fun in what would have been an intolerably dull situation—"

"React *what* way?" she demanded.

There was a note of challenge in her voice and it sparked anger in Nicholai. The little vixen was going to start fighting with him and deny what he *knew* to be true! "I shouldn't have to tell you," he replied smoothly. "You ought to be old enough to know when you are jealous."

"*Jealous?*" she cried. "There is simply no end to your conceit, is there?"

"Perhaps not, but that isn't the issue, Lisette! Are you going to tell me that you rushed up here to sulk because you needed a nap? It was perfectly obvious—"

"It was perfectly obvious to *me* that you were flirting with that poor Corkstall girl only to gratify your ego, Mr. Beauvisage, and I simply decided I had better ways to spend my time than watching you make a fool of her."

"Lisette—"

She began to close the door, but he put out his hand to brace it open.

"Lisette, you are going to ruin a wonderful day with your damned stubbornness. If you will just talk to me about this—"

"Get your hand out of the way!" She was sounding a bit hysterical.

"Look, Dr. Wistar said I could have a bath today, but I need your help to—"

"Oh! So you are just apologizing because you need me for your silly bath!" With a sudden burst of rage, she threw herself against the door and heard it click shut. "I hope you smell! I hope you rot!"

Nicholai did not attempt to reopen the door. "All right, you little she-wolf, I don't need to be beaten over the head with it. You've made your point."

Lisette heard him cross to his own room; total silence followed. After turning the key in the lock, she wondered why the taste of victory was so sour.

✵❧ *Chapter 26* ❧✵

May 6, 1793

The sunrise was spellbinding, but Lisette had been unable to appreciate it. It seemed that she had scarcely closed her eyes all night; she was consumed with misery over her quarrel with Nicholai, particularly because he had made no further move to smooth things over between them. Curled up, cold, and hurting in her bed as the new day began, Lisette realized that it was up to her to approach him. He was right; she had been jealous, and unreasonably childish.

The depth of her pain over this rift between them didn't alarm her as she had expected it to. Somehow she had changed a great deal since she had intervened in the duel. It had become impossible for her to maintain the distance between herself and the emotions that she had guarded so closely in the past. What surprised Lisette most was the realization that she wasn't frightened by the thought of loving Nicholai . . . but when she imagined him not returning her love, or simply losing interest in their flirtation, she was terrified.

Lisette dressed carefully, drank tea in the cool violet-shadowed kitchen, then prepared Nicholai's favorite breakfast of croissants, studded with raisins and drizzled with icing, paired with perfectly timed fried eggs. For good measure, Lisette added several strips of crisp bacon.

It was still early when she carried the tray upstairs, but the suspense had grown intolerable. If Nicholai had become so fed up with her that their friendship was beyond repair, Lisette decided that it was better to know now. She found him awake, propped against the pillows and staring broodingly out at the pastel morning. Blue smoke rose in curly wisps from the cheroot Nicholai held between his thumb and forefinger.

Lisette's heart turned over as she came close enough to discern the spot of blood on his bandage and the somber, sad expression on Nicholai's face. It reminded her of the way she had felt while lying awake in her own bed.

"I brought you breakfast."

His eyes flickered in her direction and he drew on the cheroot before replying, "I am not hungry."

"There are croissants." Lisette wondered briefly at her own meek voice. She couldn't remember ever hearing that particular tone, but wasn't ashamed to hear it now.

"I don't care for any."

Was he sulking to pay her back for her own pout yesterday? No. She sensed that he would never do such a thing— and the brief glimpses she had of his eyes told her this mood was deadly serious and not contrived.

"Nicholai? Could I talk to you for a few minutes?"

He nodded and moved to make room for her on the bed.

"I'm so sorry about yesterday." Her voice almost broke; she let her hands creep into his large tanned ones and stared down at them as she spoke. "I behaved like a baby. A silly *girl,* which is something I never expected to become—"

"A girl?" Nicholai echoed, letting the smile sneak through his black mood.

"You know what I mean—a childish, lovesick brat."

"An apology from Lisette Hahn," he marveled softly. "Are you aware of how much you have changed? You needn't fear your femininity, Lisette . . . I know that it must be difficult for you to let it come out, but that doesn't alter the fact that it has been inside of you all along—ill concealed by your charming displays of bravura." He tipped her chin up and traced the outline of her face with eyes that seemed crowded with secrets. "Is it true, Lisette? Are you lovesick?"

She couldn't breathe. Panic paralyzed her. Lisette wondered wildly what she should do and say. Could she admit the truth?

"Shh. It's all right." Nicholai's strong hands slid over the blue-sprigged muslin of her sleeves, across her fragile shoulders, and up the bare softness of Lisette's slim neck. They both moved forward until Nicholai's mouth covered her own with such expert tenderness that she gave a smothered gasp. When his fingers worked the fastenings of her bodice, she began to tremble, then shuddered as warm hands covered her eager breasts.

"Oh—I don't—" Her mouth seemed bruised already, yet she was ravenous for more kisses.

"Shh. Relax," Nicholai whispered huskily against her croissant-scented curls, easing Lisette back with him into the deep soft pillows.

Knock-knock.

Nicholai grazed Lisette's neck with scorching kisses.

Knock-knock-KNOCK!

She broke away, flushed and breathing quickly. "Stop! Someone is at the door!"

"I couldn't care less."

"It could be your mother, or Dr. Wistar—or the Hampshires! They could walk right in!"

"Lisette—"

She was already scrambling up, trying to fasten her bodice, tears stinging her eyes. Nicholai let out a groan, then capitulated and reached up to brush away her clumsy fingers. Moments later, modesty restored and curls hastily repinned, Lisette flew out of the room and down the stairs. When she returned, she was accompanied by Katya, Randolph, and a young man Nicholai had never seen before.

"Ah, good morning!" He welcomed them acidly, waving a hand at the plate of croissants. "Breakfast, anyone?"

It developed that Randolph's friend, an earnest young man named Hugo Kingsley, bred horses only a few miles away and had invited Katya and Randolph down for the day. Katya thought it would be just the thing for Lisette to get away from the villa for a few hours, so they had come to plead with her to join them.

"Oh, no, I couldn't possibly leave Nicholai—" Lisette objected lamely.

"But Nicky looks as if he is doing splendidly," argued Katya, "and I'm sure you must be thoroughly sick of the sight of his face."

"What is wrong with my face?" Nicholai pretended to be insulted. "Besides, Lisette is giving me a bath today."

Lisette went crimson and let out a shocked croak. "But —I'm not *giving* him the bath, just—"

"Oh, well, if that's all it is, Randolph and I could do that, couldn't we, Randolph?" Smiling sweetly, Katya patted her fiancé's arm. "I would much rather see Lisette get out and breathe the open air, away from this *sick*room, and I know Hugo will be delighted to entertain her."

"By all means!" said Hugo brightly. "Delighted!"

Realizing how neatly his sister had cornered them, Nicholai grimaced satirically and said to Lisette, "Have a *wonderful* time, Mistress Hahn."

By the time Lisette managed to return to the villa, night had almost blackened out the sky. Hugo's aunt and uncle had been at the farm as well, and Lisette had been maneuvered into helping the forceful woman cook supper, then staying to eat her share. Knowing that Katya and Randolph had driven down in their own chaise, she was certain they would be gone, and indeed they were—but another vehicle was occupying the position vacated by Randolph's. Lisette's heart sank. She tried to smile as she told Hugo good-bye and suffered his kiss on her cheek. Doubtless he thought this was aggressive behavior on his part, for, drawing back, he seemed to wink at Lisette. She, however, could only think for the thousandth time that day that Nicholai Beauvisage was radically unlike any other mortal man she had ever known. It wasn't magic or illusion after all—her day with Hugo Kingsley swept away all doubts on that score.

From the doorway, Lisette waved at the departing chaise, wondering how she could really believe that a man as splendid as Nicholai could have any permanent interest in someone as imperfect as she. Was he only pretending to find her enchanting and desirable until she let him make love to her again? Would his enthusiasm wane when the challenge disappeared?

Stepping into the entryway, she heard voices but not words. Recognizing the female pitch of one of them, her heart sank. Not again! There seemed to be only the two people speaking—Nicholai and another overeager woman. Mustering her old outspoken assertiveness, Lisette strode up the stairs, into her own room, and knocked on the connecting door. That seemed good for dramatic effect; let the hussy know Lisette had a more intimate access to Nicholai's bedchamber than the hallway.

"Excuse me"—she swept into the room—"I thought you would be anxious to know I am back. I am sorry to be so late! Have you had supper, Nicholai?" Barely sparing a glance for his visitor, she started to circle the bed, then stopped, frozen.

"Well, well, Mistress Hahn . . . we meet again," cooed Amelia Purdy. She stood against the window, just a few feet from Nicholai, the curtains fluttering about her ebony curls, ivory-complexioned face, and pink satin gown. "How good of you to play nursemaid to my Nicholai!"

Stricken, Lisette couldn't think what to do, how to behave. She fixed pleading eyes on Nicholai, who was dressed and sitting on the cream comforter, several plump pillows against his back. Was it her imagination, or did he look upset—even irritated?

"Look, Lisette—" he began.

"Did you have your bath?" she interrupted. "I hope you were sensible and let Randolph wash your hair rather than trying to yourself. The strain on your shoulder——"

"No, I didn't have my bath. I sent them away. And, Lisette . . . I would appreciate it if you would leave Mrs. Purdy and me alone for a few minutes." Nicholai's voice was even, his face unreadable.

Lisette almost flinched; she felt as if he had stood and struck her across the face. Somehow she managed to turn and walk out of the room, her back as straight as it had been while working in the CoffeeHouse the day after Ernst Hahn's death and her own loss of maidenhood.

Nicholai waited until he heard her footsteps descending the stairs before returning his attention to Amelia Purdy. The expression on her face was somewhere between a smirk and panic.

"I wonder what sort of condition you will leave that girl in when you discard her?"

"Amelia, you ought to know by now that I won't be baited—especially by someone as pathetically obvious as you are."

"Well, it is clear to me what's going on out here, and just as clear that you are only putting me to one side until you tire of her uninspired bed games." She bit her full lower lip. "Or am I wrong? Are you going to marry the tavern maid? Do you know that they call her the golden rose? Because of all those thorns concealed by her beauty. I've heard she is approximately as passionate as a block of ice!"

"That's enough, Amelia. I know this may be difficult for you to comprehend, but I am asking you to stay out of my life because there is no future for us . . . and the past shouldn't have happened either. Go home to your husband. Put your energies into pleasing *him* in bed, and you just might find out what you've been missing in life."

She was ready to show Nicholai what *he* would be missing in *his* bed, but when she had taken two steps toward the bed the chiseled contempt of his face stopped her.

"Fine! The city of Philadelphia is filled with men who would give their right arms for a night in my bed, Nicholai Beauvisage . . . and I'll wager that after a few days or weeks with the Austrian ice maiden you will be among them!"

Nicholai looked bored as he examined his sleeve for lint. "Good-bye, Amelia."

The door threatened to crack in two when she slammed it; Nicholai spared a wry smile for the drama of her exit. He decided to wait a few minutes until Amelia was far away and Lisette had an opportunity to calm down before he went to look for her. With luck, she would spare him the effort. Closing his eyes, he remembered the intoxicating sweetness of the kiss they had shared that morning. Not only did every inch of his body ache for her, but the anticipation of making love to Lisette was warmed by a deeper glow than he had ever felt before. Nicholai knew that he yearned for more than her firm breasts and delicious mouth. When they kissed, they exchanged something warm and intangible. He had a sense of the complexity of her personality—the web of emotions and budding desires, curiosities, and anxieties that clung together within her. Tonight, he wanted to hold all of Lisette in his arms and speak to her with not only his body, but his heart as well.

Irritating tears stung Lisette's eyes as she set the little deer-hide trunk on her bed with a soft thud. The room was dark and cold, which suited her mood. Stalking across to the armoire, she threw open the door and began to pull out the pretty gowns Antonia had brought to the villa. When she took them back and deposited them next to the tiny trunk, her frustration only mounted.

"Lisette?" a muted, drowsy voice called from the next room. "Could you come here for a moment?"

She stood still briefly, then crossed the rug and opened the door, just to be certain her words had the proper impact. "I would sooner jump off the roof, *Mr*. Beauvisage!" Lisette shouted into the shadows before returning to her bed. Carefully, she picked the yellow gown out of the cluster of fabrics and folded it neatly. Into the trunk it went, using up nearly all the space.

Nicholai appeared, leaning against the door frame. She couldn't bear to look at his adorably sleepy face and ruffled auburn hair.

"What on earth?" he muttered hoarsely. "If you must behave like a madwoman, couldn't we at least have a proper fire? Perhaps you have frostbite—"

"Don't you touch my fireplace!" screamed Lisette. Suddenly, blinking back tears, she snatched at his sister's gowns and threw them at Nicholai with all her might. They made strange bright puddles on the rug several feet from where he stood.

Nicholai rubbed his eyes and peered at her. "Have you been into the wine?"

"I'm warning you! Don't come near me!" She brandished a little hard-heeled slipper.

"What?" Nicholai looked around as if expecting to find a threatening stranger behind himself. "I hadn't—"

"I can guess!" cried Lisette illogically. Then, to her own surprise, her face crumpled and out of her mouth came a great hiccuping sob.

"Please . . ." he soothed, "if you are seriously planning to leave me here on my own, I hope you will at least spare me a few minutes to discuss this decision. Come into my room, where it is warmer."

Lisette saw Nicholai hold out his hand to her and found herself trusting the expression on his face. Something in his eyes told her that he cared about more than luring her into his bed—though she was certain he had not ruled that out as an objective! It was difficult to resist the allure of Nicholai's body, chiseled against the darkness, or the irrepressible flash of white when he smiled. Lisette stepped forward, slipped her hand into the warm strength of his, and went along into the adjoining bedchamber.

The fire was burning softly, so Nicholai added a log and some encouragement with the poker before turning his attention to Lisette. To his consternation, he found her seated in a chair, rather than on the bed where she usually perched. Biting his tongue, he plumped up the pillows and lit a cheroot, then stretched out on the counterpane. The weak candle and firelight left the distance between him and Lisette filled with gray shadows.

"Well?" she asked stiffly.

"What do you mean, 'Well?'! You're the one who's been throwing clothes around the room and shouting at me. Before you storm off into the night, I would appreciate some semblance of a rational explanation." Narrowing his eyes, Nicholai drew on the cheroot and tried to assess her true mood and feelings.

"Incredible! This may come as a shock to you, Mr. Beauvisage, but I don't owe you anything, least of all an explanation, and you should be grateful that I have been so dull witted until now!"

"I hope you intend to elaborate on that last comment; I am breathless with curiosity."

Lisette could almost see the cynical gleam in his eyes. The distance and the shadows couldn't disguise Nicholai. "I cannot believe that you aren't shrewd enough to understand just what I mean. I have stood by like a *fool*, smiling and slaving for a fortnight, while those silly girls have paraded in and out. You did all that you could to encourage them—flirting and leading them on—grinning when they blushed—" Her voice was rising; realizing how she must sound, she broke off and took a deep breath. "I should have left you to them days ago—let them cook and clean for you, change your bandages and sit up through the night with you—"

"Are you going to make me drag my frail maimed body all the way over there, or will you come and sit beside me?" Nicholai's voice was softly neutral; he was astounded by the raw pain that edged her words and, determined to finish the conversation, took scrupulous care not to offend her. "I want to explain something to you, but because it is such a personal matter, I would like very much to *see* you as I speak, rather than peer through the dark in your direction."

Aching to sit near him and be touched by the warm strong hands she loved so much, Lisette rose stiffly and seated herself on the edge of the bed.

"In light of your feelings concerning my female visitors," Nicholai began, "I assume you weren't happy to come home and find Amelia Purdy in my bedchamber."

"I wouldn't be happy to find her *any*where," she replied coldly. "She is a mean-spirited, vain, sharp-tongued shrew and I am disappointed to know your taste in women could sink so low."

He shrugged with wry nonchalance. "You have a point there." Seeing her back straighten completely, Nicholai amended, "It isn't what it seems, however, and perhaps one day I will explain my reasons for associating with her at all. Lisette! If you turn a degree colder I'll have to put you in front of the fire to thaw you out! Give me a measure of credit, won't you? I wasn't in love with Amelia, for God's sake! We were using each other—in bed!"

She looked stricken. The rigidness dissolved in her spine and she tried to stand, but Nicholai held fast to one delicate wrist. "Don't you see?" he pressed. "You don't have to be jealous of her. I never cared for Amelia any more than she cared for me beyond the excitement I could provide."

"You needn't worry that I'm upset over your sordid affair with that disgusting woman. I really could not be less concerned—"

"Oh, Lisette," he begged, hands shifting to her sides to draw her near. "Please, don't say it! I want you to tell me that you *do* care, in spite of my flaws."

Nicholai's emerald eyes burned through the darkness, and it seemed to Lisette that they uncovered all her secrets. It was nearly impossible to breathe, let alone speak, but she managed one hoarse word.

"Why?"

In the coral-tinted shadows, she was more touchingly beautiful than ever.

"Why?" he echoed. "Because . . . I care for you. And let me assure you that there isn't a hint of sordidness in my feelings."

Happiness swelled in Lisette, flavored by a more tart emotion. Part of her wished that he had declared his *love*— perhaps even begged her to marry him—yet this more temperate declaration was enough for now.

Nicholai studied Lisette's face, trying to read her true feelings. From the moment they first met, she had been an enigma to him, a tantalizing mystery. Slowly, she had revealed her emotions, and, little by little, her protective shell had cracked. Now Nicholai knew a great deal more about Lisette, but she remained an enigma in many ways. Her personality was incredibly complex . . . there was so much she kept hidden. What was the truth of her feelings for him? Affection, desire—of those Nicholai was certain. Love? He probed the word gingerly in his mind. His heart tightened again. It was too soon to explore that serious possibility; both of them were wary. Lifting Lisette's slim, fragrant hand, he pressed warm lips first to wrist and then palm, welcoming the rush of physical yearning that erased all thoughts from his mind.

As Nicholai eased Lisette back into the cool pillows, a stubborn voice shouted in her mind that she was a fool, a weakling, to give in so easily. What did he take her for? Could she be rendered witless by his practiced touch and a few noncommittal endearments?

Oh . . . but she longed to surrender and stop thinking. Yearning rushed over her in waves. Nicholai was exploring every curve and hollow of her face, slowly . . . almost reverently. Lisette shivered. He whispered, "Shh . . . it's all right . . ." against her ear, one hand caressing her back from the baby curls marking her hairline to the first smooth curve of her derriere. Helplessly, Lisette shivered again, and the silent voice cried once more: *Fool!*

I can't. I can't! thought Lisette. *He'll know. It's too dangerous. I can't even control my own body! I'll be just like Amelia Purdy, just like all the others. If he knew how I felt—*

"Nicholai. Nicholai, stop!" Her voice shook traitorously. "Your bath! I know how you've been longing for one." Lisette jerked away, sat up, and swallowed air in an effort to clear her thoughts. "I'll heat the water—right now!"

"What the—" Nicholai's momentary twinge of alarm was extinguished by the sight of her face—flushed and sparkle-eyed with desire. Trying to keep the devilment from his own expression, he said, "Of course, my bath! How thoughtful of you, my dear."

Lisette paused in the act of leaving the bed and peered through the firelit shadows at Nicholai, wondering what the secretive gleam in his emerald eyes foretold.

❦ *Chapter 27* ❧

May 6, 1793

A large brass bathtub reposed before the kitchen hearth.
While filling it with buckets of water from the caldron that
steamed above the fire, Lisette strove for a businesslike
attitude. After all, there was no reason to be nervous.
Hadn't she eluded Nicholai's persistent embrace—in his
bed? Now she was safely ensconced once again in her role
as nurse. This was no different from the baths she had fixed
for her father during his last months.

"My God, that looks wonderful."

Lisette finished pouring in the last bucketful of water
before glancing toward the doorway. She tried to keep her
emotional distance, but just the sight of him, twenty feet
away, made her heart turn over. Maddeningly, her face
grew warm.

"I'm glad you think so, sir. It is . . . hot work."

"Obviously." His grin was knowing. He padded barefoot
across the planked floor, clad in a handsome robe of chocolate brown velvet and carrying a decanter of wine and two
goblets.

Lisette watched him approach with trepidation. Now
that his beard was growing in, Nicholai looked decidedly
piratical, particularly when he flashed that wicked grin. He
was beside the table now, filling the glasses with wine.

"None for me, thank you," Lisette said nervously.

Nicholai looked up in mock alarm. "You *must* join me,
my *dear* nurse! Why, this is an occasion. A milestone in my
recovery. A cause for celebration!" He held out the goblet.
"I insist."

Something in his tone made her walk around the bathtub to accept the wine. "Perhaps a symbolic toast, then," Lisette whispered. "Just a sip."

One side of his mouth bent sardonically, but he said nothing as their glasses clinked in the still, dimly lit kitchen.

"Well, here's to . . . you," stammered Lisette. She wanted to slap herself. "Your recovery has been remarkably quick."

"Will you be sorry when it's complete?"

Immediately on guard, Lisette tried to read his sharp green eyes, without success. She took two nervous sips of wine, concentrating on the goblet, before replying, "How could the full return of your good health make me sorry? I know you must be anxious to get back to your house in Philadelphia and your normal routine—"

"Just as you are anxious to return to your beloved Coffee-House—?" Nicholai interjected.

"Well, of course." Flustered, Lisette smoothed her skirt, took another sip of wine, and finally let her eyes rest on Nicholai again. If only she could keep from blushing! "I—I suppose that the next milestone in your recovery will be the shaving of your new beard."

"Are you volunteering?" Nicholai taunted. "As enjoyable as that experience sounds, I fear that I must decline your offer, dear Nurse. I am planning to keep it—to remind me of you, and our idyll here together, by."

Lisette's face flamed. What could she say or do that would be safe? "That's—very amusing," she replied, sounding lame rather than light. Before he could say something that would make her even more disconcerted than she was already, Lisette rushed on, "Well, I must go now and leave you to your bath."

Nicholai caught her arm as she turned to flee. "Oh, no, you mustn't! Lisette, you have to *give* me my bath! That's why I didn't have it when Katya and Randolph were here. I didn't relish the thought of being bathed by either my sister *or* her fiancé . . . but *you* are quite another matter!"

Lisette paled under his laughing eyes. "But—I—"

"These are Dr. Wistar's strict orders!" he continued cheerfully, refilling both their glasses and walking around the table to deposit them next to the bathtub. "He is terribly afraid that I might reopen my wound while reaching to

wash some . . . out-of-the-way spot. He offered to send
Oliver out from my house, or even do the honors himself,
but I assured him that I knew someone who would be delighted to help in any way possible!"

"Nicholai!" she croaked. "You *didn't* mention my
name—!"

He grinned devilishly over one broad shoulder while unfastening his robe. "Lisette! What sort of a cad do you take
me for?"

As Nicholai turned back for a long high-spirited drink of
wine, the robe gapped open to expose his dark bronze-
haired chest. Although the rest of him was concealed
beneath the tabletop, Lisette felt her nervousness dissolv-
ing, replaced by outrage.

"Does this situation amuse you?" she demanded.

"Don't say I've made you angry!" Nicholai strove to repress a smile, with little success. "I—*of course* I am not
amused. Especially not by you, Lisette! It must be the wine.
It's made me giddy."

Lisette lifted her eyes in exasperation. "You are impossible. And you were right—I *do* think you are a cad!"

Looking hurt, he turned toward the bathtub. "Your
tongue is cruel, Nurse."

"Get in, then!" she stormed, rounding the table to confront him. "If I must bathe you, I might as well get it over
with!"

Nicholai gave her an angelic smile. "I need a bit of
assistance with this sleeve—"

Sapphire sparks shot from Lisette's eyes as she reached
over to pull the sleeve free of his injured shoulder, taking
care not to cause him physical pain by her anger. When
the robe was off and she had draped it over the nearest
chair, Lisette found that Nicholai continued to stand before her.

"Do you also need assistance getting into the bathtub?"
she inquired sarcastically, trying to ignore the nearness of
his splendid fire-goldened body.

Nicholai flicked both eyebrows upward and stepped
into the still-steaming water, wine goblet in hand. Lisette
had one quick glimpse of his wide back tapering into lean,
narrow hips and muscular buttocks as he settled into the

bath. Leaning against the high back of the tub, Nicholai sipped the chilled wine and sighed.

Lisette glared at him and reached for her own glass. "Whenever you are ready!"

Watching her drink the wine, it took all of Nicholai's self-control not to laugh out loud. He saw her eyes skitter over his tanned hard shoulders and strong neck, then turn icy when they met his own lazy gaze. Like a cat with a mouse, he bided his time.

"I have all night, Lisette."

"How fortunate for you." She drained her wine and strode across the room to fetch a large sea sponge and a cake of sandalwood soap. "My time, on the other hand, is more valuable. May I take your glass so that we can get on with this?"

Nicholai looked pleased in a way that made Lisette uncomfortable. "Your wish is my command, dear Nurse," he murmured, proffering the empty goblet. "I can hardly wait!"

"Look, Nicholai, this had better be necessary, because if you have been having a joke—at my expense!—I'll see to it that—"

"I swear—on my mother's name." What he didn't mention was that neither his mother nor his doctor had ever been able to keep him in line.

"All right, then," decided Lisette, "I suppose we should take off your bandages and wash that wound as well. How has it been today? I hope you didn't exert yourself during Mrs. Purdy's visit!"

He gazed fondly at Lisette's serious, beautiful face as she unwound the layers of gauze. A tiny drop of perspiration drizzled down from her temple. "You are so adept at this," Nicholai teased. He took a chance and kissed the wetness on her cheek and was heartened by Lisette's grudging smile.

"As I told you, this is hot work." She leaned over to deposit the pile of gauze on a chair, revealing a delicious swell of bosom to his appreciative eyes.

"Perhaps *you* should have a bath—?" Nicholai offered innocently.

Lisette couldn't resist. She smiled, then pressed a hand over the laughter that threatened to spill out.

"You are incorrigible."

"Thank you." His grin flashed in the firelight.

It was fortunate that Lisette had to kneel at that moment, since it gave her an opportunity to steady herself against the rim of the bathtub. For the thousandth time, she wondered how one man should have such a devastating effect on her. Sighing, she soaped the sponge.

"I liked you better when you leaned over from a standing position," Nicholai remarked.

"Act your age, Mr. Beauvisage."

"Don't tempt me, Mistress Hahn!"

His cool flat tone sent a thrill through Lisette that frightened her. Without another word or glance in Nicholai's direction, she began to wash his wound. Only the tender gentleness of her touch betrayed her feelings for him.

Feeling his emerald eyes studying her face, Lisette offered, "You have healed very well."

"Thanks to you . . ." Nicholai managed to murmur before giving himself up to the intense pleasure of her touch. Like feathers, Lisette's fingertips brushed his arms, neck, shoulders, rubbing and rinsing him with the soapy sponge. When she reached his chest, she used her hand to lather the expanse of crisp auburn hair that reached from the base of his throat to far down his belly. Nicholai groaned, closed his eyes, and lay back.

Contentment and desire combined to spin a web around the two of them. Silently, Lisette caressed his hard muscles with the soap, but stopped short at his navel. Feeling her touch return to his neck, Nicholai smiled and caught her wrist against his chiseled jaw.

"Aren't you forgetting the rest of me?" he chided softly.

Lisette's face flamed. "I'm going to wash your hair now." She crossed the room and returned carrying a pewter ewer. Carefully, Nicholai's hair was rinsed and lathered, and he moaned in contentment.

"You have the touch of an angel. This is heaven. . . ."

Thankful that his eyes were closed against the soap, Lisette blinked back sudden stinging tears. How she loved him! It was a joy to touch him this way, to feel his thick, glossy hair in her hands. Certainly she wouldn't have a better opportunity to memorize the details of Nicholai's body . . . and when she returned to her narrow bed above the

CoffeeHouse, she would be able to think back to these sweet moments. . . .

"Lisette, I don't mean to complain, but I'm getting soap in my eyes. Are you going to go on with that all night?"

"Oh—oh, no! I'm sorry!" She rushed to fill the ewer with clean water from the kettle, which she'd removed from the fire. "Just tip your head back so that I can rinse your hair."

Nicholai complied; then, when it was done, shook his clean wet hair and rubbed the water from his eyes and beard. He slanted a smile at Lisette.

"Now what?"

"Your back." Retrieving the sponge, she set to work, admiring the hard sculptured beauty of his body.

"Would it be easier if I stood up for a while?" Nicholai asked, trying to sound casual.

"No! And I don't see how you can expect me—I mean, certainly there are some places you must be able to reach quite easily—"

He laughed out loud. "What are you afraid of, dear Nurse? There isn't any part of me that you haven't seen— or touched—before . . . or had you forgotten? If that's the case, I'll be more than happy to refresh your memory!"

"I think you are odious to raise that subject at a time like this! Does it give you pleasure to humiliate me?" Angrily, she returned to her place next to the center of the bathtub. "Put your leg up!"

Nicholai complied with a sigh, conscious of that maddening pressure in his chest. "You are the most confounding woman!" Lisette went right on, furiously scrubbing his foot and steely calf, not sparing him a glance as he persisted: "I'm not trying to humiliate you, for God's sake, I'm trying to make you see the truth! Was it so terrible? Was I a cruel or thoughtless lover? Did I *smell?*"

Lisette had to bite her lip to keep from smiling. "Mr. Beauvisage, as far as I'm concerned, the *truth* is that you would like to take me to bed again. I mean, your baser needs must be getting quite strong by this time—and here I am! How convenient! You could satisfy your—"

"Yes?"

"Your *lust,* but all I would get would be more shame! Men are all the same: selfish—"

"Will you shut up?" Nicholai jerked his leg free, leaned forward, and caught her elbow in an iron grip. "You are a delightful, intelligent girl, Lisette, but on this one subject you are, quite frankly, demented! There is nothing base or shameful about what we have shared in the past—and what I hope we will be able to share again. As matter of fact, I can't think of anything *less* impure! I would never use you, Lisette—and deep inside, you know that. Trust your own instincts. Trust your body! It won't lie to you."

She tried, unsuccessfully, to disengage her arm. "All right, then, Mr. Beauvisage, what if I were to tell you that my body has informed me that it has absolutely no interest in you?"

His green eyes rested on her thin wet bodice. "I'd say that you should request that that message be repeated. . . ."

Lisette looked down in horror. Soaked muslin clung to her full breasts and outlined the rosy peaks that tautened just inches from Nicholai's burning gaze. It was impossible to move or speak. Her mouth opened, but no sound came out. Nicholai's eyes said it all. He looked up at Lisette with such warmth, longing—and love?—that her heart swelled and her resistance melted.

Numbly, she watched as he unfastened the tiny hooks on her bodice before standing, splendidly naked and wet, to slip the gown over her head.

"Oh, Lisette, you are so much more than beautiful. . . ." His fingers touched the pink flowers embroidered on the bodice of her gauzy chemise. "Did you do this?"

Lisette's golden lashes brushed her dusky cheeks. "It wasn't for your benefit! I—I had to do something to pass these long nights. . . ."

"You should have consulted me," Nicholai murmured, his voice spiced with amusement. "I would have been happy to entertain you—somehow!"

"Oh . . . I wish—"

Nicholai was in the midst of adding the remainder of the clean hot water from the kettle to the bathtub.

"What do you wish, sweetheart?"

One hot tear slid down her cheek. "I don't even know myself!"

Nicholai's hands cradled Lisette's face as he kissed first the tears, then the sweet, trembling lips. Nicholai groaned. His fingers flicked open the tiny chemise buttons, then rested lightly on her creamy shoulders. Already the hard ache in his loins was agonizing—and he'd scarcely touched the chit!

Lisette's arms burned and tingled as Nicholai's practiced fingers lowered the straps. Slowly, the chemise opened downward until her swelling breasts were bared to Nicholai's fiery emerald gaze.

"Oh, Jesus . . ." he breathed hoarsely.

There was a whisper of batiste as the chemise slid down graceful legs before it settled into a pool at Lisette's feet.

✤ Chapter 28 ✤

May 6, 1793

Nicholai helped Lisette into the bathtub; he smiled as she huddled self-consciously in the steaming water.

"You won't be able to hide from me in my own bath, Mistress Hahn," he remarked mischievously.

Watching him settle down across from her, Lisette tried to see only the play of Nicholai's hard muscles in the firelight—not the bold proof of his maleness that passed through her line of vision.

"I should have kept my eyes closed," she whispered. "I should have kept my clothes *on!* I should have—"

"I know, I know," interrupted Nicholai while reaching over to pluck the soap and sponge from a chair. "You should have run for your life the night we met at Belle Maison!"

"That's exactly right!" she agreed vehemently.

"But, Lisette . . ." Having lathered the sponge, he now reached forward to pry apart her concealing arms. "Haven't you heard that it's useless to fight destiny?"

"Is *that* what this is?" Her voice sounded tremulous rather than sarcastic, as she'd hoped. The reason she'd struggled against this particular destiny for so long was that she had no clue to the ending. Should she surrender completely now, body and soul, only to find herself alone and heartbroken in a few days or weeks?

The words wouldn't come. It would be too humiliating to ask him if his intentions were honorable; besides, wasn't

---

she supposed to be too independent to care? Staring at the rim of the bathtub that gleamed in the fire glow, she thought back to the time she had told Nicholai about her "woman's needs" and how she had been using *him* to satisfy them on the night they met.

Warm water drizzled down Lisette's arm, rousing her.

"Tell me about that strange smile that curves your lips," Nicholai murmured, moving the sponge up her shoulder. "Help me to understand the thoughts that glide through your mystifying mind."

Meeting Nicholai's tender gaze, Lisette felt many of her doubts dissolve. Suddenly she was conscious of the pleasurable sensation of his hard leg touching her satiny calves in the water. His chiseled arms drew her nearer and his beloved face came close enough to kiss. One slim hand reached up to smooth back Nicholai's damp hair, which seemed more burnished than ever in the firelight. She wanted to trace each irresistible feature, but then surely he would feel the love in her fingers . . . see it in her sapphire eyes.

When Nicholai caught her hand, and pressed his lips to each perfect finger in turn, Lisette hurried to break the silence. "Do you really want to know my thoughts?"

"Mmm," he smiled, kissing the tender inside of her wrist.

"I was wondering about this destiny you described . . . does it mean that there will be a happy ending—like a fairy tale?"

Nicholai took his lips from her arm and regarded her soberly. "That's the thrill of surrendering to destiny, my dear. One never knows what lies ahead . . . and I suppose the fun is in finding out." With an index finger, he did what she had yearned to do, grazing her brow, eyes, and finally each rose-petal lip before parting them and barely touching her tongue. He felt her quake. "As for fairy tales . . . no princess was ever desired as I *crave* you, Lisette, nor did one ever experience the sensations you will discover tonight."

"And you . . . truly care for me?"

Abruptly, Nicholai pulled her to her knees and met her in an intimate embrace that joined them from thighs to scorching mouths. After a deep, blazing kiss that left Lisette both dizzy and hungry for more, he answered her question.

"I not only care—I love you."

"Oh—" She had to gasp for breath, but then he was kissing her again, more gently this time, savoring the heady nectar of her lips and mouth.

"You don't have to say a word. Just relax . . ."

"I love you" echoed over and over in her mind, but soon all thoughts were swept away by an intense tide of feeling.

Nicholai sensuously caressed Lisette's exquisite body with the sponge. The memory of her touch on his own naked flesh just minutes before was branded in his mind, and he wanted to rouse her to the fever of his desire. Languorously, her eyes closed as he ran the sponge down her back. How lovely she was! As graceful as a swan and more beautifully made than a perfect long-stem yellow rose. Leaning around, Nicholai slowly lathered her silky back with his hand, massaging her tired muscles at the same time.

Gradually, he moved back and ran soapy fingertips from each curving hip upward. Lisette shuddered as Nicholai caressed the first blossoms of her breasts, then drew leisurely, torturous patterns over the full firmness. Gently, he pressed her back against the bend in the tub and lifted her upswept golden curls over the rim.

"Comfortable?" Nicholai inquired, his tone both loving and wicked.

She could barely manage a low gasp of contentment.

Smiling to himself, he rinsed her with the sponge from her throat down, then bent forward to kiss one aching pink nipple.

Lisette bit her lower lip, swallowing moans, as Nicholai's mouth burned a trail over her breasts, lingering on the tenderest places.

"Sweetheart . . ." he murmured, "as much as I wish we could spend hours in this bath, I fear that we would freeze to death. I'm going to have to finish washing you so that we can get out. But"—Nicholai drew back to give her a roguish grin—"it will still be the best bath you've ever had!"

Lisette's wide cornflower blue eyes opened with an effort.

Her entire body was suffused with a tingling heat, which was exacerbated by the warm water that swirled around her. There was a concentration of yearning so acute inside her that she knew there was only one cure.

When Nicholai lifted her delicate foot and proceeded to lather not only it but the rest of her leg, Lisette sighed with pleasure and pointed her toe in the air to make his task easier.

If not for the soap, he would have tasted every inch of the beauty she so obligingly displayed for him. After washing her other leg, he moved her ankle to rest on the bathtub rim, and slid his fingers along the graceful line of her flesh, disappearing underwater halfway down Lisette's thighs. She stared, knowing what he was about, but made no move to close her legs. Instead, she found Nicholai's free hand and gripped it tightly as, deep in the water, his other fingers brushed the sweet throbbing core of her desire. He reached for the soapy sponge and turned to tenderly wash between her thighs and up to her rounded derriere. Then the sponge fell away.

Lisette flinched under Nicholai's expert fingers. He seemed to know not only where she was most keenly sensitive, but also just how she needed to be touched. Finally, yearning seemed to fill her loins, and she trembled in anticipation. Nicholai's hand moved away and emerged from the water.

"Shall we dry off and continue our explorations upstairs?" he asked huskily, knowing that Lisette's fevered longing could not easily be contained.

Lisette could only stare dazedly. Did he imagine that she was so mesmerized with desire that she would follow like a docile lamb? Narrowing her blue eyes, Lisette decided that she would share in the control of this night's destiny.

"I'll be glad to dry off, Mr. Beauvisage, when we have finished this bath." She sat up in the water.

Nicholai felt the hairs stand up on his arms; the water had definitely cooled. "I thought that we *were* finished." One auburn brow arched a trifle irritably.

"Oh, no. I definitely recall that there were parts of *your* body that I left unwashed. Your left leg, for instance."

"Lisette, for God's sake! I'm sure that with all this soap—"

"I would be remiss in my duties as a nurse if I allowed you to take such a chance," she replied as seriously as she was able; then she leaned forward to grope for the sponge, conscious of his eyes on her gleaming breasts. They invited Nicholai's touch, but he restrained himself.

"Put up your leg, please," ordered Lisette.

Something in her bold demeanor rekindled his desire. His annoyance was replaced with an exciting rush of curiosity. What did she mean to do? After bracing his hard-muscled leg on the rim of the tub, Nicholai regarded Lisette as she began to soap his foot and calf with a deliberate sensuousness quite unlike her earlier technique. When she slanted a brief seductive smile at him, Nicholai was stunned. Long before her slim fingers found their way through the water to the top of his thigh, he wondered how he could contain the aching fire in his loins.

Gently, Lisette touched Nicholai's rigid manhood and felt him flinch. Though she was trying to appear coolly wanton, her inner emotions mixed overwhelming passion with nervous apprehension. Somehow, while washing him, she managed to keep from blushing, but when she looked up and felt the impact of his burning eyes, Lisette found it impossible to breathe. She ached to be satisfied. Nicholai's body was like a magnet, drawing her nearer, and she was powerless to resist the pull.

"Lisette . . . I can't stand much more of this—" he whispered hoarsely, lowering his leg back into the water.

Triumph and surrender mingled in her bittersweet smile. "Neither can I."

Nicholai was spellbound as Lisette straddled his hips. She brushed her swollen womanhood against him tantalizingly before his arms encircled her back, crushing her breasts against the crisp hair that covered his chest. When he kissed her dry mouth and realized that Lisette was nervous after all, Nicholai's heart melted.

"Oh, my beautiful, audacious love . . ."

"I love you, Nicholai," she exclaimed joyfully.

His hands framed her face as he pressed burning kisses from her brow to her breasts. Then, Lisette caressed his pulsing shaft, touching it tentatively to her own warm flesh. Apricot gold firelight haloed her delectable body as she straightened above him. When Lisette guided Nicholai past the taut entrance to her pleasure, he almost cried out.

His hands cupped her firm buttocks firmly so that she wouldn't slip. The water swirled around them as Lisette moved forward until Nicholai was completely sheathed within her snug warmth, over and over again. . . .

She moaned with pleasure. A tortoiseshell hairpin fell into the water as Lisette's head dropped back, setting free a spill of tawny curls.

Nicholai felt her tighten even more around his hardness and knew that her climax was surging closer. He wanted to share it fully with Lisette; to look into her eyes and let her know that more than passion had set him afire. . . .

Shifting a hand to the rim of the tub, he carefully straightened so that they sat face to face. "Am I hurting you?" he queried softly.

"No! Oh, no . . ." She smiled and nibbled at his shoulder, her azure eyes glowing. Then, to accommodate Nicholai's altered position, Lisette slid her legs around his hips and let him control the movement between their fevered bodies. As his thrusts intensified, she felt the throbbing fullness in the pit of her belly grow like a wave that towers higher and higher before breaking on the sand. They kissed urgently, climbing to the crest of the wave, then shuddered together during the explosive, exquisitely torturous descent. Gradually, they relaxed, enjoying the pleasureable fusion of their sated bodies . . . the ultimate embrace. Lisette was conscious of every inch of Nicholai that touched her flesh —his hard chest against her heaving breasts, his bearded jaw grazing her flushed cheek, his lean-muscled legs against her sore thighs, and the still-hard warmth of his manhood inside her body, pulsing contentedly.

After several minutes, Nicholai pressed an ardent kiss to her brow. "I love you, Mistress Hahn."

"And I love you, Master Beauvisage." Lisette was in a

state of total bliss. Still, she couldn't resist teasing, "I *am*, however, beginning to notice now that this bathwater is not quite as warm as it was. . . ."

Nicholai held her close and let out a deep sigh. "What water? I can't feel a thing except you, *chérie*. . . ."

May 7, 1793

A crisp morning breeze, heady with the scent of lilacs, drifted across the four-poster bed. Sunlight glinted on Nicholai's gold-washed chestnut hair and warmed his back, but it was the dull pain in his shoulder that roused him from a deep, contented sleep. Reluctantly, he awoke just enough to turn gingerly onto his back, yet there was still some pressure against the throbbing shoulder.

When his eyes flickered open and blinked in the bright sunshine, they fell on a silky trail of lemony curls. Snuggling peacefully against Nicholai's wounded shoulder was Lisette, her long lashes brushing above fragile cheekbones and one hand curled trustingly around his hard bicep. Beneath the linen sheet and ivory satin comforter, her limbs felt deliciously soft and warm entwined with his. The sensation of full firm breasts cushioned against the leanness of Nicholai's side stirred the fires in his loins to a fresh height. Ignoring the pain, he eased back onto his side.

Slowly, Nicholai's free hand slid under the covers. Deft fingers grazed the sensitive outer curve of Lisette's breast and the graceful line of one hip before touching, with exquisite gentleness, her smooth belly and the feather-soft curls below. The desire that pierced him was sharp and keen—different from the sweeping heavy yearning of last night, yet shot through with a special poignancy.

As Nicholai tentatively caressed Lisette's silky inner thighs, she was gliding into what seemed to be a beautiful new dream. Excruciatingly pleasurable sensations were concentrated where . . . someone was touching her. . . .

"Nicholai—" she whispered sleepily.

"I'm right here." Tenderly, he kissed her awake.

Lisette's eyes were vividly azure as they opened. "I—oh, my—"

"Happy to see me?" The irrepressible curve of his mouth branded her warm throat. "When I woke and found you cuddled next to me, I felt as if I'd died and gone to heaven!" More huskily, he added, "Truly, you have never looked more enchanting."

"Oh, Nicholai . . ." Somehow, the spring sunshine and their naked bodies, so cozy beneath the covers, heightened all her senses. Nicholai's warm dry touch set her instantly afire; hesitantly, Lisette slid down her own hand to curve around his steely masculinity.

They caressed each other for a long time in the lilac-scented morning, each gaining a leisurely familiarity with the other's body that hadn't been possible in last night's blazing urgency. Now, slow, tantalizing kisses and drowsy love murmurings were exchanged. Finally, Nicholai's arms enfolded her so that their wonderfully dissimilar bodies could embrace from head to toe; then Lisette found herself being eased back into the creamy satin pillows.

"I can't tell you how wonderful it is to have you here," Nicholai said softly. "Even my dozens of dreams fell short of this reality."

Overjoyed that she no longer had to struggle against her own fiercest longings, Lisette wrapped her arms around his shoulders and pressed her hips boldly against him. "I feel utterly decadent—" Suddenly, her voice broke off and she stiffened, listening. "Did your hear something?"

Before Nicholai could respond, the distant knocking was repeated. At this point, his own craving was acute and he had no intention of deferring it because of an early caller.

"Pay no attention, he whispered, pausing for a torturous moment against her thigh. "At this ungodly hour, they will assume we are still asleep and go away."

"But, what if—" Lisette broke off at the renewed pattern of knocks. Although Nicholai's hardness now burned her own aching need, she couldn't relax and take his advice. The idea of being in his bed and enthusiastically making love with him before breakfast was too new. Lisette told herself that there was no cause for shame—but it still embarrassed her to think of anyone else knowing and passing judgment on them. . . . "I think that we should see who it is, at least, in case someone is in trouble!"

"Why this very moment, for God's sake? Whoever it is can certainly wait for a few minutes!" The disruption infuriated Nicholai; his refusal to acknowledge it was taken out on Lisette. His hands caught her hips and stilled them, despite her struggles, while his unyielding manhood pressed the entry that was still sore and more taut than ever after the previous night's passions.

"Why should they wait at all?" Lisette demanded. Outrage boiled up inside of her. "So that my obliging body can provide you with another quick thrill? What do you think I am, you horny oaf? If you imagine that I am so besotted with love that I'll spread my legs at your brutish whim—"

A familiar voice interrupted her tirade. "Oh, Nicholai! Hello!" it sang. "Lisette? Are you here?"

Lisette had been battering Nicholai's chest without result, but now he was up in a flash. "Damn it! It's my mother!" he hissed angrily.

She had at least a dozen more scalding comments to make, but was forced to swallow them, temporarily, at least. Antonia Beauvisage's voice sounded closer now, repeating their names in obvious puzzlement. Sheer panic won out over modesty and Lisette sprang from the bed and darted naked across the room. Watching the dressing room door close safely behind her flying curls and creamy derriere, Nicholai fought a twinge of amusement. It would take a great deal to make him smile under these trying circumstances, not the least of which was the frustrated throb in his groin.

"For God's sake, Maman, quiet down and just open my door!" he shouted crossly.

Antonia Beauvisage hurried down the hall and into her son's room, breathing a sigh of relief. She found him sitting up in bed, naked above the plush comforter that almost touched his waist.

"Gracious, Nicky! Why ever didn't you answer sooner? Dr. Wistar told us that you were up and about, so I was rather hoping that you would greet me at the door! And where is Lisette?" Antonia perched easily on the bed, as petite and graceful as a girl, and pressed Nicholai's strong hand. "Are you all right? How is your shoulder—and why isn't it bandaged?"

"I was fine—until you came barging in at the crack of dawn to rouse me! What possesses my family? Yesterday, it was Katya and Randolph who 'happened by' before I'd even had breakfast, and today my mother has chosen an equally uncivilized hour for a visit. One would think all of you lived a stone's throw away!" Nicholai rubbed the knuckles of his fist against his bearded jaw. "Not only have you managed to arrive before my breakfast, but poor Lisette hasn't even finished dressing!"

"Oh—well, then, I apologize most sincerely. . . ." Antonia's face, set off by a fashionable royal blue riding habit and wind-tousled russet-and-silver curls, was a study in bewilderment. "However, I cannot help wondering when the hour of *noon* became so uncivilized . . . !"

After an awkward moment of silence, Nicholai echoed, "*Noon?* Are you serious?"

"Completely, Nicky." She gave him a small smile that promised not to pry into his affairs. Yet, with the natural instincts of a mother, Antonia's eyes took inventory without seeming to stray from her son's face. After forty-five passionate years of marriage, she could recognize a bed shared by lovers; Nicholai had not slept alone the night before, and Antonia guessed that little time had been wasted on sleep. A hint of a familiar feminine scent lingered in the air, and, no doubt, deep in the satin pillows as well.

"I must have been drugged by the country air," Nicholai was saying a trifle uneasily. "When I heard Lisette call out that she was dressing. I just assumed it was still early . . . but perhaps she took advantage of my lethargy to finish a new gown or just lie in bed and read or to have a bath—"

Antonia managed to nod conversationally. She was glad that Nicky didn't look her in the eye as he lied; that was one sophisticated skill she hoped he never acquired.

"I certainly don't blame either of you for enjoying your holiday." She smiled. Meanwhile, her mind was working at full speed. Was it truly possible the Lisette Hahn had become her son's lover? In spite of Caroline's and Katya's schemes to match Nicholai with the lovely Austrian girl, Antonia could not believe that the resolutely independent and frosty Mistress Hahn could have melted this much in less than a fortnight. Perhaps, now that Nicky was feeling so well, Amelia Purdy had paid a long visit in order to satisfy certain elemental appetites. . . . Antonia loathed her son's mistress, but at least his involvement with her was harmless. He would never fall in love with Mistress Purdy and was in no danger of being trapped into marriage.

Since Nicholai's return from France, Antonia had thought a great deal about her last unmarried child. Katya's romantic future, after all, was settled. Because of her own richly fulfilling marriage, Antonia had always prayed that her offspring would be similarly blessed. Over the last decade, Nicholai had suffered heartbreak more than once. He had battled for survival in France's bloody Revolution, been forced to abandon the château and work that he loved, and now bore a painful scar to remind him of the duel that had nearly claimed his life. More than anything, Antonia yearned to see her younger son at peace . . . but in reality, there were formidable barriers that only Nicholai could break down. Happiness and fulfillment would not come to him overnight, no matter how fervently she might pray or wish that it could be so.

"Maman, why am I worried that your intent expression has something to do with me?" Nicholai asked fondly.

"Probably because you have known me since the day you were born." Antonia smiled. "And also because you're smart, you rascal. Too smart for your own good!"

"Perhaps too *handsome* for my own good, but it's not possible to be too smart."

"What about conceit?" his mother rejoined. "Maybe that is the quality that plagues you in excess."

Nicholai laughed appreciatively and kissed her hand. "It is good to have you here, Maman. I apologize for the churlish welcome I extended."

"No apology is necessary, Nicky. I understand completely."

There was a soft *tap-tap* on the dressing room door. "May I come in?" called Lisette.

"By all means, Mistress Hahn," replied Nicholai, wondering how they would ever get through this unrehearsed scene in front of his mother.

Apparently, Lisette was thinking the same thing, because she wore an enchanting expression of uneasiness. Clad in a plain long-sleeved frock of pale pink cotton, with a white fichu modestly filling the decolletage, Lisette had gone one step further by wearing her golden hair in the high braided crown that Nicholai hadn't seen since the CoffeeHouse. She was the picture of polite, detached efficiency until she neared the bed and met first Nicholai's gaze, then his mother's.

"How nice to see you, Mrs. Beauvisage." Hot color flooded her cheeks. "Ah—Nicholai, now that you are awake, I will bring up a pot of tea and some muffins. Would you care for eggs?"

He was ravenous, but decided to wait and help Lisette cook a more substantial meal after his mother's departure. Remembering the day they made succotash, with bear meat, at the CoffeeHouse, Nicholai's mouth curved upward on one side.

"Nicky, are you there?" Antonia nudged him. "Honestly, will you answer Lisette?"

"Oh, sorry! I thought I had—you know how forgetful we invalids can be." He gave her a grin designed to defuse any anger she might still feel from their little wrestling match. "Muffins will be fine for now, thank you."

"All right, then, I'll be—" Lisette averted her eyes from Nicholai's face, then widened them in alarm at the sight of his bare shoulder. And the wound—surely it looked worse! "Your bandages! I—you—I mean—"

He rushed to her aid. "Don't worry, Nurse! I forgot to tell you that Dr. Wistar said my wound should—ah—*breathe* from time to time. So, I took off the bandages when I had my bath last night."

"Oh!" Maddeningly, she blushed again. "Well, I would say that enough breathing has been done. I'll put on some fresh bandages after breakfast."

Watching Lisette's graceful form depart, Antonia thought of all she had heard in recent years about the Austrian ice princess and her aversion to men and romance. She knew that Katya adored the girl, but Lisette had always been so conscientious about her work at the CoffeeHouse that she had never been able to accept any of the Beauvisages' invitations to join them for supper. So serious—and independent! How could Nicky, who had always been innately charming and quick to laugh, be involved for long with a girl like that?

"Maman, you are doing it again! *What* is on your mind?"

"Dr. Wistar told us that you are well enough to return to Philadelphia; in fact, he thinks it would be beneficial for you to complete your recovery in the familiar surroundings of your own home," Antonia replied bluntly. Unsure of how to proceed next, she paused and observed the shadow that darkened her son's face. He shifted restlessly against the pillows and the sun momentarily illuminated a long golden strand caught in the crisp auburn hair covering his chest. Antonia forced her expression not to change, instantly remembering that Nicky had bathed the night before —so Lisette's hair hadn't fallen innocently the last time she changed his dressing! "I have to agree with the doctor, Nicholai," Antonia continued. "You have healed enough to walk around, so obviously the carriage ride to Philadelphia would do you no harm. Your staff can look after you at home and you will be able to take brief walks to visit friends —and your family! In fact, we would be delighted to have you take as many meals with us as you like—or even *stay* with us at first, if the idea appeals to you—"

"Maman, what has gotten into you?" Nicholai interrupted, obviously annoyed. "I am thirty-two years old and I can make up my own mind about returning to Philadelphia—or any of those other details!"

"Certainly, I am aware of that. You needn't snap at me, Nicky. You know that I have never been an interfering mother, but—"

"I prefer to remain here for the time being," he declared flatly.

After being interrupted twice, Antonia felt herself bristle. Impulsively, she leaned forward and extended a finger to brush the blond hair from Nicholai's chest. It drifted down and settled on the white linen sheet. "The reason why you prefer to stay here is quite clear." One russet eyebrow curved upward sharply. "Frankly, I am ashamed of you,

Nicholai. Using Lisette as a plaything, to gratify your desires . . . how will she feel when this romantic fantasy is
ended and she returns to face reality at the CoffeeHouse?
I am well aware of the highly principled life Lisette has
always adhered to—"

Nicholai wanted to shake his mother. What had come
over her? "Maman, I don't like the tone of your voice;
reproach does not become you. I can understand that, in
view of my long absence, you may have trouble remembering my true age, but this outburst is trying my patience. As
for Lisette"—he took a deep breath, locking his emerald
eyes with Antonia's—"I am in love with her, Maman. I am
planning, today, to ask her to be my wife."

Antonia's mind whirled; she felt as though a sudden blow
had knocked the wind out of her. "Well," she managed
weakly, "I certainly do owe you an apology. I'm sorry for
behaving like a meddlesome, interfering mother . . . but I
lost my head . . . because I love you so, Nicky." She pressed
fingertips against the tears that stung her eyelids.

"Maman, come here," Nicholai said thickly, gathering
her close and patting her back. "You mustn't weep—I
haven't a handkerchief! As for the rest, just forget it as I
am going to do. We all say and do things that confuse those
who know us best."

"I am only concerned for your welfare—I want you to
be happy, and I have worried more because of the trials
you have suffered." She sat up, squeezing his hand, and
reached for the lace-edged handkerchief inside her reticule.
"I realize that the home you grew to love over a decade and
the work that fascinated you have been swept away by the
Revolution. Your future . . ."

"It will work out. Together, Lisette and I will make a
new future."

"Nicky, you must listen to me." Antonia's voice was calm
now, and warm with love. "I was wrong to try to tell you
what to do, but I hope that you will allow me to inject a
note of reason at this point. There is nothing that would
please me more than for you to marry a beautiful, intelligent
woman like Lisette Hahn and live happily ever after. Truly!
There is, however, more to this situation than the love that

has blossomed between you in the days you have spent
alone here. Do you know that Lisette's presence here is a
result of a scheme carried out by Caro, Katya, Meagan—
and myself? I went along with their plan to throw the two
of you together, when all my maternal instincts ached to
take care of you myself. I am so pleased that your intentions toward her are serious now . . . and because of that,
you must look past this moment at Markwood Villa and
examine other aspects of your life—and Lisette's."

"All right, Maman. I am listening."

"Well, I simply would suggest that you go slower. Marriage would not be an easy adjustment for either of you—
particulary when your love has been flourishing in an en-
vironment very different from that of your real lives. You
and Lisette wouldn't be living here and playing house after
your marriage, Nicholai. There are complex problems for
you to work out regarding your plans for the future. Lisette
already has an occupation that has been her whole life. Do
you want her to abandon that if she becomes your wife? If
not, what will you do? I know you too well, son, to believe
that you would be satisfied spending your days helping your
wife run *her* business. And, what if you should one day
have the opportunity to return to France? It is my feeling
that there are matters that you will both need to consider
over a period of time, using your minds and your hearts. In
the fire of new love, it is easy to dismiss such obstacles, and
no doubt Lisette would agree with you that the future
would work itself out as long as you love one another. After
forty-five years of marriage, I know differently. Love is the
primary ingredient, but not the only one—by far."

Nicholai sighed and rubbed his bearded jaw. "I hate to
admit it . . . but what you say does make sense."

"Don't look so dispirited, Nicky! The solution is an easy
one, and it will ensure a much more secure beginning for
your marriage. Go home—and let Lisette return to her
CoffeeHouse. Continue loving her . . . but this time in the
context of your real lives. Woo her with the care and respect she deserves. Share everyday things with her and discuss what each of you desires for the future, until you have
reached agreement about the sort of life you both want."

Nicholai sighed. The role of courting beau was one he felt both too old and ill suited to perform; also, it seemed that he and Lisette were beyond all that—and not just physically. Then, he wondered what her feelings would be. She resented his proprietary behavior so strongly that morning . . . perhaps, if he wooed her more tenderly, she would realize how greatly she was valued. Yet . . . "I will have to think about this, Maman. Some of your points seem valid, but I don't even know if it's possible—I mean, it would seem as though we were going backward. . . ."

"Let me make just one *more* point and then I'll be on my way. You know that I have never been one to care much what the neighbors say, but for Lisette's sake, you ought to consider that aspect of this situation. Already, there will no doubt be gossip when you two return to town. If you marry immediately, it will seem to validate the rumors. However, if you court her respectfully for a while before you marry, her reputation will be preserved."

"Maman—I don't really believe that Lisette would care. She knows that we have only shared our love—"

"Of course! And, Nicky, you know I feel the same way. After all, your father virtually kidnapped me at sea, and we 'shared our love' more than once before we were married." Antonia smiled impishly. "However, in this case, Lisette is well known and respected in the community. Unfortunately, people can be cruel and Lisette could be hurt as a result, and I'm sure you want to spare her that. She won't be the usual new bride, doing needlework in the parlor. At the CoffeeHouse, she comes in contact with people all day, and, as you know, some men will say anything after a bit of ale. . . ."

"Are you finished, Maman?" Nicholai was wishing she had never come to inflict all this harsh reality upon him. What a beautiful morning it had been until the sound of his mother's voice turned it upside down! "I appreciate all that you have told me—I suppose. I know that you are much wiser than I about these matters, but I still want to think about this."

Out in the hall, Lisette raised her hand, but stopped before it touched the door. She heard Nicholai's troubled tone and wondered what it could mean. All the time she had been downstairs, cleaning up the mess they had left from the bath as well as preparing the tea and muffins, Lisette had agonized over the fiery events of the previous night . . . and morning. Had it been wrong? Would he think she was a loose-moraled doxy in spite of his protestations otherwise? John, the congressman she had thought she loved, had said many of the same things—but he couldn't have loved her if he would consider using her when he was already married—! What if Nicholai had declared his love for the same reason—to get her to relax so that his lust might be satisfied? In the kitchen, she had remembered the passage from Shakespeare about love and lust; the last line had been, "Love is all truth, Lust full of forged lies."

It frightened her that she could even doubt Nicholai and she felt guilty, remembering the warm magic and emotional rapport that had grown between them and reached its zenith last night. If only her distrust of men was not so deeply rooted . . . if only Nicholai had not tried to use her so insensitively this morning. . . .

Balancing the tray on one hip, Lisette tried to make out what Mrs. Beauvisage and her son were saying. Never in her life had she eavesdropped, but there was a penetrating tone to their unintelligible words that made her wonder if she might be the subject of their conversation.

Footsteps lightly crossed the rug in the direction of the door and Lisette put her hand on the latch. Antonia, having stopped in mid-exit, turned back to speak to her son—and this time she was close enough for Lisette to make out each word.

"Don't forget, Nicky, that your sister will be married in less than a fortnight . . . and nothing must dim her brightest day." She gave her son a hopeful expression and heard him sigh.

"You *would* save that for the *pièce de résistance*," he muttered. "If *I* should marry, I'll be stealing thunder from my little sister—not to mention all the other terrible things you have listed."

In the hall, Lisette made a face. Again, Nicholai had spoken in such a low tone that she only caught words intermittently—"you," "if," "sister," "listed." He was probably going to make a list of all that he could do to help with Katya's wedding—which reminded her of her own obligation to provide the food. An inexplicable chill ran down Lisette's back.

"Nicky, dear," Antonia was saying, "I really must be on my way. I feel certain that I will see you back at home before the week's end."

Lisette realized that she would have to open the door first, or be caught eavesdropping. Mrs. Beauvisage's words were stunning, but somehow, after the spell of insecurity she had just suffered in the kitchen, Lisette was not surprised. Nicholai was going home. Of course! Did she expect him to languish forever in the bedroom of the Hampshire's country house?

Summoning all her poise, Lisette pulled the door open and entered, carrying the tray. Antonia was just a few steps away, facing her.

"Oh, Mrs. Beauvisage—I hope you are not leaving so soon! I brought an extra setting of china and cutlery."

"I wish that I could linger, Lisette, but I have taken enough of Nicholai's time—and yours. Why don't you share the tea and muffins with him?" Antonia gave her a captivating smile.

"How kind of you to suggest that!" Lisette beamed in return. "Unfortunately, I must finish packing. I may have neglected to mention this to Nicholai, but I will be returning to Philadelphia today. I know that he must be equally anxious to get back to his own home now that he is well enough to travel." She deposited the tray on the bedside table, avoiding Nicholai's piercing stare as she poured the tea. "I'm afraid that the time has come for me to return to work—though this respite has been wonderful! Katya's wedding is approaching and there are so many plans to be made regarding the food. . . ."

Antonia was speechless for a moment, then managed to reply, "It was very generous to offer your help, Lisette. I know that Katya is extremely grateful."

"It is the least I can do for my dearest friend." She was already backing toward the dressing room door.

"Well—" Antonia said uneasily, "I will see both of you soon in town, I hope."

Lisette smiled vacantly and disappeared into the dressing room.

Nicholai looked stunned, angry, and hurt. "Would you mind, Maman, waiting downstairs while I dress? I am coming with you. Suddenly, I am very anxious to get the hell out of this place."

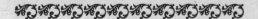

❧ *Part Four* ❧

O, never say that I was false of heart,
Though absense seem'd my flame to qualify,
As easy might I from myself depart
As from my soul, which in thy breast doth
      lie . . .
    For nothing this wide universe I call,
    Save thou, my rose; in it thou art my all.

SHAKESPEARE

❦ *Chapter 30* ❧

May 10, 1793

Descending his elliptical staircase, Nicholai breathed deeply of the sun-drenched spring air that filled the house. His lean fingers rose to touch the breast pocket of his coat, where a long cream-colored envelope reposed.

"Good morning, Master Beauvisage," Oliver said smoothly from the vestibule. Dark, tall, and imposing, he was a butler who concealed a knowledge of every inhabitant and aspect of the house behind an impassive facade.

"Good morning, Oliver." Nicholai smiled, and added for the five-dozenth time, "I wish that you would call me *Mr.* Beauvisage."

Oliver tried to repress a grin. "Yes, mast—ah—*sir.*" He stood at the entrance to the elegant dining room with its corner cabinets and their shell-carved tops. "Your breakfast is ready, sir."

"I'll just have coffee," replied Nicholai, wishing he could leave the house without stopping. He found it rather embarrassing to have so many servants existing for his pleasure, and still hadn't learned to dismiss whatever efforts they made on his behalf. Pausing at the table, Nicholai lifted the cup of steaming coffee just as Welcome appeared in the corner doorway with a tray of fragrant croissants, eggs, and a wedge of melon.

"Oh, no!" he protested, grinning. "I appreciate all your efforts, but I have an errand to run—as soon as possible." Extracting a watch from his vest pocket, Nicholai checked the time and whistled softly. "It is nearly eleven o'clock! I've grown soft, my dear Welcome, and I'm counting on

270 ───────────────────────────────── SPRING FIRES

you to do something about it. You share that breakfast with
Oliver and your lovely daughters and consider what meas-
ures should be taken to expel me from my bed at a more
respectable hour."

At the front door, Nicholai paused to face the ever-
faithful Oliver.

"Are you sure your shoulder will be all right?" asked the
butler.

"You know, I can hardly feel it today. This is the first
time I have worn a complete set of clothes in more than a
fortnight!"

Oliver allowed himself a broad affectionate grin as he
appraised his employer. Beauvisage was clad in knee boots
and buff breeches, a cream-colored shirt and crisp muslin
stock, and a double-breasted moss green coat cut away at
the waist. Just yesterday, the barber had visited the house,
apparently at the instigation of Antonia Beauvisage, and
now Nicholai's burnished hair was trimmed into somewhat
neater ruffled negligence—and his beard was gone.

"Sir," Oliver said sincerely, "you look splendid. Very
handsome, if you don't mind me saying so."

Nicholai's face lit up, a mixture of amusement and delight. "Really? Do you think so?"

Somehow, Oliver sensed the reason for his master's relieved pleasure. "Mas—that is, *Mr.* Beauvisage, I don't
think that any female alive could possibly resist your charms
today."

"Thank you, Oliver!" He shook the butler's mahogany
brown hand. "You are expert at bestowing compliments . . .
and today, I need every ounce of encouragement."

"Well, sir, I could summon *much* more if you seriously—"

Nicholai choked on real laughter and opened the arched
front door. "I'll let you know, Oliver!"

After a fortnight of bed rest, Nicholai welcomed the
chaos of Philadelphia on market day. Spruce Street teemed
with carriages, farm wagons, phaetons, sulkies, and chaises;
the dust and clatter from their wheels clouded the air. He
walked briskly toward the Delaware River that shimmered
in the distance, feeling the stiffness stretching out of his
thigh muscles with every step. Under the sunshine and clear
blue sky, Nicholai found it difficult to worry about the

encounter he would soon pursue with Lisette Hahn, that most unpredictable and enchanting of ladies. . . .

"Good morning, Mr. Beauvisage!" chorused sweet feminine voices.

Nicholai looked over to find a chaise containing the young Misses Oswald and Chew slowing near the footpath. He gave them a rakish smile and sketched a bow in their direction. "You ladies are looking especially lovely today."

"It is wonderful to see you up and about, Mr. Beauvisage!" exclaimed Miss Chew.

"You'll never know how everyone has worried!" interjected a tragic-looking Miss Oswald.

"I am grateful for your concern, ladies," Nicholai replied, trying to keep his lips from twitching while looking properly worthy of their solicitude. "Your visits during my recovery raised my spirits more than you could ever imagine."

They blushed demurely. "It was our pleasure, Mr. Beauvisage," murmured Miss Chew.

"I insist that you call me Nicholai!" He was barely able to keep amusement from infecting his voice. It was fortunate that they were several yards away in their chaise, so that they couldn't see the mocking gleam in his green eyes.

"We don't want to keep you, Mr.—that is—" Miss Oswald colored prettily before managing to say, "Nicholai. Will you be able to attend the receptions for Citizen Genêt when he arrives next week?"

"Will you ladies be present?" he inquired roguishly, one eyebrow cocked in a way that made them blush anew.

"Perhaps!" Miss Chew dared to reply coyly.

"In that case, I will look for you there. *Au revoir,* ladies."

They bade him a tittering farewell and the chaise rolled off in the opposite direction, leaving Nicholai to shake his head in relief. What a pleasure it would be to see Lisette! After the Misses Chew and Oswald, her pure, unadorned beauty; guileless manner; and clear-witted, insightful conversation would be a splendid treat.

The misunderstanding and rash anger that had marred their parting at Markwood Villa had eaten at Nicholai. He had brooded for the past three days, trying to make sense of Lisette's actions—and his own. The words *if only* seemed to begin all of his thoughts. He blamed himself for the stupid way he had allowed his passion to override concern for her feelings that last morning in bed. After all the care he had taken to be patient in winning Lisette's love, he had undone her trust at the first opportunity! Then, if only his mother hadn't chosen that particular hour to visit—and that particular conversation to have with him when he and Lisette were quarreling. . . . Of course, Lisette had contributed to the tangle of misunderstanding herself with that incomprehensible announcement about returning to the CoffeeHouse.

Nicholai had too much faith that their love was genuine to worry that it might be damaged beyond repair. He had decided to take Antonia's advice. He would court Lisette slowly, taking his time to win her complete trust. Together they would build a relationship with a solid foundation that would withstand any test. The thought of going through life with Lisette filled Nicholai with a euphoric warmth and buoyed his spirits.

"Why, Nicholai, hello!"

Nicholai blinked at the sound of a familiar feminine voice. A hand touched his arm; it was Mary Armstrong, smiling up at him, her blond curls framed by a pert chipstraw bonnet.

"Mary! It's wonderful to see you." They embraced briefly. She still smelled of roses, and Nicholai felt a momentary pang at the memories her scent evoked. "How have you been? I cannot get over the way time has improved on your loveliness, Mary."

The tender expression in his eyes made her want to weep. How handsome he looked! Putting a hand up to Nicholai's lean tanned cheek, she murmured, "I heard about your—episode with Marcus Reems. I've been praying for you, and I would have come to see you but I was afraid that Timothy wouldn't understand. He knows how much I once cared for you . . . and I think he has been rather worried ever since you returned to Philadelphia."

"I am fine now—thanks to the care I was given by Lisette Hahn. Do you know her?"

"Well—yes!" Mary realized instantly that Nicholai felt for Lisette Hahn what he had never felt for her. Tears stung her eyes. "Are you on your way to see her now?"

Nicholai laughed when he saw that they were standing less than a dozen feet from the CoffeeHouse; he had been so engrossed in thought that he might have passed it completely if not for Mary Armstrong. "As a matter of fact, I am. I've a letter to deliver to her that she apparently left at Markwood Villa by mistake."

"I see," Mary observed. "She must be an extraordinary woman." Part of her felt sick, knowing that the man she would always love had lost his heart to someone else, yet because she did love Nicholai she was glad that he had finally found happiness. "I am sorry that I don't know Mistress Hahn better."

He glanced back down at her sweet face. "I will make a point of introducing the two of you someday—properly. I think that you would get along very well. . . ." Nicholai cupped her small chin in his masculine hand. "You are quite extraordinary yourself, Mistress Barcroft. Our lives have changed, but all that we shared remains alive in our memories."

Mary couldn't breathe. She tried to suppress her tears, but her eyes filled instantly. "Oh—Nicky . . . I—" Helplessly, she pressed a hand to her mouth to keep from sobbing aloud.

"You mustn't cry, sweetheart! What if Timothy should discover us?" Smiling, Nicholai ignored the people who passed on either side of them and bent to gently kiss the salty tears from Mary's cheeks. She was a part of his past that he would cherish forever. "I still care, Mary. I'm sorry if I hurt you, truly."

Mary managed, somehow, to regain her composure. Smiling bravely, she insisted, "I am fine, Nicholai! I must have just had an unexpected attack of sentimentality. Don't imagine that I am pining for you still, because the truth is that my marriage to Timothy is wonderfully happy. We have so much in common—and we are best friends. Honestly, I am blessed."

Meanwhile, in the public room of the CoffeeHouse, Lisette Hahn stood behind the twelve-on-twelve paned window that faced Spruce Street. A dusting cloth hung limply from her hand as she watched Nicholai kissing tears from Mary Barcroft's face. In a corner of her memory, she discovered a story that Katya had told her long ago about Nicholai and the sweetheart of his youth, Mary Armstrong. As she recalled, Mary had loved him so that she waited for years, hoping for his return from France, before she finally surrendered and married Timothy Barcroft.

Lisette sighed, turning away from the sight of Nicholai kissing the petite blond's hand. *I have been such a fool,* she thought, *to have ever imagined that a man like Nicholai could feel differently about someone as ordinary as I. There are so many others girls waiting anxiously in the wings . . . and all it takes is boredom or an argument to send him off to the next, fresh challenge. And, why not? I don't blame him.*

Lisette's heart ached, as it had for the past three days. Sometimes, when the pain worsened and hot bitter tears burned her eyes and cheeks, she imagined that she might be dying. Never had she known such agony. With all her might, she tried not to think of Nicholai, but the memories crept back all the same. Last night, Lisette had lain in bed, wide awake, while the afternoon they shared in the garden when she had begun to paint Nicholai's portrait unfolded once again in her mind. Each stirring kiss, each heady sip of wine, each one of his magical smiles came back to torture her. . . .

"Honey!" cried Hyla Flowers, "I don't know what to do with you! I thought you'd perk right up when you got back to work here, but I'm beginnin' to wonder if you ain't sick." She put a plump arm around the girl and led her back into the keeping room. "Come on now and sit down here. Why don't I fix you a cup of tea? I can make tea that'd cure anything!"

Lisette smiled weakly. "That would be nice. I'll finish these pies for you."

Perched on her usual rush stool at the worktable, Lisette rolled dough to make top crusts for the delicious-looking turkey pies. She couldn't say that work was a pleasure but it did help to distract her from the ache in her chest. As for the CoffeeHouse—it had changed and so had she. Bramble, the grouchy rawboned cook on loan from the Hampshires, had taken charge of the menu planning and execution that had always been Lisette's domain. It was clear that Bramble wanted to remain here until the Hampshires returned in the fall, but Lisette knew the two of them could never coexist for that long.

Meanwhile, Hyla was nursing a broken heart of her own and had been drinking heavily since Lisette's return. Pierre, the French valet from Belle Maison, who was considerably smaller than Hyla, had caused the flamboyant woman to fall desperately in love. According to Stringfellow, Pierre had enjoyed her attentions while he was there, but the day that Lisette returned he departed immediately for Belle Maison and hadn't been seen since.

"Men!" Hyla was declaring now as she placed a steaming mug before Lisette. "They're all alike. If you'd asked me, honey, I coulda told you. Never trust 'em; they'll only hurt you in the end."

Lisette finished crimping the edges of one piecrust and wiped her hands on her cotton apron. "Live and learn, hmm?" she replied archly.

Hyla was too busy gulping down her own tea to respond, but she did watch as Lisette lifted her cup and gingerly tasted the contents. "Whew! What did you put in here? You must have given me the wrong cup!"

"No, it's the right one. I made 'em the same. Good for what ails you, darlin'—a bit of sugar and lemon and a driblet of the darkest rum." Beaming, Hyla drained her own mug and licked rouged lips contentedly.

Lisette took another sip, welcoming the burning sensation that seemed to numb the tight ache that made breathing so difficult. "A driblet?" she repeated, smiling indulgently. "More like a *deluge,* I think!"

"It's put the roses back in your cheeks, my darling. I even see some sparkle in your eyes again," Hyla observed approvingly.

"In that case, I don't suppose that your 'cure' does any harm—just this once!" Lisette finished another pie and slid it in Hyla's direction. "Why don't you put these in the oven now, then see to the tables? It will be noon before we know it."

The older woman gazed regretfully into her empty cup, then sighed and put it in the dry sink. She had just deposited three pies in the top oven and was halfway to the door when it opened from the other side, causing Hyla to gasp and lurch back against the table.

"I don't think that tea agrees with you, Hyla," Lisette remarked as she frowned at the hole her finger had put through the dough when the table quaked. "Next you'll be dropping trays if someone exclaims or motions unexpectedly."

"Sorry. I'll go see to the tables now."

The abruptness of her reply caused Lisette to glance up instantly. Hyla's wide hips were already disappearing into the public room, but Lisette didn't care. Her eyes were riveted on Nicholai Beauvisage.

"Will you look who I found trying to sneak into the CoffeeHouse before it's properly open?" exclaimed Stringfellow with forced gaiety. He peered around Beauvisage's wide shoulders imploringly. It had torn him up to see Lisette come back all sad and brokenhearted, particularly since he had found love himself, with the adoring new maid, Nancy.

"Hello, Mistress Hahn," Nicholai greeted her, the formality of his words warmed by amused affection. How ludicrous that they had allowed pride to throw up this wall between them!

"Good day, Mr. Beauvisage," she replied carefully. "You are looking very well."

"Thanks to you."

It was true; he did look splendid. One would never guess what his condition had been a fortnight ago. It was as if Nicholai had never been wounded at all . . . as if their time at the villa existed only in Lisette's yearning-filled dreams. Here he was, confronting her once again at the Coffee-House. As usual, she wore a plain high-necked long-sleeved caramel cotton frock, most of which was concealed by a snowy apron fastened neatly around her slim waist. And, as usual, Nicholai wore handsomely tailored clothes that only accentuated his rouguish magnetism. He belonged in President Washington's drawing room—not in her flour-dusted keeping room. Lisette swallowed hard and returned her attention to the latest piecrust.

"I see that you have had your hair trimmed. It looks very nice." What she couldn't mention was the absent beard.

He had told her that he wanted to keep it . . . to remind him of her and their idyll together by. That resolution had lasted all of three days!

"You are too kind," Nicholai murmured with a wry smile. He glanced over at a slightly panicky-looking Stringfellow and knit his brow over eyes that threatened and implored at once.

"Mr. Beauvisage!" cried Stringfellow. "Please do be seated! Let me bring you a cold mug of ale."

"That's very generous of you," Nicholai replied. He took the stool opposite Lisette and tried, unsuccessfully, to catch her eye. "May I be of assistance?" he inquired at length. Why was the vixen being so prickly and elusive?

"Oh, no, that's not necessary. I'm nearly finished—and I wouldn't want you to soil that handsome coat."

"Do you like it?" he teased gently, and was reassured to see Lisette's cheeks take on a dusky glow even though she kept her eyes averted. He longed to reach for her hand, to kiss each graceful piecrust-smudged finger. . . . "Perhaps you have noticed that my beard has been shaved. I know what I said to you about keeping it, but once I returned to Philadelphia and considered the fact that beards are definitely not in vogue, I succumbed to Oliver's entreaties that I shave." Gently, his dark hand touched her pale, delicate wrist. "I didn't want you to imagine, Lisette, that I—"

"Actually, I hadn't even noticed, so you mustn't give it another thought." She kept her eyes on the pie, even though the last crimp had been put in the crust. She knew that his piercing gaze would be her undoing.

Nicholai was on the verge of asking what the devil was wrong with Lisette when the door swung open to readmit James Stringfellow. With a flourish, he presented the frosty mug of ale to Nicholai, who offered thanks in the form of a vaguely insincere smile.

"Here's my Nancy!" Stringfellow announced. He drew a shy young woman of perhaps twenty-five into the circle of his arm and grinned. "Perhaps you know her, Mr. Beauvisage! She comes from your parents' house."

"Well, of course. How nice to see you again—Nancy."

Seeming to smell the tension in the air, Stringfellow decided to try to alleviate it. After Nancy had smiled, blushed, and escaped back to her duties in the public room, the Englishman perched on the stool next to Beauvisge.

"Mmm, don't those pies look ruddy wonderful! I never knew a woman who could cook like our Lisette." Ignoring her embarrassed warning glare, he plunged cheerfully ahead. "Do you know that the expression 'upper crust,' meanin' gentry, came about in England because they were the only ones who could afford that extra crust? So, you see, our food is purely top drawer!"

"That's just fascinating, James," Lisette said without enthusiasm.

Nicholai heard Stringfellow asking if the prices had been higher at market that day, but then his attention wandered as a golden shaft of sunlight suddenly slanted through the garden window to illuminate Lisette. She was wearing a mobcap today, which he didn't know she owned. Her lustrous curls were pinned up beneath it on the sides, but cascaded down behind her shoulders. The frilly little cap took some getting used to, yet he thought that she looked adorable, peeking out beneath the ruffled edge, rebellious wisps of hair curling over her brow.

"Honestly!" Lisette was saying, suddenly afire. "The prices have simply gotten out of hand. Do you know what these turkeys cost? Over one dollar apiece! They are good sized, but that does not justify robbery!" Sparks seemed to fly from her sapphire eyes. "I paid two shillings, six pence for a dozen partridges and twenty-five cents for a pound of butter! Of course, I cannot purchase just one pound or one dozen . . . and I dread the thought of raising the prices I must charge for meals. Flour is now four dollars a hundredweight!"

Nicholai was enchanted. Her curls, washed by sunbeams, whirled with each angry gesture; she had never looked more delectable. He longed to kiss the warm satiny skin concealed beneath her plain cotton dress.

"What are you smiling about?" she challenged Nicholai. "Do you find the problems of the poor entertaining?"

"On the contrary, Mistress Hahn. You have my heartfelt sympathy." With an effort, he put on a serious expression.

"I don't want your sympathy." Turning, Lisette crossed the room to wash her hands in a bowl in the dry sink. The feeling of his burning eyes on her released a hundred confusing emotions that she hadn't the strength to deal with.

"Stringfellow, go and check your bar stock. Make certain that Chastity replenished the supplies of wine and lemonade as I requested."

"Yes'm." The little Englishman gave Nicholai an encouraging wink before hurrying through the door to the public room.

Nicholai looked at Lisette's back, wondering how to proceed. He wanted to catch her in his embrace, kissing her until the stiffness in her spine dissolved and her body melted against his own. He wanted to tell her that he loved her, that he wouldn't allow misunderstanding to damage their beautiful new relationship. The notion of beginning again, of wooing Lisette slowly, seemed too great a test for his patience.

At length, she turned away from the dry sink. Her expression was starchy, yet helplessly vulnerable. Nicholai's heart ached for her.

"It's nearly noon and there is a great deal to be done, so unless you have some specific business, I would appreciate it if—"

"But I do have specific business!" he interjected hastily. "I beg you not to turn me out, Mistress Hahn. I have a letter to deliver to you."

"From whom?"

"All I can tell you is that it is addressed to you. When Katya went back to the villa yesterday to retrieve a few odds and ends I left behind, she found this under the table by my bed."

Lisette accepted the envelope that Nicholai drew from his vest pocket. "I've seen this before. Stringfellow conveyed it to me a day or two after the duel. I brought it upstairs, unopened, and set it on your bed table . . . and apparently forgot all about it!"

"I wonder why?" Nicholai couldn't resist asking. A mischievous smile flickered over his hard mouth.

"I can't imagine, I'm sure." She stared at the letter tapping it against pretty fingertips as she waited for her cheeks to cool down. "Have you eaten, Mr. Beauvisage? Perhaps you would like a dish of chicken stew while I read this."

"I would be delighted, Mistress Hahn." He stressed the last two words, hoping that she would realize how ludicrous it was for them to use such formal terms.

Lisette set down the letter and took a pewter dish over to the fire. She spooned in fragrant stewed chicken and spring vegetables, then gathered up cutlery and gestured for Nicholai to take one of the comb-back chairs before the hearth. Moments later, they were settled side by side, Lisette with her letter and "tea," and Nicholai with his dinner and ale.

"This is delicious!" he declared after one generous mouthful of chicken and vegetables. He could taste wonderful scallions and turnips, celery and small red potatoes, asparagus, savory and tarragon and sweet butter, and, of course, tender, succulent chicken, cooked until it fell in shreds from the bones. . . .

Lisette couldn't repress a smile; it lit her face. "Thank you! I concocted that recipe last night single-handedly."

"You are a woman of rare talents, Mistress Hahn—and cooking is the least of them."

Pinned like a butterfly under his emerald gaze, Lisette blushed to the roots of her pale gold hair. She reached for her teacup and took a liberal shiver-provoking sip, then broke the seal on the letter. The parchment sheet crackled as she unfolded it, turning toward the firelight to illuminate the elaborately curled script.

"It is from the bank. . . ." Lisette said wonderingly, then fell silent as she read. "Oh my . . . Lord—!" Her azure eyes widened in surprise. "Thirty-one thousand dollars . . . from an anonymous donor—!" The sheet of parchment floated down to the floor as Lisette sprang up to pace in front of Nicholai. "Why would anyone want to give *me* thirty-one thousand dollars? It says that the money was deposited in an account under my name on April twenty-seventh. Do you suppose that this could have anything to do with Marcus Reems?"

"Well—I don't see how. He was dead. And, after all, why on earth would he *give* that amount of money to you?"

"I don't know. Why would *anyone*?"

Nicholai stared at the fire for a long minute, chewing on a delicious bite of chicken, then replied, "I can't answer that, Lisette, but my guess is that someone who has known and liked you—and who could afford it—must have decided to make life easier for you. Perhaps some old man who came into the CoffeeHouse for years—and who knew your father! At any rate, I wouldn't worry about it. It seems to me that you must have a guardian angel, and as long as he or she asks nothing in return, I wouldn't complicate matters by worrying about the angel's identity."

She cast a suspicious glance in his direction. "*You* wouldn't have anything to do with this . . . ?"

Nicholai laughed, looking so splendid in the firelight that Lisette's heart jumped. "I wish I could claim the credit— and believe me, if I were responsible, I would let you know! Generosity of this magnitude could only aid my cause!"

"Which is?"

Resting his fork on the edge of the pewter dish, Nicholai reached for her hand and kissed the soft warmth of her palm. It smelled and tasted wonderful, blending a clean womanliness with delicious food scents. Their eyes met and Nicholai lost himself in Lisette's hopeful melting blue gaze. "My cause is you, sweetheart," he whispered with a ragged sigh. "You know that."

Tears stung her eyes. "I—" What could she say? How could she possibly allow herself to trust him again?

Sensing her discomfort, Nicholai generously returned his attention to his dinner and changed the subject. "Do you have any idea what you will do with so much money?"

"Why . . . I will have to think about it, of course, but I suppose I will pay the remainder of Papa's debts, including the one I still owe to Senator Hampshire . . . and then I will be able to make repairs and improvements here in the CoffeeHouse. What is left I shall put away for that proverbial rainy day—which seems to arrive quite often around here!"

Lisette's exhilarated tone and winsome smile singed Nicholai's heart. He wished that they were back at the Hampshire's villa, that he had just been wounded and that she was holding him in the darkness. Not so long ago, he had been the center of her world . . . or so it seemed. Now, she slipped through his fingers like shimmering gold dust.

"I know what you mean, Lisette. There were many times

in France when I wished for a windfall to alleviate my financial worries. More than once, our grape harvest did not meet our expectations or some unforeseen expense arose to drain my pockets at the worst possible moment. I can appreciate what it will mean to you to be free from financial oppression."

"Freedom does seem to be the perfect word." She nodded.

"Now you are not only an independent business woman, but an independent woman of means. That's quite impressive!"

She was considering the implications of his statement when a formal knock sounded at the door to the garden court. "Come in!" called Lisette.

To Nicholai's surprise, it was Oliver who stepped across the threshold. Instantly, he rose and went to meet his butler. "Oliver! What has happened? Why are you here?"

"This letter came for you at the house—by messenger, sir. I was instructed that you must receive it immediately or I would never have disturbed you here, Mr. Beauvisage."

"I do hope that nothing is wrong!" exclaimed Lisette.

She stood just inches from his side, and Nicholai's instinct was to ignore both the letter and his butler and instead crush her against the length of his hungry body.

"I can't imagine that it is anything serious. If it had to do with my family, I'm certain that someone would have brought me the news in person. Was this messenger familiar, Oliver?" Seeing the black man shake his head in the negative, Nicholai quirked an auburn brow. "Perhaps this is just our day for letters, Lisette."

At this point, Oliver bowed and took his leave, but Lisette remained at Nicholai's side. She tried not to look as he casually broke the seal on the envelope, then unfolded the creamy pages inside. The scent of gardendias teased the air. Nicholai was looking ahead to the signature on the third sheet, and Lisette's eyes helplessly joined the search. Registering the name scrawled near the bottom, she felt as though someone had hit her in the stomach; she heard herself gasp aloud.

"Nicky, *je t'adore . . . toujours . . .*" it read, followed by a single, boldly signed name: *"Gabrielle."*

Chapter 31

May 10, 1793

Lisette attempted to speak, without success.

"Gabrielle . . ." Nicholai whispered in disbelief. "I cannot believe this!"

"Perhaps—" She swallowed, then licked her lips. "Perhaps you would like to go into the study . . . for some privacy—while you read her letter."

Lisette's voice came to him through a fog. He didn't want to keep her at arm's length because of this incredible —impossible!—letter, but there was Hyla Flowers in the doorway and he had no intention of sharing secrets with her. "I believe that I will just look this over briefly in the study. If you ladies will excuse me—"

The last glimpse that Lisette had of Nicholai's dazed expression frightened her. What did it mean? She wondered, watching him disappear down the narrow corridor.

For nearly a half hour, Lisette fussed over details of the meal they were serving that noon. She spoke sharply to Chastity while the girl was assembling a tray of dishes, then lost her temper when Nancy accidentally dropped a stoneware mug that shattered the instant it struck the brick floor. Finally, she turned on Hyla Flowers.

"I want you to look after things for a few minutes. I will return shortly." Without waiting for a reaction from the older woman, Lisette turned and hurried toward the study.

When she entered, she discovered Nicholai standing and staring out the garden window. He gave no indication that he had heard her enter . . . or that he was even aware of his surroundings.

Quietly, Lisette crossed the room and touched Nicholai's moss green coat sleeve. "I do hope—it's not bad news," she whispered lamely.

He saw her then, his eyes registering a flicker of surprise. "Oh—Lisette." Automatically, he gathered up the sheets of parchment that were scattered with such seeming negligence across the faded red chaise. "I'm in rather a daze, I suppose. It is difficult to believe that Gabrielle can truly be alive. I almost wonder if I *should* believe it!"

"You don't suspect that her letter could be some kind of —hoax?"

"No—no, that's not possible. There are too many references in her letter to—ah—incidents that only the two of us would know about . . . and besides, I recognize the style of her script. It's just . . ."—he ran a hand through burnished auburn hair and smiled bemusedly—"a shock. A happy one, of course, but one which requires adjustment. I mean, I went through hell and I grieved for her . . . and at last I resigned myself to the fact of Gabrielle's death and I put her in my past. . . ."

It seemed that Gabrielle herself had tightened an icy hand around Lisette's heart. He had loved the beautiful Frenchwoman so much that he still had dreams about her— and now she had returned, as if from the dead! "Well, it's a miracle, then, isn't it? Adjusting to a miracle should be quite a happy task."

The ragged edge of Lisette's voice broke through his distraction. The letter from Gabrielle was disturbing, but he had come to realize, since Lisette, that his relationship with the *comtesse* had been less than satisfying in many respects. The deepening love between himself and Lisette, however —so keenly sweet, arousing, and fragile—was another matter. "A miracle . . ." Nicholai repeated tentatively. "For her sake, I suppose it is, but, Lisette, I don't want you to think—"

"It's been a wonderful day for both of us, hasn't it?" She interjected with false brightness. "I have the financial means to make dreams come true here in the CoffeeHouse—and you have your Gabrielle back. That's *really* a dream come true!"

"Lisette—" Nicholai reached for her hands, but she slipped away, seeing only the anxiety in his expression.

"Is Gabrielle safe?" she queried, thinking that Nicholai must have been searching for a way to tell her where his heart really lay. "No doubt the situation in France is terribly frightening. Did she ever find her brother?"

He sat down on the chaise with a sigh. "Unfortunately, the marquis is still missing, but Gabrielle is safe. She writes that she was released by some miracle and was able to escape to England with a friend of her husband. Since then, she has met new people who have offered her friendship and their hospitality in London. . . ."

Lisette saw the telltale muscle that moved in his jaw. Taking a deep breath, she turned toward the window and said, "You must be anxious to go to her."

The fragrance of gardenias floated up from the letter and, for an instant, Gabrielle's bewitching countenance appeared in Nicholai's mind, giving him a familiar pang. "You are certainly in a hurry to get rid of me," he remarked dryly. Leaning back, he caught Lisette's delicate wrist and suddenly pulled her down on the chaise.

"What do you think you are doing? Let me up!" Her cheeks flamed with outrage as he held her down easily with one arm. Inside, she burned with jealousy and fear, certain that he would be leaving her now that his true love was alive. "If you think that you can just toss me down and—"

"And what?" he taunted. How fragrant she was—like early morning in a French boulangerie. Lisette's firm breasts strained angrily against her caramel bodice, reminding Nicholai of her satiny warmth in his bed that last morning at the villa. His arousal intensified abruptly.

"And—take advantage of me all over again, that's what!" accused Lisette, her own voice husky with yearning.

"You are a hard woman, Mistress Hahn—with a short memory. When will you believe that my motives are pure?" Unable to resist a moment longer, Nicholai buried his face against the sweet softness of her throat and tawny curls. "Mmm . . . you smell like freshly baked brioche . . . buttery croissants. . . ."

"Thank you so much!" Lisette replied sarcastically. "As for your motives—well, they certainly aren't pure! Now, let me up!" She thrashed against him until her skirts were over her hips, but Nicholai's pinioning arm prevented her from restoring modesty to her shapely limbs.

He wondered if those were actually tears he saw Lisette blink back. He covered her sweet petal-soft mouth with his own, tasting and testing, while Lisette sighed and melted, her arms twining around his broad shoulders as she kissed him back. Intoxicated, Nicholai thought he would go mad when she traced the soft inside of his lips with her tongue, then drew him deeper into a kiss that was a whirlpool of sensation and acute desire. . . .

Through a blur of tears, Lisette saw Nicholai's lean dark hand on her thigh. She could feel skillful fingertips grazing upward over sensitive flesh, nearer . . . nearer. . . . His hardness was pressing against her hip through a thin layer of petticoat and she wanted more than anything to turn against him, welcoming . . .

"Nicholai?" she whispered, suddenly aware that her bodice was undone. His mouth was burning her throat, the curve of her breast . . .

"Hmm . . . ?" he answered, circling her rosy nipple with the tip of his tongue. He felt her shudder, nails biting the steely surface of his shoulders.

"Please stop!" She made a muffled whimpering sound, one hand faltering against his jaw.

Instantly, Nicholai moved upward. He kissed her flushed, beautiful, perplexed face and experienced an unsettling twinge of guilt. "What is it, sweetheart? I'm listening." The sight of Lisette's bare breast crushed against his shirt and waistcoat only increased the agonizing throb in his groin.

"Did Gabrielle write only news of her present life? If there is something else—you really must tell me."

So that was it.

Propping himself up on an elbow, he watched Lisette rebutton her bodice. "No—that wasn't all that she wrote about," he sighed, sensing the storm that his next words would trigger. "Gabrielle asked me to come to England. She has heard that her brother, the marquis, has managed somehow to escape from prison . . . and she insists that

only with my help can he be found and aided, particularly
if he is still hiding in France."

"And her husband—the *comte*?"

"According to Gabrielle, he was guillotined even before
I went to Paris last August, which is what we suspected at
the time."

When Lisette tried to take a breath, it burned. "I see. So
. . . she *is* free. I suppose that you thought to use me to
provide one last bit of pleasure and satisfaction before your
celibate sea journey. Or—do they have women on board
ships during wartime?"

"For God's sake, Lisette! I was doing no such thing! I
don't intend to travel anywhere—"

Lisette interrupted with a sound that mingled frustration
with disbelief. "Please, spare me your timely denial!" When
she struggled to sit, his arm held her fast.

"I am not going to England, you hotheaded vixen! I want
to stay here in Philadelphia and continue what you and I
have begun!"

Lisette closed her eyes in an effort to block out the sight
of Nicholai's stormy face and jewel-hard eyes that seemed
ablaze with feelings that she was afraid to trust. "I don't
believe you. I cannot! I saw you that night at Markwood
Villa when you spoke of Gabrielle. You were in agony. You
wept for her!"

"I thought she was dead, Lisette! Old loves are easily
idealized—but it's rather inevitable when one imagines that
a beautiful, soft-skinned, coquettish girl has been brutally
tortured and murdered! I told you that my relationship with
Gabrielle was fed by the mystery of her personality—not
by a deep bond of eternal love. She was a challenge at the
time—"

"That's easy for you to say now, when she is thousands
of miles away and I am right here—and you have something hard and hot in your breeches—" The sight of his
sudden flashing grin made her face flame. "I'm serious! If
there were so many unanswered questions about your relationship and feelings for Gabrielle, then I think that you
should go to England and clear them up once and for all.
Also"—Lisette swallowed hard—"she apparently needs
you."

"But you don't."

"I . . . certainly enjoy your company—sometimes—but I do think it would be fair to say that I am self-reliant. I try not to depend on men to rescue me from life's predicaments."

Nicholai gazed at the proud tilt of her graceful chin and rubbed weary fingers against his brow. "How well I know it, my sweet. There is only one thing for which you need me—and most of the time you manage to resist calling on me for help even then. . . ."

She kept her eyes open wide so that the tears wouldn't come. Aching to reassure him, yet afraid to bare her soul, Lisette moved to sit up—and this time Nicholai allowed it. "Our relationship, such as it is, isn't the issue now. If there really is something meaningful between us, it will survive a separation. I will be fine here, as you well know. Now that I'm a lady of means"—she managed a shaky smile, but Nicholai's face remained stony—"there will be all sorts of matters to occupy my time. I just think it would be best, in the long run, for you to see Gabrielle—"

"All right, that's enough. You've made your point." Nicholai was on his feet, retying his stock with swift anger. Suddenly, his shoulder hurt like hell and he was exhausted. "Do you have any idea how long I might be gone if I make this trip? Months! If I go to France to search for that damned brother of hers, it could be a year or more before I return. If I survive—*and* if I feel the journey back here is worth the effort!"

Somehow, Lisette found the strength to stand. The harshness of his voice frightened and confused her. "Nicholai, I don't want you to think—"

"That you care? Don't worry!" he interjected bitterly, turning away when she placed a pale, hesitant hand on his clenched forearm. At the door, he paused, glancing back, his face dark and dangerously cynical. "Perhaps we will meet again one day, Mistress Hahn . . . though I've no doubt that you have never trusted me enough to believe that I might return to you once I have Gabrielle—or some other available female—to satisfy my *lust*. After all, two celibate sea voyages in one year would probably kill an animal like myself— *n'est-ce pas?*" After sketching a final sardonic bow, Nicholai opened the door and was gone.

For a long minute, Lisette felt as if she had been mortally wounded. Finally, she crossed to the door, pulled it shut, and dissolved into tears that seemed to spring from her very soul.

"Dear God . . ." she moaned, "what have I done?"

Chapter 32

May 10, 1793

"Attendez!" *Pierre rushed across the stair hall just as Belle* Maison's tall-clock was striking nine. He wondered who could have the bad manners to knock on the Beauvisages' front door while they were entertaining dinner guests! Plucking a tiny oil lamp from the side table, the Frenchman threw open the door and demanded, "Who are you and what do you want?"

The flame flickered over a dark cape that fell from broad shoulders. "How rude you are, Pierre! What kind of a welcome is that?"

The little man was momentarily speechless as he stared up at Nicholai Beauvisage, who was looking quite lawless in the eerie light. "Oh, m'sieur, I apologize! Is something the matter? What brings you all the way up here so late at night?"

"I am going to England." Nicholai stepped into the entry hall and removed his cape and gloves. "I must speak with Sacha. Is he in the parlor—or the library?"

"England? *Mon Dieu!* But—your brother is entertaining guests. They are in the dining room. Would you care to join them for dessert?"

"No! Slow down, Pierre. I don't have the time or the inclination to socialize tonight. Please, just go and beg Sacha to join *me* here for a moment."

"If you insist—but Madame will not appreciate this intrusion." He turned away, only to be brought up short by Nicholai's hand catching the tail of his coat. "Was there something else, m'sieur?"

"Ahh, yes . . ." Nicholai's eyes twinkled with amusement. "I just wanted to pass along a few words regarding your— ah—love life, Pierre," he whispered conspiratorially. "Perhaps your disposition might sweeten if you were to pay a bit more attention to that aspect of your life. . . ."

"What did you have in mind?" Pierre could not resist retorting, raising the pitch of his voice an octave or more.

"I'll overlook your insolence this time—"

"That is very generous of you!"

"As I was saying . . . I happen to know a woman who apparently is very anxious to help you lighten your mood —if you take my meaning. . . ."

"Mistress Hahn?" the Frenchman replied with mock innocence. "No doubt she will be lonely once you leave for England—"

Instantly, Nicholai's face darkened and Pierre saw that he had gone too far. "My time is limited," Nicholai said stonily, "so I would only suggest that Mrs. Flowers has been badly hurt by your cavalier treatment. She may be a woman of experience, but that does not mean that her feelings are less meaningful than those of some innocent maiden."

Pierre blinked. "Yes, m'sieur."

Managing to mellow his tone, Nicholai added, "You might want to pay Mrs. Flowers a visit—tonight, perhaps. I am certain that it would set her mind at ease."

"Well . . ." Pierre considered this. "Your brother has said that there is little to keep me here this evening. . . ."

Nicholai cuffed his shoulder in a spirit of camaraderie and pointed toward the dining room, watching as the slight figure vanished around the corner. Moments later, Alec appeared in the stair hall and came toward his brother, a curious half smile playing about his lips.

"Nicky! What brings you here at this hour? Won't you join us and the—"

"Please, Sacha. I haven't much time . . . or the inclination to socialize."

"In that case, don't let me interrupt."

Nicholai stood eye to eye before his brother, thinking that somehow the years in France had even caused him to grow a couple of inches, and the physical labor had strength-ened his body so that his shoulders seemed even wider than Sacha's now. . . . "I . . . have a letter from Gabrielle."

"Your *comtesse?*" interjected a startled Alec.

"The same. It seems that she is alive—and safely ensconced with a sympathetic family in London. However, her brother is still missing and although she has some clues as to his whereabouts, she feels that only I can effect the actual rescue."

"I see," Alec answered warily. "It sounds as if all the plotting Caro and Meagan did was for naught."

"If you are referring to Lisette—that was none of their affair anyway, but I wouldn't say that our cause is hopeless. Lisette is just playing her usual willful, fiercely independent role." Nicholai paused, rubbing a hand over the stubble on his chin. "It was she who urged me to go. In fact, she damn near forced me!"

"I think I should call Caro. She will want to arg—I mean, discuss this situation with you, *mon frère.*"

He caught Alec's shoulder in mid-turn. "No!" His whisper was as soft as possible. "I don't want to fight this decision out with my well-intentioned sister-in-law. You may tell her that Lisette and I have already raked the entire complicated mess over the coals. Really, the self-reliant Mistress Hahn left me no choice. And"—he sighed, considering what words to use—"perhaps she is right . . . in some perverse way. I ought to discover what has become of Gabrielle; clear that matter up once and for all. . . ."

"Is that all that it is? A 'matter'?"

"I—hope so . . . I am in love with Lisette. It won't be easy, as our Maman has so wisely reminded me, but I plan to make our romance work—forever." His mouth bent in a smile flavored with cynicism. "She thinks I won't be back, but—I intend to surprise her. I'm counting on you, big brother, to make certain that no one else—ah—usurps Lisette in my absence."

Alec didn't know what to say. "But, Nicky . . . if you loved Gabrielle so much, what makes you think that things have changed? Perhaps, when you see her—touch her—"

"I'm human; there is no doubt about that. I suppose that I am depending solely on the memory of Lisette to restrain my baser instincts. If I do weaken, I won't waste much time berating myself. That chit practically forced me to sail all the way to England to seek out my lost love. I mean, what does she expect? I—"

"I certainly won't try to change your mind," Alec murmured. "So, do you need some form of transportation? A Beauvisage ship, perhaps?"

Nicholai grinned engagingly. "That would help."

"It just so happens that we have a large schooner that will depart for Britain the morning of the thirteenth—from New York. That's just three days away, so you won't have much time—"

"I'll make the boat," said Nicholai grimly. "I have already packed and will leave for New York immediately."

"Is there anything else that I can do? I hope that you've spoken to Maman about this. She will be devastated to hear that you are leaving again—"

"Listen, Sacha, Maman strongly encouraged me to test my feelings for Lisette. I think she's convinced that the fair Austrian maiden is the wrong girl for me, so she should be overjoyed to hear that I have gone in search of Gabrielle." He paused to give his brother a bittersweet smile.

"You've spoken to our parents, then?"

"I stopped there barely an hour ago. They were out, but I left a letter that Mrs. Reeves promised to deliver as soon as they return from their supper engagement at the Binghams'."

Alec absently shook his head. "I don't know, Nicky— this all seems too sudden. Perhaps you should put this journey off for a few days to give yourself time to think about—"

"*Excusez-moi*, m'sieur," Pierre whispered apologetically from the far end of the stair hall. "I do not like to interrupt, but I could wait no longer. If it meets your approval, I will be going out for the remainder of the evening." The elfin Frenchman gave Nicholai a wink. "I have some business to attend to in Philadelphia."

"That's fine, Pierre. I will see you tomorrow," Alec replied distractedly.

"Good night, Pierre—and good-bye, for a few months at least," added Nicholai.

"*Bonsoir*, m'sieur." He turned to give the younger Beauvisage a long, warm look. "I wish you a safe voyage and a speedy return, M'sieur Nicky."

"Thank you."

After watching his valet disappear into the shadows that darkened the hallway, Alec returned his attention to Nicholai. "I've forgotten what I was saying—but I do know that I'd better get back to Caro and our guests or she'll be out here looking for me."

"I, too, must be on my way."

"So—it's farewell again." Unashamedly, the strong, handsome brothers embraced with obvious emotion. "I hate like the devil to see you leaving—so soon after—"

"I'll be back." Nicholai managed a roguish grin. "Godspeed, *mon frère*. Give your beautiful Caro a hug and a kiss for me—and Étienne, little Natalya, and Kristin, too. It has been a great joy for me to meet your children."

"They will miss you . . . as will I."

Nicholai put on his cape and gloves, glad for the excuse to avert his eyes before Alec could see their sudden telltale glistening. Then, after one last sad embrace, he opened the door on the cool spring darkness and Alec watched from the threshold until his brother had mounted a horse and set off down the drive.

"Alec, what in the world is going on out here?" Caro had come up behind him, her whisper edged with exasperation.

He turned, closed the front door, and leaned back against it. "That was Nicky. He is on his way to England." Seeking a distraction from the stinging pain he felt inside, Alec concentrated on Caro's delicate flushed face. Her caramel brown eyes were wide with shock, her lips were parted as she searched for words; he could see her quickened heartbeat betrayed by the rise and fall of her silk-covered breasts. Impulsively, Alec reached out and caught his wife in unyielding arms. "He asked me to give you this."

Caro felt as if she had fallen into some bizarre dream when Alec covered her mouth with his. His kiss was hot and his hand strayed around to the front of her gown, searching for a way inside her bodice. What was happening? she wondered crazily. They had dinner guests in the next room who were already confused by her husband's absence; Nicky had left—for England! . . . and now Alec was behaving like some sort of madman!

Somehow she managed to twist her lips free and hiss, "What has come over you? Have you lost your senses? Release me!"

"You sound like an irate virgin, *chérie*." Alec's tone was cutting as, abruptly, he freed her. "We *are* married, you know."

"Yes, and I also know that this is not the time or place for a display of marital love!" she shot back in a hoarse whisper. "And, even if it were, a wife is not some object to be manipulated at her husband's convenience!"

Alec's fists clenched, then relaxed. "I agree—and I apologize. I was . . . upset about Nicky."

"I accept your apology. We haven't time to quarrel now —but I do insist that you explain this madness about your brother. When is he leaving for England—and *why*?"

Briefly, Alec explained the situation, reminding her of Nicholai's entanglement with Gabrielle in France, and then brought her up to date about the surprising letter from England and Nicholai's subsequent decision to go there and discover the truth.

"I cannot believe that Lisette is letting him leave Phila-delphia—to go to another woman!" Caro finally exclaimed in a high-pitched whisper. "And what about Antonia? Has Nicky discussed this with her?"

"He says that Maman came to him and urged that he not rush a deep involvement with Lisette Hahn. She asked him to go slowly and test his feelings—and to give Mistress Hahn the opportunity to do the same. Frankly, I think Maman was right. The two of them couldn't be more mis-matched. No doubt they have a fine time under the covers, but neither of them is going to want to make drastic changes in—"

"Under the covers!" Caro interrupted, pressing a tiny fist against her husband's chest for emphasis. "You have no right to assume that their relationship is based on anything besides a spiritual and intellectual rapport—"

"Oh, *please*!" Alec snorted in disbelief. "You do my brother a great injustice!"

"OOuhhrrr—*men*! I suggest that we suspend this discussion for the time being. I am not only angry at you—but at your mother as well! How could she interfere that way in a relationship that was proceeding successfully? It was none of her affair—"

"But it *is* yours?" Alec inquired with quiet irony.

"I am going out to catch Nicholai before he's out of earshot."

He gripped Caro's arm with fingers that seemed made of iron. "You and I are going back to our guests. Nicholai is a grown man, responsible for his own private life. Unless *you* want to take that responsibility for his fulfillment in the matters of love, I suggest that you pay more attention to matters that concern your own husband and family!"

"Such as my *husband's* fulfillment—under the covers?" Caro inquired with sweet sarcasm.

"Look—!" Alec's grip tightened on her soft upper arm, then abruptly relaxed. "If you insist on making a fool of yourself with my brother, that's just fine, but one of us has to pay attention to our guests."

As her husband roughly turned toward the dining room, Caro spoke up. "You are absolutely right—and your turn is long overdue!"

With that, she threw open the front door and ran outside. Since only one family was visiting, there were no exterior lanterns lit, and Caro nearly twisted her ankle running across the gravel drive in an effort to cut off her brother-in-law before he made his exit from the stables to the main road. Almost immediately, she heard the hoofbeats on the road just past their driveway; he had already gone!

"Nicky!" cried Caro. *"Nicholai! Nicky!"*

After a moment the hoofbeats seemed to pause; then they turned back toward Belle Maison. Caro stood shivering on the drive until her brother-in-law came into view.

"What is it?" he murmured huskily. "Have you changed your mind about me after all this time?"

"Don't tease me, Nicky. I want to tell you farewell, if you insist that that is what must be—but more than that, I want to urge you to stay here, to resolve your problems with Lisette—"

His gloved hand reached down to cover her mouth. "That's enough, dear Caro. I appreciate your good wishes, but the rest you will have to leave to Lisette and myself— and to fate. . . ." He gave her a grin that seared her heart through the moonlight. "Did you want to give me a kiss, then?"

Nervously, she pulled free and took a step backward. "Not a kiss . . . though if things were different, I wouldn't mind—"

"Shocking! Another word and I will be forced to confirm my brother's darkest suspicions!" His gloved hand darted out in the moonlight to capture four of her slim, delicate fingers. For an instant, it seemed that they had fallen back through time to the starry night when their eyes had met this way in the garden behind his parents' home. Nicholai had ached with the desire to kiss her . . . and he'd gone on aching inside for months after Caro's marriage to his brother. . . .

"What—" Caro swallowed with an effort. "What is it? Are you all right, Nicky?"

His smile flashed in the darkness. "No. I am repressing an acute urge to steal the kiss that eluded me ten years ago." He lifted Caro's hand instead and pressed his mouth to the tender jasmine-scented pulse at her wrist. "Your beauty is as captivating as ever, my dear sister-in-law."

"Please don't go to England, Nicky. It's a mistake. I can feel it."

Releasing her hand, he straightened in the saddle.

"In that case, you must keep me in your prayers. Now, go inside, Caro. Yours guests—and Sacha—need you more than I." Seeing the tear that sparkled like a diamond on her cheek, he picked up the reins and nudged the horse with his knees. "*Au revoir.*"

❦ *Chapter 33* ❦

Midnight, May 11, 1793

The keeping room was bathed in a dim golden luster as Stringfellow finished banking the fire and looked around to see if anything else needed doing before he took his leave. A tub of still-warm water, recently vacated by Lisette, sat before the hearth, but he knew that Purity and Chastity would see to it when they began their day's labors at dawn. Meanwhile, his own bed beckoned. Stretching, the Englishman yawned, and then inhaled the aromas of the Coffee-House with contentment. He thought of Nancy, who had lately begun to give him more than shy kisses, and decided that it was a fine life that they all shared here. Even the long hours of work were happily spent . . . thanks to Lisette. She was a rare person, and an even rarer female! Intelligent, warmhearted, fair minded, hardworking . . . and so beautiful that the merest glimpse of her never failed to awaken his most instinctive male response. With all his heart, Stringfellow wished that his mistress would find the happiness that she so richly deserved. Remembering the sight of her red-rimmed eyes and sad down-turned little mouth this evening, he ached for her. How could things have become so snarled between her and Nicholai Beauvisage?

Stringfellow's reverie was broken by a knock at the garden door. The late hour and the sharpness of the rapping gave him pause, but he crossed the wide-planked floor and called out, "What is your business?"

"For God's sake, Stringfellow, open the door! It is Nicholai Beauvisage."

The Englishman pushed aside the bolt and threw open

the door, trying not to smile. "Well, well, Mr. Beauvisage! What brings you here?"

"I would like to see your mistress." He strode into the keeping room, doffed his cape and gloves, and raked a hand through his windblown hair. "Where is she?"

"Unfortunately, she has already retired, sir."

Nicholai's eyes fell on the bathtub that reposed before the fire, shreds of steam still visible above it. "I saw her light still burning from the street," he murmured in a hard voice. "I will check to see if Mistress Hahn is still awake."

"If I let you go up there, I'd never hear the bloody end of it!" Seeing the determined glint in Beauvisage's eyes, he cast about for extra persuasion. "You're probably thinkin' that the mistress would forgive me in the end, but there's Hyla to deal with—"

Nicholai looked satanic in the shadowy keeping room. "But, Stringfellow, you and I both know that the dear Mrs. Flowers is otherwise occupied."

It was impossible for him to feign ignorance, since he had personally admitted Pierre DuBois barely a quarter hour earlier. Hyla had pouted only momentarily before leading the Frenchman off to her bedchamber.

"How did *you* know?" Stringfellow couldn't resist asking.

"I'd love to stand here and chat the night away with you, my good fellow," replied Nicholai in an ironic tone that barely disguised his impatience, "but there is a certain young lady whom I would prefer to see first."

Stringfellow winced in surrender. "All right, then . . . go on upstairs. But, if Lisette asks my part in this escapade, I'll deny everything." He paused, then laid a hand on the taller man's arm and added in a low serious voice, "If this visit causes her more pain, Beauvisage, I'll never let you near her again!"

"I hear you, Stringfellow." After a few steps toward the stairway, he turned back, his own expression softening. "Thank you . . . and wish me luck."

Although physically and emotionally exhausted, Lisette could not bring herself to blow out the candles and climb into bed. Complete dark and stillness were more than she could deal with just yet. Standing before the window, gaz-

ing down on the sleeping city, she brushed her hair rhyth-
mically. The repetitious movement was comforting somehow, but nothing could erase torturous thoughts of Nicholai from her mind.

Has he already boarded a ship? she wondered. Perhaps
he was at sea at that very moment—bound for England
and Gabrielle. Since her own bitter parting from Nicholai,
Lisette had gone over each word they had spoken that day,
again and again, wondering what she might have done differently. Now, all her instincts cried out that she should
never have encouraged this sea voyage of his to England.
What folly! He had said that he didn't want to go, that he
wanted to remain with her, and indeed, Lisette must have
been demented to argue the point. But still . . . it seemed
that Gabrielle would have appeared time and time again in
their relationship—an invisible source of anxiety and wonder. There were already too many ifs and buts between her
and Nicholai; no simple future of love spread before them.
The knowledge of Gabrielle's presence in the world would
have been one barrier too many.

Lisette leaned sadly against the window frame and
weakly pulled the brush through her hair one last time before letting her arm go limp. If only . . . and then she
silently berated herself for even half wishing that Gabrielle
had never returned from the dead. Perhaps fate had a hand
in all of this. Lately, so much of the course of her own life
seemed beyond her control.

Nicholai stepped silently into the doorway and stared
at the perfect picture Lisette made across the room. Clad
in a snowy bed gown with a pleated bodice and buttons
from the top of her neck to below her hips, she seemed to
embody the essence of innocence and womanliness all at
once. Gleaming lemony hair spilled down Lisette's back,
while her breasts were outlined temptingly against the
batiste bed gown. What struck Nicholai most of all, however, was the tear that sparkled in the moonlight as it slid
down her cheek. What did it mean?

He crossed the floor so quietly that Lisette didn't realize
that someone was in the room until Nicholai was just a few
steps away. She whirled around, and her china blue eyes
were wider than ever as she breathed his name.

"Don't worry—I'm not a ghost." Nicholai smiled.

"I—oh, my—" A wave of elation threatened to over-whelm her. Nicholai stood just a few feet away, clad in the same buttery leather jacket, fawn breeches, white shirt, and knee boots that he had worn the night of their first meeting at Belle Maison. Recognition was followed by cold realization. They were traveling clothes. "I thought that you would be at sea by this time." She strove for a casual tone and even remembered to brush her cheeks dry, hoping that he hadn't noticed her tears.

Nicholai came near enough to smell the lily of the valley soap that scented her skin. "I am sailing from New York at dawn two days hence. When I realized that I could make the trip with time to spare, I decided to use those hours to . . . try to mend matters between us." He caressed the length of her silky hair tenderly. "I didn't want to leave it that way," he finished in a near whisper.

Unable to look at his face, afraid of what she might see, Lisette dropped her eyes to the floor like a little girl. "I . . . I have felt—badly as well," she murmured.

Nicholai made no verbal reply, but reached down to take the brush from her limp hand. The sensation of his fingers brushing her own sent hot currents of longing over Lisette's body.

Slowly, he began to brush her hair with long, sensuous strokes. Lisette's scalp tingled each time the brush moved through her hair. It was as though Nicholai himself were caressing her, and her shivery pleasure soon dissolved into arousal.

Nicholai felt it, too. In the wavering candlelight, her hair shone like molten gold; it felt like a silken waterfall against his knuckles that bent around the brush's handle. Lisette's scented stirring nearness became torture as minutes passed and his hunger grew more acute. His instincts urged him to turn her, crush her in his arms, kiss her until they both were weak, then rip off all those prim tiny buttons on her angelic bed gown, and *then*—if only it were that simple! Unfortunately, Nicholai was all too aware that Lisette was not so easily swept away by simple passion. She had a power to resist that could destroy a man's confidence. It was incredible, but he felt like a schoolboy now, scared to touch

the chit for fear that she'd scream rape and toss him into
the street. Just being near Lisette was so delicious . . . and
all too soon he would be separated from her for at least a
year—possibly forever.

A rebellious curl escaped the brush and fell across
Lisette's cheek. Nicholai's free hand moved to capture it,
but when his fingertips grazed her skin, he felt how warm
she was and sensed her weakness. His own loins ached in a
way that suggested whatever would begin this night between him and Lisette would be finished—one way or
another. Gently, his hand brushed downward to the soft
baby tendrils that curled along her neck. Lisette sighed.

Nicholai needed no further assent from her. Dropping
the brush, he slid his hands around her waist while his
mouth burned the tender spot below her ear. When she
leaned back against him so that the curve at the top of her
derriere pressed his hard masculinity, Nicholai let out a
low groan. His fingers strayed upward to caress the outline
of her breasts through the batiste, finally circling to touch
the taut peaks. Then, unable to hold back, Nicholai cupped
warm fullness in each hand.

Fire spread from Lisette's belly until her entire body
seemed to be aflame. She craved Nicholai Beauvisage with
a voracity that would not be subdued. Only her natural
reticence in matters of love, especially relating to this one
man, kept her from pressing her body to the length of his
and begging him to take her right there, on the floor if
need be.

She thought, *I won't have to face him tomorrow or the
next day . . . or for months to come. No one will know.
And . . . I may never have another chance to be held in his
arms, to feel his body against mine—*

When Lisette turned to face him, the candle guttered
out and Nicholai drew a ragged breath. His arms stayed
around her, resting on her lovely buttocks. Starlight illu-
mined the bronzed lines of his face and Lisette put up a
hand to trace his irresistible mouth and chiseled jaw just as
she had always longed to do. It seemed a night to fulfill
suppressed longings. His unexpected reappearance had to
be Fate's way of giving them both a second chance to say
good-bye. . . .

She opened her mouth to his kiss, surrendering herself to the exquisite sensation of their tongues fencing, the unique and wonderful taste of Nicholai, the hard pressure of his arms embracing her, crushing her thinly clad breasts against the cold leather of his coat.

Finally, when they were both faint with desire, he lifted his head. "Lisette—I hope you know what you are doing."

Her sapphire eyes glistened in the moonlight. "I do, sir. I'm giving you a proper good-bye."

"Oh, God—" he managed to groan as she led him by the hand toward the narrow rope bed.

"There's not much room," Lisette apologized with mock seriousness.

Nicholai flashed a grin in the dark. "It will be plenty, Mistress Hahn. I don't intend to stray far from your side."

She smiled in return, then experienced a stab of pain upon realizing that soon he would be farther from her side than at any point since their meeting at Belle Maison nearly two months earlier. Could it have been just two months since she first laid eyes on Nicholai? How bleak life must have been before that day . . . and would soon be again.

They sat down together on the quilt-covered bed. Staring at Lisette through violet-shadowed darkness, Nicholai wished he could know her thoughts. His feelings for her were so keen and confusing that he sensed that she felt something—love?—with equal intensity for him. Yet, with Lisette one could never be certain. She was as beautifully soft and as enchanting as a rose . . . and just as fraught with unsuspected thorns. Ever since their first meeting, he had worked to tear down the barrier she had erected to hide her real self, but no sooner did he destroy one obstacle than did another seem to appear in its place. . . .

Nicholai reached out to touch Lisette's high-necked bed gown. His eyes held her fast as he carefully unfastened one button, then the next, and the next, until Lisette shivered as he opened the last one below her hips. With deliberate slowness, he parted her bed gown and feasted on the vision of her swelling breasts and flat belly. When Nicholai's mouth burned her shoulder, Lisette gasped aloud and lay back across the bed.

"Shh," he soothed, nibbling a trail over her collarbone,

then downward to her right breast. It swelled eagerly to meet his mouth, but he bided his time, kissing every inch, until finally his lips fastened on the rosy nipple, sucking tenderly as it puckered against his tongue.

Lisette felt the hot yearning deep in her belly, and was torturously conscious of Nicholai's hardness pressing through his breeches. She longed to tear off his clothes and ease the ache they both felt, yet the sensations his tongue evoked were so acutely pleasurable that she could only move closer when he sought her other breast. It seemed that he had lingered over her for an eternity when Lisette became conscious of the frightening pressure building in her loins.

"Stop!" she whispered hoarsely. "I can't bear any more."

"But you enjoyed it?" Nicholai inquired, his breath warm against her ear.

Lisette shivered. "Too much." She sat up and closed her bed gown over tender breasts.

Although throbbing with the need for release, he couldn't repress a smile. "What is the problem, then, *chérie?*"

She stiffened, then shuddered. For a moment, fear clutched her as she realized what must come next, but it was swept aside by yearning . . . and love.

Nicholai stared in disbelief as Lisette reached up to pull off his jacket, and unfastened the folds of his stock.

She giggled helplessly. "You look—incredulous!"

Watching his shirt open under her eager fingers, he could barely find his voice. "Well . . . this sort of behavior is not exactly in character—"

"Are you shocked? I'll stop if—"

"No!" Nicholai managed a fairly self-assured laugh. "As a matter of fact, I'm delighted! Do go on."

She blushed, but removed the shirt all the same, regarding him through lowered lashes. The moonlight emphasized the splendor of Nicholai's body and the reckless magnetism of his face. Laying a hand on the crisp auburn hair that covered his chest, Lisette gathered her courage, leaned upward, and kissed his lower lip, then all of his mouth. With a low groan, Nicholai surrendered and met her playful tongue. It took all his control to suppress the urge to roll Lisette into the pillows, pull up that damned bed gown, and seek the release he craved. Instead, he clenched his fists and suffered the torment of her feather-soft caresses, teasing kisses, and finally the wrenching sensation of her fingers unbuttoning his breeches. Nicholai slid his hand into her glossy hair and held the back of her head firmly, so that the flirtatious kiss she had been inflicting upon him deepened. Lisette couldn't break away; his mouth demanded a response that seemed to explode from the deepest part of her spirit. The kiss went on and on, like a whirlpool that pulled her under until escape was unthinkable. Finally, through a blur, Lisette saw Nicholai's silhouette against the silvery night as he stood to strip off the rest of his clothing. In the next instant, he had turned back the covers on the bed and she found herself lying against the cool pillow. Nicholai's lips hovered just near enough for her taut nipples to graze his chest through the batiste of her bed gown.

"Oh, Lisette . . ."

Her hands were caressing his hard buttocks, hips, and the muscled width of his back. "Hmm?" She heard her own voice as though in a dream.

"I'm having trouble believing that you are real," Nicholai sighed.

Lisette smiled through a mist of tears. For a moment, the heat of passion made room for quieter emotions as their eyes locked in the shadows. Lisette stared at the face she had grown to love so acutely and wondered if his image would begin to fade in her mind after a few weeks. "I'm going . . ." Her throat ached with tears. ". . . to miss you terribly."

Nicholai didn't trust his voice to answer. Instead, he kissed her wet eyelids with infinite gentleness, then traced the rest of her face until their lips came together tenderly. He lifted the white bed gown over Lisette's head, and when their bodies met at last, the pleasure was so intense that it approached pain.

Chapter 34

May 11, 1793

"Shh, sweet baby, it's all right . . ." Alexandre Beauvisage soothed his tiny daughter. Kristin had awakened just before the clock struck three and, even after being changed and rocked by her father, refused to relax and go back to sleep.

"Gwah!" Hovering on the brink of tears, she squirmed in Alec's dark strong arms.

He kissed a soft, sweet-smelling ear. "We are going to wake your mama and have her give you something warm for your tummy," he whispered reassuringly as they traversed the dark hallway together.

Caro met them in the door to the master bedchamber. Silvery moonlight haloed her gossamer bed gown and made Alec forget the harsh words they had exchanged earlier in the evening. However, instead of greeting him and their daughter, she pivoted and paced across the room.

"So—you're awake," Alec remarked, wincing as Kristin dug her fingers into the gray velvet robe he wore.

"I've barely slept all night!" she returned sharply.

"You were certainly giving a good imitation of it when Kristin began to cry!"

Caro glared over one shoulder as he sat down, cradling the baby in his arms, on the edge of the Hepplewhite four-poster. Both of them knew better than to trade any more barbs in the presence of their already overwrought daughter, but the tension remained heavy in the air. Since their quarrel earlier that evening, they had barely spoken, except to keep their guests from realizing that anything was amiss. Caro had gone to bed first, pretending to be asleep when Alec joined her and offered a tentative caress. Too many things had been whirling in her mind since Nicholai's farewell visit; there wasn't room enough for Alec yet.

"It was your turn to get up for the children, and you know it," Caro finally replied in a menacingly soft tone.

"I wasn't complaining, darling wife, but simply offering an observation." Alec's turquoise eyes narrowed dangerously. "However, I have tried every method of soothing Kristin that I know, and there are some remedies that I am incapable of administering."

Caro had resumed her pacing, but stopped at his words, tossing her head so that honey gold curls spilled back over one bare shoulder. "Honestly! Why did she have to pick this night to revert to—"

"Infancy?" Alec supplied sarcastically.

"You know what I mean! Kristin is seven months old and has been sleeping regularly through the night since before Christmas! She shouldn't need to be fed at this hour any longer!"

"Caroline," he ground out, "if you have an alternative to suggest, I would be happy to listen. Our daughter is restless and unhappy, and frankly, I'm beginning to share her mood. I want to go back to sleep!"

Sighing in surrender, Caro returned to the bed, propped up her pillows, and held out her arms to receive Kristin. The moment downy curls brushed her cheek, she felt a pang of self-reproach.

Alec settled himself on his own side of the bed and watched as Caro freed a creamy breast. Kristin snuggled into her mother's arms and began to nurse.

"I apologize. I behaved abominably," Caro murmured at length. "It's just that . . . this situation between Nicky and Lisette—"

"Is ruining the 'situation' between you and me!" Alec supplied testily. Then, softening, he bent to kiss her shoulder.

"Can't you see that it is because you and I have known such happiness that I am heartbroken to see Nicholai throw away his future with the girl I am certain he loves?" she whispered heatedly. "It was easier for us because, in spite of my stubbornness, I always wanted you more than anything else. I wanted our life together more than anything else. What disturbs me is that Lisette hasn't realized yet—or admitted to herself—that she needs Nicholai."

"Caro," Alec replied in a carefully even tone, "it's none of your business. They are both adults. Maman has already interfered and probably made things worse. I think it would be wise for us to leave well enough alone."

"I can't help being frustrated. It seems that there must be some simple solution that would fix—"

"No! That's enough." He looked down, afraid that they might be keeping Kristin awake, but his furrowed brow relaxed at the sight of her sleeping so angelically against the curve of Caro's breast. "There, you see," he whispered, "your daughter is dreaming with a smile on her face that I envy!"

"Wicked man!" Caro grinned.

"I'll return Kristin to her cradle, then show you just how wicked I can be!"

Waiting for her husband's return, Caro curled up under the sheet and coverlet and pondered her dilemma further. By the time Alec closed the door and slid into bed beside her, he was hoping that Nicholai would be replaced in her thoughts by imaginings of the love exchange to come.

Caro relaxed against her husband as he kissed her neck. One tiny hand caressed Alec's back before she murmured thoughtfully, "I just wanted to remind you that *all* meddling is not harmful. In fact, if Grandmère had not meddled ever so skillfully and subtly in *our* lives, we might never have realized—"

"Caroline . . ." he warned against her ear.

Suddenly, her topaz eyes were alight and she gripped him excitedly. "Oh, my goodness, I have just had the most wonderful idea! I feel as if I've been struck by lightning!" She held fast to his face, which had been gazing heavenward. "Don't ignore me, Alec. A plan has dawned on me that could resolve the entire situation between Nicholai and Lisette!"

"I don't want to hear it."

"But—"

"Save it for the morning."

"Darling, it *is* morning," Caro countered mischievously, "and—"

"And Nicky is hours away, en route to New York town. Nothing can be done to reunite him and Mistress Hahn at this moment, so I suggest that you put your plan away for the time being and concentrate on more *pressing* business!"

When his mouth closed over her own, silencing the words so eager to spill forth, she resisted only for a moment. As always, Alec's kiss—in fact, everything about him—assaulted Caro's senses like some sorcerer's magic. But, after ten years, she was aware that it was not magic that caused the storm between their two bodies, but love in its purest, most exquisite form. Still, even as she returned Alec's kiss and shivered deliciously when his hands found their way under the gauzy bed gown, part of Caro's mind remained with Nicholai and Lisette. She cared too intensely about both of them not to want them to discover the joyous, committed love she and Alec shared. . . .

The sun was just beginning to spread a rosy apricot stain over the horizon when Alec and Caro drifted off to sleep, locked in a warm, sensual embrace.

In Philadelphia, several miles south of Belle Maison, Alec's brother Nicholai was waking up and hating every moment of it.

"Lisette . . . it's dawn," he whispered regretfully.

Her eyes remained closed; her thick lashes fluttered on her dusky cheeks. Lisette's leg was entwined in Nicholai's hard limbs and her graceful arm curled around his wide back.

"Wake up, sweetheart." The words were like poison. Still she didn't stir, so he tasted her lips, which were a delectable deep rose color from so much kissing. Flushed and sleep-warm, Lisette's skin was soft as satin beneath Nicholai's wandering mouth. He teased and tantalized until Lisette moaned aloud and strained nearer. He had meant to trick her into revealing that she was indeed awake, but now it was impossible to stop. How could a woman be so delicious, so intoxicating?

Lisette swallowed a sob. His mouth burned, sending

waves of excruciating pleasure over her nerves. She pushed tense fingers deep into his clean burnished hair and held him fast against her breast. If only they could stay like this forever!

Suddenly, almost savagely, Nicholai turned her into the pillows and parted her thighs. Capturing her mouth in a scorching kiss, he felt Lisette's hips press upward against his own. During the night, they had made love over and over, but now their bodies met and fused with an urgency that suggested the breaking of a long, torturous fast. Tears spilled from Lisette's eyes and wet both their faces as Nicholai's hardness drove upward and retreated, then filled her again in a pattern that seemed to exemplify their entire relationship.

At last the storm was spent. Hearts pounding, they lay quiet but still united.

"It's late," Nicholai whispered with a harsh sigh.

Lisette clung to him. There was so much that she wanted to say, but the fear of rejection silenced her.

It was agony for Nicholai to separate himself from the snug enchantment of Lisette. He very nearly groaned aloud, but managed to stand somehow and search out his clothing. No dawn had ever looked bleaker.

Under the quilts, Lisette shivered as she watched him fasten shirt buttons and breeches. Her eyes memorized every detail of his face, his body, his gestures—as if she could ever forget! When at last Nicholai sat on the edge of the narrow bed to pull on his stockings and then knee boots, Lisette's pain intensified so that she found herself curling into a protective ball.

Nicholai leaned over to retrieve his leather jacket from the back of a nearby chair, then forced himself to turn and face Lisette. She looked like a wounded fawn.

"I—don't want to leave." Nicholai resisted an impulse to press a fist against the tightening ache in his chest. Instead, he smoothed damp golden tendrils from Lisette's brow, praying crazily that she would beg him to stay—forever.

"You—we both know that you have to go," she managed to answer softly.

Bending, Nicholai curved a strong hand around her neck and they shared a lingering bittersweet kiss. Then, "Come with me, Lisette."

She felt the heat of his words against her temple and stiffened. "Wh . . . what?"

"Come with me to England."

Panic washed over her, followed by a barrage of fears —of the unknown, of being out of place, of watching Nicholai fall back in love with the mysterious Gabrielle while she stood by and watched, helplessly. "But—the CoffeeHouse. You know that I can't leave it. I have a responsibility, Nicholai. Many responsibilities to many people. I'm not free to just pick up and—"

"Never mind!" Unable to bear the sounds of her excuses or the uneasy look in her eyes, he stood up and shrugged into his jacket. He felt a fool for even asking her, for hoping that she might love him more than her damned Coffee-House—enough to follow him into an uncertain future. "I don't know what possessed me to ask you such a thing, Lisette." Nicholai raked a hand through his ruffled hair, striving for a light tone.

"Well . . ." Tears filled her throat as she saw his gaze flicker from the wall to the window.

"I do have to go. I'm late as it is." He arched a dark eyebrow, and reached for one of her hands. "Farewell, Mistress Hahn."

It might have been a stranger's mouth that kissed her cold hand. "Good-bye, Nicholai." Her own voice sounded far away. "Godspeed . . ."

A moment later, the door closed and Lisette was alone.

❧ Chapter 35 ❧

May 17, 1793

Caro and Katya were visions of springtime as they breezed into the keeping room and greeted Hyla Flowers. The older woman, drenched in perspiration, took in their gowns of sky blue and peach and glowered.

"You two have a lot of nerve comin' in here dressed like that—all fresh and perfumed!"

"Oh, Hyla, don't be such a grouch. You've been spending too much time with Bramble!" Katya scolded good-naturedly. She and Caro perched on stools at the worktable before she continued, "How fares our friend Lisette these days?"

Hyla dumped an apronful of onions on the table, then hitched up a stool of her own. "Just awful!" Her voice lowered to a hoarse whisper. "Since that brother of yours disappeared, she's been wastin' away! I knew that he was nothing but trouble that first night—when Ernst Hahn died. If I believed in curses, I'd think Beauvisage put one on this CoffeeHouse!"

"That's ridiculous and you know it! Lisette and Nicholai are in love—which has you as badly frightened as it does her!" exclaimed Katya.

"Love—ha!" Hyla attacked the first onion with her knife. "If your devilish brother is so besotted, why is he off to England to bed some other chit?"

"Who told you that?" Caro inquired.

"Why—that Frenchman, Pierre. DuBois." Seeing their eyebrows raise suggestively, she blustered, "Where I learned

it makes no never mind. I say, good riddance! Men are all
the same—out for one thing. Women've got to learn to do
the same and not let their hearts get all gooey after one turn
under the sheets!"

Fearing that Hyla would take off a finger if her temper
blazed any higher, Caro nodded agreement. "You are a
wise lady, Mrs. Flowers. Lisette is fortunate to have you
here. I'm certain that the knowledge of your presence was
greatly reassuring to her during her recent absence."

Caught off guard by the soft-voiced compliments, Hyla
sniffed and allowed, "She couldn't have just up and left anyone in charge, that's true. Not that I was a bit happy about
her bein' alone out in the country with that scoundrel!
Things weren't no bowlful of cherries here, either, I can
tell you!"

Katya glanced around. "Where *is* Bramble?"

"The mistress sent her to visit her old aunt in Germantown—until she can decide what to do with her, just between us. There ain't room in the keeping room for the
both of them. Old Bramble'd like to be mistress here herself."

"Did she do competent work?" Caro pursued with studied
casualness.

"Oh, her work was fine as long as she was givin' the
orders when the mistress was off with that rogue Beauvisage. She ain't a barrel of fun, but she loves to manage
. . . and her cookin' was real good."

"Better than mine?" Lisette's tentative challenge came
from the hallway that led upstairs.

"Aw, no, honey!" cried Hyla, and scrambled off the stool
to meet her young mistress halfway. Wrapping an arm
around her, she led Lisette back to the table. "It'll be a cold
day in hell when that old crow's cookin' can match yours!"
Gently, she added, "How's that ache in your brow?"

"Better. I appreciate your concern, Hyla, but you mustn't
treat me like a child. I'm just tired, I think." She gave a
brave smile to her visitors and went to hug Katya. "It's
wonderful to see you! My goodness, the wedding is almost
here and we haven't even discussed the menu!"

"That is the least of my worries right now." She stared

with concern at her friend's pinched, pale countenance. "Are you ill, Lisette? There are shadows under your eyes and—"

"I haven't been sleeping very well, that's all. I may have picked up a bit of the ague that has been circulating in the public room, but I'm certain I will be fine in no time."

After a few more minutes' idle conversation about the impending arrival of Citizen Genêt in Philadelphia and Katya's wedding plans, Lisette politely inquired about the children of Caro and Alec.

"They are all fine . . . now," Caro replied carefully, glad for this perfect opportunity to broach the subject upper-most on her mind. "My youngest daughter has been quite ill these past few days with that nasty ague you mentioned. If not for that, I would have come to visit you days ago."

"Oh, really? Whatever for?" Lisette's voice sounded distracted and her hand trembled slightly as she smoothed a loose curl from her brow.

With a quick glance in Hyla's direction, Caro murmured, "It is a subject I would prefer to discuss privately. . . ."

"Oh—!" Lisette could hear her heart pounding in her ears; instinct told her that Caro was going to speak about Nicholai. Could he possibly have arrived too late for the ship to England? Had he returned to Philadelphia? "Hyla, would you go into the public room and make certain that Stringfellow and the girls have everything in order?"

Noting the color that stained her friend's cheeks, Katya exchanged glances with Caro.

Grudgingly, Hyla Flowers did as her mistress bid after adding the sliced onions to the pepper pot that simmered over the hearth.

"Well?" Lisette prompted when the door had swung closed.

Katya began, "We realize that it is none of our affair, but Caro and I have been very concerned about the situation between you and my brother."

"Only because we care so much for you both," interjected Caroline.

"That is . . . very nice of you," she acknowledged, her heart sinking, "but rather beside the point now, since

Nicholai has sailed for England." She paused, then added helplessly, "Hasn't he——?"

"Unfortunately, yes." Caro nodded. "Alec received word just this morning that the ship departed from New York four days ago, as scheduled, and Nicky was indeed on board."

Looking pitifully crestfallen, Lisette pressed a hand to her mouth.

"I knew it!" Caro burst out. "Nicky told Alec that you urged him to make this journey, but I knew you couldn't really feel that way. Why on earth didn't you stop him, Lisette?"

"Oh, I had plenty of reasons, but I won't claim that any of them made any sense. I felt threatened by the thought of Gabrielle, still alive—haunting him. I find it hard to believe that he could be happy with me, knowing that she still wanted him. . . ." She smiled sadly. "All my old fears rose to the surface. Also, Nicholai and I have had our share of other problems, and sometimes the pain of . . . caring so much has made me wonder if I'm not just better off working here, where I am in control and the days pass smoothly. Every step in my involvement with Nicholai has taken me just that much farther into the unknown. I was hurt in the past, by another man, and I am hurting now . . . and the idea of being rejected by him if we were any more entangled is terrifying."

Seeing the tears that glistened in her friend's sad eyes, Katya felt her own eyes sting sympathetically. "Oh, Lisette, you should have come to me. How awful that you've kept it all inside." She held tight to her pale hand.

"I've always been able to cope so well with the crises in my life . . . but this falling in love has been more difficult than the deaths of my parents or the challenge of running this business all alone. . . ." Tears spilled down her cheeks. "I was out of my depth from the first night I met Nicholai. That frightened me."

"So you retreated—back to safer waters," Caro murmured.

"I kept trying!" Lisette wiped her eyes with the edge of her snowy apron. "He seems to be in my blood, though. He won't be dismissed. Since Nicholai left, I have dreamed constantly that he has come back . . . and in my dreams, the image of him in the doorway is so real that it seems I could touch him—but when I draw near and put out my hand, I waken to my dark chamber and empty bed and it seems that my heart will burst from the pain. . . ."

"Oh, Lisette—" Katya was weeping, too, and wrapped her friend in a tight embrace.

Caro waited for a few minutes, until they regained a measure of control, then demanded, "What do you intend to do about this?"

"What can I do? Ever since the letter arrived from Gabrielle, it seems that I had to let him go and discover the truth for himself. Now, I can only wait and pray that he returns."

"Oh—horse manure!" Caro ejaculated, surprising them all. "I think it is time for you to face a few plain facts, my dear! You are in love with Nicky and it isn't going to go away. Love is a gamble—but you can't win by sitting back passively and waiting for the cards to fall into place! Do you imagine that Gabrielle is doing the same? I am certain that you and Nicky are made for each other. I love him and want him to know the kind of glorious happiness that I have found with his brother. I am begging you, Lisette, to listen only to your own heart. You must fight back. I know you can win!"

Lisette could scarcely find her voice. "But—how?" Suddenly, she felt exhilarated.

"Go after him! He loves you. You must believe in yourself. Frankly, this insecurity of yours would seem ludicrous to anyone not familiar with the details. You have no reason to be anything but confident!"

"She's right, Lisette," Katya chimed in. "I am certain you could cast every beauty in London into the shade!"

"In— London?" Lisette echoed incredulously.

Looking satisfied, Caro propped an elbow on the table and rested her chin on her palm. "Why not?"

A wave of panic swept over her. "I cannot leave the CoffeeHouse!"

"Why not?" Caro repeated calmly.

"I have responsibilities!"

"This CoffeeHouse will do just fine without you. My feeling is that right now your first responsibility is to yourself—and to Nicholai. You must save him from that scheming spider, Gabrielle! I happen to know that you have come into a large sum of money, so you can afford to make this journey, plus you will be confident of the Coffee-House's financial solvency during your absence. I also happen to know that the person who left you that money wanted you to use it to obtain your freedom from the drudgery here—if you so desired."

"Bramble will take your place," Katya said reassuringly. "And we—Nicky's family and all your friends—will make certain that nothing goes awry while you are away."

At that moment, Stringfellow saved Lisette from answering by poking his head in the door. He was wound tight with curiosity to learn what was brewing in the keeping room, and prayed that whatever it was would revive his mistress's spirits.

"Stringfellow," Lisette said clearly, "bring us some wine. Suddenly, I am parched!"

With a grin, he saluted and nearly caught the swinging door in his face. "Yes, ma'am!" Moments later, he was placing goblets and a decanter of claret before the trio, then backing happily out the door. Katya poured the wine while Lisette mulled over all that they had said.

"Obviously, you two have planned this in some detail," she murmured at length.

"The idea came to me the night Nicholai paid his farewell visit. I couldn't sleep, I was so upset! If it hadn't been for Alec's scolding about my interference and little Kristin's fretfulness, I would have ridden in to see you that night!" Caro lifted her wineglass.

Looking ill, Lisette followed suit, then told them, "It might have saved us all a great deal of trouble if you *had* come that night to shed a bit of reason on the situation." She took another sip of wine and swallowed with an effort. "Nicholai was here that night. After learning that his ship would not be leaving for two days, he decided to return for a more amicable farewell . . ."

"He was here *all* night?" blurted Katya.

Lisette blushed.

"And he still left for England?" Caro cried heatedly.

"The scenes between us seem to follow a pattern," Lisette admitted sheepishly. "Although we have made progress— old barriers are not easily broken down." She thought of telling them that he had asked her to go along to England, but the prospect of Caro's certain explosion was too unnerving. Instead, Lisette managed a weak smile and shrugged. "Perhaps, if I had realized how overwhelmed I would be by Nicholai's absence, I would have been a bit more aggressive. I didn't really think that I had any choice but to let him go. . . ."

Caro sighed heavily. "Well, perhaps you needed this lesson to bring home the truth—but it isn't one that can be extended indefinitely! We mustn't give Mademoiselle Gabrielle any more time than is absolutely necessary. I've known women like her and they can be very dangerous!"

Lisette nodded, thinking of Amelia Purdy. "You are undoubtedly right, but I don't see how we can be certain that Gabrielle is that sort of woman . . . ?"

"After you have been with Nicholai for ten years, you will understand how I know."

Her words sent an excited chill down Lisette's back. Leaning forward, she looked from Katya to Caro. "This conversation is all well and good, but you haven't told me how I am to be transported to England, or what I will do when I arrive. How will I find Nicholai—and not appear to be a lovesick female who has chased him across an ocean?" Lisette could imagine a humiliating encounter with Nicholai. Gabrielle would be clinging to his arm, and regarding her with a disdainful expression. Perhaps they would be amused by her appearance—?

"You have that uneasy look in your eyes again, Lisette!" scolded Caro. "As of this moment, I want you to practice telling yourself that Nicholai loves you and that you are the only woman in the world for him. You are intelligent, strong, witty, and clever—and completely unique!"

"It's true!" exclaimed Katya. "And I know that those are exactly the qualities that intrigued my brother from the start! Remember how you used to insult him when you two first met? He found your independence fascinating! Furthermore, he still does. You mustn't let your fear of being hurt destroy your confidence."

"Oh . . ." Lisette reached out to embrace her friend. "Thank you. I realize that you are biased—"

"Biased for good reason!" cried Caro. "Do you imagine that we would take up your cause so enthusiastically if you weren't such a spectacular match for Nicholai? He deserves only the best!"

Lisette straightened her graceful back in the old way; a familiar gleam lit her eyes. "Tell me, then: how shall I travel to England?"

Katya and Caro exchanged triumphant grins, then the latter replied, "We have plans to meet Alec and Randolph for the noon meal at the Walnut Inn, but there is also someone else who promised to join us here beforehand." Caro lifted the lovely enameled watch that hung from a golden chain around her neck. "Goodness! It is later than I thought! I believe our friend may have already arrived! Lisette, won't you make his acquaintance? He and his family have been staying at our home these past few days—and he may just provide the vehicle for your reunion with Nicky."

Lisette was suffused with an excitement that she hadn't thought she would experience until Nicholai returned in a year or more—if indeed he did return. When Stringfellow opened the door and ushered a tall, dark stranger into the keeping room, she smiled irrepressibly. In some ways, he resembled Alexandre Beauvisage, but his countenance, accented by a thin white scar that traced one side of his jaw, seemed harder . . . more dangerous.

"Mistress Hahn, I presume," he greeted her sardonically. When he smiled, silver sparks flashed from slate-colored eyes.

"Lisette," Caro announced, "may I present Captain André Raveneau—your savior!"

Chapter 36

July 2, 1793

Lisette hurried to keep pace with André Raveneau as he strode briskly down Third Street. His mood seemed forbidding and she knew that his thoughts must be occupied by their imminent departure from Philadelphia, so she kept silent.

Just minutes before, Raveneau had come to fetch her at the elegant home of Nicholai's parents who had been kind enough to arrange a sunrise farewell breakfast. In the loving company of Katya, Randolph, Caro, Alec, Hyla, and Stringfellow, Lisette feasted on sausages, broiled fowl, buckwheat cakes, salt fish, ham, and hot tea with lemon and cream. Because of a recent outbreak of what people feared was yellow fever, the group had decided against gathering at the CoffeeHouse. It was located too near the waterfront, where the first cases had lately appeared. The educated opinion was that the fever had been brought to Philadelphia by a recent influx of refugees from Santo Domingo, where a bloody slave revolt was in progress. Contributing to the problem were the unsanitary conditions around the docks and the especially hot and humid summer the city was experiencing. Stagnant pools of water made breeding grounds for disease, on the narrow, filthy Water Street in particular. The Beauvisages had begun to talk about leaving Philadelphia for Belle Maison until the danger of an epidemic passed and Katya had been forced to postpone her wedding. For her own part, Lisette was torn about her voyage to England. It had already been delayed more than a fortnight due to some unanticipated but necessary repairs to Raveneau's brigantine, *La Mouette,* and now, in light of the potential yellow fever outbreak, she was both hesitant to leave her CoffeeHouse and anxious to get safely away in time. . . . For weeks now, she had worked to make certain that every detail at the CoffeeHouse was taken care of . . . and meanwhile, the sweltering days had dragged by, heavy with fantasies of Nicholai and their reunion. Lisette experienced moments of agonizing nervousness, but they were overtaken by her yearning for the sight of Nicholai's face and mocking grin; the sound of his ironically masculine voice; the feel of his embrace, and her own fingers touching the warm bronzed body she loved so acutely. . . .

Totally oblivious to her surroundings, Lisette gave a heartfelt sigh.

"Mademoiselle, do not swoon, I beg you!" Raveneau said sarcastically. He grasped her elbow as they turned east on Spruce Street, bound for the waterfront.

"I was concerned about my business, *M'sieur* Raveneau!" she returned sharply. "You men are not alone in pursuing financial responsibilities!"

"Vraiment?" he mocked, pausing in the dawn's mist to press a hand to his linen shirt.

"As long as we are not in France, *Mr.* Raveneau, why don't you stoop to the level of us Americans and speak English?"

He bit back a grin. "Your wish is my commond, Mistress Hahn."

Feeling his eyes sweep her body, Lisette wondered, not for the first time, how she would elude this lawless-looking Frenchman between Philadelphia and England. It would be hard enough to be at sea with a crew of men, but Raveneau struck her as one who would not be dissuaded by the cool-headed, tactful rejections that had always kept the Coffee-House clientele at bay. She doubted that even a straight-forward insult would work in his case.

"Did you bring anything besides those clinging muslin gowns?" Raveneau demanded, his attention back on the crowded footpath.

"Clinging?" Her face flamed. "If my clothing clings, it is only because of the heat!"

He gave her a sidelong glance. "Did I suggest otherwise?" He laughed. "My question is purely pragmatic, my irresistible Mistress Hahn. I am concerned for your sake. Your life at sea will be a great deal more free and enjoyable if you can live it in breeches."

As it happened, she had brought breeches, at String-fellow's suggestion. Still, Raveneau's attitude unnerved her. What was his game? Caro had said he had a family, but Lisette had yet to see them—and certainly they would not accompany him on so extended a voyage! What did that mean in terms of her fate on board *La Mouette?*

"Whether I have breeches or not should be no concern of yours, sir," Lisette told him coolly.

"If you say so, *ma'am.*" Raveneau was feeling genuine amusement now, which was a relief after hours of nonstop worry about every conceivable problem that could crop up during their departure from Philadelphia. "By the way," he offered in a kindlier tone, "you should not feel guilty about leaving the city now. As I see it, it's every man and woman for themselves!"

As they ascended the gangplank, Lisette saw her two trunks and bandbox waiting on the deck. Another glance at André Raveneau sent a fresh qualm over her nerves. Would this voyage be worth the trouble if she arrived in England used and abused?

At that moment, a young red-haired man of perhaps thirty years rushed forward to meet them on the deck.

"Captain!" he cried. "I'm so glad to see you here at last. *Some* of us have been concerned for your well-being after all this time!" The young man paused, then bowed in Lisette's direction. "How do you fare, Mistress Hahn? My name is Halsey Minter and I'm pleased to welcome you aboard."

"Minter is my first officer," Raveneau explained, "and my right hand. You can always turn to him for assistance."

"It's a pleasure to meet you," Lisette said warily, extending a slim hand. She had already known too many men of the sea to give any one of them her trust—or even the benefit of the doubt!—unless he earned it. God only knew how many unsavory characters would be lying in wait for her between Philadelphia and London—!

Minter offered to show Lisette the cabin that she would occupy and Raveneau assured her that someone would be along with her trunks. As she followed Lieutenant Minter down the hatch, her last view of the French-born captain sent a fresh chill of fear down her spine. Was it possible, Lisette wondered, that Raveneau expected her to share his bed?

"Here we are!" Minter announced, ushering her into the cabin with a flourish.

Lisette glanced around in surprise. The room was small, but sunlight poured through a square window to illuminate a neatly made mahogany bed built flush with the polished floor, as well as a windsor chair that reposed before a desk and three full bookshelves. There was even a pine washstand, complete with a flower-sprigged pitcher and bowl. The entire cabin was spotless, yet somehow cozy. With a smile, Lisette walked over and trailed a hand over the plump snowy pillow, the woven blue spread tucked tightly along mahogany, and finally the brightly patterned quilt that was carefully folded at the foot of the bed.

"This seems a very personal cabin, Lieutenant." Looking up, she saw the warm pride in his eyes. "Could it belong to you?"

He grinned. "Yes, Mistress Hahn, it does. I hope you will be comfortable here."

"Why, I couldn't allow you to give up these wonderful quarters on my account!" she exclaimed. "And—you must call me Lisette!" she said trusting him instinctively.

"All right, Lisette, if you will call me Minter. It's the name that sounds most familiar to me on board ship." His open smile and twinkling blue eyes had made more friends than he could count, and were winning him another at that moment. "As for the cabin, I am honored to have you use it during this voyage. I will bunk with the boatswain, who is my friend, and I imagine that his salty companionship will be an interesting change from my own."

She crossed to lay a delicate hand on his arm. "But, Minter, I shall feel terrible, depriving you of what is obviously a private haven! It's bad enough, my coming on board because of the captain's charity—"

"It was my own idea that you should stay here. I know you from my visits to the CoffeeHouse over the years, and I've long admired your charm and poise and tact—and humor! This is the only cabin, besides the captain's, that is clean and civilized enough for a woman of your . . . value."

"In that case, I thank you for your kindness, sir!"

"You have been kind to me many times in the past— even when you were a child, your cheerful smile lightened my heart when I was lonely. It reminded me of my own daughter."

"I wish I could say that I remember you—and I'm surprised that I don't!"

"I wasn't there very often—perhaps once a year, sometimes less. But, whenever I was in Philadelphia, I found time to stop for a hot mug of coffee or a cold tankard of ale and see how you were doing as you grew."

"You don't look old enough. . . ." Lisette's voice trailed off as she noticed the tiny creases in his youthful face and an occasional gray hair among rusty orange. "You said I reminded you of your daughter! It's not possible that you could have a child as old as I am!"

He gave her another warm grin, thinking how beautiful she was . . . and how her guilelessness hadn't been dimmed by growing up near the Philadelphia waterfront. "Believe it or not, Lisette, I've a daughter who is about to celebrate her seventeenth birthday. Louisa was the result of an . . . indiscretion that occurred when I was little more than a child myself. Fortunately, however, I was able to claim her as my own when she was five."

Lisette heard a rumble in the passageway that suggested the arrival of her trunks. "You've been away at sea all these years—with a daughter at home?" she asked urgently. Minter did not strike her as that type of man.

He smiled, not offended in the least. "Until she was ten, Louisa came along with me on voyages all over the world. After the war, we sailed to China, France, Italy, Africa— everywhere. We were in Ireland when I met my wife. Louisa introduced us; she used to keep watch constantly for a potential mother, and, of course, her instincts were flawless!"

He and Lisette laughed together as two seamen lugged the first trunk into the cabin. Knowing better than to play the high-handed male role with this lady, Minter waited for her to direct the placement of the trunk.

"I do have to be on deck when we set sail," he told Lisette after the men had gone to fetch the other, smaller trunk and her bandbox, "but Captain Raveneau asked me to stay here until you were settled. One never knows when an—uh—affection-starved sailor might lose control in the presence of a lady."

Lisette sensed that Minter had been on the verge of alluding to her as the "lady" in question, complete with flattering adjectives, and she appreciated his sensitivity. "It has been a real pleasure to talk with you, Minter," she said carefully before tilting up her chin in a way that Nicholai Beauvisage would have recognized instantly. "As for your captain, I would appreciate it if you would inform him that I am an independent adult in every way. I am used to dealing with men, many of whom are less than genteel, and I certainly won't require a protector during this voyage!"

Minter's expression was bemused, but he managed a polite smile. Why, he wondered, did Lisette harbor what seemed to be hostility toward Captain Raveneau . . . particularly in view of the generosity he had shown to her? "I am certain that the captain meant only to extend a courteous welcome to his ship, Lisette," Minter said carefully. "Also, I hope that my company hasn't been too bothersome."

Realizing that she had touched a nerve of loyalty in the lieutenant, Lisette hastened to apologize. "It was terribly rude of me to say those things, Minter. Please don't be angry with me! I've adored your company!"

"I'm not angry; in fact, I've already forgotten whatever it was you said!" He gave her a boyish grin. "On the other hand, I really must caution you to keep your wits if you intend to wander around the ship alone. You wouldn't be the first woman to be accosted in a deserted passageway. I realize that you are adept at handing the men at the Coffee-House, but there you have other people all around. Only a fool would persist after you rejected him in that situation. The scene could end quite differently on board ship."

Unbidden, the dark memory of Marcus Reems's attempted rape returned to her mind. "You are right, Minter. Thank you for the advice."

"I don't mean to frighten you." The pain that clouded her sapphire eyes made him feel anxious. "Chances are that nothing at all will happen. Captain Raveneau has strict rules about the punishment for any man who assaults woman; and his crew know that he would not hesitate to follow through. I only spoke about this to ensure that you would be cautious during our weeks at sea."

"I understand." She paused as the two seamen reentered with the last of their burden. After they had been dismissed by Minter, Lisette posed a casual question. "It's reassuring to know that the crew is forbidden"—blushing, she searched for the right words—"physical involvement with women, but I am curious to know . . . is the captain bound by those same rules?"

Abrupt laughter made Halsey Minter choke. "Captain Raveneau?" he exclaimed, obviously highly amused. "Forbidden? He *owns La Mouette,* for God's sake! Who would be fool enough to forbid him *anything*—especially, ah, female companionship?" Minter drew out the last word, eyes twinkling at the implications of such an outrageous suggestion.

Somehow, Lisette managed to retain her composure. "You must admit, though, that the idea of one set of rules for the crew and another for the captain is not a very sound way to run a ship. Don't the men resent him for having a woman when they cannot?"

"No, no." Minter chuckled. "Captain Raveneau's case is different and we all know that."

"Different?" She couldn't help it; her voice rose. Was this the way it would be? After that righteous speech about protecting her from horny seamen, would Minter blithely send her, like a lamb to its slaughter, into Raveneau's bed simply because *his* appetites were somehow exalted?

"Well, you know, we indulge him," Minter was saying, cheerfully oblivious to her rising ire. "Most of this crew have served on board *La Mouette* for years, and many, including me, were with Captain Raveneau on the *Black*

Eagle during the war. We've come to understand him. He's a man who inspires a great deal of respect and loyalty . . . and affection—and terror at times."

Lisette was further confounded by the nostalgic smile that curved Minter's lips. Was this a ship of madmen? "I don't understand why you're looking so pleased! Frankly, I don't relish the prospect of spending weeks at sea with a man who is *terrifying!*"

"But that's just the point, Lisette. Although the captain is still quite capable of unleashing his fury if someone clearly deserves it, the black moods that used to well up out of his own depths virtually disappeared years ago. As a result, life is naturally smoother for the crew . . . and we all are grateful for that."

"Pray tell, what miracle wrought this change?" By now, Lisette couldn't soften the edge in her voice, but Minter remained determinedly lighthearted.

"Perhaps he used to suffer from cold feet at night!" He grinned. "If the only cure was a warm bed, the crew didn't mind, since they benefited too, in the long run."

Biting back a dozen stinging opinions of Raveneau's cure, Lisette managed to mutter, "This is the most incredible conversation I have ever had!"

"Don't worry; it's nearly ended. You'll see a demonstration of the captain's stormy temper if I'm not doing my rather crucial part on deck as we set sail!" Sobering, Minter paused in the doorway for a moment, then turned back to add, "When you know him better, I am certain that you will change your tune. Soon enough, you'll understand that all it takes to make our French panther purr is a woman's touch."

With a last smile and wink, he was gone, leaving Lisette to the sick feeling of dread that knotted her stomach. She sat down on the bed and wondered crazily if it would be possible to cancel her travel plans, disembark from *La Mouette,* and return to the CoffeeHouse without igniting Raveneau's dormant temper. If it were so imperative that his bed be warmed, Lisette couldn't expect a mere shrug upon announcing that she'd changed her mind about England. . . .

She smiled wryly, listening to the squeaks, clatter, thumps, and shouts on the deck above. It was out of the question to consider turning back now; Lisette had known the thoughts were idle, but they helped to curb her anxiety. After all, she had made a decision and leaped boldly into the fray. Every ounce of her courage and confidence would be required to deal with whatever lay in store for her in England. Lisette quailed anew as more possible scenes of humiliation and heartbreak flooded her imagination, but eventually she smiled dreamily at the more realistic image of Nicholai Beauvisage. Her mind was able to conjure up the sound of his voice, his walk, the set of his shoulders, the movements of his deft hands. . . . Sometimes, Lisette swore that she could feel him touching her, trailing his long fingers down her back, over the curve of a hip—

"Ma'am?"

Startled back to reality, she jumped up guiltily to find a boy of no more than sixteen shifting from foot to foot in the doorway of her cabin. "Yes?"

"My name's Gideon Post, ma'am. I'm the captain's steward."

He was blushing so that Lisette had to smile, but that only seemed to increase his suffering. "I am happy to meet you, Gideon. Please, do call me Lisette. I like that much better than 'ma'am.' "

Gideon nodded, smiled, blushed anew, regarded his shoes, then cleared his throat and declared, "Captain Raveneau requests that you join him in his cabin in one quarter of an hour."

"Oh!" Suddenly, Lisette realized that the ship was moving, picking up speed, swaying with the currents of the Delaware River.

Unsure of how to answer her horrified-sounding "Oh!" Gideon Post wiped sweaty palms on his breeches and offered, "His cabin's abaft of the wardroom . . ."

"Thank you, Gideon." She managed a weak smile. After he had blushed and bowed and finally departed, Lisette closed the door. Leaning against it, she wondered what could possibly save her from warming André Raveneau's bed—not only today but every day until they reached England. . . .

Chapter 37

July 2, 1793

André Raveneau rubbed his eyes distractedly and raked a hand through his glossy black hair. He was barely a dozen steps aways from his cabin, where he would be able to taste not only a hot breakfast, but also soft, delicious lips —and more, if Fate was kind this morning. Now that *La Mouette* was finally on her way to England, a great deal of tension was uncoiling inside Raveneau. The sun shone brightly, the wind was with them, and soon the ship would reach the Delaware Bay, beyond which swept the Alantic Ocean, *La Mouette's* home for at least the next six weeks. For Raveneau, too, the sea was home. No city or house could hold him for very long. These past weeks in Philadelphia, fraught with unexpected delays and complicated by the specter of a possible yellow fever epidemic, had tied knots in his disposition.

The door to Minter's cabin opened as he passed. Raveneau turned, expecting to greet the beautiful muslingowned Mistress Hahn. Instead, he was confronted by a female haphazardly garbed in ill-fitting breeches, wrinkled stockings, shoes, and a voluminous shirt that had seen better days.

"Mistress Hahn?" Amused disbelief infected his voice. "Can it be you?"

"Yes, of course, Captain!" Her smile was innocent, but her eyes were wicked. She was delighted to see him looking so startled; perhaps Raveneau might be disgusted enough to reject her! "I decided to take your advice about making myself comfortable while we are at sea. It's heavenly not to have to fuss over my appearance! For the next few weeks I intend to relax."

"Well, you are certainly off to a good start," he commented dryly, taking in the messy braids that had replaced her neatly upswept curls of an hour ago. Lisette had seemed innately clean and well groomed; he had been struck by her refreshingly unadorned beauty. Why on earth would she purposely become slovenly? Touching a dark finger to a smudge on Lisette's cheek, he inquired, "What happened here? You didn't fall into the hold, I hope!"

She tried to discern the unnerving silver gleam in Raveneau's eyes. "No, of course I didn't!" Feigning surprise, Lisette touched the dirt she'd rubbed on her cheek earlier. "Honestly, Captain, I've just been so busy these past few days that I haven't had a chance to even wash my face—let alone bathe! That's why I'm so relieved to be here, where I can rest and not have to worry about my appearance."

Raveneau regarded her in a way that made her nervous. "I see . . ."

"Now that we've had this little chat, you probably won't need to—visit with me in your cabin. I think I'll just go up on deck and enjoy the fresh air and the view. So, if you don't mind, Captain—"

"Oh, but I do mind!" Raveneau interrupted softly, one hand gripping her arm through Stringfellow's shirt. "We'll have a nice long chat over breakfast . . . and then I'll arrange a hot bath for you."

"I've had breakfast!" cried Lisette, clutching at this last straw as he led her the rest of the way to his cabin.

"In that case, you may watch me eat, Mistress Hahn. I promise that you'll enjoy yourself." Raveneau couldn't resist giving her a wicked grin that made Lisette's eyes widen so apprehensively that he wanted to laugh out loud. "I shall think of *something* to keep you entertained."

Looking ill, she strove for a firmer tone. "Captain, I must tell you that—" Lisette's voice broke off when he opened the door. She blinked.

A long desk was built in under transom windows that cut into the stern. Sunlight streamed over the stacks of books and the bright heads of three seated figures who were reading intently.

Children? Lisette was dizzy with confusion. What was happening? This was Raveneau's stateroom; a magnificent testered bed of cherry wood was built in not far from the desk, and she saw a handsome table complete with Sheraton chairs and many other valuable pieces that signaled their owner's rank. Bookshelves lined the walls.

She turned wildly curious eyes up to the captain.

With a lazy smile, he cleared his throat and instantly the three heads came up and pivoted toward the doorway.

"Papa!" cried a dark-haired boy perhaps a half dozen years of age. He leaped up and rushed forward to hurtle himself into Raveneau's waiting arms. "I haven't seen you for days!"

"You know, Nathan, that I have had a thousand things to do, readying *La Mouette* for a safe voyage and finishing my business in Philadelphia. It was easier for you to stay put. Did you board last night without any problems? I was counting on you to see that all went smoothly."

Nathan was answering, but Lisette found her attention wandering back to the two girls, who had turned in their chairs. Both were strikingly lovely. One appeared to be on the verge of young womanhood, with long sleek black curls and dark eyes fringed with thick lashes. The other girl was older, at least seventeen, Lisette guessed. Her delicate gamine's face was dominated by a cloud of strawberry blond curls.

"Nathan," Raveneau was saying as he returned his son to a standing position, "I want you to meet Lisette Hahn. She'll be sailing to England with us."

The little boy wrinkled his nose at this disheveled female intruder, but he knew better than to verbalize his thoughts. "How do you do, ma'am."

As she realized how utterly dreadful she must look, Lisette blushed furiously. "I'm very pleased to meet you, Nathan. I hope you will call me Lisette."

His hesitant eyes told her that he didn't intend to speak to her at all unless absolutely necessary, but under his father's watchful gaze Nathan replied dutifully, "All right, Lisette."

"You may run up to greet Lieutenant Minter," Raveneau

told the boy, "but I expect you back at your lessons in one hour—and you'd better not dirty your clothes!"

Nathan whooped with joy at the prospect of freedom, however temporary, from his studies. "Yes, Papa! Goodbye!" he called over a shoulder before disappearing into the gangway.

Lisette found that the sisters had risen. To her further chagrin, she saw that they were immaculately garbed in simple, charming frocks. The younger girl, who was taller, wore demure ivory muslin with a sash of rose silk, while her petite sister looked charming in a stylish apricot-and-cream-striped gown with crisp ruching edging the sleeves and low neckline. Lisette's humiliation over her own horrid appearance intensified as Raveneau led her forward to make introductions. What must they think of her? she wondered miserably. And how could she ever explain the reason for this appalling costume?

"Lisette," the older girl said before Raveneau could speak, "we are so pleased to have you with us. I am Devon. I hope that you'll think of me as your friend from this moment on."

"I'm glad to meet you, Devon." She managed a smile, but her cheeks burned as she sensed the faintly curious gleam in Devon's sapphire eyes.

"And this is my daughter Mouette," Raveneau, the proud father, was saying. "Our ship is her namesake."

Lisette and Mouette exchanged greetings, while Devon and Raveneau exchanged glances. Searching for words to fill up the pause that followed, Lisette blurted, "How is it that your mother allowed you girls to go off to sea while she waits behind? Is she ill?"

Mouette turned confused eyes toward Devon, who was staring at Raveneau in amused astonishment. He, in turn, choked on a burst of laughter.

"Our *mother*?" echoed Devon, sounding delighted. She stepped close in front of Raveneau, laid a hand on each shoulder, and continued innocently, "You, I gather, must be my papa!"

He swatted her derriere lightly, but kept his hand there, drawing her near. "Devon doesn't mean to be rude, Lisette, but she's never been able to resist an opportunity to make mischief or a joke."

"Oh." Lisette nodded blankly, her embarrassment mounting to new heights. What on earth was going on? Why did she feel like a fool who was missing a perfectly obvious point? And why was Raveneau holding Devon so closely and caressing the small of her back as if she were his—

"They're married," Mouette explained. "She's *my* mother!"

Giggling, Devon reached over to touch Lisette's arm. "Please don't think I am laughing at you! I'm grateful! To be taken for Mouette's sister is the best compliment I've had in weeks. I just couldn't resist the chance to tease André—"

"I should see what Nathan is doing up on deck, don't you think so, Papa?" Mouette queried tactfully. Her parents assented and she bade their guest good-bye before leaving the cabin.

Lisette was thinking that if she continued to blush much longer, her face would probably burn up. The entire scene had been so humiliating that she wasn't even able to feel relieved that Madame Raveneau was on hand to warm the captain's bed. What a spectacular impression she must have made on her first meeting with the captain's wife—the one person who might have supplied companionship during the long voyage!

"I have never felt more foolish," she sighed. "Yet, I still find it impossible to believe that you could be old enough to be Mouette's mother!"

"Oh, this is wonderful!" crowed Devon. "André, I can't thank you enough for bringing Lisette along."

Raveneau gazed heavenward in mock exasperation. "Try to contain yourself, *petite chatte*." To Lisette, he explained, "Believe it or not, this minx is thirty years old. Our daughter is eleven, though she probably appears more mature to you since she has her height early. It has become rather confusing for strangers now that Mouette is taller than her mother."

"André failed to mention the other qualities of womanhood that Mouette has already begun to acquire," Devon couldn't resist adding. "There's nothing harder for a father than the sight of his baby girl blossoming."

He gave her a black look. "I don't want to hear about it, Devon. I shouldn't have to begin thinking of locking her up for years!"

Witnessing this exchange, Lisette almost forgot her own discomfort. On the surface, the taunts they traded sounded antagonistic, yet their eyes sparkled with unmistakable affection.

Devon snorted delicately. "You only want to lock her up to protect her from unprincipled rakes like yourself! Wasn't it fortunate for *you* that *my* father wasn't around to protect me when—"

"*You* were the one who stowed away on board my ship!" Raveneau protested. "And, for that matter, you practically *forced* me to take you to bed—"

Coloring prettily, Devon reached up to press a hand over his mouth. "André, darling, do remember your manners!" Her cooing tone was underlaid with amusement. "There is a female guest present!"

Lisette struggled not to laugh as Raveneau pried the tiny hand from his mouth and held fast to both of Devon's wrists. In the process, her back and the curves below came in contact with her husband's hard body. Instead of offering even token resistance, Devon relaxed, happily imprisoned in Raveneau's embrace. She gave Lisette an engaging smile.

"I hope you don't think we're rude, but we've been apart for a few days and our reunions tend to be . . . absorbing! As for you, Lisette, I can't allow you to feel foolish. It's all André's fault for not telling you that I and the children were here. No one could blame you for being slightly bewildered!"

After a sharp glance at Raveneau, Lisette smiled gratefully. "I appreciate your understanding—Devon. This has been a hectic day, as you can see by my bedraggled appearance." She blushed anew, but managed to continue, "If I had known that I would be meeting *you*—or anyone!—I certainly wouldn't have entered this cabin looking like a beggar!"

Devon had a few questions along that line, but had decided to save them for André. "The first time I boarded our privateer, the *Black Eagle,* I wore clothing almost identical to yours. My hair was stuffed inside a smelly red knit cap . . . and André thought I was a boy for hours after we met. I even filled his bath and washed his back without arousing the tiniest suspicion, so if you are a fool, he must be an imbecile!"

Raveneau narrowed flinty eyes down at his wife before interjecting evenly, "Devon, *ma chère,* the passage of time has exaggerated your memory regarding a few significant details."

"The facts are what count, André, darling," she replied.

Lisette smiled, feeling the tightness ease inside of her. "Thank you for telling me your story, Devon; I feel much better."

"Good! Since you are already wearing your breeches, why don't I change into mine and give you a tour of the ship? The children don't have to continue their studies for an hour and I would love to prowl the decks and soak up some sun and fresh air!"

"That would be wonderful—but I must comb my hair and—well, tidy my appearance."

"Fine!" Devon replied gaily. "I will meet you on deck in—"

"Half an hour," Raveneau supplied. "I will walk you to your cabin, Lisette."

When they were on the gangway and the door was closed, she whirled on him, blue eyes flashing. "How dare you play games with me, Captain Raveneau!" Lisette railed in a hoarse whisper. "Why didn't you tell me that your wife was aboard? You let me play the fool not only in front of you and Minter—but Devon and your children as well!"

Raveneau smiled ruefully. "If you hadn't flattered yourself from the first moment we met that I desired only to rip off your gown and ravish you, I certainly would have told you. However, it was amusing to see what schemes you would hatch to keep me at arm's length—" He swept an ironic hand in front of Lisette. "I particularly enjoyed the speech about your natural tendency toward slovenliness. Are you sure you weren't just playing hard to get?"

Eyes flashing, she aimed an open palm at Raveneau's swarthy cheek, but he easily captured her wrist. "I'm sorry to disappoint you, mademoiselle, but as much as you may crave ravishment I shall be unable to accommodate you. Devon greedily insists on claiming all my charms for herself."

Although she saw the teasing smile that flickered over Raveneau's mouth, Lisette was in no mood for further taunting. "You are a cruel, insensitive man!" she hissed.

Following her, Raveneau couldn't resist a few more words: "Please . . . try not to take it so hard."

Lisette swung around, flushed with rage, but the sight of his face as he tried to look repentant while smothering merriment was too much. Together, they laughed as quietly as possible, leaning against the bulkhead until they were weak. Lisette covered her mouth with her hands as she giggled.

"Oh . . ." she managed to moan at last, "my stomach aches!"

Raveneau extended a firm hand. "Friends?"

Happy and relieved, Lisette placed her own hand in his and they shook. In view of her attire, it seemed an appropriate gesture. "Friends." She beamed.

"No more tricks—from either of us."

"Total honesty. I promise," agreed Lisette. "At any rate, Devon's presence solves everything."

"Even if my wife were not on board, Lisette, you would have nothing to worry about. Aside from the fact that I've never forced myself on an unreceptive woman, my commitment to Devon shapes every other aspect of my life. I cherish her too much to ever even *want* to sleep with another woman—for *any* reason."

Lisette had been regarding Raveneau in awe as he spoke. Appearing to be at least forty and probably older, he was no callow youth spellbound by first love. In fact, her original assessment of him hadn't altered; Raveneau was dangerous looking—except when it came to his family.

"I apologize," Lisette said softly. "It's just that you don't *look* the devoted husband! After our first meeting, and that rather tense walk through Philadelphia we shared this morning, I surmised that you were a hardhearted man of the sea who would never bend for anyone. I was certain that you probably had a woman or two waiting in every port, and only were putting up with my presence for one reason. . . ."

"A dozen years ago, your description would have nearly hit the mark. One could say that I grew up rather late in life—after meeting Devon." Raveneau paused in her doorway to add a subtle piece of advice. "No doubt you are something of an expert on men after your years of observation in the CoffeeHouse. But don't forget, Lisette, that people never conform to generalizations. Each of us is different, and you will be making a big mistake if you prejudge every man without evidence to back up your assumptions."

After an amiable exchange of parting words, the captain headed back to his own cabin and Lisette closed her door. Despite the time it would take to repair her appearance, the usually industrious Lisette sat on the bed's edge and spent several minutes pondering all that Raveneau had said . . . particularly his comments on the individuality of every man. For the first time, she realized how often she had anticipated that Nicholai would respond to a situation in the same manner as the familiar men in the public room, or like John, the congressman who'd broken her heart.

After several minutes, Lisette sighed and forced herself back to the present. She didn't want to further tarnish her image by keeping Devon waiting. . . .

Back in his own cabin, Raveneau found his wife fastening the buttons on diminutive cinnamon breeches. A frilled linen shirt, tailored to fit her perfectly, was already tucked snugly into the waistband. Stockings and a snowy stock lay waiting on the bed.

"What on earth are you doing?" he demanded. "Surely you don't want to go above deck *yet?*"

Averting her eyes from his wickedly engaging smile, Devon picked up the stock. "You were gone so long that there seemed nothing for me to do but begin dressing. I thought that perhaps you were otherwise occupied."

"I told you that Minter had everything under control," he replied, bemused. "It's only been a few minutes—"

"Fifteen!" Her tone was more heated than she'd intended, but now it was too late. André was drawing near;

the expression of innocent confusion that he wore only increased her anger. "You know perfectly well that I was not referring to Minter! I heard you and Lisette Hahn laughing in the passageway. How is it that the two of you have already become such close friends?"

Incredulous, Raveneau could only stare for a long minute; then he exploded. "Women! You are all expert at leaping to false conclusions! Lisette barely knows me, so her bizarre behavior has been more excusable, but I certainly expect more logic—and trust—from my own wife! What madness has your imagination concocted? Do you suspect that I spent these past few nights with Lisette Hahn instead of bedding down here alone?"

Devon blushed, for just before he entered the cabin, she *had* begun to wonder about the time André had spent on his own in Philadelphia.

"If this situation were not so ludicrous, I would be *really* furious with you!" he shouted. "Sit down and listen!" Pulling her down beside him on the bed, Raveneau lowered his voice and explained what had happened between him and Lisette. Devon listened as he described Lisette's preconceptions about him, the way she had misconstrued everything he said and did, and the tactics she'd used in an effort to avoid what she feared was her fate—ravishment by the French pirate.

"That's why she dressed and fixed her hair with such *care* after Gideon told her I desired a meeting—in my cabin," said Raveneau.

"Well, you should have told her about us!" Devon exclaimed, sympathetic and amused all at once. "Lisette must have been stunned to meet your wife and children, especially looking the way she did. It was impossible for her to explain, and I admit that I did *wonder* if she could possibly be the same beauty that Caro kept raving about!" She pressed a hand to the irrepressible smile that threatened to become a giggle. "Really, André, it was cruel of you not to tell her when you realized what was in her mind!"

"I decided that she needed to know the consequences of making judgments without proof," he replied shortly, then bent to pull off his boots.

"I'll bet you were a tiny bit insulted and annoyed that

Lisette was rejecting you so adamantly. . . ." Devon couldn't resist a bit of gentle teasing.

"Rejecting me! How could she reject an offer that was never made? I never gave the slightest indication that I was attracted; I was completely detatched, with a thousand things on my mind—not the least of which was *you,* wench!"

"Caro says that Lisette is in love with Alec's brother; that she is making this journey to find him. No doubt her head and heart are full of—Nicholai, I believe Caro said. Otherwise, Lisette could never have felt such repulsion for you."

"Repulsion!" André repeated as if he couldn't believe his ears. "Why do I have this feeling that you are saying these things to make me forget *your* latest transgression?"

Wrinkling her nose, Devon coaxed, "Why don't we pretend I never said those things, darling? I'm ashamed of myself; it must have been a reflex from the past—and you would have to agree that I once had plenty of justification for suspicions and jealousy. . . ."

"Devon, you know damn well that for eleven years I've been completely devoted to you, our children, every aspect of our relationship! It's insulting to me to think that you could believe—"

She put a hand over his mouth, scrambled onto her knees, and leaned close to his cheek. "You should be flattered! My jealousy sprang from my passion for you; my heart overpowered my head! It's been so long since you've been alone with any woman but me, and when I heard you laughing, I sat in here alone and my imagination manufactured more and more scenarios. But I was wrong. I apologize for doubting you. I love you!"

Raveneau reached up to pull her hand from his mouth, and then she was in his arms. The kiss they shared was a long and passionate reaffirmation of their love, which had survived nearly a dozen years. They had coped with Devon's fiancé, the war, separation, Raveneau's wandering eye and black moods, battles at sea, Mouette's birth before their marriage, the tragic death of their second child at age four, and a myriad of other problems and adjustments that confront married couples as the years go by. Not only had they survived, but both believed that their love was deeper, happier, and more ardent than ever. At one time, misunderstandings had sprung up frequently. A chance word or phrase could kindle a quarrel, but no longer. The Raveneaus were now the best of friends, who could banter and trade lighthearted insults because of their ability to sense each other's moods or intent.

Devon opened one eye and peeked sideways at the clock that sat on a braced bookshelf. "André . . ." she murmured as his warm lips moved to graze the tendrils along her hairline, "you know what I *want* to do right now more than anything else, but it *has* been more than a half hour since you escorted Lisette back to her cabin, and in view of the chaos she has endured so far today, I do think that I should finish dressing and meet her as I—"

"The hell you will!" Raveneau reclined against down-filled pillows and the sandy gold counterpane. Firmly, he drew Devon closer until their legs were entwined. "It's been five long days—and nights—since I've been alone with you, *petite chatte*. We have both wasted too much valuable time worrying and talking about Lisette Hahn. She'll have Minter and our children to keep her occupied until you arrive." Raveneau grasped Devon's waist, then brought her linen-shrouded breasts in contact with his own shirt and the hard-muscled chest beneath.

Passion washed over Devon as powerfully as it had the first time he'd kissed her nearly thirteen years ago. Their tongues touched in tantalizing play before the kiss intensified to communicate their feelings more effectively than words. Buttons were being urgently unfastened when a knock sounded at the door.

"Ignore it," Raveneau whispered huskily. "The children and the crew all know better than to disturb us when the door is closed."

Devon could only gasp in frustration.

"Excuse me . . . Madame Raveneau?" a soft voice called from the passageway. "Devon? I don't mean to intrude, but I wondered if you still wanted to go up on deck? I would go ahead and wait for you, but Minter warned me most emphatically not to wander around the ship alone if I could help it. . . ."

Devon managed to struggle free of her husband's restraining grasp. "If you can wait just a moment, Lisette," she called, "I'll put on my shoes and come right out. Minter is absolutely right; I know from firsthand experience!"

"I don't believe it!" Raveneau was barely able to keep his voice down as he watched his wife scramble off the bed. "Are you actually going to leave me like this?"

"André, I can't see that I have much choice." Having donned her stockings, Devon slid her feet into buckled shoes and refastened buttons. "Honestly, you needn't look as if I'm torturing you! It's only been five days, darling, and in a few minutes you'll be over this momentary discomfort."

"Argh!" After a glance at the aching bulge in his breeches, Raveneau dropped back on the pillow and groaned with frustration.

Devon was in front of the mirror, speedily tying her stock and then tidying her curls so that it wouldn't look as though she'd just gotten out of bed. "I'll be right there, Lisette!" she called.

"I'm fine—take your time!"

Devon paused en route to the door to drop a kiss on her husband's brow.

"Beware," he warned, eyes closed. "If I get my hands on you, wench, you'll not escape again."

She laughed softly. "Stop behaving like a spoiled child. Instead of pouting, think of the wonderful time we'll have tonight. We'll have hours and hours—"

"Oh, stop!" Raveneau moaned. "I can't stand it!"

Shaking her head, Devon crossed to open the door and greeted a transformed Lisette Hahn. There were no more smudges on her creamy skin or on the neat-fitting shirt and breeches she wore; shining golden curls spilled down her back.

Lisette beamed, obviously much more at ease. "Hello! It was so kind of you to offer to show me the ship. I'm looking forward to the fresh air and sunshine!" Spying the captain, she called out a friendly greeting.

Raveneau slowly lifted his head in her direction, and growled something unintelligible. Lisette had the strange feeling that their new friendship was already in jeopardy....

July 5–August 30, 1793

Devon raised her hand to knock on the door of Lisette's cabin, but paused as new thoughts crowded her mind. Suppose Lisette was already asleep, or simply not in the mood for company? In the three days that had elapsed since their introduction, the two women had developed a relationship that was friendly but far from intimate. In spite of the warm, close companionship that she and her husband shared, Devon still longed for a female with whom she could trade confidences, dreams, and gossip . . . a friend like Azalea Minter Smith, Halsey's sister, whom they visited in Virginia only once or twice a year. It seemed, however, that Lisette was keeping Devon at arm's length. From what Caro had confided, Lisette had been so busy running her CoffeeHouse that she'd had little time for friends or amusements.

So . . . tonight, as a storm brewed and finally rose to a boil, driving Raveneau out of his bed and up on deck, Devon had decided to melt the ice between Lisette Hahn and herself. Clad in her bed gown and robe, armed with a bottle of wine, two cups, and a corkscrew, she now stood in the passageway wondering if Lisette would welcome this intrusion after all. . . .

Abruptly, the capricious sea tossed Devon against the bulkhead, but the sound of a muffled exclamation from within the cabin made her forget the soreness that spread over her shoulder. Doubts erased, she struggled for balance as *La Mouette* rocked to and fro, and knocked firmly on the door.

"Lisette? It's Devon Raveneau. I hope I'm not disturbing you—"

"No! Please come in!"

Devon entered to find a wide-eyed Lisette huddled in Halsey Minter's bed. A brass oil lamp attached to the bulkhead painted the ceiling with an eerie golden light that fluttered with each pitch of the ship.

"I've wanted to go out and see what—or if—" Lisette licked her lips. "I mean, for someone like me who is used to dry land, this is a rather disturbing experience! I've been anxious for news, but each time I attempt an excursion to the door, I find it impossible to keep my balance!"

Devon grinned. "Do you mind if I join you?" Receiving a nod of assent, she soon was squeezing into the narrow bed beside Lisette and tucking the quilts around them both. "The art of crossing a deck during a storm without losing one's balance can only be mastered after much time at sea —and usually several storms!"

"What is happening? Do you suppose we'll sink?"

"Heavens, no!" Devon was twisting in the corkscrew to open the wine. "I've survived many storms worse than this one, Lisette. All that's required are extra hands on deck; plus patience to ride the thing out. By morning, I'll wager that you'll look out to find calm seas."

Lisette's anxious expression relaxed considerably. "I'm so glad you decided to pay me a visit. Fear has a way of growing out of proportion when one is alone with only one's imagination for company."

"Is this your first sea voyage?" After filling the cups, Devon held hers up and they shared a smile before sipping the aromatic Sancerre wine.

"Mmm, that's wonderful," Lisette exclaimed. "To answer your question—I haven't been on a ship since I was four, and that wasn't a very pleasant experience. You see, I was born in Austria, but my parents dreamed of a new and better life in America. During our journey to Philadelphia, we were attacked by an English warship. Nearly everything we owned was confiscated . . . and then, my mother fell ill. She died before our ship even docked in America."

Seeing the tears that gleamed in Lisette's eyes, Devon felt her own heart turn over. "My father died when I was a child—at sea, too. I can empathize with your loss. Life is never the same for those who are left to carry on, is it?"

Lisette poured out the story of her life at the Coffee-House and the gradual decline of Ernst Hahn. Devon seemed to understand instantly, offering gentle observations that suggested she had known Lisette for years rather than days. Finally, as a second cup of wine ran low, Lisette revealed the particulars of her rather limited love life.

". . . after that unfortunate experience with John, I was sure my heart had been broken forever." Her smile was both sad and wistful. "I retreated farther into the self-contained world at the CoffeeHouse. As father's health failed, I truly was needed, and I derived much satisfaction from my work. It was important to me to realize that I could juggle all the facets of the business so skillfully. People still refuse to believe that women are as capable as men . . . no doubt most of Philadelphia has thought that I've been supported by the brains and money of some man."

"Someone to total your books, pay employees' wages, order supplies in proper amounts, and especially—deal with the everyday crises that only a man could stay calm enough to handle!" Devon chimed in enthusiastically. "After all, everyone knows that women aren't born with cooking ability *and* intelligence! That rule applies doubly if the female in question has been blessed with beauty, too."

The two women shared droll laughter, then Lisette continued, "You can see, then, how someone in my position could become a bit standoffish around anyone who might make jokes about my life or question its validity . . . *without* a man."

"Your attitude must have changed, though, if you've now left your CoffeeHouse behind and are traveling across the ocean to find Nicholai Beauvisage . . . ?" Devon suggested softly.

"Oh, yes, it's changed. *I've changed!* But believe me, I didn't tumble joyfully into love; I dragged my heels every step of the way, right up to the moment Nicholai left for England and asked me to accompany him." Lisette followed that tantalizing sentence with a more detailed account of her unique romance with Nicholai. Finally, as she watched

Devon pour more wine, she said wistfully, "For a long time, I have had this idea that loving a man would require the forfeit of the identity I have worked so hard to carve out for myself. That wasn't the only feeling that loomed up to frighten me whenever I grew close to letting go with Nicholai, but it was probably the most important. I don't think it would be *possible* for me to give up everything I've worked so hard to attain, and then to just sit back and do needlework, pour tea, and have babies—all with a serene smile on my complacent face. I have finally admitted to myself that I love Nicholai so intensely that the world is a dreary, tedious place without him . . . yet even if we do somehow work out the problems in our relationship and"— she blushed and gulped—"marriage, what then? No matter *how* much I love him, how can I change the very fabric of my personality? I don't even *want* to!"

"Marriage doesn't necessarily mean banishment to a parlor, Lisette!" Devon smiled reassuringly. "Look at me! All my life I was headstrong. My father was a sea captain, and even though he died at sea, I always longed to sail all over the world. Growing up, I never dreamed of getting married, but of the far-off lands I'd explore someday. When I met André, though, I was made for him from the first minute. We think that it must have been destiny pulling us together inspite of the war and all the other obstacles— because our souls are so perfectly matched. I was only seventeen when I—ah, well, invaded his life and Mouette was conceived. I was a lot less mature than you are, Lisette, and even though I've always been independent, I had to swallow my pride over and over again just to be near André. He is such a strong man and I still feel that he's more handsome, witty, intelligent, courageous . . . well, you know—than anyone else. If he wanted to, he could probably dominate me, but our relationship isn't like that. We've been partners all our marriage, sharing life at sea and at home, and it's all become better as I've grown older. I know that my strength of character is the foundation of André's love for me. I've no doubt that the same is true for Nicholai with you. Lisette, do you really imagine that he would want you to become that boring, submissive woman you described? Heavens, if that were his desire, Philadelphia is filled with such females who would have doubtless been quite eager for his attentions. Why would he have gotten entangled with someone as prickly as you?"

Lisette didn't return Devon's grin. "I've wondered that many times myself. . . ."

"Do I detect a note of insecurity?"

"Probably. It's always been difficult for me to believe that Nicholai really loves me, or that he loves me for my real self and not for the challenge I've represented to him. Also, we've been thrown together so often that I can't help wondering if our proximity has had something to do with it. I mean, I met him—and made love with him—on his first night back in Philadelphia after an absence of ten years!" Realizing what she had said while being egged on by wine, Lisette blushed hotly.

"Don't be embarrassed to admit that to me!" laughed Devon. "I practically forced André to make love to me the first time!"

"The truth is . . . I've always been rather reserved in that area, and so I attributed my behavior that night to the fact that my father had died just hours before. So . . . it wasn't as though we'd been united by true love. After that, I rather put Nicholai off, and I couldn't help worrying that he pursued me for that reason. I mean, there were so many sophisticated, wealthy women chasing after him that I would have to be terribly vain to believe that he could have found me more desirable. . . ."

"Why?" Devon asked plainly.

"Well, because I couldn't match them in most ways! What man counts independence and outspokenness among the qualities most valuable in a woman?"

"Perhaps Nicholai Beauvisage does! Besides, those aren't your only qualities, modest Lisette. Your beauty alone would put any Philadelphia belle in the shade—and also, you are intelligent, sensitive, and courageous."

"I'll admit that my face and form are pretty enough, but I could never bring myself to paint and primp as they do, or to visit the dressmaker for the latest gowns, covered with lace and bows—or whatever—"

"Do you think that Nicholai was interested in those things?"

"Well—no—oh, I don't know! We fell in love during the days we spent alone at the Hampshires' villa, and we were alone most of that time. I can't help worrying—"

Devon had scrambled up to search Halsey's trunk for one of the bottles of wine she knew he kept hidden there. Brandishing her prize, Devon beamed and returned to the snug haven of Minter's bed. "We'll just have a mouthful or two more." She grinned, working in the corkscrew. "It sounds as if you have a severe case of insecurity! You're worried that Mr. Beauvisage cannot love you enough for a lifetime. Are you worried that he'll turn to a more glamorous woman the first time one comes along and purses her painted lips at him?"

"That's putting it rather broadly, but I'd have to agree." Lisette lifted her fresh cup of wine, sipped, sighed, and sipped again. "You see, it's not only the women Nicholai knew in Philadelphia and the women he's yet to meet that worry me . . . it's one woman in particular."

"Oh, no!" Devon arched her cinnamon brows apprehensively.

"Oh, yes! The reason he left Philadelphia was to rescue the lady he fell in love with during his ten years in France."

"I remember! Caro told me about this person—and mentioned that *you* urged Mr. Beauvisage to rush to her aid. *Why* on earth—!"

"I learned about Gabrielle when Nicholai was recuperating from his shoulder wound. He used to speak her name in his sleep; later, when he was better, he told me about her. At that time, he believed she'd been killed during the September Massacres . . . and I couldn't help feeling even then that her ghost was my rival. I am certain that she is the quintessence of female charm and beauty—fully equipped with exquisite fashionable gowns, hair that is always perfectly coiffed, jewels that are priceless but not ostentatious . . . and if the occasion demands it, that she's equally adept at making either witty or intimate conversation. When Nicholai received her letter begging him to come to her aid, I just felt that it would be better to lose him to her now rather than later. I could just imagine him dreaming of Gabrielle as time went by . . . it seemed inevitable that eventually Fate would draw them back together. . . ."

"So you took the safest course," Devon supplied. "You sent him off to England and returned to your difficult but emotionally undemanding work at the CoffeeHouse."

Lisette nodded and took a long sip of wine. "Foolish of me, wasn't it?"

"We can't go back once new ground has been broken in our lives, but certainly everyone has that urge occasionally to retreat to the past when things become risky or complex."

"I know . . . I was a coward—and I'm still scared. I'm afraid that Nicholai will already be in love with Gabrielle again by the time I arrive. Her husband is dead now—so perhaps she'll marry Nicholai immediately! And, even if matters don't progress that far, I worry that he'll feel guilty about my presence in England. I couldn't bear it if he pretended to care just to spare my feelings. Finally, I'm afraid that I'll never measure up to Gabrielle. It was one thing when he was with me in Philadelphia and she was across the ocean—but when he sees us together and compares—"

"You really are foolish!" scolded Devon. "Honestly, I'm certain that Nicholai must have *preferred* your genuine, unaffected beauty to that of the artificial, simpering females that abound in Philadelphia—and everywhere else."

"Yes, but at one point, he preferred Gabrielle's beauty, too—and he was involved with her for a much longer time than I've known him! I doubt whether Nicholai would have ever left France if he'd known she were still alive."

"Hmm . . ." Devon tapped a finger against her delicate chin. "I see your point. You would feel better if Nicholai were meeting you in London for the first time, so that you could be certain his feelings for you aren't colored by conscience and some sense of obligation from the past."

"Yes, oh, yes!"

"And you wish that you could compete with Gabrielle on her own ground, so that you won't feel so out of place now that you've left the CoffeeHouse behind."

"Yes! I feel so foolish barging over to England to snatch

him back, particularly since he may not care to be snatched! If I could win him fairly, though—and that's putting it badly—Nicholai isn't some prize to be captured! I wish, as you said, that we could meet for the first time and that he could fall in love with me all over again. I wish I could have new gowns and jewelry to match this new side of my personality that is pulling me across the ocean. "I could afford a new wardrobe, but Nicholai knows I've always scorned elaborate clothes . . . and I fear he'd think I was wearing them for the same reason all those other women do."

"To captivate susceptible men," Devon supplied with a knowing smile. "Well, Mistress Hahn, as we've been talking, I've been hatching a wickedly exciting scheme that just might make all your wishes come true!"

Lisette's blue eyes widened over the rim of her cup. "I'm breathless with anticipation! What is it?"

"We own a house in London, and when we are there André and I are able to move in the best circles—if we care to, which we generally don't. However, we'll be spending a fortnight there this time and you could visit us as our guest." Devon's eyes danced with mischief as she leaned nearer and continued, "Here comes the outrageous part . . ."

"Well?"

"I believe, with the aid of the right seamstress, hairdresser, and the application of cosmetics, that we could actually transform you into a new person—physically speaking, that is. Then, we could change your name, invent a new past—"

"I can do a credible Austrian accent!" Lisette chimed in excitedly.

"If our plan works, you really would be meeting Nicholai for the first time, for your purposes, at least! Do you suppose he would be taken in by your new identity?"

Lisette took another sip of wine and giggled. "It's insane . . . but one thing is certain—Lisette Hahn is the last person Nicholai would expect to meet in London, particularly in the altered state you described. So . . . it's possible that he wouldn't recognize me—and in any event, I intend to find out!"

Devon laughed and clinked her cup against Lisette's in a lighthearted toast.

Black waves slapped *La Mouette*'s sleek hull under an indigo sky sprayed with stardust. Lisette leaned on the rail that curved above the bow, listening to the whisper of the snowy canvas sails and an occasional creak from the rigging. Her only companion was the watch who stood silently on the quarterdeck; at this hour nearly everyone on board was asleep. By tomorrow night, *La Mouette* would be swaying securely beside London's teeming wharves. The thought sent a chill down Lisette's spine that mingled excitement with panic. How could the scheme concocted by Devon, upon which they had elaborated daily ever since, ever succeed? When Nicholai recognized her, what would she say and do? What if he and Gabrielle were already married?

Lisette sighed, then breathed deeply of the salty night air in an effort to relax.

"Mistress Hahn——" A large shadow blocked the moonlight and sent an instant bolt of fear through Lisette. Whirling around, she came face to face with the tall dark figure of André Raveneau.

"Oh—Captain—I . . ." She pressed a hand to her muslin bodice and the thudding heartbeat beneath. "Good evening!"

"I didn't mean to frighten you, Lisette. You must have been deep in thought not to have heard my creaking footsteps on the decks!" Raveneau's grin flashed in the darkness and he covered one of her cold hands with the warm strength of his. "After eight eventful weeks at sea—in close quarters—you should be calling me André."

They *had* been eventful weeks—two more than she'd anticipated, due to storms that had tossed them off course and a brief detour to France's Brittany coast. Her friendship with Devon had flourished, and she felt like a big sister to Mouette and Nathan, yet Lisette had never quite felt comfortable in the presence of André Raveneau. Her memories of their initial encounters were still painfully embarrassing. As a result, Lisette had always concocted an excuse to leave whenever Raveneau entered a cabin or joined his family on deck; he still seemed a stranger to her.

"All right, André." She managed a stiff smile. "I'm probably not supposed to be out here wandering about so late. I don't want to disturb your routine here, so I'll just say good—"

"No, you won't!" His hands held her fast. "It's time that you and I had a talk."

"A talk—?" She licked dry lips. "What about?"

Raveneau laughed, and she thought that he looked exactly like a pirate in the starlight. "Stop behaving as though you fear I'll gobble you up, *chérie*. My interest in you is purely friendly, which you would have understood weeks ago if you had remained in my company for more than five minutes!"

Hot blood rushed into Lisette's cheeks. "I didn't really— that is, I only made myself unavailable because I didn't want to be in the way. Your time with your family is precious, I know, so—"

"Let's not belabor the subject, but I do think that we should agree to be friends. Devon loves you dearly, so I can't help but like you—even though I think the scheme you two have hatched is utterly mad!"

"You are right," Lisette agreed.

Measuring her with a sidelong glance, Raveneau continued, "All the same, I'll do whatever I can to help. No doubt you think I am a hardened cynic, and certainly I used to be, but during the last dozen years I have become a true believer in the wondrous magic of love."

There wasn't a trace of mockery in his voice. Lisette looked up to search his eyes and found them clear and candid.

"You and I have more in common than you might imagine," he was saying. "Before Devon invaded my life, I was far too strong and manly to need *any*one—especially a woman with genuine love to offer. I was proud of my self-sufficiency; of my ability to share beds with beautiful females yet elude their elaborate attempts to extract a commitment."

"I've heard about men like you!" sniffed Lisette. "No wonder I remain wary of romance."

Raveneau laughed. "I told you that we were alike! I was as suspicious as you . . . until Devon." He turned a profile to her and gazed out over the shining black ocean before continuing softly, "Even after I'd fallen in love with her, my stubborn mind refused to admit it. What a fool I was! I feared that conceding that I needed and wanted her would approximate surrender during a battle. I fought what seemed to be a deplorable weakness, and struggled to return to the days when work had been my life." Raveneau shook his head at the memory.

"You're right," she admitted. "We are alike. And I feel much as you did. I tried to return to the past, when I was in control of everything, but it didn't work. So, I finally surrendered . . . and here I am."

"Still with mixed feelings, though, eh? Part of you is madly in love, and anxious to set eyes on Beauvisage again, while another part of you feels that weakness has triumphed over strength. The power of your love frightens you because you can't control it, and you are worried that this passion fever will cause you to lose the strong identity that you've carved out the past years—"

"Yes! How did you know? I couldn't have expressed it better myself!"

He smiled down at her elegant face. There was no doubt that Lisette Hahn had it all: intellect, glorious looks, a spirit both resolute and courageous, and deep wells of untapped love-infused passion. It would take a rare man to appreciate her; a man confident enough to meet her as an equal partner in life. For Lisette's sake, he hoped that Nicholai Beauvisage would turn out to be that man. "How did I know your feelings? Because I've been where you are now. Shakespeare expressed the crux of our dilemma better than I can. It all comes down to this: 'So well I love thee, as without thee I love nothing. If I might choose, I'd rather die than be one day debarred thy company. . . .'"

"That's a frightening prosposition," murmured Lisette.

"My point exactly, *chérie*. It took me a long time to finally realize that the courage to love is the strongest of all. I'd never allowed myself to be vulnerable or risk another person's rejection. . . ."

"Oh, you'll never know how frightened I am that Nicholai won't want me! The pain would be worse than anything I've ever known."

"Yet, you're willing to take the risk."

"Yes." Lisette smiled tremulously. "I have to."

"Believe me, Lisette, you've made the right decision . . . and I've a strong feeling that Nicholai Beauvisage won't disappoint you."

❧ *Chapter 39* ❧

London—September 3, 1793

After pulling on knee boots that were a shade darker than the snug buckskin breeches he wore, Nicholai Beauvisage lit a cheroot. Morning sunlight streamed through the handsome arched windows that overlooked Berkeley Square, and he paused to gaze down on the wooded gardens where nightingales sang each evening. No doubt about it, he reflected; the house, his chamber, the square—in fact, all of London—were beautiful and intensely charming. Even Gabrielle, dressing in her suite across the hall, seemed to have grown more exquisite during the past year.

Why, then, was his mood so incessantly bleak? During the long voyage from Philadelphia, Nicholai had tried to stave off the pain caused by Lisette's absence by substituting anticipatory thoughts of Gabrielle. It was hard for him to admit that Lisette's perplexing behavior had hurt him. Instead, Nicholai had decided to see what the future brought with Gabrielle; it would serve Lisette right if she never saw him again.

Now, he drew on the cheroot with a self-deprecating smile. "Beauvisage, you're a fool," he muttered.

"Bonjour, mon cher!" The door swept open and the scent of gardenias wafted across the room to Nicholai.

"Good morning, Gabrielle. You look ravishing."

It was true. A stylish dark blue riding coat over a white dress and fichu set off Gabrielle's gleaming coppery curls and creamy-velvet skin to perfection. Her leaf green eyes smiled at Nicholai under a blue hat complete with ostrich feathers and a cockade.

"*Merci.* You are looking very handsome as well." She was worried by the remoteness of Nicholai's compliment— a remoteness that had been intensifying with each passing day. "Why have you not put on your cravat and coat? Have you forgotten that we agreed to meet Angelique and Dudley downstairs at ten o'clock? It is five minutes past that time even now, Nicky!"

He grimaced noticeably, but held his tongue. It was difficult to be rude to people who offered the hospitality of their home, yet Nicholai disliked both Angelique, an old friend of Gabrielle's from childhood, and her new husband, Sir Dudley Whitloaf. He longed to ride alone, but this would have been taken as a strict breach of etiquette by the Whitloafs. Nicholai's patience was running out with etiquette *and* Gabrielle's habit of reproaching him while wearing an artificial smile. The spell she had once cast over him had been broken; Nicholai was no longer bewitched and Gabrielle was at a loss to restore the magic.

"Why don't you go down and make my ardent apologies to your friends, my dear? I'll finish dressing with all possible speed and join you in the stair hall."

Gabrielle's smile faltered as she felt the prick of his mockery. Reaching out, she touched Nicholai's ruffled chestnut hair, then impulsively curled her fingers around his neck and leaned upward to press a kiss to his hard mouth.

Nicholai suffered the desperate pressure of Gabrielle's body against his own and allowed her to push her tongue between his lips. Rather than humiliate her completely, he put one arm around her back. Part of him wished that he could respond; it would certainly make life simpler and less depressing. Whenever he realized that he'd left Lisette to chase all the way to London for nothing, and that no brother of Gabrielle's would be worth his life, Nicholai's gut knotted up. As soon as he learned of a ship returning to Philadelphia, he would tell Gabrielle that he wasn't the man to rescue her this time. She would have to find another spellbound fish. . . .

"I thought that the Whitloafs were waiting for you." Firmly, Nicholai set her from him.

Hot blood rushed into Gabrielle's cheeks. How dare he

brush off her advances as though he wasn't the least aroused? Never before had she needed to be the aggressor; in fact, she knew that it was her elusiveness that had always intrigued Nicholai. Yet, she had played at being a mysterious engima for weeks, ever since his initial arrival in London, and he had appeared uninterested . . . even bored.

"Do you expect that I am to make apologies to Angelique and Dudley on your behalf?" Gabrielle inquired icily.

Nicholai almost smiled. "Tell them that I am going out to look for rooms of my own, *ma petite*. Explain that my pride won't allow me to abuse their gracious hospitality a day longer."

"You are—leaving . . . me?" Gabrielle cried.

There was no sense inundating her with everything at once, Nicholai decided. "I am moving to rooms of my own, Gabrielle. You understand, don't you? I need to be independent. I will see you—"

"Tonight? Have you forgotten the concert at Vauxhall Gardens? You did give to me your promise, Nicky!"

That might be the best place, he mused, for him to tell Gabrielle that this had all been a sad mistake. That he was leaving for Philadelphia as soon as possible—and she would have to find another knight in shining armor to take on her quest.

"I'll see you tonight, *chérie*," Nicholai said in a softer tone. "Don't look for me until after the concert, though."

With an effort, Gabrielle gave him her most dazzling smile. "Until tonight I will wait, then, *mon amour*," she murmured, reaching out to run soft fingertips down Nicholai's swarthy cheek. Gracefully, she turned and swept from the room, thinking that tonight would be the perfect time and place to cast a new spell over Nicky. What had been accomplished once could be repeated . . . particularly when it was so absolutely imperative.

Nicholai's eyes fell on an open landau that had paused in front of the Whitloaf mansion. There were two female occupants—one with titian hair and a diminutive appearance, who was pointing at the house and saying something to her companion. The other girl—Nicholai stared, unable to breathe. It couldn't be possible. The other girl looked exactly like Lisette, from her graceful bearing and familiar gestures to the golden curls that tumbled down her neck. It was impossible! As he contemplated sprinting downstairs to the street, the landau started forward again and turned the corner of Berkeley Square.

White-hot frustration seared Nicholai's heart. Dazedly, he sat down on the bed until calm and reason filtered back in. Of course, it couldn't have been Lisette . . . the idea that she could be in London was ludicrous enough, but even if that were possible, she certainly wouldn't fail to contact *him*, and spend her time instead riding around with a strange woman! Obviously, he missed her more than he'd guessed. The vision Nicholai had just had must have been like a mirage in the desert. . . .

"Mistress Jones, I am so pleased!" exclaimed Devon as the stately dressmaker helped Lisette out of the last gown. "You have worked wonders, and in so little time!"

"Well, this was rather a crisis, wasn't it?" Dolly Jones replied generously. "Besides, when Fräulein Amstetten wears my creations out in London society, it will prove my talents once again, not only to potential customers, but also to the French couturiers who surround me here on Bond Street."

"Are they still looking down their noses at you?" exclaimed Devon. "After ten years?"

"I'm an American! Not only that, I married a British soldier during the Revolutionary War and returned to England with him, so that makes me a traitor, I suppose, in some people's eyes. British women have begun to patronize my shop as word of my talents spreads, but I find that a great deal of my business comes from displaced Europeans —like our beautiful Fräulein Amstetten." Mistress Jones gave a smile to Lisette, who was looking rather uncomfortable as she stood in her new batiste-and-lace chemise and waited for the dressmaker to finish her discourse. "They sympathize with another who is out of place in a new land —and, in the case of the Frenchwomen, they find me something of a novelty. After all, the rest of the couturiers are the same ones who plied their trade in Paris! I also suspect that they like me because I don't have any interest in their French gossip. They feel free to chatter about their friends in my presence." She paused to smile slightly and wink.

"Well, murmured Lisette in the lilting accent she had been working for weeks to perfect, "I cannot thank you enough for coming to my aid. When I had to flee our castle in Austria, I had to leave everything behind . . . except for the few pieces of jewelry I was able to fit into my reticule. . . ."

Devon chimed in with a sigh. "My friend has been through a trying ordeal, Mistress Jones, especially in light of the sort of life she has led until now. Giselle was brought up to take luxury for granted."

It took all of Lisette's self-control to refrain from giggling and rolling her eyes. "Yes, I'm afraid it's quite true. That is why I couldn't bear to mingle socially here in London until I acquired the sort of gowns and accessories I am used to."

Dolly Jones had been listening in rapt fascination. Obviously this was a lady of great wealth and breeding. Her English, though charmingly accented, was flawless! If she remained in London, Giselle Amstetten could turn out to be a veritable gold mine. "I'm truly honored that I've been able to assist you, fräulein. I hope that my work pleases you—and if there is anything that I can do to make your adjustment to this new culture easier, please don't hesitate to ask!"

Lisette managed a graciously superior smile. "At this moment, all I desire is a gown to wear when I leave this dressing room, dear Mistress Jones."

Flustered, the woman rushed out and returned seconds later with an exquisite batiste petticoat trimmed with frothy lace, a snowy fichu, a morning gown striped in leaf green and white, plus lacy knitted stockings, satin slippers, and one of the hats that a nearby milliner had fashioned to match Mistress Jones's creations.

"It is just the thing for a beautiful day like this one!" the dressmaker enthused, then waited anxiously for her client's approval.

Lisette made a show of examining each item of the ensemble, smiling inwardly as she thought how much potential for amusement this masquerade could have. "Yes . . . these will do. My friend, Madame Raveneau, will assist me so that you will be free to wrap the rest of my purchases."

"Of course. Thank you, fräulein."

Devon and Lisette waited until the door was closed and the tall woman's footsteps receded; then the two of them collapsed in a fit of giggles.

"You are certainly taking to your new role!" Devon accused teasingly. "It wouldn't surprise me a bit if Mistress Jones curtsies when next you appear!"

Lisette's azure eyes twinkled with delight. "I confess that I'm beginning to have fun . . . and after all, I do need to practice my new personality before coming face to face with Nicholai!"

Lisette had donned the petticoat and now Devon helped her into the lovely new gown. She could see that the mention of Nicholai Beauvisage's name had returned tension to the air. "On the basis of the performance you just gave, I'll wager that he won't believe it possible that you could be anyone but Giselle Amstetten, a wealthy refugee from war-torn Austria."

"Oh . . . I don't know. My insides seem tied in knots whenever I think of facing him. I still cannot believe that we saw the house where he is staying this morning! Do you suppose Nicholai was inside? And how can you be certain it is really the house? Just because André heard some rumor at one of the clubs last night—"

After fastening the last tiny pearl button at the base of Lisette's elegant neck, Devon took a deep breath. "Well, there was one other thing that I didn't tell you. Last night, André was introduced to Nicholai at Boodle's. He sat beside him at the gaming table and they conversed—casually, but at some length. . . ."

Lisette went on adjusting the fine gauze fichu that would fill in her gown's deep décolletage. Her heart beat in her throat and ears; hot color flooded her cheeks. It had been so *long* since she had even been in the same city as Nicholai

—more than three months! She longed for him with every fiber of her being, yet dreaded the prospect of actually encountering him. . . .

"Did André relate some of this conversation to you?" she managed to whisper.

"Well, he said that he liked Nicholai very much. I think that meeting him set André's mind at ease about our little scheme. He also said that Nicholai won a great deal of money, but that he seemed to take little pleasure in it. When André asked what had brought him to London, the tale of Gabrielle was briefly related . . . yet without enthusiasm. André is convinced that you needn't worry that Nicholai has fallen back into love with her."

Smoothing an imaginary crease in her skirt so that Devon wouldn't see the irrational tears that stung her eyes, Lisette asked one more husky question. "Was there anything else?"

"He didn't mention you, if that's what you mean, but then, why would he? Remember, as far as Nicholai knew, André was just a casual stranger that he met at the gaming table. However, the reason that we know where he lives is that a pompous man, well into his cups, I gather, paused to speak to Nicholai and was introduced to André as Sir Dudley Whitloaf. It seems that he and his French wife have given shelter to Gabrielle in their home, so Nicholai has been staying there as well. What is more encouraging, though, is that he told André that he's been longing for rooms of his own and might move any day." Devon smiled and touched her friend's pale cheek. "I met the Whitloafs during our last stay in London, so I can understand why Nicholai is unhappy in their home. If Gabrielle is anything like Angelique Whitloaf, you have nothing to worry about!"

Lisette expelled a nervous sigh, but fell silent as the two of them pinned up her golden curls, then added a lovely wide-brimmed straw hat with green silk ribbons that were tied under Lisette's delicate chin. Devon produced a tiny patch from her reticule, which was applied to the right and just above Lisette's mouth.

"Oh—my!" Lisette stared into the full-length cheval mirror. "I . . . certainly don't look like myself."

"Good!" Devon rejoined cheerfully. "You look like an aristocratic, mysterious Austrian beauty. Just hold your

head up as if you are confident . . . that's right! Let me see
you arch an eyebrow condescendingly—"

Lisette complied, then let smothered laughter escape. "I
don't think Nicholai will be instantly infatuated with me if
I act like *that*!"

"You'll know how to behave. Your instincts will take
over." Devon gathered up her reticule and held the dressing room door open for her friend. "All we have to do now
is contrive to bring the two of you together!"

On their way down the narrow passage that led to the
main room of the shop, Lisette and Devon paid little attention to the conversation they could hear Mistress Jones
having with another client.

"I wouldn't worry," the dressmaker was saying. "He
came all this way to be with you, didn't he?"

"*Oui*, but I do not like the feel of things lately. Nicky
has changed. . . ."

Only a few feet from the doorway that opened into the
shop, Lisette froze and gripped Devon's arm, pressing an
urgent finger over her own lips.

"Don't despair, *Comtesse*, your handsome American will
fall in love all over again when he sees you in this gown!"

"I am counting on that," came the cold French-accented
reply. "I have been worried all morning that you might not
have finished."

"Oh, no, *Comtesse*! In fact, the gown was ready last
evening in case you came for it early. You see, I have it
hanging right back here, just waiting for you!" There was
a pause, then Lisette and Devon heard a gasp of pleasure
before Mistress Jones went on warmly, "I am so glad that
you approve! Where will you be wearing it this evening? To
Carleton House?"

"*Non*, it's not that. We have plans to attend a concert at
Vauxhall Gardens . . . and I was beginning to worry that
Nicky wouldn't even come, but he has assured me that he
will be there after all. It seems the perfect place to rekindle
the flames of romance, *n'est-ce pas?*"

"Under a full moon . . . in one of those charming grottoes. . . ." Dolly Jones agreed dreamily.

At this point, Devon, who had realized who the *comtesse*
and her "Nicky" must be, pulled Lisette toward the door-

way. "Mistress Jones, we are all ready!" she called before stepping into view. Lisette had no choice but to follow.

"Ah, Madame Raveneau—and Fräulein Amstetten, you look splendid and beautiful!" the dressmaker exclaimed. "The hat is perfect for you!" She rushed toward them, then remembered her other client and turned back. "Ladies, I would like you to meet Gabrielle Marchandon, *la comtesse de Louviers. Comtesse,* this is Madame Devon Raveneau, wife of that famous dashing sea captain, André Raveneau."

"Of course . . ." murmured Gabrielle as she smiled toward Devon. "He is French, *n'est-ce pas?*"

"Yes, but he hasn't lived there for more than two decades." She paused and put on her own artificial smile. "I am so pleased to meet you, *Comtesse.*"

There was a strange undercurrent in the air that made Mistress Jones nervous. Extending a hand toward Lisette, she hurried to finish the introductions. "And this is Fräulein Giselle Amstetten. Like you, she has been forced to flee her country, to leave behind her family's castle and the possessions acquired over a lifetime. . . ."

"Welcome to London, fräulein," Gabrielle said sweetly.

"Thank you very much," murmured Lisette. She couldn't take her eyes off this woman who had so captivated Nicholai. Her midnight blue and white riding habit, the hat with its cockade, her fashionably styled gleaming coppery hair, green eyes fringed with thick dark lashes, and every other detail of her beauty imprinted themselves on Lisette's mind.

"I really must be going," Gabrielle announced, turning to the dressmaker. "If you could just wrap that up for me . . ."

"But don't you want to try it on?"

"After all those fittings? I cannot spare the time, and besides, I trust you!" Her voice sharpened impatiently.

Without another word, Dolly Jones reached for the elaborate lavender silk gown that hung behind her. Barely a minute elapsed before she had wrapped it and was presenting the package to Gabrielle.

"Good fortune to you tonight."

"*Merci.*" Gabrielle gave the dressmaker a dazzling confidential smile. "With this gown, a full moon, and my own charm and beauty, how could I possibly fail?"

❧ *Chapter 40* ❧

Midnight, September 3, 1793

Vauxhall Gardens rendered Lisette so spellbound that she was nearly distracted from worrying about the late hour and the fact that there had been no sign of Nicholai. An extended concert, featuring a celebrated soprano, had just ended, and the Raveneaus lingered with Lisette in a secluded supper box.

"Well, I suppose we should be leaving. . . ." murmured Lisette. She nibbled at the last fresh sweet cherry on her plate. "I feel badly enough that the two of you have given up your evening for this vigil—"

Devon and André exchanged amused glances. "You have a lot to learn about London nightlife! The last time André and I were at Ranelagh, a pleasure garden farther up the river, it was three o'clock in the morning before we departed for home—and we were by no means the last!"

"But—you don't think that Nicholai could still make an appearance . . . ?"

"Certainly! Now that the concert is over, there will be many new arrivals," Devon exclaimed.

"It's true," nodded Raveneau after lighting a thin cigar and lounging back against the cushions. "Besides, I heard today at Brook's, the club where I shared dinner with a potential business associate, that Beauvisage had found lodging in Saint James Street. That could explain what occupied him during the concert; perhaps he's been moving." Raveneau gave his wife a sidelong glance that suggested he wouldn't have minded being otherwise occupied during the concert himself.

"If he's moving, he may be detained for the entire night," sighed Lisette. André was refilling her glass, so she lifted it for a few polite sips, then gazed out over the moonlit fantasy of Vauxhall Gardens. In this setting, it wasn't difficult to imagine that she was someone else; certainly Philadelphia and the CoffeeHouse with its regimen of austere discipline seemed part of a past life. . . . Before supper, Lisette had strolled with the Raveneaus over a portion of the twelve-acre gardens. The gravel walkways, bordered by high hedges and sculptured trees, led one past pavilions, temples, colonnades adorned with pillars and statues, and romantically secluded groves and grottoes. All were illuminated by countless lamps that hung like stars against the indigo sky.

"My instincts tell me that Mr. Beauvisage will yet appear tonight," Devon declared.

Lisette watched as her friend responded with a muffled giggle to some remark made by her husband, then nestled into his broad shoulder for more whispered banter. To avoid the appearance of watching them, Lisette studied her own elegantly clad form. Looking like this, she found it easier to pretend to be Giselle Amstetten, for Lisette Hahn would never have indulged in such luxury or spent hours making certain that each detail of her appearance was perfect. Secretly, she was having fun with the opportunity to indulge all the frivolous impulses denied for so many years.

"After all the time and effort we took to make you look so incredibly magnificent for your first encounter with Nicholai, he simply *must* turn up tonight!" Devon exclaimed suddenly, as if reading Lisette's mind. The gown they had chosen, after lengthy deliberation, was a fairy tale creation of creamy satin with rows of ruffles above the hem and a wide gold sash that set off Lisette's slim waist and the low neckline that artfully framed her breasts with a full lace ruffle. The sleeves were long, edged with more exquisite lace, and Lisette wore no fichu, only a soft cashmere shawl shot with golden threads. Devon had contributed her own stunning necklace of gold, diamonds, and pearls with matching earrings, and emeralds and diamonds flashed with each movement of Lisette's elegant fingers. Since Nicholai would be seeing her in the moonlight, they had decided to leave her hair unpowdered, but the hairdresser had intricately woven a fillet of cloth-of-gold through Lisette's gleaming curls. He also created a froth of curls along her brow, a touch that was not only fashionable, but that also made her look exceedingly different from the Lisette who wore an austere crown of braids.

To further ensure that she would not be recognized, they had applied just enough powder and rouge to enhance some of the shadows of Lisette's face without tarnishing her radiant beauty. The patch was replaced, a shimmery rose lip salve added, and light blue powder brushed onto each translucent eyelid to make her eyes look even richer and larger than before. Even the arch of her eyebrows had been delicately heightened. The effect was stunning. With her slim graceful poise and elegant features, Lisette looked like a queen.

Observing the wistful disappointment that flickered over her friend's face, Devon turned to her husband. "André, won't you go out and take a turn around the gardens? Perhaps Mr. Beauvisage is elsewhere, hiding from the *comtesse.* . . ."

Raveneau exhaled fragrant smoke and turned his head toward the supper box some distance away, where Gabrielle Marchandon had been ensconced with the Whitloafs all through the concert. "I believe I am about to be saved the trouble," he remarked.

Indeed, Gabrielle had risen and was making her way onto the lawn. At first, their eyes were drawn to her sumptuous gown of lavender silk; then Lisette's back straightened and her head turned toward the shadowy trees in the distance. She shivered.

"My dear, what is it?" inquired Devon. "Are you ill?"

"It's—Nicholai is here," she managed to whisper.

"Where? I can't see anyone except that overbearing duke of Chedringham and—"

"He's there, on the far side; barely clear of the trees."

Devon peered obediently into the darkness. "How can you tell? All I can make out is the faintest silhouette—"

"I just *know*." Lisette's voice was barely audible. "I knew even before I saw him."

"You women!" Raveneau marveled, ironically amused.

"With such magical powers, no wonder you think you're always right."

Devon cuffed his arm. "Cad! Now, do be serious. You have a task to perform!"

"*Mon Dieu!* I was hoping you would forget my part in this outrageous masquerade," he groaned.

Lisette, meanwhile, felt positively ill. Watching as Gabrielle's shadow merged with Nicholai's under the spreading branches of an oak tree, she wondered what madness had possessed her these past months. When Devon nudged her, she made a low sound of fearful dread. "Why am I here? This is insane!"

"You are here to captivate the man you love!" Devon declared fervently. "For heaven's sake, this is no time to lose your nerve, Lisette! Don't forget, André will be with you every step of the way, and I won't be far behind. Every detail of our plan has been carefully thought out and I am positive that nothing can go awry!"

Raveneau had been studying Lisette's increasingly pale countenance. Now, he came around the table and leaned down to take her hand. His own cool fingers touched the perspiration on her palm and his heart went out to her. "Courage!" His smile was one that made most females forget all else. In this case, it did seem to reassure Lisette. "Have I mentioned that you are the most beautiful woman here tonight, Fräulein Amstetten? Might you honor me by taking my arm for a stroll in the moonlight?"

Lisette sighed loudly, swallowed, then cast a last look over at Devon. "Oh . . ."

"Stop that! You will be fine! Just listen to André and remember that you have a role to play. Concentrate on that!" Devon gave her a little push. "Go on!"

Raveneau pulled Lisette gently to her feet and hooked an arm around her slender waist for support. They began to walk slowly, the long way around the sweeping open lawn toward the far-off twin silhouettes of Nicholai and Gabrielle.

After a moment, Lisette summoned her strength and moved Raveneau's arm to her side, slipping her hand around the hard strength of his forearm. Raveneau was looking especially handsome tonight in an expertly tailored coat of dove gray over a dark blue waistcoat and a cravat so white that it seemed to gleam in the moonlight against his bronzed face. Lisette was conscious of the stares of passersby—some envious, some frankly questioning.

"Do you know these people?" she whispered finally, after one matron came to a dead stop and narrowed accusing eyes at them.

"Not by choice, I assure you! However, even though our entrées into London society have been few and far between, Devon was an instant success and remains highly popular."

Lisette smiled. "No doubt she is popular with most, but I get the feeling that many of these females wouldn't mind it if you began seeking . . . outside amusements."

"Since I never have, you shall become famous as the temptress who lured me away from my wife, Fräulein Amstetten."

After another nervous sigh, Lisette fell silent for a long minute.

"Where's the confident, free-spirited woman I admire so?" whispered Raveneau at length. He reached over to touch her cheek with his free right hand.

"I—I feel a fool! Dressed like this, wearing Devon's jewels, with all this paint—and this silly patch! To have chased after Nicholai all this way—"

"You aren't a fool. You are a woman in love, with the courage to reach out for that love. You're strong, Lisette. This is just one more area of life that you will succeed in. Love is certainly as important as work, isn't it?"

She nodded mutely.

"Then cease these childish bouts of insecurity. If you have to, pretend that you're carrying on at the CoffeeHouse in the wake of some personal crisis. Put on a mask . . . only this time, you are Giselle Amstetten, an old friend of Devon's who is flirting outrageously with me." Raveneau tipped her chin to meet his dancing silvery gaze. "Frankly, I suspect that this entire charade is fraught with possibilities for fun!"

Lisette smiled in spite of herself. "That's true . . . but I am terrified that Nicholai will know me immediately, so what is uppermost in my mind are the possibilities for humiliation!"

Privately, Raveneau agreed. He knew that Devon could walk into a room completely concealed under a cloak and veils and still he would know her. However, now that the two women had concocted this wild scheme and had progressed this far, there seemed nothing for it. "Nonsense! Remember that we men are quite dim when it comes to instinctively sensing these things. Not a bit like you females. You look and sound a completely different woman. All Beauvisage will see is a resemblance that should be excruciatingly tantalizing!"

Feeling Lisette's hand tighten on his arm, Raveneau looked over to find that they were just a few yards away from Beauvisage and the Frenchwoman. "Now, don't stare!" he cautioned.

Lisette could only swallow audibly and nod.

"He's looking very well," whispered André, smiling in spite of himself.

Her heart in her throat, Lisette let her gaze caress Nicholai one more time. Bathed in moonlight, he looked more attractive and irresistible than even she had remembered. A flawlessly tailored biscuit frock coat showed Nicholai's wide shoulders and lean hips to advantage. A snowy jabot accentuated his dark reckless face, while starlit auburn gold hair lay in casual ruffles. Yellow nankeen breeches skimmed the lean muscles of his thighs, meeting glossy boots below the knee.

"Yes . . ." she murmured, looking up into Raveneau's slightly amused eyes. "He's looking better than ever!"

"The farther apart, the dearer the heart . . ." he said dryly. "And now, *chérie,* you are supposed to have eyes for only me!"

Lisette caught a glimpse of Gabrielle's pale hand reaching toward Nicholai's cheek and her resolve flooded back. "But of course, Captain Raveneau! What female alive could resist you?" Her accent was liltingly German, her smile radiant. "If only we could be truly alone . . ."

They were standing less than a dozen feet from Nicholai now, and André was getting caught up in the spirit of the masquerade. *Who wouldn't,* he asked himself, *when confronted with a sudden wave of such enchantment?* Lifting her soft hands, he kissed them both and slanted a rakish grin into her startled eyes.

"Fräulein Amstetten, I wish for solitude as much as you . . . but unfortunately we are being watched, so do smile and pretend that you welcome my attentions. . . ."

Indeed, Nicholai had noticed them. After a brief disbelieving stare, he had tried to concentrate on what Gabrielle was saying, but to no avail. That woman with André Raveneau—God, how sharply she reminded him of Lisette! First the vision in the landau that morning, and now this. Was he going mad? Glancing over again, Nicholai shook his head slightly. No, of course it was impossible. This woman was dressed in an expensive, revealing, fashionable gown. Jewels glittered against her throat, ears, hands. Her hair, of a color he couldn't pinpoint in the darkness, was coiffed in the sort of elaborate style Lisette deplored for herself. Finally, this stranger was playing the coquette with a married man at midnight in London's Vauxhall Gardens.

I would be a madman, he told himself, *to actually believe this woman could be Lisette Hahn. I must have an acute case of wishful thinking!*

"Mon cher," Gabrielle was imploring, "have you been hearing even a word of what I am saying? Why do you look at those other people?" She couldn't have been more frustrated. First, Nicholai had not arrived until after midnight—when she had planned each moment, each word, each touch and kiss so painstakingly. And now that her scheme to recapture his love was in motion, Nicholai was being rude enough to stare at that insignificant Austrian woman!

"I—" Momentarily, he was at a loss for words. "Ah— I was just about to speak to André Raveneau." Wondering how to finish the sentence, it suddenly occurred to him that this mysterious female who so resembled Lisette might be Raveneau's *wife!*

At the sound of his own name, André glanced over with studied curiosity. "Well—Beauvisage!" he exclaimed. "What a surprise!"

"It's a pleasure to see you, Captain Raveneau." He guided Gabrielle toward the other couple and sketched a short bow.

"If I had known that your wife were such a vision of love-liness, I would have made a point of meeting her sooner."

Raveneau managed a creditable expression of uneasiness. "I don't blame you for saying so, Mr. Beauvisage, but this beautiful lady is not my wife, but a very dear friend of both of ours." He gave Nicholai a slight confidential wink. "May I present Fräulein Giselle Amstetten? The turmoil in Europe forced her to flee to London, and we only wish to assist her in settling into society as painlessly as possible." He turned to Lisette, who had dropped her eyes before Nicholai's unwavering regard. "Fräulein, this is Nicholai Beauvisage and—"

Gabrielle spared Nicholai the trouble of supplying her name. "I am *la comtesse de Louviers,* m'sieur, and the Fräulein and I have met before." She then extended her hand toward Raveneau and summoned her most dazzling smile. "It is greatly a pleasure to acquaint myself with *you,* however, *Capitaine!*"

While the Frenchwoman occupied herself with Raveneau, Nicholai reached for Lisette's hand. Somehow, she was able to keep it still and meet his sparkling emerald gaze, but when Nicholai's mouth graced her palm, a delicious, ex-crutiating flame ran up Lisette's arm and sent sparks over her breasts. After nearly four months of aching for his touch, it was no wonder, but certainly Nicholai would see through this masquerade immediately if her body continued to betray her!

"Europe's loss is my gain, Fräulein Amstetten," Nicholai told her softly.

Under his searching gaze, Lisette gathered her wits. She curved her mouth in the flirtatious smile Devon and she had practiced endlessly, then lowered her lashes. "How kind you are, Herr Beauvisage!" The disguised voice was per-fect; higher, yet somehow huskier, and of course accented, compared to Lisette's own.

Nicholai wondered if this were some wild, improbable dream. The eyes he stared into were Lisette's; there was no question! The hand he held was Lisette's. He couldn't mis-take the fragile line of her nose, her cheekbones, her elegant neck, and the creamy curves of her breasts. Yet—

Lisette could not be here, let alone in such a gown, with these jewels and hairstyle and voice—and manner!

"André, there you are!" A scolding voice preceded the diminutive figure that was crossing the lawn. "I thought that perhaps you and Giselle had gotten lost! Truly, I didn't think that the two of you would leave when I went over to have a word with Lady Margaret! It was bad of you not to wait for me."

Nicholai's attention was abruptly transferred to the woman Raveneau introduced as his wife. Clad in a beautiful white silk gown embroidered with blue and rose flowers on swirling green stems, the woman was exquisite. However, it was her strawberry blond curls and animated gestures that drew Nicholai's stare. He had seen her somewhere . . .

"I don't mean to be rude, but I do hope you all will forgive me if I steal my husband away for a few minutes—" Devon Raveneau smiled too sweetly at Nicholai and Gabrielle, but narrowed her eyes slightly in Lisette's direction. She slid one arm possessively through her husband's, then paused to glance back and add, "Oh, *Comtesse*, I heard the Prince of Wales asking for you a few minutes ago."

"The prince!" exclaimed Gabrielle. "But I didn't know he was here!"

"Oh, yes. I'm quite certain it was he. I heard him inquiring after you on the footpath behind the supper boxes." Devon pointed vaguely to the west.

Moments later, Lisette found herself alone with Nicholai after midnight in Vauxhall Gardens's densest shadows. . . .

Chapter 41

September 4, 1793.

Nicholai engaged Giselle Amstetten in polite conversation as they strolled through the trees on one of the more secluded footpaths. After weeks of rehearsals with Devon, Lisette managed to tell a convincing tale about her wealthy parents, their ancestral castle, and her colorful experiences in the great cities of Europe.

"And your parents?" Nicholai inquired. "What has become of them?"

"They stayed behind. Our castle is in a rather remote area and reasonably safe."

"They must miss you terribly." His gaze was concerned, but in reality, Nicholai studied the details of her delicate ear and the graceful sweep of her neck.

"I . . . really couldn't say. In truth, we have been somewhat estranged for a few years, and I rather think they were relieved to see me go." She turned her head, wearing the bewitching smile perfected after hours before the mirror, and encountered Nicholai's emerald gaze. Somehow, Lisette managed not to blush. "You see," she confided with a provocative glance through her thick lashes, "I don't seem to be the type of female that enjoys languishing in castles. Too much time could be lost waiting for a bold knight or prince charming who might never appear!"

"I do recall hearing rumors that there aren't many knights and princes making the rounds of castles these days. . . ." Nicholai agreed with a wry smile.

Lisette laughed softly, glorying in his company and in the sheer pleasure of watching irreverent amusement flicker across Nicholai's handsome features. However, the instant that she saw his expression become alert, Lisette stifled her laughter. Of course, he would notice! How *could* they have forgotten to invent a new laugh of her after attending to every other detail so painstakingly?

"Is something amiss?" she inquired, her accent so perfect that she was painfully reminded of her own mother.

Nicholai stopped and casually lifted Lisette's hand. They were near one of the few lamps on this footpath and she was all too conscious of his gaze, as well as his mouth, burning her fingers. "No, fräulein . . . it is only that you vaguely resemble someone I used to know."

Hearing this casual reference to herself, Lisette was stunned. How indifferent he sounded—as though their relationship had been some trivial flirtation! In a perverse sense, she felt furious and jealous of Giselle Amstetten. . . .

"Is it possible," Nicholai was saying in a voice that was both ironic and seductive, "that you could be free of romantic entanglements? There must be an ardent suitor waiting in the background!"

"Why, Herr Beauvisage, how can you be concerned about my other suitors when we have just met?" Lisette heard herself reply coquettishly.

"For your information, fräulein, it is not quite the thing in London society for a maiden to wander off alone with a man at night," came Nicholai's harsh reply. He had just employed a lamp to light a cheroot, which he now drew on before continuing, "I merely wanted to be certain that some irate fiancé wouldn't leap from the underbrush to challenge me to a duel. Frankly, I haven't the time these days. . . ."

"For *your* information, sir, I do not have any suitors who are quite that ardent after so short a stay in London. Furthermore, I am *not* a maiden!"

"Indeed?"

Lisette rushed to keep pace as Nicholai continued along the footpath. Thankful for the renewed darkness, she declared, "The fact is, I am a widow."

"No! Tragic." He had stopped again, shadows disguising his sardonic expression.

"It *was* tragic!" she assured him haughtily, not forgetting her accent for a moment. "My husband was killed last year during a battle with the French army. Afterwards, I began to travel in an effort to forget . . . and when I came to London, I decided to begin a new life, so I took back my maiden name."

"How sad." Nicholai's dancing eyes were masked by the darkness. He reached for her hand and tucked it around his arm before murmuring, "Such a difficult adjustment for one to make, as you no doubt discovered during your solitary travels."

Outrage surged up in Lisette. She knew him well enough to recognize the mockery in his voice, but certainly he did not expect Giselle Amstetten to be so perceptive! "It is an adjustment indeed, sir," came her frosty reply. "Living without a loved one can cause untold suffering that I hope you will never have to experience!"

"I appreciate your good wishes, fräulein, and my sympathies are certainly with you."

Lisette was too upset to notice how much time had passed since the last lamp. She didn't even see the secluded grotto that loomed before them. "Is it truly possible, Herr Beauvisage, that you have never been parted from a woman you love?" Tears stung her eyes as she waited for his answer.

"Love is a subject that I know little about, and which seems far too weighty for us to discuss on such a splendid night as this." Nicholai was leading her into the blackness. "There are other aspects of loving that interest me more. . . ."

Although her mouth opened, no words would come out. She stared up into his recklessly masculine face and raged silently, *What about me? What about Lisette Hahn, the woman you left behind in Philadelphia?* It wasn't supposed to happen like this. He should have been drawn to her helplessly, *against his will!* How could Nicholai be so casually cynical about love? Had she misjudged him after all?

He saw the fire in her sapphire eyes and reclined against the grotto's stone wall. It was lavishly spread with vines and ivy that cushioned his back as he drew the Austrian woman into his arms. "Relax, fräulein," Nicholai murmured. "I know exactly the kind of adjustments you have had to make since losing your dear husband . . . and just *how* you have missed him. I only want to ease the terrible suffering you spoke of earlier."

The caustic innuendo was all too clear in his voice, but before Lisette could unleash her anger, she was caught up in his strong embrace. The sensation of Nicholai's arms like steel against the satin gown that dipped low to bare half her back flooded her with hot pleasure.

"I—" she gasped. "You—"

"Naturally," he whispered leisurely before bringing his mouth down to cover hers.

Oh, it had been so long. Too long. Nicholai's lips were hard and warm as they slanted over her own until his tongue thrust into her mouth to alternately caress, assault, savor. . . . Somehow, Lisette was able at last to draw back, breathless. Nicholai's arms were unyielding, so she leaned against his wide chest until her head stopped spinning. The clean masculine scent of Nicholai's shirt and waistcoat were intoxicatingly familiar. After inhaling several times, Lisette finally managed to look up into emerald eyes that glimmered with secret amusement.

"H—how dare you?" she gasped.

"With the utmost ease, fräulein." One lean hand traced the bare creamy line of her upper back.

Trembling under Nicholai's deft touch, she retorted shakily, "I have not given you leave to take such liberties with me, sir!"

His laugh was soft and wicked. "No—but I do not recall asking."

A moan rose aching in Lisette's throat as his mouth closed over hers again. This time, he tantalized her with gently sensuous play between their lips and tongues until it took all her strength to refrain from pressing nearer to demand the deep kiss she craved. When he felt her hips arch involuntarily against his, Nicholai moved to brush scorching kisses along her delicate jaw and graceful neck.

Lisette's senses swam. She felt paralyzed by yearning more potent than she had ever known before. Her arms stole around his neck and she touched the crisp auburn hair that curled over his collar. Through a haze, she saw his lean brown fingers against the pale curve of her breast. Somehow, then, Nicholai freed it from the minimal confines of her bodice and she shivered with fearful excitement.

"You—oh, no—you simply mustn't—"

He bent to kiss first the creamy ivory swell, then the taut rosy crest. Lisette trembled in his arms. Although Nicholai's own need pressed insistently against the confines of his nankeen breeches, he managed somehow to replace the tempting breast within its satin cover.

"If you insist, fräulein," he murmured in a respectful tone Lisette had never heard before. She only wished she could see his face more clearly . . . !

Giselle! she reminded herself through the fog that clouded her brain. *I must act as Giselle Amstetten!* Taking a deep breath, Lisette demanded, "Do you always assume such familiarity with women you have just met, Herr Beauvisage?"

A moonbeam silvered the rakish planes of his face. When he smiled, a gleam of white broke the darkness, yet Nicholai's arms did not withdraw. "Not always, fräulein. Only when I feel the lady in question is in desperate need of—ah—comforting, or . . ."

Lisette's sensitized skin tingled against the lean-muscled outline of his tall body. How she had ached to be back in Nicholai's embrace . . . but if she let him see that now . . .

"Is that the reason for your involvement with the *comtesse de Louviers,* Herr Beauvisage? Are you comforting her as well?" Her cold words shattered the spell between them. "I find it difficult to believe that your motives are so charitable, sir, nor do I accept your excuse."

Nicholai arched a brow in the darkness. "I am desolated, fräulein, but may I be so bold as to ask what is *your* excuse?"

"What do you mean?" Lisette strove to keep the panic out of her voice.

"I thought that perhaps you were seeking comfort from Raveneau, the husband of your friend . . . but perhaps you would describe it differently—"

She was elated. Just as she and Devon had hoped, the sight of her with André had kindled jealousy immediately in Nicholai. Now for the hot-blooded finish to their first evening together in London, to ensure that he would dream of her later . . . or not be able to sleep at all.

"Herr Beauvisage, you go too far. You are a cad! Release me!" When he threw up his hands immediately, feigning fearful surrender, Lisette promptly delivered a stinging slap across his hard right cheek.

Nicholai made no move to follow when she lifted her skirts and turned away. Instead, he stood quietly in the deep blue night, watching the lithe, willowy figure disappear among the trees. Bronzed fingers absently rose to rub the offended cheek, while a certain bemused smile flickered at the corners of Nicholai's mouth for the first time in more than three months. . . .

"Shh!" Devon admonished as she clung to her husband's arm. "You must be serious. We can't have them notice us!"

"Milady, I assure you that I am completely serious."

They were near a tall sculptured hedge that offered concealment from the moonlight. Raveneau turned his back to it and pulled his wife against the length of his rugged body. Devon tried to keep one eye on the figures that seemed to trade secrets as they rounded the corner of the footpath and came closer to the hedge. However, her husband's warm, insistent lips were kissing tender spots on her throat and face before covering her pliant mouth; Devon forgot all else. André's hands were in her gleaming golden rose hair, then touching the soft beauty of her neck, shoulders, arms, and the sensuous silk gown that hid even more delectable charms. After a dozen years of heated passion, he still craved each fresh glimpse and taste of his wife's breasts. The idea of undressing her made him as hard and hot the few-thousandth time as it had the first. Feeling Devon sigh, he molded her body more intimately to his. Real love was certainly a splendid puzzle. . . .

Soft feminine laughter drifted across the footpath, followed by a slightly admonishing voice: "Are you certain that he hasn't guessed the truth, Gabrielle? It wouldn't do for you to become too sure of yourself or to underestimate Nicholai Beauvisage. . . ."

"How *could* he guess? Only you and I know, and certainly *I* have not confided in anyone else!" Gabrielle lowered her voice upon spying another couple against a nearby shadowed hedge. There were more people lingering behind the supper boxes and ahead of them, where late diners strolled to and from their secluded tables. This did seem to be the safest spot for Gabrielle's conversation with Angelique . . . and when she glimpsed a white breast in the starlight and the tall man bending his head to it, Gabrielle smiled with relief. Even if they did overhear, they wouldn't care or comprehend. In silhouette, she saw the woman arch her neck; the man raised his head to trail kisses over a pale throat before crushing anxious lips. The sight of dark hands sliding down the woman's back to curve over and then pull her silk-clad buttocks roughly against what must have been a splendid erection made Gabrielle flush with envy and desire.

"*Eh bien*," Angelique murmured in consternation. "It must be worse than I thought between you and Nicholai! I can see you getting hot just watching those strangers. Shame! Has he been absent so much from your bed?"

"Too much," confessed Gabrielle. She couldn't bring herself to admit that Nicholai had made love to her only once since their reunion—and that even then she had sensed his emotional distance. "I don't know what it is, but—"

"What is wrong? What do you see?" pressed Angelique after a moment.

Gabrielle was peering sharply into the darkness. Had the woman inclined her head in their direction while her lover kissed the far, bare shoulder? Probably it was imagination, but to be safe Gabrielle decided that this conversation should be in French.

"It is nothing," she said in their native tongue. "I am tired of English, that's all. As for Nicholai—what I was going to tell you is that I am certain he suspects nothing. I admit that there are problems in our relationship, but I feel that they are rooted somehow in his new life in America. He has changed."

Angelique let out an ingenuous little gasp and pressed a hand to her mouth. "Oh! Do you suppose he has fallen in love with a woman from over *there*?"

"How could he?" Now that they were speaking rapidly in French, Gabrielle began to forget about the couple by the hedge. "If that were true, Nicky would certainly have remained in Philadelphia, *n'est-ce pas*?"

"So you believe that he has come to help you even though his feelings for you have changed?"

"I am certain of it. And perhaps his feelings have not really changed after all. You know men. Sometimes their behavior is positively baffling. As long as Nicky helps me to find Henri, I don't really care what his feelings are for me."

"Liar!" Angelique laughed. "You were burning for him all summer until he arrived."

"I won't deny that Nicky is a better, more thrilling lover than any man I've ever known . . ."

"And?"

"And that his looks and careless charm are irresistible, but the truth is that he would never marry me, and even if he did, we would not suit. Nicky would not marry a woman he didn't love completely. I am not capable of that, or of sharing my life with him as I know he would want. I must be free! Nicky and I always dealt so well together in the past because we were involved in an illicit love affair. He was fascinated because I kept parts of myself hidden, unlike all those other strumpets who threw themselves at him. And I . . . loved Nicholai in my own way, but I must admit that it was the thrill of the forbidden that drew me on over the years. I mean, he could have had anyone, but it was I for whom he journeyed long miles—often to be alone with me for just a few hours!" Gabrielle sighed, remembering. "Those were such thrilling times. The queen herself would have given up her finest diamonds to share a bed with Nicholai Beauvisage!"

Angelique gave her an odd look. "But you would rather be married to Henri than Nicholai . . . ?"

"I'd prefer the best of both worlds!" Gabrielle strode over to a tree and leaned her face against the cool bark. Glancing over at the lovers near the hedge, she felt a hot twinge between her legs at the sight of the man unbuttoning the woman's gown while she nibbled at his ear and neck.

"The security of a rich husband and the excitement of a handsome lover?" Angelique queried softly.

"Don't you take that tone with me! You were no sooner in London than you had Dudley in your clutches, charming him into marriage before he knew what had hit him!"

"I may have sought a good marriage so that I could survive, but I have tried my best to do right by him! I have other things in mind besides myself!"

"So do I," Gabrielle returned hotly.

"Oh, yes!" Angelique's high voice turned shrill. "You coaxed Nicholai to come to you because he thought you needed his help in finding your brother . . . and perhaps because he thought you loved him! Now we realize that, when he came, to help you, he must have left something—or someone—special and important in Philadelphia to help you. Don't you think I can see the disillusion already in his eyes? What do you suppose Nicholai would say if he knew that your *brother* was the one claimed by the guillotine, and that the *comte de Louviers* is the person, hiding or imprisoned in France, whom you seek?"

"Henri might be dead as well," Gabrielle countered, irritated by this lecture from her usually featherbrained friend.

"But if he is alive, your husband will be able to lead you to the fortune in gold and jewels that he hid so well after the Revolution broke out."

"I won't let you shame me, Angelique! After all, I *am* the *comtesse*, and Henri's fortune should be mine! You were certainly thinking about money when you snared Lord Dudley Whitloaf!"

Angelique gasped, eyes blazing. "At least I have kept my part of the bargain; I am a faithful wife! You cannot even be truthful with your *lover*! What will you do if, after so much scheming, Henri is not alive after all?"

"I will just marry Nicholai, then, even though he would be far too possessive and strong willed to deal with as a husband. At least he has wealth—and other redeeming attributes. . . ." She smiled suggestively.

"Do you honestly believe that Nicholai would wed you after he realizes the lies you have drawn him into?"

Gabrielle arched an eyebrow. "There are ways to soften the heart of even the angriest man." Her gaze slid back to the amorous couple, who were now stealing off into the darkness. She shivered slightly, then turned back to Angelique. "Somehow, everything will work out . . . and in the meantime, you and I should not quarrel. Have we not been friends for a dozen years? You have known me in some ways better than any man, *ma chérie*."

"That was a long time ago. We were children!" Angelique's face burned in the shadows. "I would like to forget about that."

"Will you also forget to scold me about Nicky from now on?" Gabrielle trailed a white finger from Angelique's throat down toward her breasts.

"If the subject annoys you so much, then I shall not raise it again." She took a step backward. "It is late. Dudley will be wanting to go home."

As the two women continued down the footpath that curved around the supper boxes, Raveneau was leading his wife farther away, deeper into the woods.

"Lady Whitloaf is right," whispered Devon through muffled laughter. "It *is* late."

"Not late enough." His mouth quirked in a wicked half smile. "Besides, I must translate their conversation for you."

"I know French too well to be swayed by that excuse, sir!"

"But you might have missed some tiny phrase that would prove crucial, madame." Raveneau had guided her under a cluster of weeping willows and now drew her into his hard, warm embrace. All admonishments of propriety died on Devon's lips as she melted against her husband's demanding body and mouth. The tiny buttons that closed the back of her gown were deftly unfastened.

"André!" She turned her head nervously, suddenly afraid that someone would see them. All around, willow branches caressed the ground to create a lacy curtain of protection from prying eyes. Devon felt a bit less conspicuous and gave herself up to the pleasurable sensations. Then her breasts were bared to the cool night air and she gasped, shocked. "André, what are you doing?"

"I believe I am kissing your breasts, *chérie*." Raveneau's murmured response was underlaid with irony. Slowly, his tongue teased circles around each nipple. The breeze and Devon's arousal combined to pucker them into especially hard peaks that responded ardently to André's warm, skillful mouth when at last he began to gently suck on them. All the while, his hands were slowly exploring her smooth exposed flesh, wonderingly, as if this were the first time he'd touched Devon's satiny neck, back, the contour of her shoulder, the round swells of her breasts. Even her lovely arms were traced as lean fingers slid her sleeves farther down, finally freeing them completely.

"André!" Devon managed to gasp again. A familiar tingling ache was building in her loins along with a warning in her mind. "Do you mean to strip me naked?"

"That's an inspired idea, *ma petite!*" He raised his head and, smiling, captured her mouth in a hot, lazy kiss.

Devon realized that he was shrugging out of his jacket. Watching as he spread it over the lush grass, she felt weak with excitement and panic. "I—I thought that you wanted to translate the things that Gabrielle was saying to—"

"I have another, more important translation to make first." Raveneau was pulling Devon against the length of his body and the hardness that strained against his breeches.

"Oh, André," Devon murmured shakily, "aren't we too old for this sort of thing? I mean"—her breath caught as he drew her down until she lay trembling on his dove gray coat—"we are married, after all . . . and we could go home to our—own bed—"

Raveneau's hand found its way under his wife's gown and petticoats, sliding up white silk stockings to the bare thighs that felt like satin. Devon flinched and moaned softly. "Yes, *chérie,* I know all about our bed," he whispered teasingly against her fragrant hair. "We'll get there, in due time. . . ."

Their mouths met in a long, hungry kiss. She worked at buttons on his waistcoat, yearning to caress André's warm lean-muscled back. His fingertips grazed the curls between her legs, tantalizing until Devon's breath came in ragged gasps. Finally, he touched the sweet flesh that ached for him, then held his hand away. By this time, Devon had successfully wrestled with Raveneau's shirt buttons and now curved one little hand over the huge hardness still trapped inside his breeches.

"You're wet," he murmured while kissing her ear.

"Oh—you mustn't tease me!" Her hips arched in search of his hand.

"Are you certain? You don't want to go home?"

"For God's sake, André!" She pressed fiery kisses along his scarred jaw.

One lean finger returned to circle the pouting bud of her desire. "You've changed your mind, then? We aren't too *old* for this sort of thing?" The feel of her, so hot and moist and eager, was driving him mad.

Devon's only response was soft laughter. She reveled in the sensation of Raveneau's lips and tongue on her breasts and midriff. Moonlight spilled over his black hair and she reached out to feel its texture. Now he moved lower to bestow kisses that scorched the tender insides of her thighs all the way up to . . .

"André! You mustn't—not here!" She tried to pull at his hair, without success. Hot pleasurable waves of sensation spread and intensified under his wickedly skillful mouth. "This is madness!"

Raveneau caught her hands and pinned them against her sides, pausing, teasing, until finally Devon's release came in a sudden storm. As she shuddered against him, André moved upward and filled her with his urgent hardness so that she moaned aloud. Each thrust was feverishly met, slim arms clutching his wide back, and Raveneau's whisper, husky with love, tickled Devon's ear: "I must concede, *mignonne*; you are right . . . but this is a madness so sweet that I dread the return of sanity!"

Chapter 42

September 4, 1793

Lisette took a sip of tea, nibbled at her cranberry muffin, and turned once more to glance at the dining room clock.

"Is something wrong?" Mouette Raveneau softly touched her arm.

"You keep looking at the time!" Nathan chimed in, ignoring his sister's reproving stare. "It's making me quite mad!"

"Well, I'm sorry, Nathan!" Lisette shot back as if he were her own brother, then softened and smiled around the table at Mouette and Halsey Minter. "I didn't realize . . . it's just that it is past nine o'clock and we are supposed to go riding. Where can your parents be?"

She had directed the last question to Mouette, but it was Nathan who immediately retorted, "Oh, that's easy. They're probably still kissing and doing love things like that." He made a face that reflected his opinion of such pastimes.

"It's still early," Mouette said reassuringly. "Papa and I didn't leave until nearly ten o'clock yesterday, and it was at least a half hour before we encountered Mr. Beauvisage in Hyde Park."

Lisette blushed. Minter was in the midst of transferring more Irish ham, eggs, muffins, and another chunk of honeycomb to his plate, but the corners of his mouth had lifted irrepressibly. Lisette was aware that he had come here today because of the "plan." During their ride, Minter was to stay near Devon, while Lisette and Raveneau would go on ahead, side by side, in hopes of encountering Nicholai first. The idea was for him to imagine, as at Vauxhall Gardens, that the sophisticated Raveneau marriage allowed flirtations to be pursued to any end. Not for the first time, Lisette wondered whether Nicholai would react with jealousy . . . or with a more alarming combination of anger and disgust.

Nearly a day and a half had passed with agonizing slowness since their midnight rendezvous. Devon had insisted that the suspense would do them both good when she sent only her husband and daughter out riding in Hyde Park the morning after Vauxhall. "If he turns up after so late a night," Devon had declared, "it will be a positive sign indeed!" However, as Mouette just mentioned, it had been past ten before Beauvisage's handsome gelding cantered leisurely into the park. Infused with romance as she imagined herself a spy, the young girl had reported every detail of the meeting to her mother and Lisette. Of course, she had not been fooled by Nicholai's seeming nonchalance when he inquired after "Fräulein Amstetten," or when, in the midst of their farewells, he had wondered aloud whether the Raveneaus' houseguest might also be riding the next morning. Mouette and her father had agreed, nodding, that it was certainly possible. . . .

Lisette stiffened at the sound of a low, sensuous giggle that drifted down the stairs. "Oh, good!" She beamed with a sigh. "They are coming!"

When the Raveneaus appeared on the dining room's threshold, Lisette's smile faltered, for Devon wore a dressing gown of peach and ivory satin and her husband was clad in boots, breeches, and an open-necked shirt.

"Good morning, everyone!" Devon took the chair that André held for her and smiled up at him. Her dusky rose cheeks and sparkling blue eyes were framed by a wreath of titian curls. "This food smells wonderful. Why, it looks as if all of you are nearly finished! What time is it?"

"Nearly half after nine," Lisette replied flatly, thinking that they would never be ready in time. It seemed that she had lain awake all night in anticipation of this meeting with Nicholai; now her heart felt cold and hard at the prospect of another day deprived of the splendid sight of him, the sound of his voice, the possibility of being touched by his tapering fingers. . . .

"Oh, my." Devon flushed and looked over at Raveneau. Although occupied with filling his plate, he did pause long enough to give his wife a slight reassuring smile, and dropped one hand to caress her thigh under the table. Devon's blush deepened. "I had no idea . . . I—I suppose we must have overslept!"

"What'd I tell you?" muttered Nathan impishly, only to be rewarded by a scathing stare from his father at the other end of the table.

"Well, I've got to say that the two of you certainly look well rested!" Minter offered with a cheerful grin.

Devon scarely heard his words or noticed the servant that poured her tea. How beautiful Lisette was looking this morning—and how dejected! she thought. The primrose yellow velvet riding habit, trimmed with a narrow sky blue stripe, had been an inspired choice. Even the white blouse and skillfully tied cravat looked perfect. All that was missing was the matching hat, which they had had specially made so that it would cast a shadow over any exposed golden curls. A brief sideways glance told Devon that the hat was waiting on a nearby pembroke table.

"If we are going to intercept Mr. Beauvisage, I should dress immediately!" she announced, pushing back her chair.

"You haven't touched your breakfast," Raveneau protested "I thought you were famished!"

"The feeling has passed. Perhaps I am *enceinte*?" The words were spoken innocently enough, but followed by a brief wicked grin. "You'd better satisfy your own appetite also, darling, and soon! I'll expect you upstairs in less than five minutes, cravat in hand."

While a rather dazed-looking Raveneau stared after his wife's departing figure, Minter brushed bright hair back from his brow and chuckled. "This promises to be a rare morning. I can't wait to play my part—flirting with Devon in full view of Captain Raveneau!"

"Don't get too carried away," André warned darkly, "or a certain person back in Virginia will hear about it."

"I wish that I could go along," said Mouette softly, her lovely dark eyes filled with longing.

"Not this time, *ma fille*," Raveneau replied as he lifted a last forkful of egg. "Your tutor will be here at ten o'clock."

"I know . . ." she sighed. "It's just that I would enjoy seeing Mr. Beauvisage again."

Lisette had risen and crossed to the pembroke table, where she was now in the midst of settling the primrose velvet hat over her upswept curls. At Mouette's words, however, she stared back at the table in surprise. "Why ever do you say so?"

"I think he is the handsomest man I've ever seen," the girl answered dreamily. "His smile is the kind that makes one feel warm inside, and when he looked at me it was as if he thought me quite smart and pretty. Not a child at all."

"Oh, God," Raveneau groaned. "I shall have to redouble my efforts to reunite Lisette with this lecher Beauvisage before he attempts to seduce Mouette!" He felt a tiny pang, remembering that not long ago his little girl had declared that no man in all the world could be more magnificent looking than her Papa.

"André!" called Devon from upstairs.

He stood, tossed his napkin on the chair, and exited, all the while shaking his dark head in disbelief.

Nathan made a disgusted noise, rolled his eyes, and muttered, "Women!"

Hyde Park was still richly green and trimmed with rows of bright flowers on this September morn, but Nicholai knew that autumn would creep in soon enough. He appeared the picture of nonchalance as he stood near his slate gray gelding while the animal munched on grass. White breeches skimmed hard-muscled thighs; a bottle green frock coat, fawn vest, and snowy shirt and cravat fit his broad shoulders and flat belly with perfectly casual elegance. One sun-darkened hand absently flicked his riding crop against the side of a gleaming boot. Then, a glimpse of red gold hair passing through the Grosvenor Gate transformed Nicholai into an alert jungle cat. Instantly, he swung himself into the saddle and walked the gelding through the rows of immaculately sculptured trees that paralleled Hyde Park's eastern perimeter. His heart thumped in elation as he recognized Devon Raveneau—but who was that with her? The man's hair was also reddish, but a darker shade, and there was something about the way that she smiled at him and reached across to brush his hand that told Nicholai they were not brother and sister. Not for the first time, he wondered about the Raveneau marriage.

"Ah! Mr. Beauvisage, isn't it?" Feathery lashes swept soft pink cheeks as Devon gave him a flirtatious smile.

"Your memory is nearly as remarkable as your beauty, Madame Raveneau," he replied smoothly. Bringing his horse alongside her own, he caught her hand and kissed it.

Devon was astonished to feel her flesh tingle under his insolent mouth. Blushing, she heard herself exclaim, "Have you met Mr. Minter? He is a terribly wealthy merchant from Williamsburg, Virginia! Halsey, this is Nicholai Beauvisage!"

Minter could barely keep a straight face. A terribly wealthy merchant? Affecting a haughty attitude, he inclined his head toward Beauvisage and murmured, "A great pleasure, sir."

Nicholai nodded brusquely and returned his attention to Devon. "Has your husband been so remiss as to let you venture out alone?"

"Oh, André is not far behind . . . unless he and Fräulein Amstetten have gotten lost!"

Minter couldn't resist. *"Again?"*

Narrowing his eyes, Beauvisage stared past them to the pair of horses and riders that was just then passing through Grosvenor Gate. He heard Devon Raveneau and her wealthy friend say something about going, and he bade them a distracted good-bye, his eyes never leaving the graceful figure in yellow velvet who approached on a lovely cinnamon mare. She was laughing at something Raveneau had said, but Nicholai could swear she'd seen him.

"Regardez!" the Frenchman was saying. "What a coincidence! Giselle, *chérie*, we have encountered M'sieur Beauvisage once again!" One black brow curved high in pseudo-surprise.

" 'Tis a small world, indeed, sir." Lisette cast a laughing glance at Raveneau, then turned to regard Nicholai with a serenely beautiful countenance. "We meet again, Herr Beauvisage. I trust you have recovered from the rigors of your night at Vauxhall?"

"As a matter of fact, I enjoyed myself immensely, fräulein." He paused as though listening. "I am certain that I hear your lovely wife calling, Captain Raveneau."

André bit back a smile and pretended to hear a non-existent summons. "Ah, *oui!* I thank you, Beauvisage." He turned back to meet Lisette's sparkling blue eyes. "Do you mind if I leave you here with M'sieur Beauvisage?"

"No, no," she managed to reply without laughing. "You go ahead. I will meet all of you at home."

Suddenly they were alone. "André and Devon Raveneau have a unique marriage," reflected Nicholai.

"That is true." Lisette knew they were not speaking of the same thing, but she couldn't resist replying in kind, since his choice of words had made it so easy. However, sensing that he intended to probe further, she deftly changed the subject. "How have you been of late?"

"Barely a day has passed since our last meeting, fräulein."

The familiar ironic tone of Nicholai's voice made her heart pound with yearning. "Oh, really? It seems much longer!"

"Fräulein Amstetten, you wound me!" Yet his mocking smile told a different story.

Rather than answer, she turned her horse away and Nicholai followed her through the trees to the open lawn beyond. When their horses bent to nibble the lush grass, he dismounted and gently lifted Lisette down.

"Did you wish to discuss something with me?" she inquired, burningly conscious of his strong hands spanning her waist.

"Yes. I will be leaving Britain two days hence . . . and somehow, I thought you might wish to know."

"Leaving!" gasped Lisette.

"Why, Fräulein Amstetten, I almost believe that you care!" One arm curved up around her slim back; his other hand caressed her neck, tipping her head up for his kiss.

Lisette struggled for an instant, then succumbed. At first she was conscious only of his mouth opening her own, the delicious sensation of his tongue, the pressure of his arms and hands embracing her, but then, as Nicholai hardened and grew against her velvet-sheathed belly, Lisette flushed and pressed her hips helplessly nearer.

"How cozy!"

Nicholai stiffened immediately. Dropping his hands, he straightened to meet Gabrielle's taunting gaze. Behind her, the Whitloafs tentatively walked their horses toward Grosvenor Gate.

"We'll wait for you at home, then, Gabrielle . . ." Angelique ventured.

"Might I have a word with you alone?" the Frenchwoman inquired of Nicholai.

"I have to be going, anyway," Lisette interjected, her tone carefully detached. "My horse and I both need our exercise."

Nicholai glared at Gabrielle. What timing! Still, there seemed no choice. . . . "I was coming over to speak to you this afternoon, but I suppose this is as good a time as any. If you could grant me a moment's indulgence—?" Sarcasm lingered in the air as he turned back to Lisette and lightly took her elbow, guiding her to the mare who had wandered a short distance away. "I apologize for the interruption, fräulein."

"Actually, I am rather grateful for it!" A dimple winked next to her pretty mouth. "I only hope that the *comtesse* is not too angry with you."

"She'll recover," Nicholai said noncommittally. He lifted her hand, studying it as his mouth scorched the soft palm and inner wrist. "I fear that I should bid you good-bye, fräulein. I regret that I shall have to forgo the pleasure of getting to know you better."

Lisette saw the irreverent gleam in his eyes, felt his hands slide up to her breasts as he lifted her onto the horse. It was as if the primrose velvet and fine white linen had been burned away; for a moment she couldn't breathe. Traitorous tears stung her eyes.

"B—but . . . Herr Beauvisage, are you certain that we shall not meet again before you sail?"

Nicholai grinned in a way that sent hot blood rushing to her cheeks. "I suppose it is possible, Fräulein Amstetten— if you are planning to attend the Prince of Wales's reception the evening after next."

"As a matter of fact," Lisette declared boldly, "I wouldn't miss it for the world!"

Chapter 43

September 6, 1793

"*Where could he be?*" *the* comtesse de Louviers *hissed* under her breath. The ballroom of Carleton House was growing uncomfortably warm; many of the guests had wandered out into the gardens or to the sumptuous tables of food in the Gothic Conservatory. The Prince of Wales had made his entrance more than an hour ago, which meant that Nicholai was disrespectfully late. This might be her last chance to change his mind and recapture his love. If only that Austrian harlot would give up and go home!

Gabrielle's lilac eyes were venomous as she stared at the woman who was dancing with the prince. Tonight, Giselle Amstetten appeared more enchantingly beautiful than ever. A stunning gown, fashioned of sapphire velvet, emphasized her slender waist, high rounded breasts, and elegant neck. Deep ruffles of cloth of silver bordered the hemline, while more silver accented the bodice and was tucked into ruching that edged the low neckline. Artfully, Fräulein Amstetten had left bare the creamy distance between her upper bosom and throat. Instead of dripping jewels that would distract an admiring eye from her natural charms, she wore a wide exquisite collar of sapphires and diamonds that served to accentuate her elegant throat and delicately perfect face. Even though the Austrian woman had used cosmetics, including the usual patch near the corner of her mouth, the effect was far from artificial. From her curls, pinned up in charming disarray and lightly powdered to complement her gown, to the silvery slippers that peeked out as she danced

an Allemande with the prince, Giselle Amstetten was a
work of art.

Gabrielle turned away, sick inside. If it was not for that
woman, all would be well between her and Nicholai! He
was bewitched; that was the only explanation! Remembering their last conversation, in Hyde Park, was torture, yet
she couldn't help going back over the things they had said,
wondering how the outcome might have been changed. . . .

Nicholai's speech had been simple: whatever love or
magic had once bound him to Gabrielle no longer existed.
It had been a mistake for him to come to London. He was
in love with someone else now and his first commitment
was to her, which meant that he would not be able to help
Gabrielle search for her brother in France. He would be
leaving England very soon to begin a new life with the
woman he planned to make his bride and hoped that Gabrielle would be generous enough to wish them good fortune.

"If you continue to frown with such repeatedness, you
will find yourself with wrinkles, *ma chère amie!*"

Gabrielle looked over to discover Angelique's reproving
smile and worried gaze. "You should concern yourself with
dear Dudley's well-being rather than mine—or my
wrinkles!"

"I am not able to stop caring for my friend."

"*Eh bien*—I am not able to stop caring for Nicky!"

"Your pride has been wounded worse than your heart,
chérie, but both will mend. It is difficult to accept that
Nicholai no longer loves you; that he seems to prefer another woman."

Gabrielle whispered a string of French epithets while
staring across the ballroom at Fräulein Amstetten. The
music had stopped and she was engaged in conversation
with her friend, Madame Raveneau.

"Do you not realize, though," Angelique was continuing
blithely, "that some other man will fall in love with you
now, and I do not doubt that in the first storm of passion
and romance he will happily go to the ends of the earth
for you!"

"I do not care about the ends of the earth. I need only
to cross the channel—and I want Nicholai to be with me!"

Angelique could only sigh, yielding to her friend's stubbornness.

Across the ballroom, which was crowded with lavishly garbed guests, Lisette and Devon enjoyed the breeze that wafted through open french doors leading to the gardens.

"I tell you, I have seen him!" Devon insisted.

"Why would he come so late? It is like the night at Vauxhall. He takes some kind of mean pleasure in prolonging my agony by making me wait, and I'll wager that this entire evening is his idea of a joke. He never actually said he would be here, you know, but of course I spent a full day primping—"

"Will you be quiet? Mr. Beauvisage will be coming any moment. You have to keep your wits about you and remember how important it is to extricate him from the *comtesse de Louviers*'s trap. You can't come right out and tell him that she's made a fool of him, so you must phrase your warnings very carefully."

"I know that, Devon!" Lisette snapped. In spite of herself, she was scanning the main entrance to the ballroom and was annoyed at herself for reacting so predictably.

"Well, I can't help worrying that you will *lose your temper!*" retorted Devon with meaningful sarcasm.

Instantly contrite, Lisette looked down at her friend who had gone to so much trouble for her sake. Devon and André could have spent all their days in London alone and with their children, but they had chosen to share their home, time, and imaginations with Lisette. "I apologize. My . . . nerves are frayed."

"Understandably." Her smile was both forgiving and affectionate. "That is why I though to remind you of those details anxiety might sweep from your mind."

"Are you truly certain you saw him?"

"Absolutely. He must have been waylaid for conversation—probably by some eager female. I hear that every mama in London has her eye on Nicholai for her daughter . . . and that just as many are sizing you up as the perfect wife for their sons!"

Lisette gasped. Instinctively she glanced around and was

astonished to find at least a half dozen pairs of male eyes
staring at her with open admiration and obvious desire. "I
can't believe it! I have been so preoccupied with Nicholai
that I haven't even noticed—"

"Your modesty is one of your most becoming traits,"
Devon assured her, laughing softly. "And . . . don't look
now, but here he comes. The man obviously has eyes for
only you! Don't forget, now, that if persuasion and reason
don't seem to be effective, you may have to find some other
way to keep Mr. Beauvisage from journeying to France."

"Believe me, with something this important at stake, I
won't get so dizzy with passion that I forget all about it."
Helplessly, Lisette looked past Devon and immediately
spotted Nicholai's tall, broad-shouldered figure winding
through the crowd across the ballroom. Hundreds of candles in the chandeliers struck sparks over his ruffled auburn
hair. He was so fiercely magnificent that Lisette's heart began to race the first moment she saw him. Nicholai's frock
coat was dull gold velvet over an ivory shirt and stock, and
a waistcoat of warm brown and golden brocade.

"Don't stare at him until we have you dancing with
André!" scolded Devon. "I suspect that your eyes could
send fire even across this ballroom."

And then, Raveneau appeared and swept Lisette into his
arms with a roguish grin. She saw Nicholai just a few feet
away as they drifted farther into the swirling pairs of
dancers.

"We are wicked," Lisette told André, unable to repress a
smile.

"Well, it's important that Beauvisage not become too certain of success with you, particularly in light of the *comtesse de Louviers*'s influence."

It was like being at the center of a raging fire, for all
eyes seemed to be on them, from the Prince of Wales's to
Gabrielle's to Nicholai's to the dozens of pairs belonging to
London's most eligible bachelors. Then, Raveneau was
stopping just as Lisette noticed familiar dark fingers against
his shoulder.

"Might I steal a portion of this dance?" inquired Nicholai.
"The choice is Fräulein Amstetten's." Even as André

responded, his own gaze was being pulled toward the french doors and the enchanting figure of his wife. She was clad in a low-cut gown of hyacinth and ivory silk, her strawberry blond curls spilling down in seemingly artless disarray, and Devon's unique complex beauty was a match for that of any woman present.

"I don't want to make a scene. . . ." Lisette murmured. She heard Nicholai's ironic chuckle, then her body was being held close against his hard chest, hips, and the tantalizing bulge at the apex of his lean-muscled thighs.

"I am sorry to be late," he whispered as they danced.

"Oh, are you late?" Lisette strove for an offhand tone. "I hadn't noticed."

His laughter said that he didn't believe her for a moment, but he replied, "You wound me, fräulein. I was hoping that you had come here tonight for the sole purpose of seeing me one more time before my ship sails. I thought that perhaps you chose that exquisite gown just to please me, and that you might have dreamed, briefly, of the moment when we would be alone and my mouth would drift down to that enticing décolletage. . . ."

"Herr Beauvisage!" Lisette's gasp was hot as she felt her nipples stiffen in betrayal. "You forget yourself!"

"I do?" He stopped suddenly amidst the other swaying dancers and looked around in comic dismay. "I don't think so, Fräulein Amstetten. In fact, I would take an oath that I am right here at Carleton House with you!"

"I am not joking!"

"Neither am I." Warm lips grazed her temple, then the satiny curve of her ear. "Perhaps we should discuss this further in the garden."

"Well . . ." Lisette answered doubtfully as a sweet weakness swept over her body.

"A wise decision, Fräulein Amstetten."

No sooner had they strolled out into the cool cloud-strewn night than the *comtesse de Louviers* was cornering Lady Angelique Whitloaf in a corner of the ballroom.

"Do you see what has happened? Nicky means to bed the vixen. I know it!"

Angelique sighed and wished her husband would come

along to escort her to supper. "If that is so, I cannot see what you may gain by fretting over it, *ma chère amie*. Why not leave them alone and concentrate on a new plan to find your husband? If you really care about Nicholai so very much, I would think that you would be made happy to see that he may have found new love—"

"With that Austrian trollop? *Quelle horreur!*"

At last Angelique spotted Lord Whitloaf as he turned away after a brief conversation with the Prince of Wales. "Dudley! There you are. I am famished; won't you take us to supper?"

Her eyes fixed on the french doors, Gabrielle shook her head. "I am not ready to go yet. I shall meet you both in the Gothic Conservatory after a little while." She glanced at Dudley and added one last parting shot aimed at her friend. "Angelique always *has* had a much more enormous appetite than I. *Vraiment*, I could tell you such stories. . . ."

Lord Whitloaf's wine-dulled eyes widened in bewilderment, but then his wife was tugging at his arm and he allowed himself to be led away.

Gabrielle allowed herself a small sly smile. Thank God for Angelique's guilt over the curiosity they had satisfied for each other when they were both twelve. Their bodies had begun to bud and bloom; Gabrielle had initiated the first shy exploration one morning in the gazebo when their parents had gone riding. . . .

Across the ballroom, diamonds sparkled as a sapphire-gowned figure appeared in the french doors. Gabrielle saw Fräulein Amstetten laugh and she saw the dark hand that drew her back into the secret fragrant night. After a long minute, the woman appeared alone and made her way through the crush of dancers until she was at the side of the Prince of Wales. They exchanged pleasantries, his face registered regret, he kissed her hand, and then the Austrian woman was leaving the ballroom. Gabrielle couldn't decide what to do. Her mind whirled, taken by surprise, but after a minute she resolved to find Nicholai. Just then, he came through the french doors, the picture of nonchalance, and made his way to the prince. Watching, Gabrielle felt her ath burn in her lungs. Of course, they couldn't leave together, but it wasn't hard for her to imagine their reunion in the carriage that would take them to Nicholai's new town house.

Obviously, he cared nothing for *her* suffering—after all they had shared for so long in France! Now, blinded by lust for that Austrian hussy, Nicholai thought only of himself. Did he imagine that she would allow them to humiliate her before all of London without so much as a whimper of protest?

Gabrielle's lilac eyes took on a harsh dazzling light as the pieces of a plan fell into place in her shadowed mind.

Chapter 44

Midnight, September 7, 1793

*The interior of the coach Nicholai had hired was comfort-*able, with seats of padded velvet, but so cramped that a pleasant sort of panic caused Lisette to flush as soon as the door closed and an all-too-familiar body settled next to her.

"So, Fräulein Amstetten, where were we?"

Thin wheels crunched over bits of gravel as the coach picked up speed. Alarmingly conscious of the hard masculine arm that pressed against her in the darkness, Lisette swallowed audibly before replying, "I—I told you that there was a matter of grave importance that I wished to discuss with you, Herr Beauvisage."

"Ah, yes!" A brief white grin betrayed his amusement. "I, too, found our 'discussion' in the garden to be highly enlightening, and I am anxious to continue it!"

"That's not—"

Nicholai's hands encircled her waist, turning her easily into his embrace. For an instant, Lisette was conscious only of the intoxicating scent and texture of his shirtfront, then one lean arm was around her back while the other slid up until long fingers were in her carefully arranged hair, holding her face still to receive his kiss.

Oh. . . Hazily Lisette wondered why the sensation of Nicholai's mouth against her own ignited such a blaze of desire from the deepest corners of her body. Just when she thought her memories of their lovemaking must be exaggerations, he managed to interfere and remind her that reality cast fantasy in the shade.

Nicholai's mouth slowly worked on hers, urging her soft lips to open and yield the sweetness within. Their tongues met and played. Fiery currents of longing swelled Lisette's firm breasts and burned downward to her loins, while her slender arms twined about Nicholai's strong shoulders and neck.

Knuckles rapped impatiently on the side of the coach.

"For God's sake!" Nicholai's dark head went up. "What the——"

Lisette realized then, as he did, that the coach had stopped outside a handsome well-lit town house.

"It seems that we are here," he muttered ruefully. "Why don't we finish this—uh—*conversation* inside?"

"I really do have something I want to discuss with you!" Lisette insisted as he opened the carriage door and stepped lightly to the ground. Apparently Nicholai hadn't heard, but for good measure she reminded herself once more of Devon's admonishments at Carleton House. Above all, she must dissuade him from journeying to France.

A wrinkled, tired-looking butler met them at the door. Nicholai immediately sent the old man off to bed. Lisette gazed around in wonder. The narrow house was three stories tall and decorated with flawless good taste. Fine paintings lined the long hallway that passed the stairs and led back to what she assumed must be the dining room and the servants' quarters. A fire bathed the parlor to her left with soft, intimate light that made the furnishings look all the more elegant and inviting.

"Shall we sit down? After you, fräulein." Light mockery infected his voice.

Lisette perched uneasily on the far side of a mahogany and satinwood sofa upholstered in pale green striped satin. Turning her head, she discovered that Nicholai was removing a bottle of champagne from a silver bucket filled with ice. He apparently sensed her stare and glanced over to give her a wink that struck Lisette as indecent. Champagne! Was such extravagance a nightly habit, just in case he persuaded a gullible female to accompany him home, or was this preplanned to celebrate his seduction of a wealthy Austrian widow? Had Nicholai no thought for the girl who waited in a CoffeeHouse in Philadelphia? Gazing into the fire, she heard a sudden pop, and a moment later he was sitting down beside her with two crystal goblets of golden, effervescent wine. Lisette accepted hers reluctantly.

"Thank you, Herr Beauvisage," she murmured primly, avoiding his desirous eyes.

"To your rare beauty and grace, fräulein." Nicholai touched his glass gently to hers in a way that made her feel as if he'd caressed some intimate part of her body. "Just looking at you is making me warm!"

Words dried up in Lisette's throat as she watched him set the glass on the end table before standing to strip off his frock coat and vest and drape them carelessly over the opposite arm of the sofa. The firelight emphasized the contrast between Nicholai's bronzed face and his neatly tapered ivory shirt.

"How did you ever manage to find such a wonderful place—with servants and lovely furniture?" Lisette heard herself ask a trifle too loudly as she felt his body settle next to her own once again.

"All this belongs to an old friend of my family. The death of an elderly relative took him to the country unexpectedly and he was kind enough to offer the place to me."

"How very fortunate! Is he returning soon? Perhaps that is part of the reason you are leaving England?"

"No. He'll be in Yorkshire until November," he replied without further elaboration.

Out of the corner of her eye, Lisette watched Nicholai idly straighten pleated ivory cuffs. Her gaze slid to his fingers. They were long, deft, and golden brown, with well-tended nails. The hairs on the backs of his hands glinted in the firelight and Lisette remembered how strong they were, with calluses earned during a decade of physical labor in the vineyards. She remembered, too, the sensation of Nicholai's fingers and hands on her naked body, the smell and the taste of them against her open mouth. . . .

"Fräulein, you are flushed," he was murmuring huskily. "Are you also too warm?"

She was mesmerized by the sight of one of his hands coming toward her face. When he cupped her chin in his palm and laid his fingers against her cheek, Lisette nearly gasped in reaction. She ached to turn her mouth and kiss, inhaling—

"You feel feverish, fräulein. I hope you aren't ill!" Nicholai's fingertips blazed a feather-soft trail down to the cleavage formed by a bodice that displayed the high curves of Lisette's breasts. "How quickly your heart is beating. Shall I send for a physician?"

Finally, she detected the hint of amusement in his voice and realized that he knew exactly what her ailment was. Slowly, slowly, Nicholai's hand stole away from her thudding heartbeat and traced the warm curved flesh on either side. Shocked by the violent response of her body to such simple caresses, Lisette closed her eyes and swallowed a sob. Between her legs, she felt hot and congested and now suddenly so wet, even on her thighs.

"*Fräulein Amstetten*, look at me." Nicholai's voice seemed to cut the air like a sword.

Swept by a wave of panicked anxiety, she complied. His eyes were emerald flames, scorching her, and she would have turned away, but he caught her delicate chin in a steely grip. Nicholai's other hand brushed one of her erect nipples, outlined against its sapphire velvet cover. Lisette trembled and tears stung her eyes. At that moment, it seemed that she would die if Nicholai did not make love to her.

"I want you to come upstairs with me," he told her bluntly. "To bed."

She nodded; he released her chin. Seeing him reach for his champagne, Lisette suddenly realized how thirsty she was. She drank down the rest of her glass and the thousands of bubbles felt like tiny pinpricks in her mouth and throat. Wait! What about Gabrielle? That was why she had come —to warn him!

Nicholai stood up and said with heavy irony, "Don't worry, my passionate *liebling*. Whatever you wanted to discuss with me will keep until—later."

Had he read her mind? Lisette hadn't the strength to hold the thought, for Nicholai was propelling her toward the stairway, his hand riding on the small of her back in a way that sent shivery sensations down over her derriere. They ascended to the bedchamber in silence. It was a spacious room furnished with handsome Sheraton pieces, including a curtained field bed.

Lisette pretended to look around, suddenly shy, and wandered over to the fireplace, holding her hands out toward the soft coral flames that provided the chamber's only light.

"Fräulein Amstetten, is it possible that you are now *cold*?" Nicholai exclaimed in mock dismay. He came up behind her so softly that when Lisette turned and discovered him only inches away, she gasped.

"I—I suppose that you should call me—" She paused to lick her lips.

"Giselle?"

Something in Nicholai's voice alarmed her. Was he different . . . in bed with other women from the way he had been with her? He couldn't feel any *love* for Giselle Amstetten . . . ! "Yes, of course. Giselle," she whispered. At this point, there was no choice. Unable to go on meeting his penetrating stare, Lisette turned back to the fire in an effort to collect her wits.

Nicholai bent and kissed her nape, smiling when her hips jerked slightly, involuntarily. He began to slowly unfasten the tiny velvet buttons that followed the elegant curve of her back. "Be patient, Giselle. I will give you everything you need—and more."

Uneasiness vanished as arousal surged higher in Lisette. It seemed that she would go mad if he didn't hurry with her gown; she burned to feel his skin against her own. *He doesn't realize it,* she told herself, *but the reason he wants Giselle Amstetten so badly is because she is actually Lisette Hahn. He's making love to me . . . to me!*

Nicholai's warm hands were sliding inside her open gown, under her arms, until they curved teasingly around her gossamer-covered breasts.

"You've missed this, haven't you?"

Lisette moaned and gasped, "Yes!"

"Have you missed this too?" He turned her to face him and, grasping her hand, placed it on the hard thick ridge of his desire. Lisette was excited and ashamed all at once as she thought, helplessly, that he believed she was someone he barely knew. It was obvious that Nicholai meant her to take her turn and unfasten his breeches. He began to kiss her with a lazy sensuousness that banished every thought and sensation save passion. Her shaking fingers worked at the straining buttons until suddenly his manhood sprang into her hand, steely-hard, yet warm and pulsating.

"Oh . . . Giselle—" Nicholai gave a harsh groan.

Confusion pierced Lisette's own arousal. "I—you don't think I'm a—doxy . . . or a—"

"No, no, of course not." His tone was soothing as he pulled off his clothes. "You are a widow, after all. You know the pleasures of the bedchamber—and it isn't fair that you should be completely deprived of one of life's greatest delights."

"But . . . what about love? At Vauxhall, you told me that I remind you of someone you once knew. Did you love *her*?" The words spilled out in a flood. What would he say? Would he laugh?

"Love her?" Nicholai seemed to consider the implications, meanwhile slipping down the thin straps of her chemise. "Certainly she was a beautiful, fascinating woman . . . but now I think that perhaps her eyes were not so blue as yours." Baring Lisette's taut breasts, he nuzzled them and continued, "Her breasts were not this firm and full, nor so delicious. . . ." She had to bite her lip to stifle a groan as Nicholai sucked tenderly on each nipple in turn until she pressed closer, caught in a raging storm of desire. Her priceless velvet gown, silk chemise, and ruffled petticoats slid down to pool around her ankles. Stepping over them, Lisette barely noticed as Nicholai tossed them aside. Tenderly, he removed her silver slippers and she stood before him naked, except for white silk stockings secured by sapphire velvet garters.

"You are beautiful, Giselle," Nicholai said huskily. The tone of his voice and the heat of his gaze on her naked body intensified the throbbing between Lisette's thighs. "You are more glorious than any woman I've ever seen." He kissed the creamy flesh above each stocking.

"Even . . . ?" she managed to breathe.

"I've never known anyone who could compare." With tantalizing slowness, he removed the garters and then the stockings, his fingertips tracing fire down her soft thighs.

"Your legs are longer. . . ." Nicholai's mouth was hot as it pressed nibbling kisses inward along Lisette's waist, then down over the swell of her hip. "Your belly is smoother. . . ." Suddenly, she felt his warm breath stir the feathery gold curls that concealed her womanhood. The effect upon her body was convulsive, yet somehow outrage triumphed over passion.

"Oh! How dare you!" As strong hands molded her buttocks, drawing her closer, Lisette struggled mightily. The beast had never even bedded "Giselle Amstetten," and yet he dared to venture where only the most intimate of lovers would be allowed—! And for him to say that this fictional woman's body was in every way superior to Lisette's, obviously just so that she would weaken and allow him to have his way with her—it was too much to be borne! "Loose me, you molester of women! Brute!"

Nicholai sat back on his heels with a grin just as one of Lisette's flailing hands flew out to catch him across the side of his jaw. His amusement turned to annoyance. Hard-muscled arms flexing, he grasped her waist and rose, lifting her easily.

"Animal!" Lisette railed. She could not believe this was happening. During all the stirring, sensuous encounters she had had with Nicholai, he had certainly never *forced* her. Now, after carrying her to the bed, he cupped her buttocks and pulled her hard against his insistent masculinity. Wildly, she struck out, but Nicholai ducked, laughing, and caught one recalcitrant hand. No sooner had he pinned it to the small of her back than Lisette's other fist struck him in the nose with surprising force.

"Bitch!"

"Bastard!" she hissed in return. "I have completely misjudged you; you're a typical man! A stupid pig!"

Mercilessly his steely fingers captured her rebellious wrist and pulled it back to join its twin. Meanwhile, Nicholai forced her thighs apart with his knee. Just before thrusting his aching hardness deep inside Lisette, he admonished, "Don't be a sore loser! Or did you imagine that you were the only one capable of putting on an act?"

She didn't know what he was talking about, but fully realized his physical intent. Crazily, she bucked against him,

which only served to facilitate Nicholai's hot driving pene-
tration. "Oh, God!" she whimpered. It felt so good!
Ashamed, yet imprisoned by age-old instincts, Lisette
eagerly met the thrusts of the bronzed male body that
covered her own. "I hate you!"

"Oh, no." Nicholai laughed harshly. "You aren't *that*
skilled as an actress. You love me—or you wouldn't have
followed me all the way from Philadelphia to London,
Lisette!"

Chapter 45

September 7, 1793.

"Bête!" *Gabrielle spat. "What takes you so long?"*

On the verge of tears, Angelique hurried down the long staircase before turning back to speak to her companion. "I had to make certain that Dudley was truly asleep, didn't I? If he should discover us leaving, I know that he would follow—all the way to the new home of M'sieur Beauvisage, and there is not any explanation in the world that I could offer if that were to happen!"

"Would you prefer to explain your love affair with another female?" Gabrielle whispered with a small wicked smile.

"D'accord!" Angelique wanted to scream, but somehow managed to exclaim softly, "You are a cruel person to blackmail me with something that happened when we were little more than children. I did not realize—"

"Would Dudley accept your excuses?"

"Perhaps." She lifted her chin.

"Would you care to find out?"

"No." Angelique breathed nervously.

Gabrielle opened the door. At four o'clock in the morning, even Berkeley Square's nightingales were asleep. "Shall we go?"

Luxuriating in the lean-muscled arm that held her near, Lisette nuzzled Nicholai's shoulder and sighed contentedly. "You smell wonderful!"

"So do you." He smiled.

"Like croissants and brioches?"

"Even better!" Nicholai grinned and lifted a snifter of brandy to his mouth. "You taste better, too."

"Flatterer!" She laughed softly. Surely this was a dream and morning would find her back in her bed in the Raveneaus' house on Hanover Square. Dream or not, she would enjoy to the fullest sitting with Nicholai against plump down pillows, sipping brandy as moonlight streamed through the parted bed hangings. His body, warm, hard, and familiar against her own, was a potent source of euphoric pleasure. "Tell me, now, when did you realize that Giselle Amstetten was actually me? Did I forget my accent in my anger tonight?"

Nicholai choked on his brandy, apparently hugely amused. "Please! You underestimate me, my sweet. I knew it was you at Vauxhall!"

"Liar! You only say that to make me feel foolish! If you knew it was me, why did you not say so?"

"And miss that stellar performance? Watching you play the wealthy, love-starved widow, garbed in satins and velvets and dripping with jewels, has been the most fun I have had in months!" He touched the spot where she had worn the patch. "I especially liked that little detail. Would Lisette Hahn have ever affected such—"

"Stop gloating!" She cuffed his hand away. "I want you to tell me how you knew—exactly when you realized, and why."

"Actually, I knew in my gut even before Vauxhall, but my logical brain convinced me I was having an hallucination." Nicholai glanced over to find Lisette looking charmingly perplexed. How lovely she was! The first thing he had done after soundly making love to her was to take down her hair and brush out the light dusting of powder. Now, her long tousled curls gleamed gold in the moonlight, reminding him of his first night at Markwood Villa, when he'd wakened to find an angel with cool soft hands perched on the edge of the bed. . . .

"What do you mean?" prompted Lisette.

"I—oh, sorry. For a moment there, I was—oh, never mind." He smiled and kissed her with feeling as tears pricked his eyes. "Let's see . . . where was I? Oh, yes. Well, before Vauxhall, I saw you and Devon Raveneau draw up in front of Whitloaf's mansion in an open landau. You two were pointing and whispering—for God's sake, Lisette, you needn't look at me so accusingly! I wasn't spying on you; I just happened to look out my window!"

"Oh . . ." she moaned, "when I think of all the trouble and expense Devon and I went to—and all our plans were thwarted even before we began to carry them out!"

"Not exactly. As I said, I thought you were a figment of my lovesick imagination . . . until you appeared again that night at Vauxhall—and still I told myself that it was a coincidence. I reacted just as you and Devon meant me to, until she came over to be introduced and I realized, after a moment's confusion, that she had been the other person in the landau that morning—accompanying a girl who had looked much more like my Lisette, with loose long blond hair, a simpler dress, and no paint or patches. . . ." Nicholai paused to set aside his brandy, then took her snifter and placed it on the nightstand also. Yearning to feel her warm lush body against the length of his again, he drew her with him under the covers. "Still . . . I wasn't certain until we were alone in that grotto. Did you imagine that I could forget your kiss? The sweet taste of your mouth?" Nicholai demonstrated, for emphasis, until a ravenous Lisette lay atop his big body and feasted on his intoxicating kisses. "Did you actually think that some other woman could have skin as soft as yours?" he murmured at length, running his hands up her thighs, lingering on the firm curves of her derriere, then softly caressing the elegant line of Lisette's back. "And your breasts . . ."

She smiled, remembering how he had managed to expose one breast that night at Vauxhall . . . doubtless to aid in confirming her true identity!

"But, Nicholai—what about Gabrielle? When you saw her again, did the magic return? If I hadn't turned up in London, would you be in her bed tonight? I find it a bit difficult to believe that you are planning to accompany her to France solely out of a sense of obligation!"

"I wouldn't accompany the chit across the street if I could avoid it, let alone to France," he replied evenly.

"I'm not one to accept every glib story offered, you know," Lisette was continuing, seemingly unaware of

Nicholai's words. "I wasn't born yesterday! You mustn't think that I'm spreading tales just so that I can have you all to myself, because that's not it at all. It isn't right for her to practice such deception and get away with it, especially when your life could be in danger as a consequence—" All at once she broke off, straightening her arms to stare down at him through silvery blue shadows. "Did you say that you would not accompany Gabrielle to France?" Her voice was a perplexed whisper, as though she were certain she'd been hearing things.

"I did. I wouldn't have gone with her even if it were really her brother she's been searching for instead of that slimy *comte.*"

"You know?" gasped Lisette. "How long?"

"I've suspected for a long time, and made up my mind to sever ties with Gabrielle before I knew the truth for certain. Actually, I probably would have turned back for Philadelphia the first day if not for my chivalrous instincts"— Nicholai's voice was acid with sarcasm—"and my genuine affection for Gabrielle's brother . . . who, it would seem, has been dead for some time."

Lisette shook her head as though in shock. "I cannot believe my ears! You've stolen all my thunder. The shocking exposure of Gabrielle was my excuse for coming home with you tonight. I was sacrificing my pride to save you from boarding that ship for France—" She paused and stared down at him, arching one delicate brow. "Where *were* you planning to go?"

"Nowhere at all without you, sweetheart," Nicholai drawled, then gave her a mischievous smile. "I was just getting bored waiting for you to conclude your little game . . . and even more impatient to have you right where you are now, so I forced your hand."

"You are shameless. An unscrupulous rogue." Lisette was smiling as he drew her face down and brought their mouths together in a slow burning kiss.

"There is another reason why I couldn't sail to France with Gabrielle tomorrow," he murmured at length.

"Mmm. What?"

"I have other plans for tomorrow."

Lisette rolled onto her side and hooked a graceful leg

over Nicholai's lean hip. "Pray enlighten me," she responded absently. Her fingers were in the soft crisp hair that covered his chest, while her mouth sought an unsuspecting nipple.

"Well . . ." Nicholai clenched his teeth as she sucked hesitantly. Somehow he managed to finish, "I cannot possibly go to France because I will be very busy at church." Lightning shot from her persistent mouth to his groin. "Busy—" he ground out, "—marrying you, you insatiable vixen! God's eyes, stop that before you drive me mad!"

All at once, his arms were around her, pressing her into the pillows, and Lisette's lilting laughter filled the bed. "I promise to behave, milord. After all, I'd be unwise to marry a madman, wouldn't I?"

Nicholai breathed deep of her golden mane of curls and wondered if acute happiness could shatter one's heart. "I love you excessively, Mistress Hahn."

Their lips were clinging, pausing, tasting, while Lisette's slim fingers boldly curved around the hard proof of Nicholai's passion for her. "Mr. Beauvisage, I—"

He silenced her with a deep warm kiss as she guided him into her sweet, cozy, feverish body. Nicholai didn't need to hear her say that she loved him. He was all too aware that nothing short of kidnapping by an army could have brought Lisette to London and caused her to act out that touching masquerade unless her love for him was so powerful she hadn't been able to bear life without him. Nicholai was well acquainted with such desperate emptiness. . . .

They made love slowly, glorying in each exquisite sensation.

Afterward, they had no wish to break their bodies' embrace. Flushed and rosy, Lisette sighed dreamily and trailed a fingertip over a muscled arm and shoulder, then traced Nicholai's neck, jaw, and every chiseled feature of the face she loved so well. "I adore your hair," she whispered. "It ruffles so attractively . . . and I always thought that it looks as though the sun painted it ever so lightly with its own brush."

"The brandy's gone to your head," Nicholai replied fondly, amused.

"I've always been afraid to compliment you, to let you

know how special you've always been to me. Exposing my feelings now is terrifying and—"

"And?" he prompted.

"Exciting. Liberating."

They kissed tenderly for long minutes, communicating with an eloquence that far surpassed words.

"I cannot believe that we are actually going to be together from now on," Lisette whispered in wonderment against Nicholai's shining hair.

"How do you feel about that? Are you worried that marriage will usurp your identity?"

"It's hard to break old patterns." Lisette smiled, pausing for a moment to choose the right words to explain the changes her thinking had undergone since their parting in Philadelphia.

"I've been thinking a lot about the old problems in our relationship—and those old habits that tripped us up so many times," Nicholai was saying. Lisette beamed in the darkness, amazed at the rapport between their minds.

"What have you decided?" she asked.

"One of the main reasons I love you so much is that backbone of spirited independence that makes you shine in any setting. Admitting our love and need for one another doesn't mean that one of us has to submit to the other's will. We've made the mistake of making our relationship a contest of wills so much of the time. If you had ever surrendered and begun deferring to me—"

"Like a good, obedient girl who always lets the man have his way?" Lisette teased.

He groaned. "That must be the main cause of boring marriages. Promise that you'll never be *obedient!*"

"I swear it!" She giggled delightedly.

"I'm sure that the solution must be a marriage of lovers and friends—with common goals and mutual respect. We'll each have an equal say in decisions and *we'll have to learn to compromise!*"

"Perhaps we could still argue sometimes just to spice things up—" Lisette was laughing, but she tingled with excitement at the picture Nicholai painted of their future together. "We don't want to be reasonable to the point of stuffiness!"

"Granted—you vixen!" Abruptly, he caught her up and began to tickle her. Lisette shrieked with outraged laughter and was squirming to free herself in a way that rekindled the embers of Nicholai's desire. Then, just as they sank into the pillows, wrestling and kissing at the same time, a loud banging at the front door broke the spell.

"What the devil?" Nicholai exclaimed irritably. "Let me up. God only knows who is out there at this hour. I'd better answer it before the servants are roused."

Logic told her that it was probably nothing—a drunken acquaintance from one of the nearby clubs on Saint James Street—yet Lisette couldn't help admonishing, "Be careful, Nicholai."

The door knocker thumped again as he pulled on a brown velvet dressing gown. "Don't fret, love. I'll be right back."

Nicholai's bare feet were silent as he hurried downstairs. "Who the hell is it?"

"I am so sorry to bother you at this hour, M'sieur!" a familiar French-accented voice piped up from the top step outside. "It is I, Lady Angelique Whitloaf!"

He opened the door in consternation. "Angelique—do you have any idea what time it is? What the devil is going on?"

She was looking very pale and small. "Please, I implore you as a friend to let me come inside. I need only a minute of your time."

He shook his auburn head in exasperation and led the way into the parlor. "What is it?"

Angelique's heart was beating wildly. She went to the fireplace and turned around so that Nicholai would be forced to have his back to the door. In a trembling voice, she told him the story that Gabrielle had drilled into her head—all about the terrible sad condition of her friend who had done nothing but weep ever since he broke her heart. Explaining that Gabrielle had forbidden her to speak to Nicholai, Angelique said that this had been the only time she could come—to beg him to reconsider.

"This is insane—at four-thirty in the morning?"

Around his shoulder, Angelique saw the front door open slowly, silently, and then Gabrielle was tiptoeing across the entryway. It was obvious that Nicholai was not going to stand still for much more of this conversation. How was she to keep him here? Then Angelique glimpsed a flash of silver near Gabrielle's hand before the other woman passed up the stairway. *Fool!* she screamed in her mind. *I've been a blind fool to believe that Gabrielle meant only to frighten or threaten that girl. She's going to kill her!*

Angelique bolted around Nicholai and ran wildly into the entry hall. "Gabrielle!" she cried to the copper-haired figure who had nearly reached the upstairs hall.

"Go back, or I'll tell Dudley!"

She's mad, thought Angelique dazedly. With a speed she never realized she possessed, she was running up the carpeted stairway. "I don't care. That's not important. You cannot do this—for your own sake, *ma chère amie!*"

It was all over in a few seconds. Gabrielle wheeled around as though she would stab her own dearest friend, and the two women struggled. Somehow, Angelique managed to wrest the knife away, but not before Gabrielle lost her balance and tumbled down, down, down the long staircase.

Lisette, hastily clad in Nicholai's voluminous white shirt, came into the hall. Angelique stood silently, her face a mask of pain, while Nicholai knelt beside Gabrielle far below. After a long minute he glanced up.

"I think she's dead. . . ."

Epilogue

Doubt thou the stars are fire;
  Doubt that the sun doth move;
Doubt truth to be a liar,
  But never doubt I love.

                    Shakespeare
                    Hamlet: Act II

October 21, 1793
Château du Soleil
St. Briac-sur-Loire, France

Nicholai and Lisette Beauvisage sat on a hillside, protected
from the sun by spreading branches with leaves burnished
by autumn's flame. The remainders of a generous wedge of
cheese, a long, crusty baguette, apples and peaches, and
half a cold roasted chicken rested on a flowered cloth in
front of them. With a sigh, Lisette sipped the last of her
crimson Bourgueil wine, savouring the faint raspberry flavor.

"This is heaven. . . ."

Nicholai slipped his hand into the silky mane that tumbled down her back and drew her closer until their mouths
touched and tasted. "My love," he whispered thickly, "*you*
are heaven."

Hearing the emotion in his voice, Lisette felt hot tears
well in her eyes. How blessed they were to be sharing such
a rare, glorious love! As Nicholai leaned back against the
tree trunk, she snuggled into the hard warmth of his shoulder, conscious of the texture and fresh scent of the snowy
white shirt he wore. The widest blue sky Lisette had ever
seen stretched above them, dotted with wisps of cottony
clouds. Below, the broad azure Loire River wound lazily
between banks of golden sand, past picturesque villages,
fairytale châteaus, and vineyards where succulent bunches
of grapes were ripening for the harvest.

"How much farther to . . . our home?" she asked.

"Well, let's see. We've just passed Saumur, so we should
arrive at the château within two hours. You do realize that
it isn't a replica of your average American dwelling? I'm

afraid that Château du Soleil leaves even the Binghams' mansion in the shade."

"You needn't apologize!" Lisette teased, then added wonderingly, "I feel as though I've wandered into someone else's dream . . . like Cinderella, waiting for the spell to wear off. I expect to find myself at any moment back in the CoffeeHouse, rolling out piecrusts."

"I assure you that I won't allow that to happen. This is *your* dream—for better or worse, as someone once said— and I intend to share it with you." Nicholai watched his bride attempt to stifle a yawn through her smile and, whispered, "Why don't you have a nap, my princess?"

"Oh, no . . . I couldn't possibly . . ." She yawned again. "I'll just rest my eyes for a minute or two."

Nicholai watched her fall asleep, smiling fondly, but then his expression sobered. Their journey through France had been a grand adventure as well as an unconventional honeymoon for Lisette, so he had tried to minimize the risks. As long as they had presented themselves as Americans on holiday, they were safe, even welcomed with open arms. However, if word should leak out that the wealthy owner of Château du Soleil was back in residence, God only knew what would happen. Nicholai prayed that the group of servants who had grown up at the château and had given their fervent promise that they would guard it until his return had been able to keep that vow. In a month, he and Lisette were to meet the Raveneaus and *La Mouette* in Saint Nazaire. From there they would sail back to Philadelphia, to remain until the Revolution in France had run its course.

So much had happened, good and bad, since the night in London when Nicholai and Lisette had revealed their true feelings to each other. By some miracle, Gabrielle had survived her fall down the staircase, but it would be a very long time before she would be in any condition to cause trouble for anyone. Her broken bones were mending at the Whitloaf's house, where Angelique had been dutifully keeping vigil by her side in the hope that warmth and love could heal her mind as well. For his part, Nicholai hoped never to see or hear of Gabrielle Marchandon again.

During the month Lisette and Nicholai had spent together in London, they talked, made love, planned their future, and took long walks. All the old barriers were broken down as they shared feelings and old fears and new dreams. Even the crisis with Gabrielle bound them closer together. And so, because Château du Soleil figured so importantly in their conversations, Nicholai resolved to show it to Lisette so that she could discover for herself if she wanted to make a life there someday. He smiled now down at her sleeping face. Thus far, she had been unable to stop exclaiming her delight in every detail of France. She loved it with a passion that threatened to surpass his own.

On the dark side was the news that they had heard three days ago . . . Queen Marie Antoinette had been guillotined on October 16. Lisette had wept, but Nicholai's raw, sick grief went much deeper. He had known the queen. They had shared many pleasant conversations. In spite of Marie Antoinette's selfishness, he had admired her beauty and charm. To think of her suffering so degrading a death before cheering crowds tore Nicholai apart. What next? How far would this madness have to go before people opened their eyes to their own senseless barbarity?

With his free hand, Nicholai reached into a saddlebag and withdrew the letter that had arrived at the Raveneaus' the day before he and Lisette were to sail on board *La Mouette* for France. Now, his eyes skimmed Alec's neatly written sentences once again:

My dear brother,

I hope that all is well with you and that this reaches you in London. Everyone here is anxiously waiting to hear that you and Lisette have untangled your differences. . . .

The yellow fever is finally fading away in Philadelphia. It's taken a staggering toll. Thank God Lisette left when she did; the waterfront was the worst area. Hyla Flowers fell ill shortly after Lisette's departure, but she managed to recover here at Belle Maison with the help of Pierre's ministrations. They were

married the first week of August. So many others
were not that fortunate. Samuel Powel is dead . . .
the list is too long and depressing to make now.
Among others who contracted the fever and survived
are Alexander Hamilton—and our father. I put off
writing until I was certain that I could give you good
news. He remains weak, truly a shadow of his former
self, and I would worry still if not for Maman's firm
conviction that father will be dancing again by
Christmas. . . .

Nicholai paused to rub his eyes, conscious of a tight knot
of emotion in his chest. Relief and—fear? He had reread
Alec's careful sentences so often, each time freshly astonished to realize that his father could easily have died—and
still might. He wouldn't live forever. It had always seemed
that there was plenty of time for Nicholai to tell his parents
everything that was stored in his heart. Now he was glad
that he and Lisette were returning to Philadelphia so that
they could spend time with his father and mother.

The rest of Alec's letter concerned other tidbits of family
and political news. He related that Pierre and Hyla DuBois
were anxious to purchase the CoffeeHouse from Lisette if
she decided not to come back. Bramble, it seemed, was
reinstated in the kitchen of the Hampshires' Pine Street
house.

God knows she's needed there. Lion and Meagan just
arrived back in Philadelphia last week—with their
three babies! They have two sons and a daughter,
born a month early, but rosy with good health. Lion
is bursting with pride and Meagan, though appearing
a bit stunned by it all, is obviously delighted and
radiant. I've forgotten the babies' names and Caro
can't help me now because she's gone in to see Father
with a bouquet of late roses. I *do* recall that one of
the boys is named Benjamin, after Lion's great friend,
and the others have very nice names that don't rhyme.
Your sister and Randolph had a fine wedding, at
long last, although we did miss Lisette's tortes! The
two of them seem very happy . . . and Katya has

begun to read again, which I take as a good sign.
We're all well—and would appreciate an occasional
scribble of news from you! Take care.

Sacha

Lisette stirred, nuzzling Nicholai's chest, and he lost no
time in returning the letter to his saddlebag.

"Mmm . . ." she murmured contentedly. Her smile was
frankly sensuous and long feathery lashes brushed her
dusky cheeks.

Nicholai couldn't resist. Gathering his wife into his
strong embrace, he moved so that the two of them were
lying full-length on a bed of deep, fragrant grass. Lisette
responded warmly to his kiss, all her senses glorying in the
magic of those moments. She wanted to tell Nicholai how
happy she was, how much she loved him, but she couldn't
bear to raise her mouth from the intoxication of his kiss.
Besides, he knew . . . Nicholai knew everything. . . .

A misty dusk was gathering when Lisette saw Château du
Soleil for the first time. For a moment, she was unable
to breathe, but finally she sought Nicholai's eyes and
murmured.

"I thought I was only joking about being Cinderella!"

White stone turrets, machicolated towers, and a cylindri-
cal keep were all surmounted by chimneys and pepper-pot
roofs. Terraced flowerbeds lay around the castle like jewels,
while off to one side the spires of a Renaissance chapel
shone in the twilight. Farther away, Lisette saw the vineyards that staggered up and down the steep slopes that
served as the château's protected perch above the Loire.
Behind were woodlands, and in the distance loomed the
mysterious, dark Forest of Chinon.

Nicholai wheeled his horse around and laughed softly
down at Lisette. "Naturally, you are not Cinderella, my
love. It was Sleeping Beauty who came to life here at
Château du Soleil." Seeing the momentary puzzlement that
crossed her face, he twined a finger through one long,
burnished curl and explained, "It is commonly believed
that Charles Perrault was inspired to write 'Sleeping Beauty'
after visiting here."

Lisette smiled dreamily. "Château du Soleil . . . Castle of the Sun. What a perfect name." It was true, for although the towers and turrets were now tinted pink and violet by the twilight, a golden haze lingered that could not be dispelled. Nicholai's horse had begun to ascend the long drive that curved up the hillside, and Lisette followed, but reined in her mount so that she could gaze lingeringly at the beauty unfolding before her. "I really cannot believe this is happening to me! Can this enormous château actually belong to you?"

Nicholai fondly shook his head and walked his horse back to join her again. He realized that he had forgotten what a stunning first impression the château made on a new visitor—particularly one who was contemplating the possibility of spending a lifetime there. "Technically, all of this is my father's since he is the current marquis. Upon his death, Sacha would inherit, but since Father has never used the title and believes in the principles behind this revolution, none of those factors carries any weight in this situation. Father told me while I was in Philadelphia that Château du Soleil was mine if I ever desired to return here; he felt that my work and love for this land earned possession for me. When France's new laws become clear, he will sign Château du Soleil and all her holdings over to me." Nicholai reached for Lisette's hand. "To *us*."

His emphasis on that simple word brought tears to Lisette's eyes, and she had to force herself to concentrate as Nicholai explained the history of the château. It had been built one wing at a time, beginning in 1450, and originally the courtyard that now opened to the Loire had been closed in so that the château had been a military fortress. It was a distant Beauvisage ancestor, Thomas St. Briac, who razed that wing and then allowed further sunlight to invade by opening bay windows onto the courtyard.

By the time Nicholai and Lisette had tethered their horses and met the astonished servants who clustered in the high doorway, Lisette felt as if she was coming home. Even this group of strangers felt somehow familiar as they greeted Nicholai with unabashed affection and joy. Upon learning that Lisette was actually the new Madame Beauvisage, they surrounded her with hugs. Bottles of the château's best wine were opened to celebrate both Nicholai's homecoming and his marriage. Nicholai was as anxious to show his bride around the château as she was to see it, so they carried their glasses and sipped as they walked.

As she observed the transformation that Nicholai was undergoing, Lisette had to smile to herself. He kept up a running conversation as they walked, in English on one side as he described the features of the château, in rapid French on the other as he conversed with the woman and two men who had been most responsible for preserving the castle and vineyards in his absence. Whenever wandering bands of revolutionaries had arrived with the idea of sacking the place, these warm, trusted servants had persuaded them that they had run off the marquis and claimed Château de Soleil in the name of the people. This was not to say that these servants did not believe in the spirit of the revolution, but they knew in their hearts that Nicholai Beauvisage did, too. He had proved this to them through his actions over the years.

As Lisette explored the château, she continued to feel as if she were in a dream. There were floors patterned with black and white marble, and more white marble graced the elegant staircase that curved to the upper floors. One bedchamber had been decorated in red and white Chinese silks for the use of the king on his visits. There was a gallery with a coffered Renaissance ceiling that took Lisette's breath away. Each room seemed more magnificent than the last and Nicholai had to smile at the enthusiastic reactions of his Philadelphia-bred wife.

Finally, after an extravagant, home-grown meal in the château's dining room, Nicholai and Lisette retired to their private chamber. The massive bed was hung with drapes of sapphire-blue velvet that were securely closed before the couple snuggled together under the covers.

"Tell me . . . are you pleased?" Nicholai inquired softly, knowing the answer. "Do you think you could make a life here?"

"Oh, Nicholai, I *adore* the château! I do wonder though how shall I keep myself occupied? Not that my duties as your wife won't be enough, yet—"

"Shh." Nicholai silenced Lisette with his finger, then

grinned when she began to nibble on it. "I am shocked, madame, to hear that you might be less than content, spending all your time catering to *me!*" Nicholai teased. Then he continued more seriously, "Don't you know, my love, that I adore every part of you? When we return to France, I certainly do not intend that all your talents and intelligence should be wasted."

"Really? What *is* your intent, milord?"

"I would deem it an honor, Lisette, if you would consent to join hands with me and help to restore our family vineyards. I want you at my side, Lisette."

Lisette imagined a future where she could escape the duties of lady of the manor and wander through the vineyards with her husband, assessing the progress of clusters of plump grapes. She could visualize the two of them deep in discussion, huddled in the cool limestone wine caves, then side by side sampling the latest vintage of effervescent Mousseaux or crisp Vouvray. The possibilities for challenge and fulfillment sent a shiver of excitement through Lisette.

"Won't you answer, my love?" Nicholai queried, softly tentative. Had he said something amiss?

Lisette tried to find words to reply, but there were none. She pressed her naked body against the length of his and expressed her feelings with a long, hot kiss. At last she murmured, "I only wish that we didn't have to leave in a few days. . . ."

"Well, it should only be for a year or two—and in the meantime, we will be able to resolve all our affairs in Philadelphia."

"*Affairs?*" she echoed, thinking of Amelia Purdy.

Nicholai laughed aloud and kissed her cheek. "The only affair I desire is with you, Madame Beauvisage, and well you know it!"

"If you insist. . . ." She smiled, thinking absently how utterly comfortable his body felt against her own. "But, what shall we do in Philadelphia for all that time?"

He chuckled again. "Well, for one thing, you will manage your CoffeeHouse and decide if you wish to sell it to Hyla and Pierre DuBois."

"Will you help me?" Lisette interrupted, suddenly alarmed by the idea of being away from Nicholai.

"Help *you*? Impossible! However, I might watch and admire you at work."

This extravagant praise called for another kiss, but eventually Lisette caught her breath and asked, "What else shall we do to pass the time until we can return here?"

"Well, we could read and talk . . . and you could paint. I will surely help with the family business, particularly since Father is under the weather. . . ."

"And . . . ?"

"And, I can think of one particular activity that we might share."

Feeling his mouth graze her neck, then slide downward, Lisette could barely find the strength to inquire: "What might that be?"

"The creation of a baby."

"Oh!" Laughter bubbled up inside her. "That would certainly keep me busy!"

"Ma chère," Nicholai paused to lift her hand and kiss each finger. "It is a project that requires a dual effort . . . and I for one hope it is not accomplished overnight!"

About the Author

Best-selling historical-romance writer, Cynthia Challed Wright has been hailed by her loyal readers as the "successor to Kathleen Woodiwiss."

When Cynthia is not hard at work researching and writing her latest novel, set in 16th-century France, she spends her time sailing, attending the ballet, and sharing the pleasures of her 18th-century Connecticut country home with her husband, Richard, and her daughter, Jenna.